The Curious Kitten

Halloween Madness - Book 4
A Starlight Investigation Short Story

Marnie Atwell

ISBN: 978-0-6483158-6-5

Chapter One

Five hungry kittens raised their noses as they attempted to sort through the scents wafting on the breeze that crossed their forest floor. Their makeshift home provided little protection from the onslaught of smells that assaulted their olfactory nerves.

The rustling from dried leaves produced a shiver of fear in the youngest of the females. Her eldest brother, Champ, raised himself to his full height to provide protection. He allowed her to snuggle closer to him, his body heat helping to soothe her fears. His eyes peered into the distance, seeking the image of his mother.

Champ's attempts were unsuccessful, his eyes having been opened for only one full cycle of the moon. With a few more months behind him, he would be able to see far into the distance. For now, he could barely make out objects more than a metre away.

"Don't worry, Shadow," he said. "Mother will appear at any moment now. You'll see."

She pressed herself deeper into his ginger fur, a striking contrast to the black of hers. Eyes closed tightly against unknown terrors, she whispered, "There is something bad coming. I can smell it."

Champ breathed deeply, acknowledging the smell of bloodied, damp fur. Not having any experiences to call upon, he was unable to give a name to the scent. "Yes, I can smell it, too. But, I can also detect the smell of Mother. She is close."

"Will she get to us before the other smell does?" Ash, the second youngest female with fluffy grey fur, asked. She wandered over to stand beside Champ, creating a more significant barrier for Shadow to hide behind. Mind you, Champ was a roly-poly kitten who constantly glutted himself on his mother's milk making him quite a bit larger than his siblings.

"Her smell is stronger than the other. She will reach us first," Champ assured her. "Where are you going, Stubs? Don't you think you should stay and help me care for our sisters?"

Stubs glanced over at Champ. "I'm pretty sure you've got it under control," he replied matter-of-factly. His blue eyes glistened with intelligence and curiosity as he raked his gaze over his siblings. A slight frown marred his face as he spotted his older sister, Snow, sleeping on a pillow of grass. How anyone could sleep through an entire conversation, let alone ignore the auras of tense emotions was beyond him. Having black fur himself, he kept to the shadows as he made his way towards the oncoming danger.

"I asked you a question," Champ growled, posturing for the benefit of his sisters.

"I don't answer to you," Stubs replied, continuing to move forward without so much as a glance in his brother's direction.

"Go, get yourself killed then. With your stumpy legs and spindly muscles you wouldn't be much help to the females anyway."

Stubs turned to glare at his brother. "The reason you are the best choice to protect our sisters is that you are the most likely to be targeted for food. While our predator is chowing down on you, our sisters will have time to run away and perhaps find a hiding spot before it finishes its meal."

"What a terrible thing to say," Shadow hollered. Ash gazed at Champ and conceded that what Stubs said held a modicum of truth. The predator could kill them all before sitting down to eat. On the off chance it went for Champ first, she would run for her life and worry about the consequences of her actions after, if she were able to make it to safety.

"Where are you going?" Ash asked sweetly.

"To discover what is coming before it arrives," Stubs replied, crouching low as a loud rustling came from a few metres ahead.

Stubs laughed at himself for being so scared. He rose and took a couple of steps forward when his mother leapt into view. She looked frightened, but he could see the determined look on her face as she barely stopped to acknowledge him.

"This way, Stubs," she demanded, not even bothering to turn her head as she reached his siblings.

"What happened, Mother?" he asked.

"Not now, Stubs. Stay here!" she ordered, grabbing the back of Ash's neck with her mouth and carrying her further into the forest. She returned after a few minutes, scooping Champ up by the neck and disappearing from view. When she returned, she looked at Stubs with a very pleased expression. "Thank you for not wandering off," she grinned.

"What happened to your leg? You are running funny, and it smells wrong. What's that stuff on your fur?"

"Later, Stubs," she picked him up and prepared herself to run.

"You should take Shadow. She'll be scared left alone with Snow, who is still asleep."

Mother cat lowered him gently then moved to stand in front of Snow. She noticed the rise and fall of her chest and let out a sigh of relief. Although Snow was a heavy sleeper, the mother cat was astounded that her daughter had managed to remain asleep. She gave her a gentle nudge and jumped when Snow, who had become startled, flexed her claws and squeaked with fright.

"Mother, you scared me!" she cried.

"You need to learn to be more aware of what is going on around you when you rest, Snow. You are putting yourself, and your siblings at risk by sleeping so soundly."

"We are safe here, are we not?"

"No, we are not. We need to go deeper into the forest. Keep your brother company while I take Shadow to safer ground."

Mother cat scooped Shadow off the ground and ran with a more pronounced limp.

"What's going on?" Snow asked Stubs as she washed the sleep from her eyes.

"I don't know," he replied, glancing in the direction his mother had taken. He sniffed the air, surprised the scent of danger no longer assaulted his nasal cavity. His ears twitched as he listened to the sounds of the forest. He wasn't able to detect anything out of the ordinary. "I'm sure Mother will tell us what we need to know when she is ready."

"You should go next," Snow said, licking the fur on her chest.

"No, you go," he returned, crouching into a hunting position as a skink came into view.

"Mother is not going to leave you to last," Snow scoffed. "It would be doubtful that you would still be here when she returned. She seemed tired and hurt. She doesn't need the stress of having to look for you and being separated from us any longer than is necessary."

Stubs bristled at the truth of her words. He wouldn't want to wander off. He was a curious creature that was easily distracted. He pounced for the lizard, disappointed to find it had managed to evade his clutches quite easily. His mother returned and took him by the neck.

"Told you," Snow smirked.

He wanted to keep his eyes open for the journey, but they closed of their own volition. When they arrived at their new destination, he shivered with the drop in temperature. It was dark and gloomy. Gone was the handful of flowers and leaves that were soft beneath his feet. They had been replaced by dust and small pebbles. "Where are we?" he asked.

"A cave," Champ replied.

"What is a cave?" Stubs queried, never having heard the word before.

"This is a cave," Champ answered, surprised that Stubs had even asked.

Chapter Two

Stubs growled with frustration, wishing his eyesight was more advanced. He could see the light at the opening but could not determine the distance, nor see any obstacles or pitfalls that lay in between.

Putting on his brave hat, he ventured toward the exit, one paw at a time. He could hear the low mutterings of his siblings but was not interested enough to listen with both ears. The pebbles hurt the pads on his paws. The silence of his surroundings burned his ears. Stubs had barely been there a few minutes before he'd decided to hate his new home.

The light disappeared as an object filled the space. Stubs gasped with fright and crouched down low; a soft growl rumbling in his throat.

"Be calm," his mother's voiced cooed. "It is just me," her voice muffled with Snow's body hanging contentedly from her mouth. He was getting to his feet when his mother stumbled over his body. Snow was flung to the side as his mother fell. He tried to apologise, but his words were lost beneath her thick tortoiseshell fur. The mother cat groaned Snow's name as she tiredly got to her feet.

"I'm okay, Mother," Snow called, also getting to her feet. "It is very dark here."

"Yes, I know. We will be safe here," her mother stated, moving the kittens until they were huddled together. She lay on her side so they could feed.

"Did you bring some mouse or snake?" Ash asked.

"No, love. I did not have time to hunt. I will fetch you something to eat once I have rested. Come, drink some milk, for now."

Stubs moved in to take his share when he felt a paw push his head into the dirt. Even after pointing out the dangers of his gluttonous behaviour to him, Stubs was amused that Champ continued to treat him in this way. He chuckled quietly to himself. What Champ didn't realise was that he was actually doing Stubs a favour. By shortening his meal, Champ ensured Stubs was not so full as to fall into a food coma. It enabled him the chance to investigate his surroundings and practise his hunting skills.

As soon as Champ had filled his tummy, he released Stubs and waddled closer to his mother's face. There he lay down to take a nap while snuggled against her neck. She licked him a couple of times then fell into a troubled sleep. Stubs drank enough to take away the hunger pains plus two more swallows. He stepped back and listened to the sounds of his sibling's sleepy breaths. "Are you awake, Snow?"

"Yes, I'm awake," she replied.

"Do you want to help me explore the cave?"

"No. Let's wait until Mother's awake and she can show us around."

"We could be waiting for ages," Stubs whined.

"Fine, go exploring then, but don't go outside."

Stubs was not going to lie to his sister. Because he wasn't sure he wouldn't end up outside, he chose not to reply. He discovered it was difficult stumbling around in the dark. Especially when the light source was streaming in from above. '*The opening must be up-hill,*' he thought, which seemed to be confirmed by the ache in his leg muscles as he moved.

Reaching a wall of the cave, he took one step after another, ensuring his fur remained brushed alongside the hard, cold surface. By the time he reached the opening, he was panting from the exertion and feeling the beginning pangs of thirst.

Stubs didn't want to disturb his mother further by shuffling down for another drink. Instead, he chose to search for another source of hydration. With a quick glance back into the cave, he placed his paw into the light and felt the thrill of adventure coursing through his veins.

His eyes blinked many times as they adjusted to the brightness. He raised his nose to the wind, performing shallow breaths. The air smelled crisp, but more importantly, free from danger. Stubs took in his surroundings and grinned with wonder. The tall trees provided plenty of shade and protection from the elements. Where there had not been much vegetation at their last place of rest, this area was filled with a variety of plants that had thick green leaves and dainty flowers. Pink, yellow, blue and white coloured the landscape with the sweetest fragrance Stubs had ever had the pleasure of experiencing.

"Oh, Mother," he squealed with delight. "This place is extraordinarily beautiful."

Stubs bounded along the carpet of broadleaf grasses, basking in the dappled sunlight. He frowned as his mind considered his new living arrangements. He had never seen a cave before but was pretty sure he had not just come out of one. It was more like a tunnel, perhaps created by a wombat or a hare. Shaking his head to clear his thoughts, he continued his search for interesting things to look at.

Stubs needed to keep his wits about him or risk the chance of becoming lost. His curious nature had gotten him into some hairy situations which had resulted in him having to be rescued by his mother. He did not mean to be a burden to her and would take extra care while making the journey. His mother didn't smell right, she was limping quite badly. She needed rest. If he didn't find anything in the next half hour or so, he would make the journey back to their new home.

The forest was alive with the sounds of wildlife. Birds were chirping happily in the treetops; while lizards, rats, and mice were scurrying through the underbrush. The temptation to pounce on the moving objects was strong, but Stubs managed to ignore his instincts. He stepped beneath a shrub with soft, purple flowers and froze. He had never seen anything so magnificent in his life. He licked his lips as he crouched down low, his eyes never straying from the vision before him.

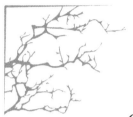

Chapter Three

Scout ventured through the forest, enjoying the solitude of her flight. She breathed in the smell of rotting vegetation and smiled. This was the environment she felt at home in.

There was so much to explore in the forest. She could spend months there and still find new things to delight her senses with. The thing she enjoyed most about this piece of Australia was the preservation of nature. Not a skerrick of litter was to be seen. The people who lived in this community either never went into the forest or took their rubbish with them when they left.

She found many trees that would make the perfect home for a fairy. She gazed around her surroundings, imagining the woodlands filled with them. She felt a pressure in her chest and placed her hand there for comfort. As she fluttered to the nearest branch to rest, she wondered what had come over her.

In the three thousand years she had lived on Earth, not once had she missed her homeland or its occupants. Now she felt herself pining for what was. Her view was limited from where she was perched. While the trunks and branches were long and thin, there were many of them situated closely together. Not happy to be left alone with her thoughts, she leant forward and exhilarated in the fall before her wings spread open and lifted her up.

She moved further into the forest, looking for something to distract her from her musings and the loneliness that ensued. After flying for a few minutes, she found it. With a gasp of pleasure, she fluttered to the ground. "This is amazing," she said aloud with no-one but herself to hear. A small village of fairy-sized mud huts and cobble-stone pathways lay before her. Scout wandered inside the nearest shelter. There was a cluster of round tables that had seating for four. Tablecloths in black material with purple flowers adorned their surfaces. Square plates and round goblets made of clay sat on each table. They were empty and without dust. Somebody had been there recently.

"Hello!" Scout yelled, walking outside. "Is anybody here?" She was met with silence. She could feel eyes on her, but couldn't see who they belonged to. "I won't hurt you!" she cried, hoping to allay their fears. Still, they remained hidden from view. Not a sound to indicate what direction they lay in. It seemed that the huts were all empty. She didn't check them all, but it was quite apparent that whoever lived in this village were currently elsewhere.

'*What a wonderful discovery to share with Briella,*' she thought. *'Perhaps by the time we get back, the inhabitants will have returned.'* Scout had no trouble finding her way back to the pub. "Wait until you see what I found in the forest, Briella," she said as she flew in through the window.

"Scout, you're home," Force said, stating the obvious.

"Hey there, Force. Where are the girls?" she asked excitedly, projecting her thoughts.

"They've returned home."

"Of course," she said, flying towards the door.

"They're not next door. They have returned to the coast," he qualified his earlier statement.

"Oh," Scout uttered as she hovered in place. After she took a few seconds to gather her thoughts, she turned to face him. Being careful to keep an accusatory tone from her voice, she asked, *"Why did they leave?"*

"April said there was an issue with one of her units that required attention."

"You sound as though you don't believe her," Scout fluttered towards him.

"I don't."

"Why not?"

"I believe she is using her property as an excuse to avoid facing her feelings for me. I would like to pursue a relationship with April, Scout. I think, if she were honest with herself, April would like to pursue a relationship with me, too."

"Force, I need to tell you something." He eyed her body language and sighed.

"What did you do?"

Playing for more time, she said, "What makes you think I *did* something?"

14

"You are wringing your hands together and biting your lip. Your eyebrows are furrowed, and you are crossing and uncrossing your feet while hovering there in front of me. I suspect out of fear of my reaction."

"Why do you have to know me so well?" she whined, slapping her forehead with her hand.

"Scout, we have worked together long enough for me to recognise a few signals in your body language. I will not hate you, regardless of what you have done. Tell me what it is so that we can move forward," he swiped his hand in the air to indicate she should land on the bench in the kitchenette.

She stood on the hard surface, fumbling with her words. *"I told a lie when you asked about your energy levels."*

"You said that the excess energy had dissipated."

"Yes, I did. What I didn't tell you was your energy signatures have amalgamated with one another, Force."

He tapped his fingers on the benchtop, "What does that mean?"

"It means that your feelings for one another will deepen. More quickly than they would have had your energies not joined together."

"So I would have fallen in love with her anyway? My feelings for April are not entirely because I used too much power when healing her?"

Scout fluttered up to Force's cheek and rubbed her hand over its surface. "You and April have been in denial for a great many years about your feelings for one another. The healing merely brought your emotions to the surface. You will need to tread carefully. April is so afraid of getting hurt, she would prefer to go her whole life without knowing what it is like to love you than run the risk of losing you."

"She is not going to lose me," he spluttered.

"You can't know that for sure," she answered, thinking about Toren's demise. "You can't promise April you will be there forever. What you can do is promise that you will give her all the love that is inside of you to give. You can promise to love her for as long as you shall live. You can promise that you will protect her with everything you've got." She landed on Force's shoulder to give her wings a rest.

Force smiled, "So, are you giving me your blessing, then?"

"You have my blessing," she smiled and was delighted to find it was genuine.

Force grinned like a man who was standing on top of the world. He leaned back on the stool and steepled his fingers. "So Scout, what are you so excited to share with Briella?"

"Hmmm, I don't know if I should tell you," she narrowed her eyes while contemplating her options. Was this something she wanted to keep just between Briella and herself? She wasn't sure. Scout could tell that Force was going to push the issue, so she figured she would need to come to a decision quickly. He was, after all, her Gatherer and a good friend.

"I suppose I'm out of favour now." Force lifted his eyes to stare at a cupboard attached to the wall as he relaxed his hands on the surface of the bench.

"What is that supposed to mean?" Scout slammed her hands on her hips with a scowl.

"Nothing. Don't worry about it."

"That's a low blow, Force. Guilting me into telling you something that should remain between best friends."

"I thought we were best friends, Scout. I guess Briella holds that position now."

"That is *so* unfair. I was going to share the most exciting discovery I've made since arriving in this town, but you can forget it. Briella will never take your place in my life. But, if you start carrying on with that sort of nonsense, you are going to find yourself missing out on a lot of opportunities you should be a part of." Scout fluttered into the air and headed for the window.

"Where are you going?"

"OUT!" she projected at him.

Chapter Four

Scout's cheeks puffed in and out as she tried to control her disappointment. She knew Force had been goading her, but couldn't work out why. Nor could she understand her reaction to his taunts. What was wrong with her?

She made her way back to the village, landing softly on the cobblestones. "Hello," she called with a smile in her voice. "Is anybody home?" Scout sighed deeply as she glanced at the buildings that lay vacant. So many thoughts crossed her mind that she didn't know where to begin. An overwhelming sadness filled her heart. Scout gracefully sank to the ground, placing her elbows on her thighs and her head in her hands. Then she began to cry; mournful sobs that wracked her torso and caused her nose to run.

She was so caught up in emotion that she hadn't sensed his approach. For the first time in a long time, Force had transformed himself into a fairy to follow her into the forest. He hovered close enough to reach his hand out and touch her. Uneasiness at the cause of her sorrow stopped him from taking the final step. His eyebrows furrowed as he gazed upon her. His mouth moved from side to side as he contemplated his actions.

The depth of her unhappiness gutted him. He had never heard anybody cry like that without having been tortured by a monster beforehand. *What did that make me?'* he wondered. He wasn't sure what he was going to say, but he couldn't stand to hear her cry a minute longer. He opened his mouth to say her name, but the sound that reached his ears made the hairs on his skin stand on end.

Scout screamed as she peered over her shoulder. Force hovered a few centimetres off the ground, a terrified expression on his face. Behind him, she could see a growling black kitten that was preparing to launch itself at Force. Keeping her voice calm, she sniffled, "It's a young kitten, Force. Don't do anything rash or you might hurt it."

Force's eyes nearly bugged out of his head, "You don't want *me* to hurt *it*?"

"It's just a baby," she managed to get out before Stubs' paws hit his back and he face-planted into the dirt. Scout laughed so hard she got the hiccoughs. While Stubs sat on Force's back with a smug expression on his face, Scout reached into her pocket and pulled out a bunch of tissues. After wiping her eyes and blowing her nose, she said, "Are you all right, Force?"

"Sure, just dandy," he grumbled.

Scout stood carefully, ensuring her movements were slow and smooth. "Hey there, kitty. Come on, off you get." She clicked her fingers, tempting the kitten closer. Stubs tipped his head to the side and mewled. "I won't hurt you," she cooed softly, stepping closer to the kitten. Stubs growled a warning. Scout stopped advancing and began waving her pointer finger at the kitten. "You are behaving like a very naughty pussycat." Stubs rocked on his haunches and launched himself at Scout, who flew up into the air. Stubs missed his target and pulled off a perfect forward roll. He stumbled to his feet, hissing and spitting.

The second the weight was removed from his back, Force was up and gauging the situation. The kitten was no longer a danger to Scout, she was safely out of reach. From the agitated sounds coming from the kitten, Force realised that not only was he in danger, but the kitten was at risk of hurting itself. There was only one thing to do. Force transformed himself into a kitten of the same size and colour. It took a few minutes to find the connections that would allow him to mind-link with Scout while in cat form. The second they connected, Force began to converse with Stubs.

"Hello, my name is Force," he meowed.

"My mother calls me Stubs," was the reply.

"You seem to be a bit angry, Stubs."

"I am not angry," Stubs assured him. "Just frustrated."

"Why?" Force queried.

"My mother needs me," he said.

"Then why aren't you with her?" Force asked.

"You don't understand," Stubs cried. "She smells funny. Bad."

"Is she injured?"

"I don't know. She is walking funny, and her leg smells bad."

"Where is she?"

"Hiding."

"Show me. I can help," Force nuzzled Stub's cheek with the top of his head. His ears twitched from the sensation of Stub's fur brushing against them.

"No, you will hurt her," Stubs growled.

"No, I won't. I promise. I can heal her."

"How?"

"I just can. You saw me change from a fairy to a cat."

"Can't everybody?"

"No, only a few special people can do this."

"People. My mother said to be wary of people."

"She is right. Some of them are dangerous. I am not one of them. Please, will you let me help her?"

"No," he shook his head from side to side, before running off.

Force considered following, but a quick glance at Scout had him standing his ground. Though she had the slightest smile on her face, her eyes glistened with unshed tears. Stepping closer, he said, "About earlier . . ."

Scout held her hand up to stop him from speaking. "I know what you are going to say, Force. You are sorry and shouldn't have said what you did, blah, blah, blah. Force, you haven't changed. That's the same sort of stuff you have been telling me for centuries. I've changed in the past few days. I'm having a hard time adjusting to always having somebody else around. Then, when I am alone, instead of enjoying it, I find myself beginning to feel lonely, or worse, guilty for loving the solitude."

"Is that why you were crying?" he frowned.

"I was crying because I found this beautiful village . . . you might want to transform into a person my size to see it better." He obliged and Scout held her hand out to him. His grip was gentle but firm. "And when I looked inside, it was clear that the inhabitants of the buildings had vacated them not so long ago. I felt myself longing to meet them, with no idea how long they would be away or if they were even planning on returning.

"I was so excited to think that we would have a community of our own living here that I felt a deep sense of disappointment when I discovered Briella had gone back to the coast with April. I became overwhelmed with sadness when I returned to find the owners of these establishments had not reappeared. I'm afraid I lost it, Force, and burst into tears."

He opened his mouth to tell her it was more than a few tears but was smart enough to keep the thought to himself, in this instance. As they reached the peak of a small rise, Force felt excitement bubble up inside him. At that moment, he felt like a little boy exploring a mysterious jungle.

He ran towards the buildings, pulling Scout forward. She yanked her hand out of his, moments before losing her balance completely. Her wings fluttered furiously, preventing her from a nasty fall. "Well, I never," she muttered, reaching up with her right hand to brush her fringe to the side. She viewed his child-like antics with a smile on her face. *'Aw, how cute.'*

Chapter Five

Stubs ran home. He alternated between glances over his shoulder and keeping an eye on the path. It took him twice as long to return. He was gasping for breath and thirstier than ever upon arrival.

In his fright, he didn't notice the small scratches that covered his face from diving through bushes to hide his short stature from view. He was terrified that his little venture out would lead to the discovery of his family's location by the male and female in the woods.

Who knew what they would do to his loved ones. His mother had warned him on many occasions of the dangers in going out on his own. She had also used many words to provide him with a horrifying picture of the humans that stole little kittens from their mothers so that they were never seen again.

While she told her stories, he pictured creatures much larger than the two he had left behind. She hadn't mentioned the fact they could take on the forms of other animals. Perhaps, that was what made them so dangerous. Maybe, she had only ever seen them in giant form.

Either way, there was no telling what she would say or do to him if he were to articulate what he had been up to. Hopefully, she would still be sleeping when he entered the cave, or tunnel as he had come to think of his new home. Stubs crept over to the opening and stuck his head inside. The darkness had wrapped its arms around his family, making them invisible to his eyes.

He took a deep breath and thought brave thoughts before taking a few steps inside. Stubs stood still for a few minutes, allowing his eyes to adjust. The first thing he noticed was a slight movement in his peripheral vision. His body began to shake. He could have let fear take over, but he was smart enough to know that if anything dangerous had been in there, his mother would have taken care of it, sick or not.

"Hello, who's there?" he said, puffing out his chest and protracting his claws.

"Where have you been?" Ash's voice cut through the darkness.

"Checking out our surroundings. I thought I might be able to find mother something to eat," Stubs answered steadily.

"Why?"

"She is not well and needs some help. We can't rely on her forever to satisfy our needs. It is probably for the best if we start to learn how to take care of ourselves, don't you think?"

"A mother takes care of her kittens, Stubs. It is the natural order of things. Why can't you just be happy with the way things are? Why do you want to change things all the time?"

"Survival of the fittest, Ash. Those that are willing to take risks and try new things will have a greater chance of survival."

"Or a shorter lifespan and an earlier grave."

"What are you two arguing about?" their mother asked.

"Sorry to wake you, Mother," Stubs said, rubbing his head against her chest. "Did you have a good sleep?"

"Yes, fine. Come away from the entrance," she said, grabbing Stubs by the neck and expecting Ash to follow. She carried him to the others and placed him gently on the ground. "Look after each other while I get us something to eat. Stay here, all of you."

"We will," the kittens chorused.

"Stubs?" she questioned.

"I said it too," he whined.

"Promise?" she said, needing some extra assurance before leaving him behind. She knew he had been out but was too tired to search for him. Luckily this time, he had come home safely without the need for any intervention from her.

"Yes, I promise," he said, swallowing his irritation to appease his mother.

"I won't be long."

Once they could no longer hear the padding of their mother's paws, Snow wriggled herself over the top of her siblings until she was sitting beside Stubs. She didn't want the others to hear, so she whispered in his ear, "What did you see out there?"

"It's very pretty outside, Snow. There are dainty flowers in exquisite colours, and oh, the perfume; It's simply divine."

"What else?" she asked, her eyes growing more prominent as images began filling her head.

"The trees are taller, and the leaves are a darker colour. The shrubs are not as dense, therefore, easier to huddle inside to hide."

"Ooh, it sounds lovely," she squealed a little louder than she meant to.

"What are you two going on about?" Champ grumbled.

"Nothing you would want to talk about."

"Who says?" Champ growled.

"Nobody," Stubs said, hoping Champ would let the conversation die a natural end. The 'harrumph' Stubs received as a reply told him his strategy was right on the ball where his brother was concerned. He waited a few seconds before continuing, "You are going to love being out there, Snow. I guess you will have to wait until Mother says you can go outside before you see it, though. You being such a good girl and all."

"I don't always do what I'm told. I only stayed behind to keep an eye on Shadow. She was feeling a bit scared after the move, and I didn't want her waking Mother. We both know how that would have ended."

Stubs did know. They would have been in a lot of trouble, and he would have been given an extra scolding for leading Snow astray. "Next time Mother goes to sleep, I'll show you what it's like out there, as long as you promise we won't be gone long. Champ, I'm sure, would have no qualms about waking Mother to tell her you are missing."

"Yeah, you could be right about that."

"What are you going on about, Stubs?" Champ snarled, moving closer to the duo.

"I was asking where the best position is to have a nap. I'm a bit tired."

"Well, the best position does not belong to you. We all get first pick of the softest, most comfortable place to sleep before you."

Stubs sighed before nipping the tip of Snow's tail which she used to lead him to a snug corner in the back of the tunnel. He lay down and closed his eyes. "Do you mind if I stay with you while you sleep, Stubs, even though I'm not tired?"

"Of course not," he mumbled before sitting up in a hurry. He narrowed his eyes as he said, "Unless you are planning on doing something while my eyes are closed?"

"No, I wouldn't do that. Lie down. You'll be safe with me."

He fell asleep within seconds of his head hitting the dirt.

Chapter Six

Force spent the rest of the afternoon exploring the village and its surrounds with Scout. He had hoped Stubs would make another appearance. He would like to be given another chance to convince the poor little thing to let him help his mother. Force worried that the mother might die without assistance leaving Stubs, who was too young to fend for himself, to perish also. Force had already decided to take Stubs home with him if he refused to give up the location of his mother. Until he spotted him again, there was nothing more Force could do.

"I suppose we should head back," Force said, noticing the darkness creeping in.

"You go," Scout replied. "I'm going to stay out here tonight."

"For what purpose?"

"You know I like to sleep in the forest. I don't like being enclosed in human buildings."

"Then why didn't you say something before April began building you a house?"

"I don't know. She seemed to find happiness in creating it for Briella and me. I didn't want to disappoint her. I will only need to sleep in it when Briella and April come to visit. Besides, Briella will need somewhere to stay when she comes. She doesn't like sleeping in the forest.

"She lives in her house within April's home at the coast, but that is not natural. Briella needs to start acting like a fairy. The Purge is coming. She will need to be prepared for its arrival, and she can't do that while living in April's pocket, so to speak."

"What does The Purge have to do with anything?"

"We will be relocated to Fairyland prior to the commencement of The Purge. Briella will become an outcast if she continues to act like a human. She will be in unfamiliar territory because there will be no way for her to get back to Earth."

Force looked aghast. "Perhaps she should stay here then. We could hide her."

"That won't be necessary. Dynopiah, the wood nymph we met a few days ago, said that we had at least a decade to prepare. Briella will be ready by then."

"What makes you say that? The Starlight Investigation team are not going to let the two of you live together full-time. You both have areas of Australia that are your responsibility to keep safe. Where do you think Briella is going to live when she is not here?"

"In her house at April's place," Scout sighed.

"Don't worry about it now, Scout. We've got plenty of time to devise a rescue plan for Briella. Do you think the fairy that was assigned to this area before you built this village?"

"No," Scout shook her head. "While these are lovely, they are not our style of dwelling."

"Who do you think could have created them?"

"Probably some of the local children. They probably bought them at the shops and then set up a play area where they could let their imaginations run wild."

"But the furnishings are free from dust. That means somebody has been here recently."

"Jacinta spends a lot of time in the woods, Force. Now that she has become friends with Calamity, she has lots of children to play with. Perhaps it is another group of kids. We might never know. We can't very well stay here until their return. It could be days, or even months before they come back to play."

"You're right," he said. His thoughts went back to the kitten. "Have you spent much time in this part of the forest?"

"No, that was the first time I've ventured here," Scout admitted. "Have you?"

"No. There must be a water source nearby for the mother cat to be raising her kittens there. Would you mind helping me find it, Scout?"

"Not at all. Why does it matter?"

"If she is injured, she may not be able to hunt effectively."

"So, if you can find the water source, we can leave some food there for them to eat," Scout finished for him.

"Exactly," he grinned broadly.

"What kind of food are you thinking?"

"Well, I was hoping you would continue surveying the area while I ducked to the shop to pick up some dry food."

"Sure, good idea. That way, the food won't go off before she can find it."

"Stay safe," he said as his body grew to its usual size. Without a backward glance, he headed towards the pub to retrieve his bike and his wallet.

It took her half an hour to find the small creek that meandered through the woods. She shook her head at herself. *'Girl you are always heading off in the wrong direction when you don't have a monster's signal to follow,'* she thought. She landed carefully, mindful of disturbing any paw prints that might be visible along the bank. Strolling with downturned eyes, she searched for any sign of a feline's presence. A few minutes before Force's return, she found them. Allowing the mind-link to take place, she guided him to her location.

"This would be the perfect place to leave the food, Force. See the paw prints in the dirt?"

He placed the container of food he'd brought with him on the ground before shrinking himself for a better view.

"I agree," he stated with interest. He pointed to a spot over her shoulder, "Why don't we wait over there by those trees?"

"As long as it's downwind, it should be a great spot to lay in wait," she stated.

But the mother cat never came.

Chapter Seven

Stubs was getting itchy feet. It had been two days since he'd had the opportunity to leave the tunnel. His mother had ventured out for little bursts, always returning before he and Snow could make their preparations to go. Stubs worried that his mother wasn't eating and said as much. She simply smiled in return.

Having been inside the tunnel for so long, his eyes had adjusted to the darkness. He figured there had to be a light source coming from somewhere further along the hollow because he was able to tell the difference between night and day without having to move closer to the entrance. Not being given another chance to exit through the opening, he convinced his sister to explore their new home further.

"Where are you two going?" their mother queried.

"We are checking out our new home, Mother. That's okay, isn't it?" Stubs replied.

"Don't go too far," she warned, not having had a chance to explore their new home herself before relocating her family.

"We won't," Snow said excitedly.

"Can I come?" Ash asked.

"Of course," Snow replied before checking with Stubs.

He simply stared at her. She bowed her head, knowing she had displeased him.

"Does anyone else wish to come?" he asked. When he didn't receive a reply, he looked to his sisters and said, "Come along then."

After half an hour of walking, they realised they were indeed in a very long tunnel. The further they travelled, the darker it became. There were a couple of places that had small holes in the ceiling that allowed light to filter through. Once they moved past those places, though, it took a while for their eyes to readjust to the gloom, wasting precious minutes.

"This is boring," Ash grumbled.

"Turn around," Stubs commanded with a deep sigh. He had known she would start complaining sooner or later when he'd allowed her to come. "We'll head back for a drink. I'm getting thirsty anyway."

Feeling deflated, Stubs trudged back to his mother with his sisters. He was going to go out of his brain if he had to stay in the dark for an hour longer.

"Did you have a nice time?" their mother asked.

"No," Ash growled. "It was boring."

"Is that right?" mother cat asked, spotting the scowl that Snow gave Ash. "Snow?"

"It was nice to be able to stretch my legs for a bit," she answered.

"I suppose you are all feeling the same way," mother cat said.

'I'm not!" Shadow cried. "I like it here."

"You like it here because you are hidden away, Shadow. You need to learn to embrace life. You can't hide in the darkness your entire life."

"Why not, Mother?"

"You need to learn to hunt and fend for yourself. I won't be around forever."

"You'll be around long enough to take care of me until I'm old," Shadow pouted.

"Get up, all of you. We are going on a grand adventure," their mother stated.

Stubs was so excited he almost bumped into her on his way to reach the exit. Mother cat leaned forward and gripped the back of his neck between her teeth. Lifting him up, she grinned when squeals of outrage poured from him. Slowly, she limped towards the opening, giving her young a chance to keep up. She ignored Stubs outburst knowing the position of her hold and the rocking motion of her movement would lull him into submission.

Mother cat led them over the damp terrain that would take another day or so to dry out after the downpour of the previous night. The raindrops glistened on the blades of grass, the leaves of the trees and the petals of the wildflowers that grew in abundance along the water's edge.

THE CURIOUS KITTEN

The kittens gasped with awe as their eyes took in the beauty of their surroundings. They breathed in the crispness of the air and enjoyed the cool morning breeze as it ruffled their fur. Everything that moved in the wind became prey to be stalked or hunted. She led them to a bend in the creek that had a safe platform for them to learn from. Placing Stubs at her feet, she said, "It is time for you to learn how to drink water."

"What is water?" Ash questioned.

"Why? I like your milk," Shadow sulked.

Mother cat showed them where to put their feet so they wouldn't lose their balance and fall into the creek. Next, she showed them how to use their tongue to scoop up the water. The kittens tried this new technique with varying amounts of success, beginning with Champ and finishing with Shadow. "I am so proud of you my little kittens," she said quietly, focussing her attention to the other side of the bank. Scout knew she had caught the attention of the mother cat when the feline herded the kittens together and crouched into a predatory pose.

Mother cat licked her lips as the creature landed on the petals of a daisy flower. She glanced from right to left, looking for a way to cross the river without getting wet. To her annoyance, there weren't any low hanging branches to climb, or dead tree stumps with which to cross the quickly flowing stream of water. She determined she would need to get her feet wet if she wanted to secure a tasty meal for her kittens.

"Stay where you are," she warned her kittens as she began to stalk her prey. The movements of her front legs were slow and precise. As for her back leg, well, the pain that came from being in that position was almost enough to make her abandon the idea.

"What is mother doing?" Snow whispered.

"Hunting," Stubs answered softly. He was too interested in watching his mother hunt so he could learn how to do it, to tell his mother that he knew the creature.

Mother cat's hesitation was short-lived. The pride in Stub's voice encouraged her to resume a stealthy approach. She stepped into the stream, bracing herself against the cold and the pull of the water. The creature seemed to be unaware she was being hunted. The mother cat reached the middle of the creek, careful to place her paws amongst the pebbles.

The fire in her leg was almost unbearable, but she continued to move forward. The opportunity to show her babies how to catch their food was too great to pass up. Her leg was getting worse with each passing hour. She needed to do something to ensure her kittens survived should her injury get the better of her. Almost to the edge of the bank, she heard a sound she hadn't wanted to hear, the fluttering of wings.

"NO," she yelled as she watched the creature fly away.

A glance over her shoulder told her why. Three little kittens were bouncing excitedly on their paws. Stubs was perfectly still, learning with watchful eyes. Snow was asleep at his side.

THE CURIOUS KITTEN

Mother cat extended her claws and swiped at the bank in anger. A growl ripped through the air as she unleashed her frustration. After gaining control of her emotions, she limped back to her kittens and led the way home.

Chapter Eight

Scout watched them leave from a safe distance, determined to find the location of their home. Although aware the mother cat hunted her, Scout knew she would have had a relatively good chance of being captured had the feline not been injured. Once she discovered their hideaway, Scout hurried home to notify Force.

She flew through the window, *"I know where they are!"*

"Who?" Briella asked, thrilled to see her friend.

"Briella," she cried, fluttering to her friend and hugging her firmly. "It's so good to see you. Where's Force?"

Briella raised an eyebrow, "Good to see you, too. He's next door, saying hello to April." Scout took off for the door. "What's got you in such a hurry?"

"There is an injured cat with kittens that needs help," Scout threw over her shoulder. "Wait until you see what I discovered in the forest."

"What is it?" Briella asked, chasing after her friend.

"I'll show you later," she said, "It's too impressive to ruin with words. I can assure you it will be worth the wait. How did it go back home?"

"Great," Briella said.

"You seem to be more at ease with yourself," Scout observed.

Briella shrugged, "Nothing went awry while I was away. Halloween is getting closer, and my magic has behaved itself over the past couple of days. Perhaps, the danger is over."

Scout felt a little disappointed to think that the drawings Briella had completed may not have a way to come to life to give the people in their new community a thrill on All Hallow's Eve. She did feel relieved, however, that Briella was no longer feeling fearful of what might happen if her emotions were to become excited.

The fairies flew into an uncomfortable situation that was developing between Force and April. She appeared to be experiencing discomfort at having him stand too close to her personal bubble. He seemed to be annoyed that she was trying to distance herself from him. Scout entered the room and said, *"I've found them, Force. Come quickly."*

He spun around on his heels and asked, "Who?"

"The cats," she said, annoyed that he had forgotten them so quickly. When she glanced at April, she could hardly blame him. He definitely had his work cut out for him.

"Lead the way," he said, instantly transforming into fairy form. April and Briella remained rooted to the spot, surprised expressions on their faces as Scout and Force exited the room swiftly.

April glanced at Briella, "Any ideas?"

"Scout said something about an injured cat."

April frowned, "Why would that make him leave in such a hurry?"

"Apparently, she's got kittens."

April quickly composed herself and hurried out the room.

"Where are you going?" Briella yelled.

"To give them a hand," April answered. She found them quickly and followed on foot. Stepping inside the forest, she contemplated turning herself into a fairy as well but decided one of them should stay in human form. Their healing abilities didn't work while they took the appearance of another being. She wasn't as agile as Scout and Force who could zip around obstacles quickly, sometimes flying right through the middle.

She tried to keep her footsteps light, and to avoid stepping on anything that would make a lot of noise. The last thing April wanted to do was alert the cat of their presence and have her runaway without receiving the medical attention she required. Scout landed on a branch and pointed to the burrow. "They are in there."

Force glanced down and nodded. He flew to the entrance and contemplated walking inside, but thought better of it. Force felt Scout behind him before he saw her. "What do you think?" he asked her.

"I think we should send you in there in your cat form. If you look like a kitten, the mother might be less inclined to hurt you. Then you can ascertain the situation and report back with information that could make the retrieval go a lot smoother."

"Won't she be able to smell that I am different?"

"Probably. She will be more defensive than normal too. Either way, you will probably get scratched up, if not bitten," Scout grimaced.

"Nah, I'll be right. The mother cat will be able to sense my intent. She will know that I am not there to hurt her or her kittens."

"If you say so," Scout said.

Force morphed himself and entered the burrow cautiously. He wanted to appear as though he was lost and in need of help. The mother cat sensed his presence and growled menacingly. He froze on the spot, afraid of what she might do. Her next move was quite surprising. She deferred to Stubs, who quickly moved between his mother and the newcomer. "Don't hurt him," Stubs cried.

"You know this kitten?"

"Yes," Stubs answered.

"From where?"

"Out there," he answered.

"Please, can you help me? I seem to have become lost and can't find my way home."

The mother cat stepped forward, her kittens looking on curiously. She sniffed Force oddly, her nostrils curling up at the bottoms. "You smell of human," she growled, grabbing Stubs by the leg and dragging him behind her.

"I live with them," Force acknowledged. "They have been good to my mother and me."

"Then how is it that you became lost?" she probed suspiciously.

"I like to explore my surroundings," he glanced towards Stubs. "and got carried away."

The mother cat accepted his explanation without question. She had a kitten afflicted by the same traits as the newcomer. She was not well enough, however, to take on the responsibility of another kitten. With regret, she said, "I am sorry young one. I am not in a position to help you."

Force was stunned by her reply. She must be feeling worse than he had realised. "Could you at least take me to the edge of the woods? I am sure that once I am out in the open, I will be able to find the farmhouse I came from."

"You live in a farmhouse?" Ash asked, taking a step forward. "What is that?"

"A big house that is cool in summer and warm in winter," Force replied.

"That sounds wonderful," she sighed.

"What do you do for food?" Stubs asked.

"The humans give me food to eat, plus whatever my mother catches when she hunts."

THE CURIOUS KITTEN

"You are fed by your mother and the humans?" Champ asked.

The mother cat was unsurprised by his response. She knew she was not feeding him what he needed with her leg the way it was. She wondered if she should allow her kittens to be raised by the humans who were looking after the newcomer. His fur shone with health as did his eyes. Would she be doing the right thing by trying to care for her kittens when there might be a better option?

"Would your humans be willing to take care of my kittens?"

"Sure," Force replied. "But why would you not want to take care of them yourself?"

"I am injured. I cannot care for them any longer."

"What are you saying, Mother?" Ash asked.

The mother cat ignored her, staring at Force while she waited for an answer.

"My humans would take care of you too if you would like to live with them."

The mother cat looked at him sadly, "I don't think so."

"You are going to abandon us, Mother," Stubs growled. His eyes glowed with animosity.

"I love you all immensely. I want you to grow up to be healthy, happy felines. You will not have that opportunity if you stay here with me. You will all die of starvation," she told them truthfully, no longer able to hide the seriousness of her injury. "This kitten can provide you with an opportunity to flourish."

45

"A loving mother would stay with her kittens," Stubs grumbled with an accusatory tone.

"I will see you safe," she promised. "Come, kittens, let us see if we can find this young one's home."

Chapter Nine

Force snuggled into the mother cat's coat. He rubbed his head beneath her chin and tickled the fur on her chest. "Let me check to ensure it is safe out there for your kittens. Wait until I return before making your way outside."

"That is not necessary, little one."

"I insist," he said, making his way towards the opening.

Stubs lurched out of his mother's reach, "I'll come with you."

Once they were close, Force said, "My friends are waiting outside to help your mother. Do you think she will be upset when she sees them?"

"Maybe," he muttered. "Is she going to die?"

"No, we are going to heal her. There are too many of you for my friend to carry on her own. I will need to turn back into my human form to get you all back home. You will have to go in there and encourage her to come out first. Tell her that I have decided to stay out here as a lookout."

"Okay," Stubs agreed, making his way back inside.

Force established a link with April and quickly apprised

her of the situation. She was ready to act when the mother made her appearance. The moment her head poked out of the hole, April fussed over the kitten in her hand. "Who is your friend, Smoogie?" She leant down and placed Force at the foot of a native ginger plant. She then turned her attention to the mother cat. Remaining in a kneeling position, she called to it tenderly, "Hey there, kitty. I won't hurt you." She clicked her fingers quietly, "Come here, and let me take a look at you."

The mother cat meowed softly, "Is she safe?"

"Yes," Force mewled back.

The mother cat crept forward, the pain in her leg evident. She stayed just out of reach of April as she studied her intently. April held the back of her hand out to the cat, making sure to remain a few centimetres away. The cat sniffed her, recognising the scent from the newcomer. *'This must be the kitten's human,'* she surmised.

"Your leg doesn't look too good, does it? I'd like to have a closer look if it's all right with you?"

Force moved forward and rubbed himself over her leg. April chuckled quietly, "Yes, I know. You don't like my attention being on anyone other than you." She picked him up and returned him gently to the base of the ginger plant. "Stay there, Smoogie."

By this time, the mother cat had moved within reach. April reached out slowly and ran her fingers over the cat's back. "Now, let's have a look at that leg." April grabbed the cat beneath the tummy and lifted her off the ground, tucking her firmly against her body. Then she ran her hand over the leg and scanned the flesh, bone, muscle and tendons for the source of the problem. She was horrified to discover the cat had a serious gunshot wound and that the injury had since become infected.

April murmured softly to the cat as she extracted the bullet and sent healing energy into the wound. The cat struggled slightly as her leg began to heat but soon settled down again once the pain started to lessen. After a few minutes, the leg was good as new. April rubbed the cat's cheek and got a nip on her thenar eminence (the part of the palm below the thumb) for her troubles.

"Ouch," she howled, giving her hand a couple of shakes. "Naughty kitty."

She put the mother cat on the ground and viewed her irritably. She glanced at Force, "Nice friend, you have there, Smoogie."

Stubs meowed bravely as he raced to stand by his mother, protecting her. The mother cat gave an answering meow, warning him off. Humans were definitely not creatures you'd want to be tangling with. Force padded towards the mother cat, "Will you let my human take care of you and your kittens?'

"No," she stated decisively. "My leg is healed, and I am quite capable of taking care of my kittens."

"Until next time," he cautioned. "You know, if you were to live with my human, you and your kittens would have a safe place to roam, hunt, and rest peacefully."

"What makes you so sure?"

"My humans are highly respected in the human world.

People wouldn't dare come onto their property to shoot their animals. My humans would likely shoot back, and get away with it."

"Is that the truth?" she asked.

"Yes."

"Fine. We'll give it a trial for a few days, see how it goes."

"Great," Force replied. "I'll let my human know."

The cat looked at him funny. Force decided it was time to let her in on his secret. She thought he was joking until he transformed himself. She became spooked and ran back down below. Stubs ran in after her.

"You lied to me, Stubs."

"No, I didn't, Mother."

"You told me that kitten was safe."

"He is."

"He is a human," she hissed, furious at him for placing them in danger, "who knows where we are."

"The lady fixed your leg, Mother. They are good people."

"That is beside the point."

"You said you would look after us. We would have died if she had not healed your leg. I think we should give them a chance."

"He is dangerous, Stubs."

"Why?"

"Because," she struggled to find the words to explain her feelings. "He is not right."

"He is special. Like the woman. Imagine what our life

would be like with them in it."

She did. They could bring them danger just as easily as protect them from it. She looked at their faces. She could tell, they had believed the human's words and wanted to live somewhere like that.

"A few days," she cautioned.

"Thank you, Mother," Stubs grinned. He hurried outside to see if the humans were still there. Force and April were where he left them. He meowed at them excitedly. It took Force a couple of seconds to make the connection with Stubs while in human form. "I missed that little buddy. Say again?"

He was surprised when Stubs complied. Force passed the information onto April, suggesting they carry one kitten in each hand. That meant the mother would have to walk along beside them, which wouldn't be a problem now that her leg was better. Provided, of course, she had the energy to make it that distance. She hadn't been eating sufficiently. Force figured they should make a quick stop for some dry food and a drink of water before beginning the trek home to the pub.

He waited for Stubs to send the cats out before they made their way to the creek. The mother cat was grateful for their hospitality and would have overeaten had it not been for Force's cautionary words. The walk home was uneventful, but they ran into a bit of trouble when they arrived at the pub.

Chapter Ten

Force and April used the back entrance to avoid bringing any attention to themselves. Unfortunately, Robbie had taken that moment to dash to the toilet before the next lot of patrons started making their appearance. He hopped from one foot to the other, as he said, "You can't bring them in here."

April blinked her eyes in surprise at the gruffness of his voice. "They are tiny kittens in need of a home. Their mother has been injured and needs a few days to recover."

"That may be the case," his face softened slightly, "but I'm running a business here, and they are not allowed."

"Nobody will even know they are here once we have hidden them behind closed doors," she said.

Robbie was going to wet himself if she kept him any longer. "I'd love to oblige your wishes, April . . ."

"Then do it," she butted in. "We'll be gone soon, and they will have loads of room to run around in at our new place. They are too little to leave out there with no supervision."

He peered at the cat weaving her way between their legs. "They have a mother," he replied.

"What if she gets shot again? She might die this time."

"She looks okay to me," he jiggled on the spot.

"Well, she's not," April's voice roughened slightly. "I wouldn't argue with you if I wasn't concerned about their safety. I will make sure they don't make a mess and will clean it up if they do. Please, Robbie. Just a couple of days?"

"Fine," he said, running for the bathroom. "You remember this when you are being railroaded by a suspect."

"Where do you think I learnt it from?" her raised voice followed him through the door. He chuffed slightly before letting loose with a curse. She grimaced guiltily hoping she hadn't caused him to have an accident. They hurried up the staircase and fought over which room the cats would be situated in. April won the argument. Force hoped his decision to concede would gain him favour at a later date.

Briella was excited to see them return until she spotted what they held in their arms. "What are those things doing here?"

"We are going to take care of them," Scout answered happily. "Aren't they cute?"

"Sure, for now. They will eat you when they get bigger," Briella warned.

"No, they won't. They will be our friends, protecting us from other predators."

"You think?" Briella viewed them distastefully. "I'll be staying with you until they leave."

"They are coming with us to our new home, Briella."

"I see," she fluttered to the window and stared outside. The mother cat jumped up beside her and startled her. She too, peered out not giving Briella the slightest bit of attention.

"I don't think you have any worries about your safety," Scout stated.

"Sure, while everybody is looking. Wait until she gets hungry and wants to feed her kittens."

"There will be plenty of food for them to eat," Scout assured her.

April collected her handbag from the countertop. "You girls be right here while I grab some kitty litter and a tray?"

"Hardly," Briella said sourly. *"I'm going next door."*

"Do you want me to give them to Force to look after?"

Briella studied her face. *"No,"* she admitted, noticing the stress lines had disappeared from her forehead. *"They'll be fine here."*

"I won't be long," April promised.

Force wanted to go with her but thought it best to keep an eye on the fairies. He was awarded a grateful smile from April. Determined to get away from the kittens, Briella suggested Scout show her the surprise she had been saving for later. Scout's face became highly animated as she pictured the images she was about to share. *"You'll be right here, Force?"*

"Of course. The cats and I will get to know each other while you are gone."

He grabbed a couple of shallow bowls from the cupboard and filled one with water and the other with dry food. He sent April a text requesting a few tins of different flavoured wet food for the kittens to try. He worried that their milk teeth were not strong enough to withstand the biscuits. The mother would not be able to hunt for them until settlement of their new home took place.

Force watched the fairies leave through the window with a touch of jealousy. He wanted to walk through the village and observe Briella's response to seeing it for the first time. A small black kitten flopped its body against his foot, sending the feeling of missing out far away. He scooped the kitten from the floor and carried it to the centre of the room where the coffee table was. He sat down and soon had kittens trying to climb all over him. The mother cat sat at the window, peering into the distance.

Chapter Eleven

Briella had a spring in her step as she wandered through the village. She assumed the persona of a voyeur as she perused the quaint cottages with their cobblestoned borders. Various expressions adorned her face as she absorbed every sight, sound and smell. Her heels clicked loudly on the hardened surfaces, squelching unpleasantly when she went off course.

She peered inside a building, leaning casually against the doorframe. Her arms were crossed over her chest, and her legs were crossed elegantly at the ankles. "Hmmm," she murmured as her eyes raked over the furnishings. "The occupants have style."

"It's nice, isn't it?"

"It's all right." Briella stepped further into the building, her eyes never staying still. "There are no doors or windows, only openings."

"Our houses back home were like this, open and airy."

"Small and unsecure," Briella contradicted.

Scout held her tongue. She wasn't about to get involved in an argument. She could tell that Briella was more excited than disappointed by her discovery. That was good enough for her. "Do you think these belong to fairies or humans?"

Briella whipped her head around swiftly. "These were not put here by one of us."

Scout was disappointed by the conviction in her tone. Even though she had come to the same conclusion herself, there had still been some hope in her heart that fairies other than the Locator Fairies shared the Earth with them. Scout found the loneliness creep in. She gave herself a mental shake, hoping her outward appearance remained unchanged. "How is our house coming along?"

Briella's face brightened. "It is finished. April just needs to put it together at the new property. I thought I let you know that before we left for the coast. Sorry."

Scout waved her apology aside. "Let me show you the garden before we leave." Scout escorted her outside and took her down the wavering path. In the middle of the village was a small plot of soil with the most gorgeous bunches of dahlias growing in the dappled sunlight.

Briella gasped with delight as she lowered herself to sit among their leaves. She ran her fingers over the petals, which were soft and smooth. "How beautiful," she breathed softly.

Scout grinned broadly, "I thought you'd like them. Want to take a couple home?"

Briella gave her a quizzical stare. "You don't think they will hinder our flight home? They are a bit big."

Scout studied the flowers critically. "I believe you are right," she determined. "We should come back tomorrow with the jeep."

"Great idea," Briella laughed happily. An ominous growl had them jumping with fright. That, combined with the thought of going for another ride in the remote-controlled car, had the production of fairy dust kicking into overdrive within Briella's body. It burst from her pores like an exploding powderpuff. Luckily, Scout was outside of the firing line. Unfortunately, Stubs was not.

He had been looking for his family when he heard the fairies talking. The yearning for his mother temporarily forgotten as curiosity took hold. He tried to fight the compulsion to seek out the source of the noise, for that was what got him separated from his family in the first place. He had heard a rustle in the bushes and curiosity had gotten the best of him. By the time his curiosity had been satisfied, his whole family had disappeared. But once again, he was unsuccessful. The emotion was too powerful.

He had snuck up behind the fairies, hoping to pounce on at least one of them, if not both. Their wings fluttered slowly, the anticipation of their capture increasing exponentially. He lowered his front legs and wriggled the stump of his tail, preparing to launch, let out an ominous growl akin to "Geronimo" when the assault of Briella's fairy dust occurred.

He sneezed explosively, the dust irritating his eyes enormously. He rubbed them with tender paws. He could hear the shocked voices of the creatures but wasn't able to see them. His eyes hurt too much to open them. He cried, wishing his mother were there. He felt tiny hands rubbing the fur on his chest and fluid pouring over his eyelids. Soon, he was able to pick out the shape of their bodies from the grass. A few more minutes enabled him to see a fuzzy version of their faces. Fifteen minutes later, he was able to make out their features entirely. He blinked a few times, but not because his eyes were still hurting. He could have sworn the fairies were taller before the dust cloud smothered him.

"Oh my goodness, Scout. Look at what I've done!" Briella shrieked with dismay as his body transformed before her eyes.

Scout's incredulous gaze swept over the changes in his physiology. "It's okay, Briella. Don't panic."

"Don't panic? It looks like we left a kitten behind, and now I've turned him into a monster. What if there are more of them out here?"

"He is not a monster and you didn't leave him behind, I did. As for leaving more behind, I doubt it. They would be together, don't you think? I bet this is Stubs. He was the one Force and I met first. He seems to be a very curious kitten who tends to wander off. I bet that's how he got left behind."

Briella shook her head, totally ignoring Scout's explanation. All she could do was fixate on the effects of her troublesome magic. "Of course he is a monster, Scout! Just look at him. He is the size of his mother. Look at his colouring. Where did those grey and white stripes come from? Where has his shiny black fur gone? What if he doesn't change back? He looks like a white tiger cub, but with a thinner head."

"Briella, you've got to stop panicking. Your magical mishaps always right themselves by dawn. Why don't we get him to follow us home and let Force and April deal with him."

"His mother is there. She won't recognise him. She will think he is a threat to her babies and might hurt him."

"Well, what do you suggest?"

"I don't know what to do," Briella cried unhappily.

Scout gave her a cuddle, keeping a watchful eye on Stubs. She wondered if they were in more danger now that he was the size of an adult. She hoped he still had the outlook of a young kitten, playful but not too serious. Scout had to admit he could kill them both with a single swipe of his paw if he got too carried away.

Stubs sat down and swished his tail. He peered at it with surprise. Gone was the stub that had given him his name. In its place was a long, normal-looking tail, albeit the wrong colour. He mewled with happiness that he had a fully functioning tail, then noticed that the fur on his leg had also changed shades. His heart grew heavy with despair that his glossy black fur had been replaced with white and dark grey stripes.

He tried to communicate with the fairies, but they couldn't understand him. Stubs knew that they were somehow responsible for the transformation in his appearance. He wanted to know where his mother was and felt the fairies might be able to help find her. He worried that she would not recognise him if he did manage to find her.

Chapter Twelve

Briella paced in a tight circle, being careful to keep her wings as still as possible. She couldn't stay motionless to think, and she didn't want to give him an incentive to attack. Underneath his new façade, he was a baby who had not learnt to take care of himself properly.

His mother had not had the opportunity to teach him to hunt effectively for his food. He was also unskilled in defending himself against another tomcat or predatory animal. Briella was desperate to work out a way to keep him safe until he reverted to his usual self and could be reunited with his mother.

Briella turned to Scout, "He is going to die, isn't he?"

"Why would you say that?"

"He can't take care of himself."

"We can take care of him," Scout said calmly.

"How? I can't use my magic without things going wrong."

"We won't need magic to look after him. There is dry food at the creek. We left it there for his mother, but he is big enough now to eat it himself. Actually, it is probably just as well he is the size that he is. Otherwise, he would go hungry."

Briella scowled at her, "If he wasn't this big we could have reunited him with his mother. She could have fed him and protected him."

"One of us would have gone to the pub and waited for April's return if she was still out shopping before Force could come back to collect Stubs. That would have left one of us alone with him. A baby but, potentially, a dangerous, predatory animal. I think it worked out better this way. We can take care of him until the morning if we have to. April or Force will come looking for us when we don't return."

"Do you have your phone on you?"

"No," Scout replied. "I tend to leave it at home these days with Force remaining in the area."

"We could send a distress signal."

"This hardly constitutes a situation that warrants an action as drastic as that. We will be fine, Briella. You are worrying too much. Let's see if we can get him to follow us to the creek."

Scout and Briella walked backwards so they could keep an eye on Stubs. He watched them with keen eyes, lowering his front legs into a killer's crouch. Briella turned her head in Scout's direction but was too frightened to take her eyes off him. She whispered out the corner of her mouth, "Do we fly?"

"Not yet," Scout murmured back. "We are too close. He will capture us before we have lift-off."

"When?"

"I'll let you know," Scout answered, hoping she would get the timing right.

His irises flickered in size as his eagerness grew. The capture of a fairy would be a considerable boost to his confidence. He had watched his mother keenly when she had taken them to the river. While his siblings had not been able to contain their excitement, he had sat quietly and observed the way she had manoeuvred her body while hunting her prey.

Had he not growled behind them, he would not have been covered in fairy dust and would have had one of them in his grasp already. A mistake he would not make again. He could not come at the fairies the same way his mother had. As far as he knew, Scout had been unaware of his mother's presence. The creatures in front of him were fully aware he wanted to catch them. How to accomplish that was something he was not sure how to do.

His opportunity came when Briella's heel got caught in a piece of grass. She lost her balance and was falling when he took a swipe. He scooped her up in his paw and grinned as he brought her closer to his face. She panicked and screamed at the top of her lungs, the sound hurting his ears immensely. He shook his head swiftly from side to side and let her go. She landed with a thump in a cloud of dust. Getting to her feet, she brushed her clothes down with a scowl. Scout held her belly with her arms as she cried with laughter.

Briella stamped a foot, "Stop it, Scout!"

"That was the funniest thing I've seen in ages," she giggled.

"I don't think it is funny at all," Briella stormed.

"Of course not," Scout hiccoughed. "It happened to you."

"At least he didn't eat me."

"Thank goodness for small mercies," Scout agreed still chuckling.

"Will you stop it?"

"I can't. I wish I had captured that on video. You would be laughing too."

"Highly doubtful," Briella sniffed. "Let's get back to the job at hand, getting this guy some food. It will be dark soon."

"Sure. How about we try to confuse him. You fly left, and I'll head right. Hopefully, he won't know which of us to go for first. By then, we will be too far away."

"Sounds good," Briella said. "On three?"

Scout nodded and counted. They flew up into the air, and as expected, he hesitated long enough for them to get a reasonable distance away before coming together again. Scout hovered in the air, encouraging him to track them. Then, she fluttered away, thrilled to see him weaving around bushes and leaping over fallen branches to keep them in sight. When they reached the spot where the dry food was located, Scout found a low-lying branch to land on.

She pointed to the forest floor, hoping he would understand her desire to look for the biscuits that were scattered there. Stubs looked at her uncomprehendingly, but then his nose sniffed the air curiously. He searched the area expectantly before detecting the path to the delectable scent. In his excitement, Stubs pushed his nose into the dirt before pulling back slightly. He had found one of the biscuits and scooped it up with his tongue.

He crunched on it satisfyingly before seeking out another. After a few minutes, he found he was thirsty and headed towards the creek. He stood how his mother had taught him and after a few failed attempts, managed to drink his fill of water. A flurry of wings brought his head up with a snap. A pigeon had landed not more than a few metres away. Stubs licked his lips and lowered his body to the ground. "Hmmm," he meowed softly.

Chapter Thirteen

The fairies covered their faces with their hands. They knew what Stubs hoped to achieve and that what he attempted was a natural instinct in felines. They just didn't want to watch the outcome of his actions. Should he be successful in his attempt to capture the bird, he would surely kill it and begin to consume its carcass. If he failed, they didn't want to see the disappointment that would surely be plastered across his face.

Briella tapped Scout on the arm, "If he kills the bird and eats it, do you think we could go back home for the night?"

Scout narrowed her eyes, "Leave him out here on his own, *all night*?"

Briella twiddled her fingers. "It was just a question."

"You were terrified for his welfare before. What has changed?"

"Nothing," she shrugged, trying to appear blasé. "I just thought if he could take care of himself . . ."

"And what happens when the sun comes up, and he transforms back into a kitten, or a fox comes trotting by and decides he would make a great meal."

"We could be back before dawn and the chances of a fox trotting by is . . . "

"Highly likely," Scout interrupted. "I've seen one hanging around for the past couple of nights. It is probably the reason the kittens' mother got shot in the first place. It is most likely hungry and looking for an easy meal. What could be easier than him?"

Briella settled herself on the branch, her legs swinging gently beneath her. "You are right. We should watch over him and make sure he is okay."

"You managed the night out here when the scarecrow came to life," Scout reminded her.

"That was different. He was like a ninja warrior."

"From what I heard, he was copying your moves, Briella."

"The cat won't do that. He won't be able to protect us if we get into trouble."

"We won't need protecting. Besides, once the cat has finished with the pigeon, we will head back to the village. It will offer us protection from any night creatures that might come across us. We will be able to keep an eye on the cat while he sleeps. In the morning, you can go and get Force, because April will be busy with the mother cat and kittens."

"Sound good to me," she cringed as they listened to him kill his prey. "I think I am going to be sick."

"Why don't you go and find us some food to eat?"

"What?" Briella retched. "How can you think of food at a time like this?"

"It will be dark soon, Briella and we won't be able to see very well to fly. It can get quite dark in here at night with the canopy of the trees above us."

"Fine," she stated. "It beats staying here listening to that."

Briella flew away and collected some mushrooms, placing them on a table inside one of the cottages. She chose a building near a plot of dirt large enough to allow the cat to stretch out if it wished to. Then she gathered a selection of wild berries to keep them hydrated throughout the night. Figuring she couldn't delay her return any longer, she made her way back to the branch to find Scout waiting patiently for Stubs to finish his dinner.

Briella felt like she was returning to a crime scene. Feathers were scattered everywhere, some with bits of flesh still attached to the calamus. She wondered if she would ever feel like eating again. Briella did marvel at the swiftness with which Stubs devoured his meal and the fact that he hadn't wasted any of the bird. She wondered if the head had been eaten before quickly pushing that thought away. She really didn't want to know. "How're things?" she asked instead.

"Fine," Scout said. "He should be ready for a nap now that he has eaten. We should probably make our way back to the huts."

"Great idea. How are we going to get him to follow?"

"I don't know. He is not likely to chase us after that huge feed."

"If he doesn't come with us, you should sprinkle him with dust and levitate him there," Briella suggested.

"That will work," Scout said with a nod. She wasn't going to leave him there alone for the night, but she didn't want to remain out in the open herself. Stubs couldn't understand their words but decided to follow them anyway. He had a belly full of food and was feeling quite content, though he did not want to be left alone. He seemed to work out the gist of their pointing and figured they wanted him to settle on the blanket of dirt for the night. He puffed up his fur to keep himself warm and curled himself into a ball. He closed his eyes and was dreaming of running with his siblings in no time.

Scout and Briella sat at the table and shared one of the mushrooms. Scout chose to finish her meal with a slice of strawberry while Briella elected to munch on a blackberry. Then they chatted throughout the night about a variety of subjects. The thought foremost on their minds was the relationship between April and Force and how that would impact their lives.

"I don't understand what her problem is," Briella lamented. "She likes him, he likes her . . ."

"Look at what happened to Toren. How would she cope if something happened to Force?"

"Would it hurt any less, just because she decided not to date him?"

"Maybe," Scout shrugged. "I've never liked anyone enough to want to date them."

"Liar," Briella laughed. "If you could have made yourself permanently big, or Force could have made himself permanently small, you would have had a crack at it."

"True," Scout grinned. "I imagine it would hurt more to lose someone you were dating than someone you were good friends with. Having said that, you can't live your life in fear that your loved one will die. Think of all the happy, special moments you would miss if you lived like that. We have got to do something to convince April to give them a chance. Imagine how happy she will be when they begin living their lives as a couple."

'Yeah, imagine," Briella whispered, a conniving grin on her face.

Chapter Fourteen

Snarling from outside had the fairies jumping to their feet. They dashed outside to see a large tabby arching its back and hissing at their kitten. Briella raised both hands to her mouth while Scout couldn't manage anything other than a face-palm. They viewed the scene with horrified eyes unsure of how to proceed.

"Do something!" Briella shrieked.

"Like what?" Scout shouted. Now that she was faced with a daunting situation, all ideas flew out of her head.

"I don't know." Briella yelled. "If I get any magic on them, who knows what will happen."

"They will most likely become the size of a panther," Scout answered helpfully. "What if I put the other cat to sleep?"

"Then what, you levitate him somewhere else?"

"I could," Scout nodded slowly, seeing the holes in her plan. The cat would eventually wake and return to finish what it started. "We can't let the kitten fight the cat. He will get hurt."

THE CURIOUS KITTEN

Briella looked around for something that could help them. "How about we grab one of those branches lying over there and chase the cat away?"

"Do you think we would be able to lift it? It looks a bit heavy."

"You could magic it, and make it lighter. We only really need the end bit with the leaves. It should be enough to scare the cat away."

Scout flew to the branch with the most foliage. She sprinkled a bit of dust and with Briella's help, lifted it off the ground. They fluttered to a spot above the two cats then swished the end between them. The tabby ran a few metres before stopping. He spun around and glared at the fairies. Stubs ran in the opposite direction. He got as far as the other cat before completing the same actions. The cats eyeballed one another. Scout and Briella gripped their weapon more tightly. "Seriously?"

The fairies flew after the tabby cat, screaming a battle cry at the top of their lungs. They held their weapon in front of them, the tip wavering wildly as they struggled to maintain its weight. The tabby took off in fright. Even though he left the safety of the forest to run across the open meadow, they continued to follow. Stubs chased after him. "Don't," Briella yelled out to him, but he didn't listen. Stubs was running, and he was enjoying the chase. He hadn't thought about what would happen if the cat stopped and faced up to him. He only wanted to play.

Stubs growled. He didn't mean to issue a challenge. It was an involuntary action. The cat spun around and arched its back, yowling menacingly. Stubs screeched to a stop, hissing instinctively. The cat rushed forward and took a swipe at him, cutting the bridge of his nose. Stubs howled in pain, upset the cat was behaving so viciously towards him. The cat wanted him out of its territory, but he had nowhere else to go. All Stubs wanted to do was to play and to find someone to help him locate his mother. The cat did not know that Stubs was just a kitten. How could he? The cat treated Stubs the same as he would any other cat and took another swipe.

Stubs cried again, striking out in self-defence. He managed to catch the tabby on the tip of his ear, bringing a scream of outrage to the fore. The cat retaliated swiftly, pouncing on top of Stubs. He bit him on the side and kicked him with his back legs. Stubs screamed with pain. Briella shouted at Scout, who flew over the top of the fighting felines fully prepared to sprinkle her dust.

The cry of another cat caught the tabby cat's attention. He lifted his head and listened keenly. In the blink of an eye, the cat tore himself away from Stubs and bounded in a southerly direction. Stubs grumbled to his feet, licking his fur with long, tender strokes. The fairies looked at him sadly. Briella said, "I wish we had brought a lantern with us. Then we would be able to discern his injuries. Do you think they are serious?"

"I don't think so," Scout shook her head, "but he might get an infection if we don't take care of it soon. Cat bites can cause a nasty abscess. "

"Can it wait until morning?"

Scout shrugged. The extent of her interest in the local fauna, extended to which creatures posed a danger to herself and which she could ignore completely. "We can try to coax him to the pub so that April and Force can look him over."

"You don't sound confident at all," Briella scowled. "We can't leave him here, bleeding."

"The pub is too far away for us to be able to keep his attention. We could lose him before reaching the halfway mark. If only the cat had taken off in the pub's direction."

"Yeah, that would have been helpful. Don't worry, Briella, he'll be fine. Cats fight all the time. It can't be too big a deal, or there wouldn't be as many of them around."

"They have huge numbers in their litters, Scout. Perhaps, that is because most of them don't make it to adulthood."

"Fine. How do you want to do this?"

"I don't know. I was hoping you would have a good idea."

A cat meowed in the distance. Stubs stopped bathing himself and listened. The fairies dropped their weapon and Scout flew in front of his face and hovered. "Don't you even think about it," she scolded. He swatted a paw at her. She just managed to raise herself in time. "Oh, you are a naughty boy." He gave her a calculated look but became distracted by the cats caterwauling in the distance. He took off at a fast pace with the fairies in hot pursuit. "Obviously, his injuries are not too severe."

"Hmmm," Briella responded. "Maybe you should have hit him with your magic after all."

"Indeed," Scout said, slightly out of breath.

Chapter Fifteen

They came upon the tabby who was circling a grey female with ginger patches. She had a slim face and a sleek body. She was hissing at him plenty while he returned growls in low tones. Scout and Briella searched for anything they could use as a distraction. Stubs was about to get himself into a world full of trouble. He puffed out his chest and shouted, "Pick on someone your own size, ya bully!"

"Oh, oh," Briella cried.

"We have to do something," Scout murmured. "Don't panic. Don't panic."

The tabby cat said, "Mind your own business, boofhead. This does not concern you."

"I won't let you hurt the female."

"I'm not going to hurt her, idiot."

"That's right because I'm going to stop you."

The tabby cat laughed. "You and who's army?"

Stubs took a couple of steps forward. The tabby cat growled menacingly. Stubs was frightened beyond belief but refused to acknowledge his fear. He took another step forward. The tabby declined to accept Stub's challenge. He went for the female and wrapped his mouth over the back of her neck. Stubs leapt towards the tabby. Scout flew to the rear of Stub's neck and landed abruptly. Her heels dug into his skin before she managed to place herself in a sitting position. She had barely grasped his fur with both hands when he began to twist his body savagely.

Briella looked on with a mixture of shock and amusement. She didn't know whether to laugh or gasp. She conjured an image of a cowboy riding a bull and couldn't really see any difference between that and what she was currently witnessing. Briella was desperate to give Scout a hand but was afraid of releasing more fairy dust. All she could do was keep watch and be ready to offer assistance if Scout happened to fall or become injured some other way.

Stubs was terrified. Something was biting him on the neck, and no matter how hard he tried to dislodge it, the rotten thing wouldn't let go. He decided to seek another method of detachment. Stubs sat on his backside and spun his head around. He nipped at his neck and managed to grip Scout's leg between his teeth.

He tugged at her roughly. Her scream was lost beneath the noises of the felines. She let go of his fur, hoping he would do the same to her limb. He did not. Not to be deterred, Scout swung herself up and flicked her arms at his mouth. Fairy dust flew from her pores and landed on his face. He opened his mouth and coughed long and hard, spitting up a hairball in the process. Briella hovered like a parent who could see the danger approaching their child but was uncertain of which path to take that would keep them safe.

Scout flew onto Stubs' shoulders and fisted his fur gently. When he didn't make any sudden movements, she tugged slightly with her right hand and waited to see how he would respond. His ear twitched faintly, but he didn't attempt to throw her off. She kicked her legs lightly, wishing she had allowed Briella to give her a riding lesson.

Stubs flinched and looked set to protest, so Scout stilled herself and waited patiently. She hoped that he would not be distracted by the other cats that appeared ready to take their leave. Scout leant forward and rubbed his fur in smooth, circular motions. Stubs relaxed beneath her fingers, so she continued the action for quite some time.

When she felt he was suitably calmed, she tried again. A light kick of her legs had him standing on his feet and looking over his shoulder. His eyes widened slightly when he spotted her there. She grinned at him self-consciously, hoping he wouldn't realise her lack of riding skills. Scout wished she could trade places with Briella. It seemed she was going to have another opportunity to step out of her comfort zone. Scout spoke gently to him, even though she knew he wouldn't understand a word she said. She hoped that he would get the gist of her tone and comprehend that she meant him no harm. Although she was still unclear how she was going to get him to go where she wanted.

"We should have filled our pockets with cat biscuits!" Briella yelled at Scout.

Scout snorted, "Yeah, that would have helped a lot." They would have only been able to carry two each.

"We could have flown ahead and dropped them like Hansel. The kitten would have followed behind, eating them as he went."

"Who's Hansel?" Scout asked.

"You know, Hansel and Gretel."

"No, who are they?"

"Never mind. It was a great idea, but as we don't have any biscuits, I don't know how we are going to get the kitten to go anywhere tonight."

"Why does he have to go anywhere?"

"It's not safe here. We are out in the open, and the moonlight is so bright we are too visible to predators. We would be safe back in the forest among the trees."

"Like we were when the tabby came?"

Briella grimaced, "Good point. At least they are gone now, and the kitten didn't even notice."

"Yeah, we got lucky there. This little fella seems to notice everything. Have you noted how curious he is?"

"No, but that gives me an idea."

Chapter Sixteen

Briella shoved a hand into her pocket and pulled out her notebook and pencil. She quickly sketched the outline of a turtle dove and shaded it enough to make it appear 3D. She tore the page out of her book then sprinkled some fairy dust on it. The bird flew off the page, catching Stubs' attention.

The bird flapped aimlessly, unsure of its surroundings. Briella called to the bird and instructed it to follow her. She zoomed towards the forest, the bird trailing close behind. Stubs gave chase, though he still felt full from his last meal. However, the memory of the sweetness of the dove meat could not be shaken, and he figured it would be just as delicious the second time around.

They raced across the meadows, the moon supplying enough light to ensure they headed in the right direction. Scout held on for dear life. Stubs didn't seem to mind the tightness of her grip. She noticed the way his fur rippled when she tugged too harshly. His eyes never strayed from his prey and his paws never faltered in their stride. It didn't take Scout long to begin enjoying the ride. Although, after a while, she discovered her bottom was becoming quite tender.

"Are we there yet?" she muttered beneath her breath and then laughed. The quickest way to upset a parent was to ask that question. She considered screaming it at Briella but didn't want to upset her friend's feelings. Briella had come up with the perfect solution to getting Stubs to a safer place to spend the night. Scout certainly couldn't have done as good a job. There were some benefits to Briella's magic being on the fritz.

They reached the edge of the forest, and things became a little more complicated. Once they stepped inside, their light source would disappear. Thanks to Briella's great idea with the bird, it sparked another in Scout. She flew up to join her friend. "Do you think you could draw a lantern, Briella? You could make it come to life, and I could fill it with fairy dust."

"What a great idea," Briella said, clasping her hands in front of her. "I don't know why we didn't think of this before."

"I didn't know you carried a notebook and pen with you," Scout returned.

Briella rolled her eyes, but as she had turned to look at Stubs, it was lost to the darkness. Briella convinced the bird to land on a nearby branch. Stubs sized up the tree, wondering if it were possible to scale its bark. Scout encouraged Briella to draw quickly, afraid that Stubs would catch the bird, infecting him with Briella's magic.

The moment the two lanterns were created and filled with fairy dust, they moved inside the forest. Stubs had not had a chance to attempt the climb, but the idea remained in the back of his mind. He leapt over logs and skirted around bushes, though the fairies wondered how he was able to complete such feats with his eyes looking up rather than where he was going. Scout was highly impressed. Briella was rightfully terrified. "How could you live out here with these dangerous creatures?" she asked Scout.

Scout sighed. Briella had lost so many of her fairy instincts by living a comfortable life with April. Scout realised it was going to be a more significant task than she had initially thought in teaching Briella how to live as a fairy, once again.

"I am a fairy. How else am I supposed to live?" Scout answered.

"Like me. Luckily, April is building us a house. Imagine the dangers you would have to face by making this forest your permanent residence." Scout thought about her previous home in the Gold Coast Hinterlands. As far as the wildlife was concerned, the danger was no different. The human element, however, was a different story. There were far more chances of being detected by a human in this area of the country than her previous home.

'Yeah, lucky."

They arrived at the village, and Briella helped the bird settle in for the night. She found an abandoned nest for the dove to use as its temporary home. Then she returned to Scout to find that Stubs was nowhere in sight.

"Where is he?" Briella shrieked.

"In the bushes. He's going to the toilet."

"Oh!" Briella huffed. "I should probably go myself."

"Use the outhouse. It's over there," she pointed, making sure the light picked up the action.

"There is a building just for that?"

"Yes, Briella. A communal bathroom."

"How gross!" she exclaimed.

"You could always go in the bushes with Stubs," Scout suggested.

"The outhouse will be fine," Briella assured her.

Stubs returned while Briella was away. He looked around for the bird but could not find it. He raised his nose in the air, but could not detect its scent. He lay on his tummy, with his front paws spread and his nose touching the dirt. Then he closed his eyes and began to snore.

Briella came back quite concerned. "Should he sound like that?"

Scout shrugged. "I don't know. I generally stay away from cats wherever possible."

Briella watched the rise and fall of his chest. When his rhythm stayed consistent, she settled in for a chat. "Do you think April or Force will keep the cat and her kittens?"

Scout didn't have to think about it at all. "Force will definitely hang onto them if the mother cat consents to stay." She nodded in Stubs direction, "I think he will push to keep this one, either way."

"The mother cat won't allow that," Briella frowned.

"Oh, I think she will. This one is going to be heaps of trouble. He seems to be easily distracted."

Briella appeared doubtful. "He didn't take his eyes off that bird for anything."

"No," Scout agreed. "But he did take his eyes off those two cats."

"I nearly had a heart attack when he challenged that tabby."

"Me too."

"I can't believe he thought he was going to hurt her."

"He is just a kitten," Scout reminded her.

"True," Briella murmured. Stubs ears twitched as they spoke. "Should we go inside?"

"Yeah, we should let him get some sleep."

Chapter Seventeen

The first rays of the day breached the horizon chasing the shadows away. The extreme change in the skyline was lost among the trees in the forest. The fairies were taken by surprise by the gradual lightening of their surroundings.

They were laughing so hard, they missed the quiet meowing of the kitten they were supposed to be caring for. Stubs, curious as ever, peered through the window of the hut. He gave Briella such a fright, she launched to her feet. Scout pushed back from the table, afraid of a possible dust shower. Briella's expression became crestfallen when she witnessed Scout's response. Scout sported the appearance of a guilty person when she noticed how her action affected her friend.

"I'm sorry, Briella."

"Don't be," she replied, heading for the door. "I'd be afraid to be around me too if I was you."

"I just spent the entire night with you, Briella. I am not afraid to be with you. I am a little cautious of what your magic is capable of, however. Please don't hold that against me."

"I won't," she replied, but Scout was doubtful of her tone.

It sounded like she would definitely hold it against her. She had to distract Briella, and Scout knew just what to say. "I think you should sprinkle April with your fairy dust."

"What did you say?" Briella shrieked. "How could you suggest such a thing?"

"Easily," she shrugged, "We know from the kitten that your magic is not going to kill or maim her permanently. She will get a fright and worry that her life will never be the same. But then dawn will come, and she will discover that it wasn't so bad once she takes the time to think about it and she might be more open to taking a chance on a relationship with Force."

"You've got rocks in your head," Briella shook her head. "I am not doing that." She stepped outside, and her heart melted when Stubs rubbed himself against her. "You are so gorgeous," she cooed gently, wrapping her arms around his neck. She stopped abruptly when she realised how dangerously she was behaving. "Oops, nearly did it again."

Scout was stunned by Briella's reaction. She had been terrified by the kittens at the pub, not wanting to be in the same room as them and then lying to April about her feelings. Now she acted as though she was meeting an old friend that she had longed to catch-up with. Scout observed the gentle way Briella approached the kitty, and the tender strokes she applied to his cheeks. The kitten meowed loudly. "He must be hungry," she said. "Wait with him while I go get Force."

"Okay," Scout yelled after Briella, who had already begun the journey to the pub. She eyed the kitten cautiously. "How did you manage to get separated from your family? I can't wait to hear your story. You need to stay here for a minute while I take care of something. Don't go anywhere," she waggled her finger at his face.

Stubs stared at her with curious eyes. He watched her fly away before he realised he had missed an opportunity to practise his technique. His instincts to hunt weren't as strong in his kitten body. He scrutinised his surroundings for something interesting to do. His ears pricked forward as a rustling sound came from his left. He stretched out his body and listened intently. Another crunching of leaves had him crouch-walking in that direction. By the time Scout reappeared he had miraculously disappeared.

"Oh dear," she exclaimed, hovering a couple of metres off the ground to get a better view. She spun in a circle but was unable to see him anywhere. She cupped her hands around her mouth and called to him. Though she listened carefully, she was unable to detect a response. Scout flew to the nearest branch and sent out an energy burst. Searching for an indigenous creature of Earth didn't reap a reply. "Briella is going to kill me," she spluttered, choosing the direction of the creek to begin her search, and hoping for the best.

It took her a few minutes to locate him, which wasn't bad considering she was in the forest. She watched him with quiet amusement. He was following a blue tongue lizard twice his size. What he planned to do with it when he caught it was anyone's guess. The lizard would more than likely bite him before Stubs had a chance to work out how to wrap his little mouth around the reptile's body.

A field mouse raced through some leaves to his left. Stubs jumped slightly, his claws popping out of four paws. He spun his body around and chased after the rodent.

"Wait!" Scout yelled, wondering how long it would be before Briella returned. She kept him in her sights until he ran out of puff and squatted on the ground defeated. His little head rested on his front legs, and he closed his eyes. Scout wanted to tell him what a great job he had done tracking but knew he wouldn't understand a word she said. Instead, she merely kept an eye on him to make sure he was safe while she waited for the others to arrive.

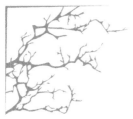

Chapter Eighteen

Force and Briella arrived soon enough. Briella flew down to Stubs' level and checked him over carefully. He raised his head with a semblance of interest that didn't last long. He lowered his head, still exhausted after his latest burst of energy.

Briella turned to Scout, "What is wrong with him?"

"He's been chasing our local wildlife. He is just tired."

"He must be hungry," she surmised.

"I doubt it. Not after the feast he devoured last night."

Briella didn't look convinced. "Let's get him home to his mother so she can feed him."

Force picked the kitten up and studied him closely. "You look just like the kitten at the pub. How did I miss you?"

Scout flew nearer to Force, "Judging by his earlier behaviour, I would say he was off exploring something when you counted them."

"But I was talking to him at the time," Force replied.

"Then perhaps his sibling looks the same as him and

was off somewhere else."

Force nodded, "That is plausible. Come on, little guy, let's get you home."

The fairies used Force's shoulder as a means of transport home. Force took his time walking through the trees then over the open fields. He breathed in the fresh air and took joy in being outdoors. Children's laughter that would not have been heard with natural human hearing brought a wistful smile to his lips. His thoughts turned to April, and for the first time in three thousand years, he wished that he could father a child of his own.

Force waited for the fairies to flutter away before sneaking the kitten in through the backdoor and heading quickly up the stairs. He managed to beat them to the room. They found the window of their usual entry and exit was closed but they couldn't have entered anyway because their way inside was blocked by the mother cat who continued her appraisal of the surroundings through the window. Force entered the room, and the cat jumped from the windowsill. She padded over to him and meowed long and loud. He knelt down beside her, holding the kitten out in his hand. "Is this what you've been looking for?"

She pressed her nose to Stubs' and purred contentedly. She meowed gently and began washing his face with her tongue. Force placed him gently on the floor and opened the window. "Sorry," he told the fairies. "I forgot we closed the window. April was afraid the mother would jump out and hurt herself."

"Do you think she was looking for him?" Briella asked.

"No doubt," Force replied, brimming with happiness. "I'm glad you found him. I'd hate to think what might have happened to him if you hadn't. Just imagine if he'd come across a tom cat or a fox or some other predator. I shudder to think."

"Me too," Scout smiled. "Imagine if we hadn't been brought here by the Jealousy Monsters. His mother would have died, and all of these kittens would have followed her."

Briella said, "You don't suppose Destiny . . ."

They looked at one another then laughed. Linking elbows, Scout said, "Up for some breakfast?"

"Sure," Briella stated with a stomach growl for emphasis. They flew to the cupboard to retrieve their mushrooms.

Titles by Marnie Atwell

Starlight Investigations
Jealousy Monsters
Vampire
Phantasm

Halloween Madness
The Pumpkin Patch
The House of Horrors
The Spirited Scarecrow
The Curious Kitten

About the Author

Marnie is an Australian author who lives in South-East Queensland with her husband and two children. When she is not dreaming up new adventures for her characters, Marnie enjoys creating pictures in Daz 3D; playing the piano; reading paranormal romance novels; and spending time with family and friends. Not necessarily in that order.

Visit her website at: www.marnieatwell.com for more books, contact details, and free downloads.

The next book in the Halloween Madness series is:
The Sneaky Skeleton

Lightning Source UK Ltd.
Milton Keynes UK
UKHW011433030720
365982UK00003B/722

A View from
the Observation Deck
of the House of Cards

I.W. BORTER

A View from
the Observation Deck
of the House of Cards

The Five Elements cycle
The Air trilogy
(on Power)
vol. I

To my muse,
Dorothy

ABOUT THE AUTHOR

I.W. Borter was born in Poland in 1986. He writes originally in English, his second language. As he says, *I find it delightfully melodious and malleable. Ever since I can remember, I have been reading books exclusively in English, even Polish books in translation.* He currently lives in Warsaw.

C'est un roman simple sur des choses compliquées!
Timoléon du Bois

BOOK ONE

◆

IT'S NO USE LOCKING THE STABLE DOOR...

◆ ◆ ◆

"The world, the entire world as we know it, is going to end soon," these words, these utterly unwarranted and harsh words said a man, an invisible man, a nondescript man, a mysterious man, who might as well not have existed at all. I overheard him through the door of the largest and most expensive hotel in town. And thus I had no reason not to believe his rather muffled judgment. No reason whatsoever. So I believed him. I believed him sheepishly.

I did that quite willingly for I heard it through the door. And there is hardly anything more relevant and momentous in the history of mankind than the invention of the door. Of that certainly not unhinged guardian of privacy. Of that ultimate crime stopper. Of that invincible barrier erected between nature and civilization. Between barbarity and refinement. Between coldness and warmth. Between all the classes and kinds and types of people. Like a dutiful chaperone separating potential lovers. Thus, understandably, its merits and achievements earned throughout centuries are simply and amazingly stunning, and nothing short of stunning. For it was doors, and doors alone, that had been letting the first people in and out of their crude and primitive huts. And now they also selflessly guard everyone's intimacy. They dutifully protect everyone's secrets. They obediently shield everyone's fortunes. And they even, if not above all, keep the benighted masses at a safe distance from those wealthy and powerful ones of the world. They do that like a palpable counterpart of the smell of urine that marks the inviolable spheres of influence among dogs while remaining unobtrusive to everyone else. They also keep separating the unemployed ones from their potential employers. They do the same thing for actors and chiefs of movie studios. For artists and possible recipients of their art. For singers and their listeners. For writers and their publishers. And for everyone who has ever tried to get to the other side of the inhospitable threshold of nothingness and finally become someone. They are so magnificent and astonishing in their performance of utter imperviousness that many claim that a single door, when installed as a part of the bigger whole, as a fragment of some great construction or other, not only does not weaken, let alone imperil, the stability of its structure but even strengthens it and toughens it considerably. Like a single toothpick inside a canapé. So, some even insist that all the otherwise feeble and dainty houses of cards would have been incomparably steadier, more reliable, more trustworthy, and far more useful, had they only possessed at least one door. A door of spades. A door handle of hearts.

And if doors constitute such a tremendously vital and irreplaceable part of our society, not so much a window as a door to our souls, then, consequently, a doorman must be the most respectable occupation in the world. He must be. He simply must be. As their protector, as their caring guardian, and the high priest in one. For every doorman, being that remarkably privileged person, sees everything and hears everything that takes place on both sides of such a wooden membrane. Of that swinging barrier. Of that passable frontier. And thus he sees and hears more than anyone else. Even while remaining free of any voyeuristic inclinations. Like a male cashier in the shop with women's lingerie. He sees and hears more than those powerful elites gathered on one side of it and the ordinary masses crowding right on the other one. A talented and skillful doorman is like an excellent medium, capable of establishing and maintaining a firm as well as reliable connection between two opposite sides of such a demarcation line. A deft doorman is like a priest, perfectly striking a balance between two parallel worlds. The spiritual and the more palpable one. A great doorman, a truly brilliant one, can be compared only and solely with the finest and most dedicated servants of gods. Of any gods, really. But in this case, of the still living and kicking and breathing, yet because of it, no less powerful ones.

That was why I was so proud. I was so immensely proud of my prestigious and enviable occupation. And that was why I had been doing it, performing it, and diligently devoting myself to it, for so incredibly long.

Many people today, mostly young people, are fooled and deluded by a certain fallacy, by a certain common fallacy. And it is a fallacy that opening doors for others is so simple, so trivial, and so laughable a thing that it is utterly unworthy not only of their attention but also of the equally precious time of their eventful yet still incredibly short hotheaded youth. They eagerly dismiss it. They zestfully disparage it. And they naively believe that this only ostensibly banal activity could, and even should, be left to machines. They state that it should be left to various engines, servomotors, pneumatic actuators, and the whole tangle of ever-vigilant sensors. All of them incurably coldblooded. All of them devoid of even the smallest molecule of human warmth and gracefulness. And so they could not have been more mistaken. And so, sooner or later, they will eventually find it out for themselves. But surely not in the most delicate or subtle manner available. Like a husband hearing the tremolo of his wife's excited wailing coming from their bedroom as he returns home earlier, far earlier, than usual.

And I do not intend to educate or enlighten them in any way. I do not want to do that. Not at all. Not in any degree. Neither the slightest nor the smallest one. Or regardless of its size. I simply do not feel obliged to do that favor to that wild bunch. To that unruly pack of inconsiderate ingrates. To that throng of doltish and spoiled hooligans. I refuse to do that in order not to be perceived by them, or by anyone for that matter, as yet another impossibly embittered old man incessantly admonishing youths like them. For I am not like that. Not in the least. I do not belong to that heavily wrinkled circle of perpetually grumbling elders, akin to monks chanting their embittered prayers. I am not one of them. I am not one of those grumbling ones. In fact, grumbling for so long and so insistently that the smallest and most innocent flicker of a smile that wanders into their countenances can incur a serious risk of making the skin of their faces crack and crumble, and then, consequently, kill them ruthlessly with a hardly amusing hemorrhage. Oh, no! No, sir! I am not like that! Not that I care.

I can only state, without unnecessarily trying to provoke such inane, groundless, baseless, and other less, accusations and a howl of wrongful indignation, that they should really and truly listen to me. All of them. While not excepting anyone. They should let me administer to them a dose or two of common sense as if it were prescribed by a conscientious doctor. For I know, I really know, what I am talking about.

They ought to listen to me. Like people thronging to an ancient oracle. They ought to do that, that is, to listen to someone who has been, repeatedly, tirelessly, unstoppably, closing and opening doors for other people for five long decades. Or even longer than that. Much longer than that. They ought to listen to someone who has been doing it for so long. This inconspicuous activity. This underrated work. This belittled job. For I have been doing it for so long that a metallically musical and highly nuanced squeal of hinges has become to me the most wonderful melody. For it has become to me even more moving and beautiful than the most acclaimed classical sonatas and symphonies. Finally, they ought to be convinced by the words of someone who has been repeating it so many times during all those years. Like a grown man who cannot help repeating one and the same kindergarten grade. For I have been doing it while polishing to perfection the way of grasping door handles, and while performing a series of deep bows toward all those coming in and going out. They ought to listen to someone who could and would testify, with unfeigned seriousness and a clear conscience, that this very activity, and the dignified occupation connected with it, are in some way related to art. And high art especially, decidedly. Anyway, they should be elevated to that noble level of art, if they still are not for some inexplicable reason.

One should know, or, at the very least, be aware of a certain fact. Of a certain deceptive fact. For what seemingly gives the impression of a simple and unassuming act of taking hold of a door handle at the sight of an approaching guest, is, in fact, a remarkably complex process. It is as intricate a process as playing a game of chess with the live pawns in a corporation. For it comprises various arcane techniques of holds and grabs and pulls that have been, consistently, meticulously, and devotedly, modified and refined and improved ad infinitum over countless generations. And thus they markedly differ from each other in terms of the pressure being applied by a hand on a door handle. Of the angle and the position of that hand. Of the quickness of its grip. Its firmness. Its elegance. And its gracefulness. And all that, in truth, partly depends on the shape of such a handle, and partly it is a faithful reflection of the social status of the person for whom a doorman is about to open the door.

And so the final product, that is, the wide-open door, respectfully and hospitably, is a resultant of so many disjointed factors, of so many accidental catalysts, and impromptu modifiers, that I resolve not to reveal all of them now. Not right now. I resolve not to do that to spare everyone being bored unwarrantedly. Like a child who upon paying a visit to its classmate wanders right into a lengthy parental lecture on the things that one should do and do not at its age.

But also I refuse to do that in order not to commit treason on a great scale. On an unthinkable scale. Like a child who unwittingly gives away the details of a surprise party. For it would be treason. For it would be high treason, that is, the act of divulging all the precious trade secrets of my greatly endangered, if not almost utterly extinct, profession to the herds of ever-curious laymen and dilettantes. And I do not want to give them away. Especially to those for whom, one ought to, literally, ironically, slam the proverbial doors in their faces. One should do that. Sooner or later.

Because all those only ostensibly banal techniques and no less supposedly shallow components of that, after all, perennial ritual, which is, undoubtedly, opening doors for other people, are not without significance. They do not remain unnoticed. They do not remain unappreciated. It is like with even the silliest and most trivial details in the art of diplomacy. Because it is in the uncommonly fertile field of diplomacy that, on each such trifle, on each smallest inadvertence, can depend the fate of entire countries and continents. Even of the large portion of the world. Even of the entire world as we know it. For it is there that such little and unassuming things may jeopardize the habitually delicate and brittle world peace, akin to a fragile wine glass. For only there this or that otherwise negligible detail can be suddenly regarded by the finicky experts at, and connoisseurs of, the diplomatic protocol, as a deliberate and unforgivable affront to someone's dignity. To some foreign dignity. To some diplomatic dignity. And this or that laughable innuendo can be tragically misconstrued as an open declaration of war. For where else if not in the very art of diplomacy, incessantly requiring the surgical level of precision and attention to detail, is it possible to pit two hitherto friendly and inherently neighborly nations against each other by a little subtle nuance as a badly placed chair? Or a treacherously filthy fork? Or a poorly folded handkerchief in a breast pocket? For, apparently, it might be capable, depending on the way of folding it, of communicating a wide range of information and encrypted messages. Like a pocket-sized version of a flag semaphore. And thus, it can serve as a recondite kind of language that is understandable only to the lucky few, and still only among the most avid linguists and translators. For not only once or twice over the Machiavellian course of the history of the world, it turned out that myriads of unsuspecting poor beings almost paid a rather handsome tip to this or that clumsy waiter with their, after all, invaluable lives, after he had accidentally served a drink in a dirty glass to an ambassador of a foreign power during a lunch break in a peace conference, or, which was much worse, after he had failed to perfectly align the silverware with a plate. Or with each other. At least, I remember reading such an edifying anecdote at some time or other.

That was why, while still on duty, for countless years I had been doing my best not to offend the people for whom I opened doors, humbly, but never obsequiously. I had been doing it, while being perpetually aware of the unflagging importance of my duties. I had been doing it while being aware of their both potential and proven influence on the global politics, of their tacit impact on the global order and harmony. Let alone on the game of geopolitical chess. Like in the case of a lopsided table affecting a game of billiards. It also meant that I paid particular attention not to enhance the importance of those who, obviously, did not deserve such special treatment. No more. No less. Thus, I was utterly unable to imagine a situation in which one would be careless enough, in which one would be foolish enough, or incompetent enough, to open a door in the same manner for an ordinary mailman, or some other tedious deliveryman, as for a distinguished high-ranking official from a foreign country. With the same amount of respect. With the same kind of elegant reserve. While paying the same honors. As well as while using the same strength to grab and pull a door handle. It would be nothing else but a typical and crude insult to the former and an unearned ennoblement to the latter. A mistake of this scale and caliber was both unimaginable and unthinkable to me at the time. It was inconceivable to me to the extent that my, after all, quite substantial mental capacity, seemed to be simply insufficient

9

to complete such a demanding task, such a daring task, such a blasphemous task. I seemed to be unable to visualize, to envision, this kind of absurd and unacceptable situations. Like a child who cannot imagine what its parents may be doing in their bedroom after the revealing lights are turned off. It was insufficient to do that with an adequate care for, and attention to, all the necessary details, and all the always-welcome nuances. That was exactly why one, in this case, no one else but I, had to be constantly and tirelessly on one's guard. That was why one had to be wary and watchful all the time. Without mercy. Without respite. That was why one had to be constantly alert. Even in the place like this. Especially in the place like this. In this inarguably the greatest and most impressive hotel in this entire city. In this entire Western country. If not on the whole continent. And bear in mind that there is not a single note or false tone of exaggeration in those paeans of praise.

For, indeed, it was a place to which many flocked in droves. For, indeed, it was a place to which many drifted eagerly. As if succumbing to the grip of some luxurious magnetism. As if following the singular for man-made kind of gravity. Like in the case of a vortex of a roulette sucking in the players' souls. It was a place where used to stay celebrities of all kinds, of all heights, sexes, sizes, and statures. It was also a place where noble ambassadors kept spending the nights with their wives. Or ambassadresses with their husbands. And other diplomats of various ranks and importance with their distinctly less formal and unsanctified companions of the opposite sex. Or of any sex for that matter. It was a renowned place. It was an exquisite place. It was a fine place where the rather scarce spare time chose to spend the dashing and resplendent crowned heads. And those a bit less decorated, heads of states. It was finally that marvelous place where the smallest mistake on my part could cost me dear. It could cost me, me, as an employee and a humble citizen. But also it could inflict grave consequences upon thousands, if not millions, of innocent people living in remote and hardly ever dusted corners of the world. Living in far away countries of which I had never heard before. And, most probably, never would. Like a lazy Santa Claus who visits only the children from his own neighborhood.

And this was why I had kept carrying on my shoulders that insufferable burden. That tremendous burden. Right on my osteoporosis-tormented back. For all those years. For several eventful past decades. But I had been doing it with pride and obviously laudable dutifulness. But I had been doing it like an exemplarily diligent beast of burden. And do not be fooled by my unassuming appearance. Do not be fooled by its demure sister, my inconspicuous figure. Do not be misled by the respectably white hair protruding and peering timidly from under my cap. Like claws from under a cat's paw. For it was the very cap that I had proudly been putting on top of my head since the memorable first day of my service. Frankly, it had been so long time ago that it now seemed to be almost in the different epoch. In the different time. In the different space. And that cap, that incredibly faithful cap, that indefatigable cap, despite the inevitable passage of time, and owing to my enormous care for it, retained its original, intact, mint condition. So do not believe everything that your fallible senses prompt you all the time. So do no believe them implicitly. For, regardless of my age, I am still, I had always been, and I will surely be, perfectly aware of my position as a nameless pawn, and my role as an expendable player, on the tricky stage of international politics. Now. Before. Forever.

And yet, in spite of that, after all, disconcerting and uncomfortable fact, the job was still the source of pride and ineffable pleasure for me. It was. It still was, although I was forced to settle for living with that relentless crushing moral weight. I was forced to live with it. Like a detective who failed to solve too many horrible cases and is now haunted by the ghosts of unavenged victims. It was, although I was forced to endure that baggage of responsibility. Easily verging on pure madness. Easily bordering on downright inhuman. It was, although I had to live with it each and every single day. At every hour. At every consecutive minute. And even according to other fractions and units of time. And thus also during the nights. It was, for I simply had to do that. I had to do all that. For the sake of the whole civilized world.

And it was chiefly on account of that I had been adamantly refusing to take a single day off. For all these decades of my sacrificial service. For all the both innumerable working hours as well as overtime. I had never had one in my life. Not even one. Not even half of it. It had not crossed my mind. It had not done that. Not for a moment. Not even after cautiously looking left, and then right, and then left again. Not even before entering it with a confidential gait of an adolescent still being deluded by the faith in, and the illusion of, his youthful invincibility and immortality. Like a petite birdie believing that the world ends beyond the outline of its nest. For why would I? For why should it? And, consequently, why should I do anything like that? After all, it would have been nothing else but torture, pure torture to me. It would have been a painful and implacable torture to me. It would have been like a need to apologize to one of his school friends by a child who desires to become a ruthless politician capable of crushing and devastating his future opponents with a wide arsenal of various lethal slanders, gossips, and dirty tricks. If I had taken such a day off I would have been bored anyway. And what kind of benefits, of measurable and relevant benefits, would it have brought to the delicate balance in the geopolitical game? It would have been one great waste. A horrible one. A tremendous one. Unthinkable even. Like the impatient doctor closing the eyes of a not-yet-quite-dead man. Besides, during the nights, I would have been only rhythmically tossing and turning in my sleep. Or even hours before falling asleep. I would have been doing that due to the nagging awareness, if not this unbearable sense of guilt, that I committed some gross negligence of my duties or other. And so, I would have to do something anyway in order to adequately atone for that grave offense. Even if symbolically. Even if ostensibly. Even if only a little bit. If not to compensate for it. And also to overcompensate for it if needed. For I would have started flailing my arms. For I would have begun doing that while striving to open and close my faithful pillow. Or to pull up and down a no less loyal duvet of mine. If only not to become idle for longer than a sole instant. If only not to feel useless and utterly redundant. Like an old calendar that one tries to adjust to the current year to avoid being forced to buy a new one.

It was also a fact, a rather healthy fact, that I had never been sick over the course of my impressively long-term career. So, it looks like, when one wants something strong enough, passionately enough, and long enough, almost everything is possible. Almost everything is within your even if elderly reach. And work, hard work, tireless work, proves to be the best kind of remedy known, not so much to man as to a working man, for all illnesses imaginable, for all ailments tormenting humanity for centuries. For, do intrepid generals lie around in their beds with cold compresses lounging on their heads, and with cups of hot tea in their feverish hands, when their soldiers have the dubious pleasure of having the mud masks done by falling on their faces in the middle of a swampy battleground, clueless and fatherless and unprotected? Do they do that when their subordinates dance deliriously to the murderous accompaniment of vicious cannonades? Or, do dignified heads of states allow themselves such moments of weakness? Do they allow themselves such moments with boxes of tissues near at hand, and with strings of variegated pills, akin to a peculiar type of necklaces, when there is being decided the fate of their nations, the lives of their compatriots, during the habitually momentous international conferences? I doubt that. I highly doubt that. And so how could I do such a thing myself?

That was why I decidedly preferred to wait it out, if not literally sweat it out, for some time. I preferred to do that while going to work swathed in yet another layer of shirts and sweaters. I was going there with a scarf wrapped tightly around my neck and tucked neatly under my flawlessly ironed uniform. Like a leaf that is being squeezed into a book, as a dry kind of bookmark. I preferred to do that, I preferred to do anything for that matter, all that was necessary and indispensable not to offend with its crude appearance the exceptionally refined tastes of the guests of this hotel. And even, at least, in my visibly unbiased view, there was nothing wrong with refraining from coughing. Even for all day long. There was nothing wrong with that. Even when my lungs started falling apart at their old wrinkled seams. Even when they began fraying around the edges from the insane internal pressure trying to tear them to the jagged fleshy pieces. For they were like twin crumpled paper bags that were about to be popped impishly. There was also absolutely nothing wrong with taking a break to get out of the building and cough oneself away. Once an hour. Once a day. There was nothing wrong with that when others relished their lunch or enjoyed a whiff or two of a cigarette smoke between the obligatory morning gulps of coffee. Thus not only once or twice it happened that I had coughed myself into a quite serious condition.

But there were times when I lacked the strength to go on. But there were times when I was plagued by a temptation to dismiss all my previous efforts as pointless, as ludicrous, and as downright dangerous. And there were times when I was ready to give up. There were times when I was ready to surrender. To throw in the towel. Or even the whole supply of them from the hotel's impressive stock. And then I wanted to crawl under a warm and cozy blanket and assume a rather threadbare fetal position. Like a sick man's handkerchief that having seen all that it is about to clean up and deal with decides to crawl back into his pocket. But I resisted it. But I

14

boycotted it. And I defied it gamely. For I always managed in time to summon to my mind the images of all the martyrs and prophets who had suffered while investing aggressively in high ideals. Those were the ones who had bought the stocks of noble intentions, of lofty ideas, and of moral integrity, without expecting the payday anytime soon. And, besides, I still feel quite well. If not remarkably well. And, besides, I have lived to a decent age, to a rather respectable age, in spite of all this. As a tree that creaks and crackles plaintively but still refuses to go down for good.

And even at such evidently sporadic moments of weakness, unfortunate and lamentable, utterly unworthy of someone of this respectable position, I would eagerly bend in half. I would bend like a rickety switchblade. I would do that as thunderous coughing spasms convulsed my entire defenseless body. As they maltreated it. As they battered it internally. They were doing it while devastating my lungs. They were doing that just like a writer who unmercifully crushes and punishes the incalculable sheets of paper for his own crippling inability to articulate his thoughts and ideas in the proper manner. And I would feel as terribly as if some internal and unnamed force endeavored to dissect me and eviscerate me alive. And I would feel as if it tried to do that without bothering to use any, even symbolic, even partial, anesthetics. And even, from time to time, I would feel as if that force strived to play a tasteless concerto on my entrails. I would feel as if it tried to do it while using all the possible tendons and fleshy tubes as strings, and my other, fuller, softer, organs as percussion instruments. But even then I would do everything in my power to avail myself of such moments. Of such rather unsettling moments. I would do that to turn them ably to my own spasmodic advantage.

So I would cleverly use those painful opportunities. So I would use them while choking and gagging and coughing convulsively, to practice the depth of my bows, the sureness of my grips. And I would practice them avidly. And I would practice them devotedly. For they accompanied me. For they assisted me faithfully, in the course of my working hours. As a shadow that keeps stalking an avowed stalker. They did that as I kept holding and releasing door handles. They did that as I kept nodding to the guests and receiving their nods in return. And they formed an integral and inextricable part of my professional life. It was like a mellifluous voice in the case of a famous tenor. Or like an uncanny resistance to asinine jokes and other instances of creative idiocy developing in a teacher.

It is no secret. It is no secret at all. So I will not betray any confidential information or classified tactics if I state that the depth of every bow in the natural and highly visual way reflects the rank of the person for whom it is intended. It is nearly as easily recognizable and infallible an indication of one's stature or importance as the number of stripes lingering on an officer's shoulder board. Or stars on a general's helmet. Or scars on a brawler's jaw. For those things also both trigger and determine the proper style of greeting. At once. Without any unnecessary delays. And in this case, in this special case, it instantly sets in motion the gears of the adequate diplomatic protocol. And it automatically adjusts itself to the position in the hierarchy of every single guest. It is like an indiscreet soft-spring suspension of a car that is unable to mask the excessive weight of the passengers.

But all that is not only about marking a rather broad distinction between one guest and the other. It is not even about sketching some vague rules or even less transparent differences. Or about not so much going as dignifiedly marching from one radical extreme to another. Certainly not. For this work and this position requires from one a lot of self-sacrifice, even more humbleness, and the highest precision possible. For what we are talking about here are the differences that are measured in millimeters. Or even in something smaller than that. For in the morsels of one's devotedness. And although they, for an outside and carefree observer, may look just silly and irrelevant, for a person concerned they surely form a startling contrast between an unmitigated insult and a blatant overestimation of one's importance in the world. They do. They surely do that.

As it often happens in the case of such venerable occupations, one has to look for the source of the problem in the tissue of the rich and seemingly interminable history of that particular ritual. For, after all, it appears to be understandable that, over the centuries, there had developed a plethora of rules and exceptions. Like mold on a forgotten piece of food lost in culinary action. There had developed the countless special ways, the exceptional ways, of showing respect to those privileged ones in society. In every society. It had been happening since the furry times of prehistoric people unveiling entrances to caves for their primordial leaders, through knights opening doors to various chambers and dungeons for their kings, to the present times of doormen devotedly serving their politicians. And each one of them required individual attention. And each one of them required a separate place on the scale of bows. Like each speed on the crescent of a speedometer. Thus with each next generation, there would be only more, if not unthinkably more, of them. Much more.

That was why I hardly envied my still unborn successors. I surely did not envy them. Although, probably, they would be resorting to the same array of proven tricks and self-made learning aids in order to facilitate their learning process as I had done in my time. As I had done in my now almost prehistoric time. I mean the ones like surreptitiously painting miniature scales on the walls behind them. Or no less secretly concocting them from a series of barely visible cuts in a wallpaper. Or from the lines sketched with a pencil or crayon. But that would depend on the color of a particular wall. So that this singular cheat sheet would not stand out from it too much. And such a trick would rush to the aid of that beginner.

It would help him to assume the right position and perform a bow of the expected and acceptable depth. It would help him till he managed to develop in his back the proper, almost mechanical, reflexes, allowing him to do his job automatically. Completely unwittingly. Even mindlessly. In the best possible meaning of that word. It would do that till his spine started resembling a serrated ratchet mechanism furnished with an unerringly precise scale. And due to that, at the sight of an inevitably approaching guest, an imaginary pawl in his backbone would instantly fall into a correct gap between the right vertebrae. Like a ball gamboling around the carousel of the roulette that finally chooses its favorite slot. And it would prevent him from making any mistakes, any risky motions. But, to their unconcealed dismay, all that requires from one, it mercilessly demands from one, a lot of experience. It demands from one a bit more practice. And, additionally, it also demands from one a pinch of strenuous training, before one attains proficiency in this profession, that one could be proud of. Truly proud of. Yet please note that I remarked that without a trace of haughtiness. Of superciliousness. Or even of an innocent tinge of conceit. I remarked that in such an amicable manner even though I myself could, and I am perfectly willing to do that, serve as a shiny and staggering example of the well-invested time, training, and opportunities. Like a nicely kempt lawn that pays one back for all the efforts by sensually caressing one's bare soles. For I am fully entitled, after so many years of active service, to a dash of complacency. Not much, but only to a dash of it. But never in the amount exceeding the limits of good taste. Or even better manners. Much better.

And thus I felt authorized to think this way. And thus I felt entitled to talk this way. For, in my particular case, in spite of my idiotically overrated age, all the mental processes and motions and a range of my professional reflexes remained in an ideal and intact condition. For, in my particular case, they had been correctly preserved. Impressively maintained. And dutifully synchronized. It was as if I were an antique musket whose barrel had not been savoring gunpowder for a few centuries, but which, if a belligerent need arose, would be capable of doing some considerable harm no less efficiently than its far younger and far more modern colleagues. And quite often I caught myself thinking, and frequently I was amazed to discover, that all that took place inside me unknowingly. All that took place inside me unnoticeably. And nearly without any conscious participation on my part. It was as if my organism were a remarkably programmed self-sufficient vehicle. It was as if it had a perfectly adjusted wheel alignment as well as an exemplary remaining tire tread depth. It was as if it were able to drive and move efficiently and uninterruptedly even when its driver decided to take a coffee break. For, in my case, it was a matter of milliseconds. And it would take me just a couple of those to correctly assess the importance of an advancing guest. And it would take me so little time even if he found himself in my blind spot. Sweet spot. Or any other kind of spot that was in any way connected with me. Or even if I noticed him out of the blurry corner of my eye. Then a few more of those fractions of a second would have to pass before I subconsciously calculated the distance separating me from that person. And me from the door. Several of them would have to perish irrevocably before I established an exact number of steps that this very guest had to walk before he approached me. It would have to happen before I managed to convert them into various units of length and speed, depending on his supposed nationality. For our hotel prided itself on its priceless ability to adapt to the needs of all its clients. Like a comfortable mattress that servilely adjusts itself to one's body, without a single rustle of demur. Then, as the next handful of seconds elapsed, I would painstakingly scrutinize and inspect our immediate vicinity. They would be greedily consumed by my frantic attempts to analyze a farrago of the most relevant external factors. The slope of the floor.

The carpet density. The freshness of the air. For they could have a greater or lesser, more or less direct, influence on our impending, yet always brief and overly formal, interaction. And then I would surreptitiously begin counting those steps in my head. And then I would try to figure out when there came an optimal moment for me to initiate my polished bow. Like an actor instinctively starting to speak on his cue. I would do that, all the time remembering about the inevitable smoothness and gracefulness of my movements. I would look for a moment when I could lovingly outstretch my hand toward an impassive door handle and complement that routine with my wide, welcoming smile. A warm and sincere though still studious smile. Then I would start performing the ingredients of that ritual in reverse. Like a rewound film tape. I would do that despite the fact that this very guest was long gone and absent and had already forgotten about me completely. And I would do that without losing anything. Not even an ounce of my elegance. Not even a dash of my attention to detail and my famed fastidiousness. I would do that like a ballerina who instinctively moves around her house in that distinctly light and dancing manner even when no one is looking, and no tickets have been sold.

However, not everyone made it through the ordeal of a trial period. Because not everyone went through that first phase of his professional initiation, that unrelenting challenge, and that merciless rite of passage, as smoothly and swimmingly as others. For to some of my fledgling colleagues had happened larger or smaller mishaps. Larger or smaller blunders. Though all of them equally unfortunate. Though all of them equally troubling. But, surprisingly enough, most of the hotel guests were astoundingly willing to overlook and forgive them. At once. Right away. They were willing to do that after noticing the whole sprawling landscapes of inexperience painted across those abashed and unskilled faces. For it was as if those pale novices were wearing a singular kind of war paint. And even, some of the guests, with playful smirks and while winking at them solicitously, would eagerly take over their duties. And thus those magnanimous guests would be opening doors for themselves. And thus they would be bowing to themselves jokingly. And they would be playing those roles if this or that rookie turned out to be too petrified or too inefficient to work and lost in a maze of infinite possibilities of refined bows and grips. Like a child in a supermarket. It was also not uncommon for such inept apprentices to help themselves, not only by cunningly, furtively, glancing at the already mentioned scales penciled discreetly on the walls behind them. All of which were akin to memorable lines made during the regular measuring of the growth of a little child. They would also cheat by illegally using their legs during the bows as counterbalances. Thus they would clumsily strive to stabilize their insufferably youthful bodies and retain their equilibrium. Like an oil pump that incessantly bows to the earth in gratitude for its sticky treasures. This method, naturally, was a glaring breach of all the possible protocols and codes of conduct. But it was still an acceptable one. It was still an admissible one. It was still perfectly acceptable in the case of such callow practitioners of this honorable profession.

With time, however, all those contrived crutches would eventually cease to be useful to them. With time, all that would cease to be necessary to them. And they would be forced to cope with their demanding tasks without that. Without all that. As if all that were a pair of training wheels affixed to a child's bicycle that were being shed in the learning process. So they would gradually stop resorting to such awkward artificial aids. So they would gradually purify and refine their technique. And by measuring the time that they needed to become fully independent, to liberate themselves, to stop hopelessly depending on those things, those crude things, one could learn the true class and worth of a particular doorman.

Besides, that period of unheard-of leniency, that period of uncommon forbearance, would not last as long as it appeared to some. And as others wished it to be. It would not last. That specific protective period. That peculiar time. That closed season for amateurs and defenseless fledglings. Unfortunately, it would constitute a quiet and calm prelude to a hunting season replete with a flurry of dangerous activity. Of far more dangerous activity. For, soon afterward, the same thing that not that long ago, a mere moment ago, was being treated with exceptional compassion and tolerance as a fully understandable, and even, at times, quite charming, blunder of a beginner, would become, without any prior notice or any kind of courteous warning, a display of one's sickening incompetence and laziness. It would be perceived as such. It would be, although neither the scale nor type of that mistake had drastically changed in the meantime. As it happens with an adolescent whose mischief no longer passes for childish antics. And woe to all those who failed to discern that turning point in time. And woe to all those who failed to see in time that undetectable point of no return. The point that, after all, did not figure in any crumpled maps or various glossy guidebooks. For, after attaining it, after crossing it, all the things that, till recently, they could easily get away with, from then on would be brutally hailed as unacceptable. All that would be regarded as intolerable. And all that would be scoffed at. And frowned upon implacably.

But that singular moment seemed to be particularly dangerous, if not downright sinister, to all those who correctly noticed, identified, admirably realized, and decided to avail themselves of the lack of any consequences for their gaffes. Even symbolic ones. Even provisional ones. Like in the case of a celebrity who gets away with the most improbable excesses. Especially, as that impression was additionally being corroborated by that overt leniency expressed by guests toward their more or less innocent oversights during the initial period of their work here. It was dangerous to those who ostentatiously ceased to work on improving their skills. It was dangerous to those who hoped that this rather dysfunctional state of unlimited mercy, of forgiving them everything, and of turning a blind eye, or two of those, to each and every one of their slips, would last forever. For it is always like the honeymoon phase of every relationship that sooner or later is being unashamedly verified by the bittermoon one.

Basically, I might, or even should, just as well have warned them. I should have berated them and informed them about this perfectly natural course of events. I should have warned them about all the tragedies and downfalls that were certainly going to happen to them. It was only a matter of time when. It was only a matter of time where. I certainly could have made such an effort and do that after discerning the first timid yet already telling symptoms of their disturbingly reckless behavior. But on the other and far less, not so much warm-hearted as warm-palmed, hand, I did not intend to do one's work for him. Surely not. Nobody had cautioned me against anything. Nobody had deigned to help me. So why should I? Why? It may sound insufferably banal or even downright silly, but everyone has to count on himself. Such are these times. Such is this world. And such was also life in this hotel. Such was life in this fabulous and outstandingly open microcosm. In that equally dangerous plush jungle. For such was life in here where behind every deceptively harmless and lavishly ornamented balustrade or seemingly calm embroidered curtain, could be lurking a ruthless predator. It could be there, waiting for a proper occasion to leap at one and stab one in the back at the first opportunity, at first sight of its victim. It could, if only one lost the sight of its markedly predatory silhouette even for a moment. Even for a single moment. Although, most certainly, keeping up with the style and undeniable class of this place, as a murder weapon would serve a rather expensive and generously encrusted paperknife. Yet a knife nonetheless. And that was why one had to be incessantly and tirelessly on guard. Without exceptions. Without excuses. Without any extenuating circumstances. That was why one had to be in the state of constant combat readiness. With his guns cocked. With his anchor lifted. And with his cannons loaded permanently. And that was why here, nowhere else but here, and especially here, one had to count on himself and trust only himself alone. And even that ought to be done with a considerable dose of suspicion and skepticism. For even though such an impressive amount of varnished wood, leather upholstery, and soft materials, could easily lull one's vigilance, a plush-wrapped dagger surely would hurt as painfully as a shamelessly naked one.

I know something about that, believe me. I know that. For it was no one else but I myself, who had once, while bursting with confidence in myself and my skills, swayed, staggered, and faltered threateningly in the middle of one of my sensational bows. And they, after all, inarguably were my forte. I faltered like the otherwise splendid dancer who suddenly confuses the order of steps and ruins the whole choreography of the show. And due to that unforgivable slip on my part I had an impression that, for a flicker of a second, I had imperiled the lives, or at least health, of thousands of innocent people being total strangers to me. I must have done that. I surely must have done that horrible thing. But, in my defense, I had done it recklessly. I had also done it unintentionally. For while balancing spectacularly on one foot with my outstretched hands, like a bird in flight, I had felt like a pilot of a bomber. I had felt like such a pilot who is about to deliver a lethal package to an entire unsuspecting city stretching and sprawling listlessly far below his feet as an oversized version of a map. All that had at all happened for, initially, my unforeseeable stunt, that clumsy acrobatics of mine, had been regarded as an ill-conceived and inept assassination attempt, yet because of it no less threatening, on the life of a military attaché from one of the embassies. For that man, at the time, had been visiting our hotel. For that man had been visiting it in the company of his lovely and simply gorgeous lady friend, most certainly working as a young and supple dancer in the nearby nightclub, and as a rather uptight rigid spy after hours. As far as I knew. For I had seen a lot on my duty.

It was without a doubt the most serious diplomatic crisis that I had ever provoked during my professional life. I had provoked it as foolishly and unnecessarily as a husband uttering the wrong name in the presence of the right wife. And that professional part of my life was the most important of all. But, paradoxically, those international catastrophes triggered by such more or less deliberate, more or less purposeful, instances of irresponsible behavior, or even by a medley of simple misunderstandings, were not the worst ones. They were not. They were not the gravest ones. They were not the most fateful ones. And indubitably they did not belong to the group of the most disturbing cases. For much greater, and sadly often irreparable, damage every single doorman could easily, and at any given moment, cause by mishandling all the things that he overheard during his working hours. All the private things. All the intimate things. All the embarrassing things. All the things that he then thoughtlessly repeated and imparted to someone else. As a kind of occupational trivia. As harmless curios. And which things then, in turn, somehow, after percolating through the wooden membrane of a door could reach the wrong people at the wrong time, but while giving them the right pretext for taking action. Any action, in fact.

As I have mentioned it before, a doorman bears a striking resemblance to a priest. But mostly to a priest willingly immured in a confessional, who hears everything and knows even more than that, and, above all, who observes the unrivaled sanctity of the seal of confession. But, unfortunately, even I happened to be eavesdropping on our clients. Even I happened to be listening in on the incomplete fragments and bits and disjointed shreds of their conversations. Often of an

25

immensely private nature. Often of an intimate nature. Yet I happened to be doing it only incidentally. Always unintentionally. And always against my remarkably strong will. And mark my words, for it would be unseemly for me to lie about this inordinately delicate subject. For I am perfectly aware of a potential scale and proportions of a fierce backlash that I would bring upon the reputation of my profession if I did that. But still, I did that even though, after all, the perennial ethics of doormen, that famous code of behavior, that door-related etiquette, forbade such deplorable practices very clearly. It forbade them very unequivocally. Very resolutely. Not to mention that it refused to recognize any justification or excuses for it. And so it was like a seasoned teacher who has seen too much and too often to believe a single word that comes out of the mouth of a student after he has allegedly lost a notebook with his homework in his dog's mouth for the second time in less than a month.

To be honest, if for some reason, for some specific reason, for some really convincing and cheerfully clinking reason, I had decided to reveal to the ever-curious public the content of all those overheard casual chitchats, discussions, repartees, curt quarrels, and other verbal duels, then not only one or two strictly gossip magazines, but also purely pornographic magazines, would instantly have blushed with sheer embarrassment and shame. And the printing ink used in them would have started smudging rapidly. It would have started smudging like mascara on the eyes of a professional weeper. It would have started making the words blend and merge to the point of indecipherability. It would have started doing that while listening to one of such stories of mine. For such were the things of which I had all too often become an accidental witness and an involuntary listener. For such were the things about which I had heard as a troubling result of the collusion of a quirk of fate and the recklessness of the clients of our hotel. And it would have happened if I had suddenly resolved to do that. It would have happened if I had done something like that. If I had ever divulged even a small dose of those secrets. Perhaps while succumbing to the temptation and merrily rustling incentive offered by one of the infamous tabloids. For, after all, I admit, and it would be an example of deplorable hypocrisy on my part if I did otherwise, that every man has his jingling price. But, if I had done it, if I had really done it, it would have happened against my innate honesty being so deeply ingrained in my trustful and upright perception of the world that it was like a bit of shrapnel in a veteran's leg. It would have happened against all the rules that had been indelibly etched in my mind. Like a love confession that is carved on the trunk of a tree. And which values I, in turn, had been laboriously etching in the minds of others. Of my followers. Of my acolytes. And of my professional successors. For all those things that I happened to be hearing on an everyday basis, all the words of the people who were being caught by my incessantly vigilant ears at the least appropriate moments of their sacred privacy kept significantly exceeding and surpassing that what could be possibly devised by the entire hosts of authors. By genuinely talented authors. By any authors for that matter. They kept surpassing the best efforts of those endowed with even the most fertile imagination, producing crops several times a year, without the need to be watered or fertilized excessively. I mean all the things that were being said when those guests did not expect any invigilation of this kind. I mean all the things that were being said when they had their guards lowered either naively or nonchalantly. Like lazy boxers. And when they had the masks of their fake and studied poses either misplaced or removed carelessly. Like relaxed actors who take a rest behind the scenes in their half-removed costumes. And I mean all the words of the impromptu confessions of love. And I mean all the words of the saucy and salacious announcements of the indecent things that one of our clients wanted to do to the other one when left alone. Or even before that. Who knows. When the sun capitulated and decided to set finally. And when something else rose daringly. I also mean all the words of grumbling and complaining about the people located high, if not terribly high, above them on the ladder of social hierarchy. I also mean all the words of sheer contempt mixed in perfect proportions with the tones of vicious contentment with the failures of those over whom they towered triumphantly. Both in terms of their position and wealth.

From time to time, however, those bits of information that I managed to overhear, though I stress that only in an unplanned and accidental manner, turned out to be quite interesting. They turned out to be even mildly intriguing. But always infallibly edifying. It was a rather obvious fact, considering that they came mostly from the people of the upper classes. They came from people being located at least a bit higher than I. Far higher than I. Because the price for an overnight stay in this fabulously exquisite hotel significantly exceeded the financial capabilities of any commonplace mortal. If not of several consecutive generations of such nonentities. And thus, they came directly from the people who were so infinitely that nearly insanely more affluent than I was. Who were noticeably more erudite than I was. Far better educated than I was. But, above all, who were far more sophisticated and far more familiar with the vernacular of the wide and great world than I would ever be. For, after all, my own entire world came down to that little faithful door handle, fastidiously polished by my hand throughout the years. It was as in the case of rocks being smoothed caressingly by the slowly yet meticulously oozing water. For my entire world came down to the beaten and slightly worn-out patch of the splendid hotel carpet. My impervious bastion. My unassailable post. For it was there that I had been standing tirelessly for the five decades. The full five decades. Or even more.

And if I had ever felt an irrepressible urge to go and travel to the remote and exotic places, or to experience an exciting adventure full of petrifying surprises and bloodcurdling dangers, I could always have headed toward the staff canteen in the back of the hotel. I could have done that. For, in order to get there, one had to surmount an inhospitably, if not just hostilely, high threshold. And it had almost succeeded in killing me once or twice in the past.

That was why it happened, every now and then, that mere seconds after my surprisingly fruitful eavesdropping, I would immediately hasten to take the fresh news for a spin. Like an exhibitionist who after buying a new coat instantly rushes to the nearest park. And I would hasten to check them in the always-tricky practice. All feverish and tremulous with excitement. And I would invariably hasten, succumbing to the violent fits of curiosity, to try them out. To break them in. All the things that I overheard accidentally. But only by chance. All the things that I furtively picked up with the still perky antennas of my oversensitive ears. And not a single reasonable person could blame me for that. And thus, I would put into practice all the disjointed shreds, all the incoherent bits, and even all the vague outlines, of conversations and theoretical reflections on this or that matter that I learned surreptitiously.

Once, for instance, I was expertly, as usual, opening a door, as it turned out, for two stately dignified men. Their speech, as I could not help noticing, was detectably affected by, and tinctured with, the patina of a clearly melodious foreign accent. But they also gave an inescapable impression of coming straight from a burlesque. It was due to the impressive and downright comical contrast between their physiques. For the first one was quite tall and lanky while the other was of a rather short and plump type. Their intimidating self-confidence and the both springy and commanding nature of their gaits were akin to that of officers on the prowl. Their distinct body language seemed to be written only and surely in the imperious capital letters. And all that mixed with their breathtakingly elegant and expensive suits were the only things that prevented me from dissolving my professionally emotionless expression with a boyish smirk at their sight. So, as I was opening the door for them, I heard them anxiously discuss an impending stock market collapse, a veritable catastrophe. It was about to be caused by a sex scandal in the highest echelons of one of the largest and most omnipotent corporations that ruled the market. And, as a result, it would reinvigorate its direct competitor. It surely would give its competitor more scope to act. So, they kept alternately assuring and reassuring each other solemnly that the thing was certain, that the thing was unfortunate, and that the disastrous scandal was inevitable. And the notably quickened pace of their speech, although still perfectly rhythmical and almost regal in its nature, betrayed that it was a matter of days. If not even hours. Let alone minutes.

And so, the very same day, I rushed with all my might to the nearest brokerage office. I rushed there, and while sweating and coughing and panting heavily I strived to stutter out, between my alarmingly wheezing breaths, akin to the asthmatic groans of a pierced accordion, the name of that other company that they were talking about. And which I barely overheard. And, after a few abortive attempts, more or less botched attempts, as well as after a miniature investigation in which was involved the entire staff of that office, we finally managed to deduce the right name and the right company. And I bought several shares of it. And I bought them with the little money that I had kept till then stashed under my bed in my never-washed sock, the safest place and greatest deterrent of all. Then the whole deplorable affair soon proved to be true. The appalling scandal broke as predicted. It broke with almost surgical precision. As the repeatedly squashed nose of a brawler. Yet without the expected support of any anesthetics. Apparently, it was all about some fowl and dogs. For everyone kept mentioning chicks and bitches. What a horrid and sick idea! Then a long-time leader and founder of that international corporation fought gamely though briefly with a relentless spate of accusations. He fought with a veritable deluge of calumnies and slanders. He strived to salvage the faint vestiges of his reputation. Like a man whose all dirty linen is being washed in public without the aid of any detergents. But then, when a fine vessel of his hitherto unblemished name started sinking due to the unremitting inflows of charges against him, he eventually, yet reluctantly, gave in. He surrendered. And he resigned from his office. His company lost the priceless trust of its clients. Its stocks plummeted rapidly. Its main competitor naturally gained from this confusion. So, in turn, the other stocks skyrocketed at once. Unfortunately for me, they were not the same ones that I had purchased so impulsively. So foolishly even. And in such a hurry. For I had apparently misheard that name. I had not heard a part of it at all. I had misconstrued the rest of it. And I had even failed to notice, in all this excitement, in all this commotion, that the company that I had chosen operated in a completely different line of business than the recently compromised one. It could happen to the best of us. That is, to me.

Some other time, when my dear and loving wife was still alive, when she was still endearingly alive, I listened in, but the same as before by sheer accident, and only by accident, on a pair of young guests. Evidently, they were insanely in love with each other. Evidently, they were madly fascinated by each other. For she, resplendent in her merrily rustling evening dress, could not take her hazel eyes off him. And he, invincible in his wrinkleless suit, was clearly unable to keep his uncommonly nimble hands away from her brassiere fastening as if they were a fish that was lured by an unapologetically cunning hook. And I heard them panting evenly. And I heard them panting huskily into each other's ears. I heard them talking passionately in that sultry dialect of unbridled lust. Thus they described what exactly they intended to try out in bed that night. And which was supposedly the latest sexual trend from the glamorous world. From the refined world. From the most enchanting world of all.

And, immediately after work, I dashed back home. I dashed there like a boomerang that cannot wait to meet its owner. I ran to my hallowed sanctuary. I ran to my protective oasis. I ran to my caring wife. I ran while repeating in my addled mind all the consecutive actions that had to be performed in that exact specific order to achieve the desired effect that this adorably youthful duo was so enthusiastic about. I kept busily pondering the excitedly unusual ways, the marvelously innovative ways, of using this or that body part. I kept contemplating all the rather unorthodox and numerous applications of this or that seemingly commonplace orifice. I kept doing that till I faced my beloved spouse. And I did that confident, proud, beaming earnestly, and completely naked. For I had farsightedly taken off all my clothes on the way from the door. Like a banana that has shed its peel to indulge in the trite slapstick joke for the umpteenth time. And then I ceremoniously announced that I was going to show her, and let her taste herself, the fanciful trends from the alluringly exotic distant lands. And then she finally learned, and then she finally found out, and then she comprehensively fathomed what exactly was demanded from her. She learned what was expected of her by this brief and challenging foray into the nuances and intricacies of the cultures of those faraway nations. And then she acquainted herself with all the more or less disturbing details of those eccentric things that were going to happen to her. That awaited her. That threatened her menacingly. Like a surprise party that can prove to be fatal for a man with a serious heart condition. And when she heard about all the things that would happen to her body parts that were completely unprepared by usually cautious Nature for such excessive antics, she treated me to a quick and succinct rehearsal of our own indigenous customs. And they were incomparably closer in their style and character to our mentality and our national temperament. Thus, she punched me and pummeled me several times. She punched me over and over again. She hit me on the head with her purse that, as if out of sheer weighty spite, was filled to the brim with some jingling junk. After which indubitably painful incident I spent the forthcoming night not only utterly and inconsolably alone, but also the only pleasure left to me was an old, fatigued, and no longer needed petite pincushion. Of course, robbed of its usual prickly inhabitants. It was supposed to serve me as a modest bolster, though a bolster nonetheless, until I abandoned such asinine ideas.

And so, it was in this way that I kept hearing things and forgetting things. Also unwittingly. Also not by design. And also without malicious intent. Or any sinister ulterior motives whatsoever. Because I was not some incurably inquisitive gossipmonger. Because I was not some impenitently prying busybody. I was not some chronically meddling home-made and self-declared spy. I was not someone who was all too interested in the minutiae of the lives of others. I was not someone who listened in on those others during his idle working hours, only to go around blabbing and wreaking havoc and telling complete strangers what he heard and what he did not hear at all.

And in the same way, I was reached by those words. In the same way, I was reached by the most terrifying, traumatic, and enigmatic words that made my obviously vintage blood freeze in a maze of my already draughty, leaky, for rather old, veins, namely, "The world, the entire world as we know it, is going to end soon."

◆ ◆ ◆

For a long time, I was forced to keep repeating in the privacy of my innermost thoughts that just-heard sentence. I was forced to keep repeating it like a novice secret agent trying to memorize a no less secret code. I was terrified. I was paralyzed. I was scared stiff. And thus oddly motionless. It was as though I were a clumsy character from a fairy tale who had accidentally turned himself into stone, and who now strived with all his rocky might, with all his lithic power, to summon to his now rather stony mind, a proper antidote spell, capable of breaking, crumbling, chiseling, or, at least, reversing that curse.

So I kept reiterating it. So I kept repeating it obsessively. So I kept doing that in the vain hope that with each repetition it would sound a little bit less menacingly, a dash less threateningly, a pinch less gloomily, than just a moment before. Like a dish whose original spiciness wears off with time. I kept doing that in the hope that it would lose so much as a fragment of its distinctly ominous character. That it would drop its sinister note or two. I kept doing that as if hoping that, eventually, somehow, I would manage to discern in it a hint of positive tones. Even if they were subtle overtones, discreet undertones, or any other kind of tones imaginable. Even if they were the vestigial remnants of their echo. In this regard, I resembled a bewildered worker who upon hearing that his career is over, that he is being fired indisputably, tries to find in the words of that, after all, irrevocable verdict, at least some dregs of praise. Of appreciation. Or of acclaim. No matter how weak or diluted.

And on account of that laborious rumination and that endless replaying of this sentence in my mind ad infinitum and ad absurdum, I lost myself unreservedly. I immersed myself in the depths of my internal world. For I suddenly developed a fondness for replaying it compulsorily. As if it were a particularly pessimistic kind of mantra. Or a remarkably catchy song. And I forgot completely about the whole world. I forgot about it and the, a bit smaller, yet far more wonderful, hotel reality surrounding me. I did that like an absent-minded parent who, having forgotten to pick up his child from school, allows it to sleep over in the classroom, yet without even cordially asking it for its consent. But I forgot myself to the extent that I stood there, suspended in the middle of performing an impressively low bow, with a partial smile, and with the only partly opened door. I did that as though I were a street mime artist who heard not enough clinks of coins in his hat and thus could not complete his movement, to the dismay of beguiled children, out of his own pecuniary spite.

And so, the door remained misleadingly ajar. It kept yawning languidly although there was no one in its vicinity. There was no one in sight. There was no one who could be worthy of that privilege. Also only partially. Also only to a limited degree. And this fact was a rather glaring instance of abject indelicacy on my part. For it, and I by means of it, inadvertently deprecated not only the value of that splendid ritual itself, but also it disparaged and belittled all those who had received such honors in the course of its till then irreproachable history. For one could wonder, if an empty corridor deserved the same amount and scale of genuine attention and celebration as the most distinguished of guests. And if so, then how much did they really mean to the hotel? To its owners? To its personnel? And if little or very close to nothing, then, did closing that door make sense? Any sense at all? And if it was true, if there was so much as a misplaced modicum of truth in that downright embarrassing supposition, then perhaps (horror of horrors! terror of terrors!) that once respectable task might as well have been entrusted to photocells, to the mechanical parts connected through odd umbilical cords made of tangled cables with the comparably soulless electric motors. All of them blinking and humming coquettishly. All of them infallibly precise. All of them faultless. But also, all of them would be undiplomatic and not caring for anything else than the next drop of oil or two. Unlike those a bit less perfect likes of me. Unlike me myself. And if anyone had ever drawn such an unjust and injurious conclusion from this little tableau, the petrified I, the motionless door, the deserted corridor, then it would have meant that I had contributed to it inadvertently. It would have meant that I had corroborated that blasphemous turn of events. The one that I feared unthinkably. The one that I abhorred most of all. Then, I would have been like a fierce pacifist who unwittingly, by virtue of the ferociousness of his antiwar protests, succeeds in producing enough sparks during their unforecasted drizzle that, upon landing on the flammable ground of national sentiments, trigger the much-feared war.

Unfortunately, which was odd and which had never happened to me before, the wretched door remained open. It was still open in spite of the fact that he had disappeared long ago. The elusive messenger. The almost ethereal deliveryman of these words. Of the baleful news. Of the horrid news. For he quickly scurried away. And then he smoothly blended into that expanse of uninhibited luxury and affluence reigning supreme in this very place. In this very country. In this superb hotel. He disappeared there as a cry for help in the middle of an overture to a cacophonous concert. And he disappeared there as promptly as he had emerged from it, seconds ago. Mere seconds ago. He had done that to rudely stir the peace of my elderly mind. He had done that to ruthlessly turn my world upside down, my entire meticulously kempt orderly world. As if it were a shiny shaker. He had done that to upset it along with my, till then stable, perception of its exigencies and intricacies. He had done that to turn it upside down along with its carpeted streets of winding hotel corridors. Along with its town square of an imposing hotel lobby. Along with its archipelagoes of neat and polished intimate tables in the hotel restaurant. And with the exciting cliffs of hotel balconies. And so, it turned it over impulsively. It turned it over as though it were a snowball that has to be shaken and stirred forcibly once in a while to get rid of the sediment. The accursed sediment. And due to all that, before that man vanished, before he became nothing less than a troubling memory to me, his actions toward me resembled a particularly disconcerting modus operandi. And I recognized it. And I recognized it without any problems. For it resembled the actions of the obviously less palpable cold shiver that tap-dances triumphantly on one's back when one learns that the closest, the dearest, childhood friend of his has just died, perished abruptly, turned into nothing, from some merciless illness or other. For it is then that one is being brutally pulled out of the soft and comfortable illusion of safe, stable life. One is being pulled out of it, like an underwater creature that falls for a hook posing for a metallic fate of every fish. For it is then that one realizes that cold breath of death has just missed him by inches. By a mere handful of them. Hitting the next one in line.

Suddenly, I was deprived of the velvety cushion of self-deception. Suddenly, I was robbed of my saccharine illusion. For I then, swiftly, unexpectedly, noticed, on account of his prophecy, the fragility of all that. I noticed the brittleness of everything that was, according to his words, allegedly going to end so soon. I noticed it like a long-distance runner who spots the first faint holes in his shoes in the middle of the run. After not much more than an instant it seemed to me so obvious, so incredibly conspicuous, and so embarrassingly self-evident, that almost impossible to be missed by anyone endowed with a pair of eyes. With a pair of decently maintained eyes. It seemed to be obvious even though I had no inkling whatsoever of its existence barely a minute ago. For, apparently, I needed that violent push. For, apparently, I needed that cruel jolt. That unseemly poke. I needed it to startle me out of some stupor. For it was as if I were a heavy pendulum that lost its momentum. I needed that to let me look at all the things around me through the verbal prism of those prophetic words. I needed that yet not only to see all those things, to recognize their shapes, their colors, their fabric, and their names, but I also needed that to notice them properly and realize what they meant at the same time.

So, it was then that at the sound of those dreadful syllables there appeared before my eyes a full catalog of dangers and threats and potential tragedies. They belonged to a group that, till then, had been safely concealed behind the glossy layers of wallpapers. They belonged to a mass that had been cunningly covered with the heaps of elegantly decorative drapery. It was a mass that had long been paganishly buried under the heavy yet enchantingly soft layers of thick bed sheets and towels and duvets. Each one of them with the hotel's name handsomely embroidered in its corners. It had long been buried there like a spicy magazine that an adolescent hopes to hide from his parents. And then, I at once noticed a constellation of those risks and hazards hitherto only discreetly simmering beneath all that. Underneath all that. And right under all these layers insulating us from them. I noticed it even through that thin, yet until recently astonishingly durable, deceptive film of the illusion of opulence that was, after all, supposed to guarantee us the everlasting peace. And I saw those risks very clearly. And I saw them with all their harrowing details and no less traumatic nuances. And I saw them for the first time in a long time. In a really long time. Because till then I was blissfully convinced that such horrors of life had long been hidden, muffled, deftly and adeptly contained. And kept at bay. And buried for good. Once and for all. I was convinced that they had long disappeared under the fancifully decorated carpets and ornamented plaster ceilings that had been selflessly laid one upon another by the successive generations. Like a fluffy coral reef. I was convinced that they had been laid there since the time of the last war and the equally horrible times of unrest. Those horrors. Those unspeakable horrors. All of which he had brilliantly squeezed into that one ominous sentence. Like a poet who is capable of embedding the whole gamut of profound emotions in a single delightfully melodious verse.

They could not escape my notice now. They could not do that even though for so long I had been hoping, truly, genuinely, that these atrocities, along with their echoes, would not return anymore. For I had hoped, just as the rest of society, of this marvelous society, of this refined society, especially that older and more experienced part of it that easily remembered a bit more than the winter temperatures from the last year, that they had already been immured somewhere. That they had been deposited underground. I had hoped that they had been stashed there, in that poorly-ventilated realm of the past tense. In that abysmal warehouse of history, dutifully storing on the shelves of the layers of soil the evidence from all the past epochs. Like an elderly man suffering from the compulsive hoarding disorder. I had counted on that there was not a chance, not a single chance, let alone a full-fledged possibility, that they could have survived the unstoppable inflows of affluence. I had counted on that they had been stifled by the influx of unalloyed prosperity, of healthy and peaceful lifestyles. I had counted on that they had shared the fate of a poor wretch whom a few gang members decide to embed into the foundations of a stylistically daring building, to drown him in cement, to treat him to a pair of the ever-fancy cement shoes, and thus to elevate the rank of their crime to the level of pure art. And I, also in good faith, had counted on that. And I had deluded myself. Diligently to a fault. I had counted on that it was exactly what had really happened to them. But, in truth, I had only selfishly yearned to attain the peace of mind. I had done that although there was no evidence of them meeting such a fate. No proof of that. Not even the most trifling and misplaced one. But I still had counted on that, although no one had ever dared to peel off all those carpets, all those towels, and all those duvets, to take a quick and cursory look underneath. But I had done that although no one had ever dared to make sure, once and for all, whether those horrors and unrepentant demons of the past that had once caused such misery had, indeed, suffocated there. Whether they had, indeed, died in there from the lack of public attention and interest in them. Like a now utterly forgotten and moth-eaten past celebrity.

Nonetheless, now they seemed to be returning from that banishment. And once again they gained ground. And once again they gained popularity and support. At least, within the confines of that single fearsome sentence. It was just as with one's long repressed childhood fears that return later on in one's mature years to haunt one and to torment one mercilessly with childish vigor.

And thus, present in this particular sentence, they ably turned the worst threats as well as warnings that had ever been intended for me, thrown at me, as well as that I had ever encountered during my long life, into the most subtle and endearing compliments conceivable. For every danger that I could possibly imagine paled in comparison with their breed to the point of hemorrhaging all the blood contained in it. And they surfaced in this single seemingly harmless sentence. And they surfaced in this sentence that, after all, apart from my doubtless righteous indignation, passed completely unnoticed in this wonderful place. For, a mélange of its terrifying sounds and tones, those intrinsic components of this message, quickly settled on, and soaked into, the highly absorptive surfaces of the invitingly soft silky carpets. It became detained there unlawfully. It became muffled and silenced there. It became arrested there, on a charge of their glaring incongruity with the imposing grandeur of this hotel. With the magnificent interior design of this edifice. It was accused of incompatibility with the delicate and refined language of all the conversations being conducted here. Regardless of their length. Regardless of their importance. For they were always conducted in the same glorious tone. Always in the respectfully lowered voices. And always with the regally restrained giggles of those extremely cultured people, for whom there was hardly anything more impolite than a hearty guffaw or two.

Besides, that horrible, cruel prophecy had to be silenced that way. As a bit too talkative accomplice in crime. There was no doubt about it. I do not claim otherwise. It had to be silenced that way mainly on account of its rawness as well as its unpalatable crudeness. For it would certainly have offended the tastes of our guests, had it not been brutally pacified in time. It had to be treated this way, uncompromising and unhesitant. Before anyone heard it. Before anyone noticed it. And before it managed to cause so much as a passing stir. It had to be dealt with that way before it, within a second, within a single crepitant breath, ruined and marred the impeccable calm of this place that had been established there by means of the distilled sweat and dreams and sacrifices of countless past generations. And they, the ghosts of those generations, now lingered there above the unsuspecting heads of the guests, of the unsuspecting guests. And they lingered there like a piñata that is about to start raining candies. For it sounded in here strikingly out of place. In this remarkable setting. In this hermetic realm of elegance. To which only a few chosen privileged ones had unlimited access. It sounded here as vulgarly as a loud curse word in a cathedral. Or as a warm word of praise during a session of a parliament. Otherwise, it would exactly have been as a verbal gunshot capable of rudely punching a hole in one of the finely decorated walls. And it would have been a hole akin to those left by bullets, yet naturally being of a more symbolic and intangible nature. And it, even if still rather small and inconspicuous, even if for the time being deceptively harmless and clearly innocuous, could fairly easily have led to the uncontrolled decompression not only of that single room, of that single cabin, but also of that entire exquisite microcosm. Then it would have resulted in a series of boorish turbulences. All tragic in their consequences. All horrible in their aftereffects. And then, inevitably, thus giving my most intimate fears a good and lengthy airing, it would have resulted in the collapse of the whole system. Of its minutely designed structure. And then it would have resulted in its being perversely sucked out through that hole into the cold void along with all the fruits of this very civilization. I could not let it happen. Not I. Not now. Not ever.

41

And with my entire, after all not too young, not too springy, body I rebelled against that. I fiercely opposed the return of those redoubtable fanatic demons that, at the time, seemed to be dangerously inevitable and imminent. And it was due to this protest, it was due to this visceral and genuine protest, that I even, somehow, regained a fraction of my long absent youthful zeal. I even restored a flame of my former energy. Just like a match that rubs its sulfur-drenched perm against a box, its home, its itinerant refuge, its ignitable shell, to produce a vivacious flame of self-immolation. And also several of my most prominent wrinkles became miraculously smoothed out. Not to mention my hair that won back its charming boyish luster. In places. In patches. Here and there. And each one of my internal organs seemed to be separately, voluntarily, as well as of its own accord, joining that impromptu revolt. Thus they, as a belligerent internal gang of mine, started shaking and swaying my frail old body in outraged unison. It was as if I were a perpetually wrinkled banner, no matter whether it was tickled by playful wind or not, that was being brandished during a demonstration.

And yet, what could be done? And yet, what could possibly be done about that matter? What could be done about that colossal predicament? Even by someone enjoying a relatively prominent, though not leading, position in that overly lenient society? What could be done even by someone wielding enormous influence and considerable power within the realm of world politics, yet manipulating it always from the cozy shade of the back row? As a puppeteer pulling strings from above the miniature stage. What could be done even by someone endowed with innate cleverness, sagacity, and uncanny political acumen? That is, by someone like me? Especially by someone like me? Most probably nothing. Or very close to it.

That was why I watched pityingly the sheer enormity of what we had achieved. That was why I watched in awe the magnitude of what we had attained. And what was now at stake. That was why I admired the vastness of what we had built laboriously. With more or less joint work of our countrymen. For, let's face it, not everyone had been working with the same alacrity and devotion as I had done my part. Not everyone had been fatiguing his legs and hands as I had done. The humble and obedient I. And so, I relished seeing what we had managed to create since those dismal events of the past. I mean the events which I myself remembered now, perhaps fortunately for me, only as if through the haze. Yet still the gunpowder-soaked haze. Akin to a translucent curtain in the theater of shadows. And so, seeing the now endangered overwhelming splendor, our recent pride and joy, and understanding and appreciating better than anyone else, due to my immemorial age, what we had to lose, and to which we might return, a tide of tears pushed and elbowed its sentimental way to my eyes. Like a movie buff on his way to a long-awaited premiere. And yet they remained as invitingly open as all the doors that I had ever laid my hands on. But those tear ducts of mine did not belong to a group of my body parts that I used and misused and exploited the most. Especially now. Especially at my age. So I needed a little more time to start them up smoothly. So I needed some time to warm them up properly. To break them in. In order to get the tears rolling down my petrified face. And so only the third and even fourth batch of them met, in a satisfactory degree, a farrago of regulations and quality expectations for their shape and form. And only then it began looking exactly like the ones that everyone hoped to see. And when nothing could possibly stop or detain that veritable flood anymore, only then there appeared the tears of the finest vintages, first-rate quality, and the richest emotional bouquet available.

For I was scared. For I was really and truly scared that, when the ghastly menagerie of various demons and evil spirits as well as other eerie bogeymen from the past, somehow managed to escape, when they broke free and came into contact with the air of today, there would take place a chain reaction on an unprecedented scale. It would surely take place. And it would be eminently difficult to subdue or reverse quickly. It would be all the more dangerous that along with it there might emerge from the past a miscellany of downright hideous designs of hats, suits, and rather unflattering skirts, those unrevenged crimes against fashion, which had once, fortunately, mercifully, sunk into tasteless oblivion.

Suddenly, it might turn out that it would be impossible to drive them back into their former cages. Into their tight and sequestered cages and cells of nothingness. It might turn out to be impossible to put them where they had been languishing patiently for the last several decades or more. Like wine maturing in the venerable oak barrels. And one should bear in mind that immuring them in there the first time had already verged on the lay version of a miracle. For I knew perfectly well that it would not take much to make those visibly stale fears, outdated sentiments, and rancid prejudices start swelling, bloating, and becoming dangerously purulent. Like some really nasty lacerations. For it would not take much to make them begin spreading rapaciously. While availing themselves slyly of the current highly favorable cultural and ethical situation. Of the prevailing moral landscape. While using it as the dreamy kind of nourishment. As a fabulous growing medium. And due to their unstoppable growth, they would quickly prove to be simply much too large and far too expansive for their former claustrophobic cells. From then on being sadly unable to contain them anymore. Like a little old apartment of a haughty nouveau riche. Soon, they would start spreading on their own exuberant account, while puffing up, growing up, and expanding greedily. They would do that like an obscure and unstudied, or rather, once studied and cured but then forgotten, illness that is being recklessly unleashed and set free by a group of archeologists who invade the morbid peace of some ancient tomb or other. And we would all be utterly defenseless against such an epidemic. And we would all be defenseless against such a modern supernumerary plague that had once been ignobly overlooked in the scriptural passages. For we had lost, if not forfeited voluntarily, if not abolished deliberately, our immunity to it. For we had lost it after a social organ responsible for protecting us against it had atrophied and withered and perished irrevocably. Long ago. Dreadfully long ago. Like an ability to make incredible excuses when one loses his childish fantasy and grows up. For we had lost it after the last pharmacist who was familiar with a recipe for an infallible antidote to it had died so long ago that no one remembered how to pronounce his name properly anymore.

That was why if it came to this, if this putative epidemic transformed into a fatal fact, we would not stand a chance with it. And that was why we would be dropping like suicidal snowflakes on the first, and thus still pretty warm, day of winter. We would be doing that under the pressure of such an ancient and crude and vulgar intellectual infection for which there was no effective cure any longer. We would be doing that because it had been gotten rid of. Somewhat recklessly. Somewhat precipitately. But certainly foolishly. It had been gotten rid of after that kind of threat had been declared no longer truly frightening. No longer dangerous to anyone. And after it had been hailed as a faint echo of the bygone cruel barbaric times. Like the sight of a primitive furry man playing hula-hoop with a stony prototype of the wheel. For it was as if its sole presence, of that remedy, kept making everyone uncomfortable by summoning to their minds a slew of horrible memories. And by reviving in them those abominable demons of the past. It was as if the sole presence of that cure was jarringly incongruous with the zeitgeist of these times. Of these cultured times. Of these delicate times. It was as if its rhythms were discordant with the prevailing mood. The benign and gentle mood. For, in the meantime, since their brutal heyday, the world had managed to shed its habitual

45

callous mask. It had managed to lose it and then it had developed a more delicate, more lenient, as well as chronically forbearing, one. It had become far too forgiving to be able to take any decisive actions. Any uncompromising actions. Any bold actions if necessary. Any relentless actions if unavoidable. And so, I was stuck here, in this hopeless situation. I was stuck here, like a prehistoric animal in a tar pit. For it had become unable to take any actions that could prevent the relapse of that social disease from happening. Often tragic in its consequences. Often catastrophic in its outcome. And thus it had become unable to preserve the peaceful status quo. And it was a disease of that bizarre kind that, more than only once before, had caused sudden death of dozens of its hapless victims. Without so much as prior notice in the form of an irritating rash. Without any alarming paroxysms of convulsive coughing, severe sneezing, and uncontrollable drooling. Or any other easily discernible symptoms. Perhaps except for the insufferable trigger finger itching and the joint shouting of absurdly radical slogans.

That was why all my seemingly unfounded fears had in truth better foundations than most of medieval castles or cathedrals. That was why those fears of mine warned me that all that we had created and constructed, with enormous difficulty, with inconceivable toil and effort, but also with an incredible flourish, we could lose now very quickly. We could lose that now. Like a poker player who bets too rashly. We could lose that as our ability to oppose such threats, to fend them off, to keep them at bay, was incomparably weaker than at the time. Than the first time. Than in the past.

And yet, perhaps, the truth and nothing but the truth was being prompted to me by the timidly smoldering embers of hope. It was the truth that, after all, everything was not lost yet. And, perhaps, that was exactly why everything started seeming to me inexpressibly, as well as illusorily, unreal. After another fear-sodden moment. After yet another dreadful

instant. And then, soon afterward, I could not resist that particularly obstinate impression. For, right after the echo of his
foreboding words had sunk for good into the tissue of that
boundless luxury, it was impossible to divine whether it had
been there in the first place. It was impossible after it had sunk
into the ubiquitous soft upholstery covering everything and
everywhere. Like the smell of a lover into an empty bed. It
was impossible after it had sunk into the fabric of sprawling
carpets and endless draperies, with their gauzy folds flowing
and heaving lightly, soothingly, almost hypnotically, but certainly without end. So there was not a single trace of those
words left there, anywhere around me. It was just like in the
case of the evidence for the existence of a bogeyman inside
the child's room after its dreamy crime scene is being contami-
nated by the first stray sunrays of the newborn day. For, right
after all that, the echo, as well as its very author, that nightmarish messenger, appeared to me so irrational, along with the
content of his words, that nearly surreal.

Thus, I had to find him. Thus, I had to get hold of him.
Now. Right now. And then I had to ask him. And interrogate
him imperiously. And even torture him if necessary. I had to
do that to get out of him the confirmation of his previous
words. I had to do that to force out of him the comprehen-
sive answer to the question implied by his involuntary warning. That is, when was going to happen that "soon." That
infamous "soon." The one that he had been talking about so
menacingly.

And I walked at a quickened pace. And I walked while balancing precariously on the verge of breathlessness as well as the
helpless limping of the weary old man. I traversed, in search

of that mysterious man, of that ominous specter, an unending maze of hotel corridors. Both imposing and luxurious. Both fantastic and stunningly real. And I traversed the very corridors that kept intimidating one with their sheer opulence and grandeur to the point that one could not help asking himself what kind of marvels and supernumerary world wonders could still be hidden behind the line of those doors. Which veritable labyrinth I knew so well. With which tangle of elegant passageways I was so perfectly familiar. Which I had learned by my servile plush-upholstered heart countless years ago. And with which I had acquainted myself as well as if it were a constellation of holes riddling a pocket of an old coat of mine that I kept covering and uncovering unwittingly with my unruly fingers. Like a deft flutist doing the very same thing with her decidedly more audible instrument.

I kept searching. I kept looking incessantly for the little unassuming traces, any traces, really, that he had recklessly left en route. That he had unknowingly left behind. Like a snail leaving a slimy trail. This nasty runaway. This inordinately vile fugitive. But I strived to do it as discreetly as possible. But I strived to do it while taking great care not to exaggerate, not to overdo, my endeavors in any way. And thus I strived not to make a fool out of myself. I strived not to do that by incurring a volley of amazed glances of our guests by comically walking around on all fours. I strived not to do that by looking for his footprints impressed on the fluffy surface of the carpet, with my nose amusingly hovering mere inches above the floor. Like a peculiar, for wrinkled, metal detector gliding right above a fertile minefield. And I doggedly looked for his hardly perceptible handprints on the walls. Of his both hands. Or only of a single one. And I looked for the handprints that he had presumably left there while propping himself up in order to retain his balance after steering out of a dramatic skid near this or that hellish sharp turn. Or a diabolical one. Because the civilizational hell followed with him. Like the insufferable odor stalking an onion aficionado. And I also desperately tried to spot any telltale broken twigs or stems of the flowers bowing deferentially to all the honorable guests from the bouquets sitting on the tables lined up against the corridor walls. Like demure girls and timid boys during a senior prom. And I strained my eyes to see the details. And I strained my eyes to see the little details. The unobtrusive details. I mean those so ostentatiously insignificant details that were capable of easily escaping the notice of an untrained and unaided eye of an unsuspecting passer-by. Like the hopscotch grid chalked on the sidewalk when one is too old to play. For they would pass unnoticed by anyone who did not belong to my one-man posse. For they would easily pass unnoticed by anyone who was not as well-versed in the tricks and secrets of the dying art of chasing people down hotel corridors as I was. At least, at that still sprightly time of mine.

But I not only looked for him. Alertly and attentively. But I not only looked for him while examining painstakingly every piece of furniture. Every trifle. Every bric-a-brac. For also I inspected everything that might, after treating it a bit roughly, after maltreating it a little bit, yield any useful information about him. They might do that. Like an initially reluctant potential informer who changes his decision and converts to lawfulness after savoring a dash, a mere hint, of the overly safe accommodation provided by the state. Because it should be duly mentioned that I had mastered the most challenging interrogation techniques and highly practical methods and tactics of extracting information from inanimate matter. I had mastered them to the always stubbornly elusive perfection. So I could, without too much effort, without too many attempts, force even the most inconspicuous element of interior design (a door handle, a light switch, a naked bulb) to sing. To snitch. To spill the beans. Or rather, nails and bolts. Depending on its type. I could do that even to the most adamant one that this hallway fugitive did not even expect to turn its back on him.

49

And also to the ones that he did not suspect of possessing any incriminating data about him. For everything might have a lot to say about him. Even the tiniest hook carrying a painting, past which he had run breathlessly. Even an insignificant headrest of an armchair that he had nonchalantly poked with his elbow during his sprint. Or even a door frame that he had stroked fleetingly while running away from me. Each one of those small things. Each one of that lifeless staffage. Each one of those parts of the bigger and unmistakably opulent picture. They might have a lot to say about his tactics and motives. And thanks to their selfless cooperation they could guide me to his still fresh trail. And so, I not only simply looked for him, but I also harnessed to that search all my senses. Also the ones that had grown intolerably stale and rusty and misaligned from disuse since my last chase. However, being of an incomparably less dramatic nature. For, at the time, it had been merely a leisurely pursuit of a hotel guest who had apparently forgotten, in a fit of his stingy absentmindedness, to slip a handsome tip into my always-receptive pocket. So they needed only a little bit of maintenance work. So they needed only a little care to regain their former famed efficiency. Like a car of a Sunday driver that is being awakened from its slumber during a business day.

And thus, I walked hastily. And thus, I walked hardly managing to place my feet in proper order so as not to make any of them feel passed over or offended. And all the while I smelled and tasted and savored everything in my way. I greedily searched for any invisible and impalpable yet distinctly aromatic traces. I did that like a thoroughbred hunting dog, though already limping a little bit, as well as suffering from an insufferable syndrome of loose dentures. Thus, I touched and caressed and groped everything and everyone. I felt compelled to do that. I had to do that. Regardless of whether it was a whimsical lampshade of a flirtatiously blinking wall bracket light. I had to do that whether it belonged to the hardly lively family of inanimate matter, or, on the contrary, to that of the excessively animate one, in the form of a lithe cleaning lady from the top floor. And thus I remorselessly grazed with my incessantly searching hand every single thing that found itself in my vicinity. The frigid brass door handles. The lustrous tabletops. The comfy sofas. And the exceedingly upright walls. It was as if I were a blind person fiercely striving to read the tips and hints covering all the objects or persons, and, ironically, being visible only to his defective eyes, for being written in a peculiar version of the Braille alphabet composed of various cracks and scars and creases, describing the world far more accurately than any image would ever do. And thus being worth a thousand pictures or more.

And, meantime, I was helplessly mystified. I was utterly bewildered. Because I was not entirely sure what I was looking for. Because I was unable to recall any trivial detail of that accursed fugitive's physical description. Not a single one. Not one innocent trifle. Not even the outline of his chin. Not even the topography of his cheeks. Nothing at all. It was all the more surprising given that he had just sauntered listlessly right past me. It was all the more disturbing that I had just overheard that disconcerting prophecy of his. The same one which had put me rather indelicately in a state of shock. For then it put on full alert all my senses and sensory receptors. Like the smell of a mailman does to almost every guard dog. It awakened all of them. From those buried in my fingertips to those located in the ends of my dignifiedly grayish hair. And it had rocked my life to its very foundations. Now wrinkled. Now consumed by nascent rheumatism. But it did not do that as a curt unannounced earthquake but as a whole family reunion of such earthly shivers. And that was why, if anyone had recklessly ventured to stop me and ask me for assistance in the preparation of a composite sketch of that messenger, of that formidable harbinger, my genuinely evasive answers and ambiguous suggestions would have painted a painfully ordinary outline of a face. It would have been completely empty inside. Like the dentition of a boxer. And thus it would have been thus matching the description of everyone and no one at the same time. Like a universal size of cheap socks. And due to that troubling fact, I would surely have been considered his clumsy accomplice and asked to share the sentence with the man whom I apparently tried to protect so ineptly.

Undoubtedly, it would have happened despite the fact that I had once been priding myself, since my youngest years, on my splendid memory. Of the finest kind. Of a truly photographic type. However, it did not require any flashes, shutters, or a host of additional lenses. Not even the rest of such an unwieldy equipment. But now I could no longer vouch for the quality of the film used in it. But now I could not vouch for any smallest part of it. For it had lost most of its stunning qualities with time. Thus it was like the smile of an aged seductress.

And also I had no certainty whatsoever as to the type and tone of his voice. And, what was worse, with each timely passing second his voice, or, at least, a remarkably faithful copy of it, if not its vocal facsimile, kept fading and withering and diminishing unstoppably. It kept doing that while irrevocably losing all its distinctive mannerisms. All its inimitable idiosyncrasies. It kept fading away although it had been recorded and preserved and then stored in that continually shrinking archive of my memory. For its rooms and offices were being brusquely overtaken by force and then unlawfully occupied by the ever-greedy department of senility. Thus there was left only a raw, insipid, and austere message. Thus it was being completely peeled off of any embellishments and adornments softening the blow delivered by it. Like in the case of a fist being stripped of a boxing glove. And the more often I remembered him, the more often I carelessly replayed his voice in my memory, the more worn-out and fatigued that recording became. It was like an invaluable manuscript from the distant past that implacably cracks and fades and crumbles to pieces with each turn of its page, with each flexing of its spine, devolving into dust, of the kind that travels through time inside a hourglass, thus justly and deservedly meeting the fate that it had escaped the first time.

Then I carefully scrutinized the line of doors I quickly walked by. I scrutinized it as if I were an officer inspecting his troops. Then my heart contracted furtively from an unscheduled pang of pain and an irrepressible overflow of emotions. Like a love letter that is being squashed by a heartless object of that fatally misplaced affection. It contracted even though my mind went to great lengths, bordering on the Marathonian distance, to distract me and divert my attention from all that. It contracted although my mind ably tried to focus on a mishmash of unfathomable signs and clues pertaining to my impromptu investigation. It was a pain. It was an agonizing pain. It was a pain that could not be possibly alleviated by any miraculous pills or syrups. It materialized impudently right when I admired and appreciated all that was so ineffably dear to me. All that was so infinitely close to me. All that was so splendidly invaluable to me. For, not infrequently, this or that exquisite hotel trinket, this or that glorious piece of hotel furniture, or a decorative balustrade, meant far more to me than the members of my own family. And decidedly, much more than most of my colleagues.

Perhaps my motives and beliefs seemed to be a dash bizarre. Perhaps they seemed to be rather disturbing. If not downright preposterous. Perhaps they seemed like that at first and always-imperfect for biased glance. But, after all, I kept spending with those objects, and not people, most of my time at work. It was with them, those adorably lifeless entities, those soothingly calm items, that I found it most convenient to establish and maintain the firmest bonds and closest relationships. Like a child that adores its blanket to the soft excess. For it is incomparably easier to understand the needs and intentions of an ignobly soiled door, requiring only a quick and deft wiping with a cloth to restore the famed brass glint in its knob, than to decipher the entire complex interplay of gestures and grimaces as well as obscure thoughts underlying each one of them, that accompany all conversations with the more lively people.

And so I gazed at this accumulation of things. And so I gazed at it but not as if it were the work of my whole life. Not as if it were an outcome of my sacrificial toil. Not as if it were the precious something that was suddenly supposed, during the far less laborious instant, to collapse and fall apart and chaotically crumble to dust. But rather I gazed at it as if it were a dreamy and peaceful haven, as if it were a remarkably tranquil oasis, on that fiercely tumultuous sea of contemporaneity. I looked at it as if it were a cozy refuge on which one could count earnestly. In which one could trust implicitly. On which one could place high hopes. His medium hopes. And any other hopes. I looked at it as if it were a safe place. I looked at it as if it were a place with which one could associate his safety, as well as that of the future and still unborn generations. And which, unforeseeably, had become unstable and therefore markedly endangered. It was like a house of cards that is about to be devastated and annihilated insolently by the slightest jolt of a rickety table serving as its clearly unreliable foundations. Soon. Very soon.

Meantime, my restless eyes perfectly mirrored the hectic state and condition of my dazed mind. For they kept perpetually searching for something. For they kept tirelessly hunting for anything that could betray him and inform me where he had gone. For the half-baked and half-seasoned ideas and questions kept simmering and stewing discreetly in there. In that intimate mental oven of mine. Like popcorn that one has left in a hot car. For my brain, horribly crevassed from age, teemed with a slew of disconcerting thoughts and visions. It teemed with troubling worries. It teemed with the most inconceivable misgivings. It teemed with them as I wondered intensely what I had actually heard. Because, at first, I had to rule out the risk of a mistake on my part. I had to do that, utterly, categorically. And beyond any doubt. I had to be certain about that. I had to be sure about that before I took any action. Before I resolved to avail myself of my unique and much envied position on the international political scene. And of my rather tenuous relations with most of the indubitably powerful people of the world, yet being relations nevertheless. I had to be absolutely certain about that before I employed them to stop that tragedy. To ward it off cavalierly. To prevent it laudably from ruining our marvelous times. But to accomplish that I had to find any conclusive evidence. Even though I was well aware how absurdly difficult that task was. Like building a comfortable and delightfully furnished suburban house out of sand. I had to get any proofs that this man had said what I had heard. This sinister prophet. This vicious fugitive. And that he had meant what he had said in my inconspicuous yet ever-vigilant presence. I simply and truly could not afford to provoke the smallest misunderstanding. The silliest innocent confusion. The tiniest yet greatly amusing disgrace. I could not risk anything of that kind that would surely ensue if, for instance, it transpired that this man had not said what I thought. That this man had not said "the world, the entire world as we know it" but "work." And only I, due to a despicable collusion of my mounting giddiness, considerable age, and various shameless acoustic tricks and shenanigans, had heard what I wanted to hear. Like a boy who keeps drooling over a girl even though he has just been indelicately turned down by her. Whereas, in truth, all that was about his demotion. Whereas, in truth, all that was about his job loss that had certainly shook the world. Yes. But only that miniature and limited for his personal one. And, perhaps, I had heard everything correctly, but it was he who had meant something completely different. For after losing his job he still had to return home. He still had to go home and impart the bad news to his blissfully unsuspecting wife. That potentially fatal information. But fatal to him. And only to him. And this confrontation also could lead to the unscheduled end of the world. Yes. Once again. But this time of the one formed by his family life.

That was why I was forced to gather proofs. Lots of them. And they had to be the most irrefutable proofs. And they had to be the most unshakeable proofs. Not to mention the most indubitable proofs available. Like in the case of a young scientist hoping to challenge some old and long established theory or other. I had to gather them before I would even start thinking about stepping in and taking action, any action, really. I had to gather them before I would even dare to make the smallest and shiest move on the immeasurable chessboard of international politics, requiring from one a simply staggering level of theatrics. For if the whole thing proved to be a mistake, nothing else but a silly and laughable mistake, after I had set in motion all the imposing and dignified, and thus terribly cumbersome, wheels of the geopolitical machinery accompanied by various cogs and ratchets, there would be no turning back. There would be no rescue for me. For I would make a fool out of myself. And my so long and so eventful that almost perennial a career, which I polished and cultivated fastidiously, as well as the outcome of the years of opening and closing doors servilely, all that would be instantly jeopardized. All that would be momentarily put at risk. And those formidable cogwheels would pull me in. The very same ones that were just about to help me. To salvage me gallantly. And to protect this world tightly shrouded in the veil of unbridled opulence. They would crush me barbarously. Like the grip of a warm-hearted bodybuilder who may also become one's formidable opponent when handled inappropriately. And they would do that without so much as a faint flicker of remorse flitting across their voracious cogs. Besides, I had to be absolutely certain about all the aspects of this predicament of mine. For I was always careful not to abuse my political power. My special influences. Never. Not even under such unusual circumstances.

Thus I strived to decompose this ostensibly innocent little sentence into its prime factors. Hastily yet precisely. Thus I strived to do that as a combat engineer gingerly tampering with the potentially lethal insides and intestines of a still ticking time bomb. In this case, it was a no less potentially catastrophic cultural explosive charge. And I did that quite nervously. And I did that in order to get rid of any doubts. Any second thoughts. Any irritating displays of distrust of myself marring the otherwise impeccable clarity of my judgments. At the same time, I conducted a cursory, yet never-perfunctory, examination of its every single element. I did that while analyzing and diagramming the accursed sentence in a more or less grammatically palatable way. I did that while looking for any treacherous traps. Any hidden explosive surprises. Or any wires in a color palette not matching the one mentioned in the screening room of collective imagination.

And, a mere second before I ventured to remove an intangible detonator from it, I held my breath. I held it with a drop of sweat teetering on my bushy brow. Like a tightrope walker balancing over the precipice on a treacherously fraying rope. And I waited for something. And I waited for a torrent of images and snapshots from my entire life to flash spectacularly before my eyes. And I waited for it because I saw it, more than just once or twice, in the incurably trite movies. So when it did not happen, so when the eagerly awaited vision did not come, I felt disenchanted. I felt cheated. And even slightly offended. I felt like an archeologist who finishes his education while deluding himself and expecting to experience during his professional life a mishmash of exciting chases through ancient tombs and duels with ruthless grave robbers only to spend the rest of his career on poring over some insipid lump of soil or other. Thus, I had to do all the work myself. So I imagined an ending film tape that was about to start fluttering helplessly on a still spinning reel, like the tail of a fish that gets caught in the vertiginous embrace of a working propeller.

And only then, all of a sudden, some mysterious force, some inexplicable force, summoned to my mind, on my behalf, a flock of fleeting images and reminiscences of all the fine places, of all the fantastic places, and of all the phenomenal locations that I used to frequent in the past. Those were all the fine places with which were associated the more or less moving, the more or less mawkish, moments of my life. And they were now helpless. They were now defenseless. They were now callously imperiled. And there was also a deluge of images and memories of my so distant that almost dubious youth. And it seemed, at the time, to be no less fantastical and surreal than any given fairy tale. There were also the much fresher images of the present, as well as the somewhat flamboyant predictions about the future. That imminent future. And the more remote one. And, both of them, stood now timidly in the impenetrable shade of an enormous question mark. Like a fat man striving to hide from the eyes of his ruthless pursuers behind a skinny lamppost. There were, as well, the melancholic images of my almost prehistoric childhood, dating back to ancient times, which were terribly difficult to recollect and determine. For one had to first cut off my hand, or any other limb of mine, cut it in half and count the growth rings concealed in there to be sure, to be absolutely sure about my age. Those were the images. The truly horrible images. The appalling images. Those were the proofs of unthinkable horror and atrocities that had once reigned supreme in my region of the world. In my once tormented fine distant country. And their now faint and almost utterly faded, yet no less terrifying, memory, still haunted me. It still plagued me. It was like a mad photo lab technician who, partly dutifully and partly obsessively, sends out to his clients the countless prints of their photos, although they had been first developed whole decades ago.

And it was those last images that prompted me to take a stance. It was those images that prompted me to intervene. They prompted me to feverishly oppose the unexpected return of such an unspeakable tide of sheer barbarity and terror. For it was a tide that had once remorselessly washed off the deck of my life my childhood house. My childhood dreams. My childhood fantasies. And, above all, my beloved parents and siblings. Now I saw those images once again. A whole torrent of them. I saw them once more. Wild and kaleidoscopic. I saw them being so varied, so unique, and fervently mingling and merging with each other. Like the swirling clothes inside a washing machine that one watches at close quarters. And I saw them chaotically blending and permeating each other. Like the flavors in the ground leftovers. I saw them doing that in this little intimate orgy of distorted facts and overblown details, akin to a testimony of a slurring drunk driver. And then I was unable to distinguish that which was, from that which is, and from that which might be. Without even a little dose of certainty. Of any certainty, really.

Half-dazed, half-paralyzed by fear, I reeled spectacularly while ricocheting from wall to wall. I was like a ball in the pinball machine that took a severe beating from an abusive plunger. And I saw, as if through a thick haze of incurable guilt, the faces of all the people whom I used to pass on the street. Those were the faces that I had been seeing every day. For many years. On my way to work. To my beloved work. And those were the faces to which, till now, I had not paid any attention. Not even a passing one. Not even a nominal one. Those were the faces that I used to ignore stubbornly, always doing my best. As if they were nothing more than an inevitable element of my surroundings with which one has to come to terms. To some terms. To any terms. Sooner or later. In spite of my not adoring it too much. But only now, when they became seriously endangered, when something threatened their existence, they induced in me the feeling of sadness. Even a fit of despair. And without a doubt they only strengthened in me the overpowering sense of loss throbbing in my chest. And it was throbbing there like a worm inside an apple. For I really and truly wanted to protect them. For I wanted to save them. All of them. Without exceptions. I wanted to do that even though I had not cared for them no longer than a moment ago. A mere instant ago. Even though I did not know anything about them. Not a single thing. Not a sole trifle. I felt exactly as if I were a child who while facing that acne-covered threshold of adolescence yearns to save as many of his old toys as possible, out of pure sentiment, out of pure regret, although they would be, from then on, just gathering dust, that tailored coverlet of dust trying to pass for an ennobling patina of time.

But then I caught a promising glimpse of an image of my dear late wife. I caught it amid that flashy and gaudy lot of my maudlin memories. And then there also appeared the snap-shots of all the moments, of all the better or worse moments, which we had spent together. Then, after yet another while, I noticed a constellation of neat little portraits of my daughter. I saw them forming those infinite miniature serpentines akin to the photo booth strips. All depicting my daughter. And, above all, my beloved tiny daughter. For she, although already adult and independent, remained to me a child. She remained a lovable child in my somewhat faulty and aged yet loving fatherly eyes. And thus she seemed to be suffering from varying degrees of arrested development, in which my paternal love was in possession of both the keys and handcuffs. For, because of it, the curse of growing pains would never befall her. For, because of it, she was free of the nagging insecurity marring one's youthful days. And no ophthalmologist, no contact lenses, and no marvelous corrective eye surgery, were capable of changing that perception of mine. For she was still a child to me. An enchanting child despite everything.

And it was then that everything that was not enclosed

within the smooth and innocently delicate outline of her face ceased to exist for me. At once. And all of a sudden. Without any prior notice. Without so much as a fair warning. Without even cordially asking for my consent. Because she, my gleeful daughter, my intractably joyous offspring, eclipsed the entire world for me. Because she eclipsed it with her dainty and loving self. And her likeness, her endearing mental portrait, was being continually screened on the inner side of my eyelids. It was being screened there like a movie on the wall of a garage in some makeshift cinema. And it was so faithful, it was so uncannily lifelike, that it became durably etched in there. It was like an afterimage of the sun that is being preserved in the retinas of a doctor glaring at it too intensely, too obstinately, out of professional habit, while striving to notice on it the notorious sunspots and trying to deduce whether they are merely overgrown liver spots, or the first symptoms, the warning shots, of some far more threatening ailment.

But then it suddenly subsided. But then faded away that impressive collage of scattered bits and scraps and clippings of my rather vague thoughts and memories. And it occurred to me that I had reached the main and stunningly airy banquet hall. I had reached it in this mayhem of my internal confusion. I was so confused, in fact, that I almost overlooked the sophisticated floral pattern winding and writhing lightly, almost frolicsomely, on the lustrous hardwood floors. Like veins on a leaf. I almost overlooked a chandelier crowning it, hovering above it, above everyone in there majestically. As an overgrown diacritical mark. I also almost overlooked that it, this hall, this superb hall, was currently bursting with the elegant people, with the flawlessly resplendent people. It was brimful of fabulous sparkling drinks and even far more astonishing dishes. But, above all, it was located exactly two floors below my perennial post by the door. And it meant that I had somehow traversed two flights of wide and otherwise imposing stairs without even noticing that fact at all.

61

I needed only a brief moment to snap out of that stupor. I needed only to snap out of that highly unprofessional kind of trance, to fully and utterly comprehend where I was. And among whom I now found myself. But then, I felt delightfully self-confident and determined once gain. After that instant of puzzlement and stifling uncertainty. After I shed the last vestiges of my doubts and misgivings. I felt almost like at home. Or even more at home than there. And I felt like that when I was being engulfed abruptly, if not protectively, when I was nearly being sucked in, by that boundless and variegated mass. Of dignified figures. Of honorable guests. That elegance incarnated. That multi-headed epitome of impeccable manners. And that uncontested paragon of unforced gracefulness. It was a mass of those undeniably wealthy people, of those immensely influential people, of those incredibly powerful people, without excepting anyone, among whom, strangely enough, I had never felt like a stranger. Let alone a poor stranger. I had never felt like that despite that enormous gap yawning triumphantly between our social statuses. Our financial statuses. Or any other statuses. For it was among them, among this splendid lot, this distinguished lot, that I knew my role and place. For I was now among those to whom I had been attending for years. For I was now among those whom I had been obliging for endless years. And toward whom I had kept assuming that air of unalloyed servility. Almost instinctively. Like a collapsible chair that strives to please its master and owner regardless of the time or place. And I kept assuming that air not only at the mere sight of them, but also while sensing their close proximity and the temperature of their both marvelous and intimidating bodies. For they were the same ones to whom I had been looking up for so long that I could not imagine any different, perhaps even more equal, relations with them. Not even for a second. Not even for a playful instant. For they were the people, those people among whom I felt fulfilled and happy. Really, truly, happy.

And so I was happy there. For, under other circumstances, in other surroundings, I would feel a certain discomfort, a certain annoying discomfort, that only increased with age. I would feel it whenever I was being confronted with a new, challenging, for strange to me, social situation. I would feel it although I had never considered myself a man with an impaired, in any way, capacity for interpersonal relationships. I would feel it although I had never seen myself as one of those socially awkward creeps. And I would feel it although I had never discerned in myself any, even faint or repressed, fears of relationships. But I had always tried to do everything in my power to avoid them. I had always tried to steer away from making any new acquaintances. That was why I would twist and writhe and squirm spasmodically, yet only internally, right beneath that wrinkled cover of mine, whenever someone suddenly, and without any warning, accosted me during some family celebration or other. I would do that. Even if it was some distant and youthful relative of mine. Usually, his name would be a total mystery to me, as well as his acne-stained face. For I had seen him for the last time when he still had not realized that one could dine out somewhere else than at his mother's tit. But that quite embarrassing fact would not prevent him from talking to me for hours. Not in the least. I would endure a similar kind of ordeal whenever some newly hired young worker of our hotel found it absolutely necessary to share with me his unremitting appreciation for my work. He would find it necessary to express his admiration for my tenacity in clinging to my respectable job. And, from time to time, he would ask me about any tips or hints about his duties. Not to mention that he would thank me profusely for my nodding to him abstractedly in greeting. Now and then. Here or there. And this little and inadvertent gesture on my part he would supposedly cherish in his memory, believing that it gave him the right to pester me. From then on. With impunity. But the worst instances of social hell were to me those mostly forced conversations with casual passers-by. And thus insufferably artificial. And thus horribly awkward. And thus utterly predictable. I mean with those who would somehow feel obliged to reciprocate for my giving them directions, or my telling them the time of day, by striking up a brief chitchat with me, hardly having anything in common with a marathon of creativity. Or with a spurt of originality. They would feel compelled to do that only because, by a mere twist of malicious fate, they occupied the seats right next to me. Such behavior was simply intolerable. It was just unthinkable. It was truly unacceptable. And not only to me. The exacting me. But also to everyone endowed with at least a dash of social sensibility. Any sensibility, really. And each such encounter cost me a lot. It cost me so much, in fact, that I might easily become emotionally insolvent.

That was why I perceived it as a true social blessing. I mean that chance to be there. Right there. Among them. It was a unique chance to commune with them in those circles of affluent elites. And that was why I kept crossing, every day, tirelessly, the threshold of that hotel with such unconcealed joy and unfeigned relief. Excited. Breathless. And every time I looked as if I miraculously escaped with my life. I looked like that after reaching that place. I looked like that after emerging from the formidable depths of the filthy urban jungle. I was like a castaway who thankfully clings to the sandy folds of a beach after fighting for his life with the sea endeavoring to playfully duck him under the water every now and then. But in here, there were no doubts. There were no uncertainties. There were no fears. There was no place for any baffling ambiguities, or any grotesque social charades, to solve and decode diligently. There were no vague regulations. There were no opaque rules of the social game, through which pointedly confusing maze one would have had to trudge and meander helplessly in order to survive in ordinary society, whereas the more sly and calculating ones would likely have been bending and breaking them impenitently. As though those rules were a spine of a supple dancer. Especially if such sly ones were completely void of even a vestigial moral fiber, righteous backbone, or a dash of decency circulating in their veins. But this place was free of that kind of shenanigans. This place was ethically pure. This place was enforcing a quarantine on every ethically dubious action. This place was kept in an exemplary moral order. And this place was where I had finally found my own place in this cruel world.

But still, from time to time, I would happen to overhear, more or less accidentally, the little hermetic groups of young and hotheaded bellhops. I would hear them uttering the whole litanies of grievances, charges, and slanders. All exaggerated. All totally groundless. All uncommonly base. I would hear them reciting the entire cavalcades of objections while grumbling and revolting indignantly against this or that aspect of their professional lives. They would do that while conspiring ineptly in the remotest and forgotten nooks and corners of this hotel. Like a platoon of mice planning an assault on the fridge. And they would do that while voicing their inane tirades as well as simply outlandish grudges. They would do that while claiming that they were terribly mistreated. That they received outrageously low wages. That all the decisions directly impacting them were being made secretly behind their unsuspecting backs. And that they demanded more. Much more. And that they wanted to take the place of all those distinguished guests of ours. And not someday. And not in the always-elusive future. But now. Right now. Like zealous young actors who are anxious to replace their older colleagues on theatrical posters. I only smiled pityingly. I only smiled for I could not do anything else for them. Besides, a mixture of their almost boundless ignorance and foolishness with a heady hint of audacity amused me greatly. Their naivety being, in truth, their little personal disasters on an inconceivable scale cheered me up much better and far more effectively than the most proven joke that was the sight of a man heading heedlessly toward a banal banana.

And thus, I found that mental tossing and turning of theirs, full of incoherent movements and succumbing to the tritest of fallacies, extremely entertaining. For I knew, for I was perfectly aware, for I understood, how much comfort and happiness gave one the ability to know one's place in a hotel. In any hotel, really. For I knew how immensely important it was, how crucial it was, how inevitable it was, to cultivate one's relations with those strong and powerful ones in the hotel hierarchy. Often painstakingly. Often self-sacrificingly. For I had long realized how strategically essential it was to approach them and fawn on them and systematically ingratiate one's way into their favors. And I was fawning on them as a caress-starved cat that refuses to be dislodged from one's leg for so long that it becomes an integral furry part of it. For I had long calculated and learned how to properly appreciate the astonishing worth of all that toadying and flattering. Especially, as it still remained the best available and most reliable social currency. Utterly immune to any crises. Totally impervious to any market crashes. Particularly in comparison with such asinine youthful dreams and doltish insinuations, which, by their definition, were bound to devalue pretty quickly. Like the white smoke-written doodles left by a plane on the canvas of the sky.

Thus I smiled indulgently. Thus I smiled condescendingly. For, contrary to them, the rebellious them, the subversive them, the revolutionary them, I did not expect any kind of improvement. Not in the least. I did not demand any grandiose reforms. Much less the miraculous and much-vaunted changes. I did not want my simple, modest life to become significantly better, easier, quicker, more comfortable, far more complicated, or even more affluent. I did not want any of that partly because it still was not in such a parlous state. Not even anywhere close to it. But mainly because I was already content with it. I was truly and really satisfied that at least it was not getting any worse.

And only then it occurred to me, only then it struck me with the full force of sudden realization, that soon they could lose their colossal fortunes. Or perhaps even suddenly. Even now. Right now. They could lose them. All of them. Without exceptions. It was as if that belated realization were being transmitted to me right through the pleasant proximity of those dazzling earthly counterparts of celestial bodies. Listlessly orbiting somewhere near me. Gracefully drifting somewhere next to me. It was as if it were a kind of socially transmitted disease. For it dawned on me that their tremendous influences, and that their otherwise well-established social positions, well-rooted in the fertile turf of history, were all now in peril. All of them. In unspeakable peril.

Thus it could quickly turn out that I might soon lose my dreamy and ideal mental support. Without the aid of any merciful anesthetics. Without the caring assistance of any medical personnel. Thus I might lose my cherished footing in life. Thus I might lose my sacred order of all things, as well as my seemingly inviolable hierarchy of values in life. Thus I might lose all that that was forming my moral backbone. My reliable and inflexible ethical scaffolding. And without it, I would become nothing else but a soft mass of inert and crumpled skin. Thus I might lose everything that was so ineffably dear to me, that undauntedly formed a core of my lifestyle for so my years. For I would be unable to keep on serving them obsequiously and satisfying all their whims and cravings, as they would no longer be able to afford that, they, all those suddenly impoverished elites, to come here again.

Then, the sheer enormity of that impending catastrophe, already lurking around the nearest corner, already prompting me to let out a howl of indomitable terror, already failing to curb my galloping fears, provoked the wave of wild and insatiable anger that overcame me. That assailed me and conquered me in the first round. It was like a fiendish fire devouring my insides and scorching my internal organs. Without mercy. Without

67

remorse. It was like a fire turning my chest inside out while transforming it into a kind of hellish oven on earth, which radiated so much heat that it was capable of smoothening and ironing all the ruts and crevices forming the rich topography of my skin. I was mad. I was furious. I was insane with anger. I was so angry, in fact, that my typically tremulous limbs, also poisoned with the first seeds of rheumatism, resolved to break the usual rhythm of their involuntary vibration and motions, and started trembling dreadfully off-key. Like a fork rattling on one's teeth. I was almost unmentionably outraged and enraged. I was angered not only because suddenly something threatened the proven and hallowed social order to which I was so accustomed, and without which I could not imagine my life. I was furious, not because I was rudely forced to abandon my beloved post by the door for the first time since the beginning of my now almost eternal career to launch a frantic pursuit for that savage messenger. But I was beside my doddery self because that man, by means of his reckless words, by dint of his unspoken threat, put at risk the future of all the wealthy people of this splendid Western country. If not world. Whereas their ongoing prosperity was a guarantee of the current world order. Whereas their regular and undisturbed incomes kept ensuring international safety. For they were better, much better at keeping and providing peace than a long parade of men adorned with rifles on their shoulders. And their unending professional success was a foundation of the safe and calm lives for a myriad of less fortunate, that is, less prosperous, citizens. And I did not mean me. I really did not mean me. For there was hardly more than a few symbolic years of living ahead of me. I did not mean me for I could already see the triumphantly fluttering outline of a checkered flag not that far in front of me. What I meant, or rather, whom I meant, was my daughter. And, above all, my frail and dainty daughter. And as a responsible and caring father, I could not let anything happen to her. Not now. Not tomorrow. Not ever.

Thus now I was forced to look out for that malicious

messenger amidst that bevy of the stately cruising dazzling bod-ies. Thus now I was forced to do that in the hope that, even though I did not know what that culprit looked like, he would finally and foolishly betray his position by his overly nervous behavior. He would do it while suffering from the unendurable mental weight of his offense. Or even, he would instantly bolt away at the mere shaky sight of me, flailing all his limbs at once. As if trying to sketch a flightless angel on the snow. But the only thing that I achieved without any troubling doubt was glaring consternation creeping over the faces of the rest of the perfectly innocent guests. For they, due to my unannounced presence in there started feeling uncomfortably guilty. They started wonder-ing whether they were the reason of my pursuit. They wondered whether I came there to catch them red-handed, red-eyed, or red-anything for that matter. They wondered whether I was there to claim my right to their beloved money, to the tip that they had shamelessly grudged me before. And so, they began slip-ping me money, abashedly, surreptitiously, and en masse. They started putting it in my pockets, as well as inserting it into my utterly unprepared hands when I walked past them. As if I were a priest collecting alms during the Mass. They started putting it there even though it was not what I meant and wanted. And due to that intrusive overcompensation for their imaginary faults and mistakes, for their immaculate innocence, in fact, they caused a quite embarrassing stir as well as confusion around me. And thus it must have, certainly, scared off that cunning fugitive. And thus it must have ruined my well-meant previous efforts.

But it was not that unforeseen inflow of generous though belated tips clinking and rustling alluringly, and promisingly playing a symphony of appreciation in my pockets, that trig-gered a series of vertigos, that series of unbearable vertigos. It did not cause those vertigos tormenting and maltreating me without a momentary respite. For they ensued when I started hunting intensely for that vile messenger and troublemaker over the impeccably brushed coiffures as well as amid the no less finely dressed legs of other guests. And it was then that I managed, naturally by sheer and unaided accident, to catch, out of the corner of my eye, now left, now right, now the mind's one, a glimpse or two of the statuesque figures of these dignified and aloof people. Now they conversed anxiously. Now they whispered to each other in that, rather unflattering to them, but also quite inappropriate in general, nervous manner. For it clearly detracted from their majestic, if not simply godlike, air. Like a drop of blood on the skin of a supposedly immortal prophet.

But I could not hear their exact words. I could not hear any of them. I even did not want to. For I was certainly not eavesdropping on them rudely. As it would be tactless and unworthy of my respectable occupation. Yet while assuming a pose of studied casualness and feigned indifference, I discreetly had my ears not so much to the ground as watchfully turned in their direction. Like a prying neighbor on duty. And thus I cunningly operated still well within the strict and safe boundaries of the hotel etiquette. I did that to overhear, to catch a single disjointed scrap of those agitated conversations here and there. I did that to snatch all that chipped off from those secret consultations conducted in lowered voices. I did that like a dog hunting excitedly for the crumbs and bits of food raining from its master's high table. And then I strived to put them together in the laudably hermetic editing room of my mind. So I was like another dog that tears the whole parts of fabric out of the careless mailmen's trousers, only to arrange and rearrange them later on as though they were a peculiar and somehow uniform jigsaw puzzle.

Then I descended to a rather humiliating position of a crawling toddler. Then I turned to the left in order to inspect a suspiciously jerking and quivering leg that I discerned amid the forest of other legs. It was like an apple tree that one shakes and maltreats a bit too indelicately to get the fruits. But it turned out to be merely a delightfully ornamented flower stand being repeatedly nudged by a grotesquely obese man. And he, in turn, was cornered by a terribly garrulous old lady, as he kept, in this more or less conscious, more or less desperate manner, signaling for help. It was then that I was reached by a tremulous voice, breaking from time to time, as if due to some mechanical flaw of its transmitter. It conveyed that all was not well in society, that there were no prospects, no chances, no opportunities, for improvement of any kind. It conveyed that all of that was only becoming worse and worse every day. Every single day. It conveyed that soon, very soon, if not any day now, the first outbreak of protests was going to erupt violently. It had to. It simply had to. And all of them, the affluent them, the powerful them, were now not so much sitting leisurely on a little innocent powder keg as on a whole abysmal arms depot that was ready and willing to blow up any minute. And thus they were like a pyromaniac who cannot resist chain-smoking even while perching on a crate bursting with fireworks.

Then I progressed even lower. Then I progressed right to the basic floor level. It was as if I tried to wipe off surreptitiously some embarrassing stain or other marring with its sticky presence the otherwise unblemished cleanliness of the glistening ocean of the hardwood floor. Then I decided to direct my now slithery steps toward a curious scene that looked from afar as if a tall man were, tactlessly and far too importunately, groping from behind a gorgeous young lady. But he, in truth, turned out to be a monstrously large dark fur that must have weighed exactly as much as a fully-grown lecherous man or even more. Then, I was assailed from an utterly different direction by yet another wave of anxious whispers. They communed intimately with my auricles. They indecently caressed my earlobes. They playfully tickled my eardrums. Like the most delicate and tender otolaryngologist. And then they informed me discreetly that those infamous belligerent protesters were already there. Right there. Somewhere out there.

But quite near. They imparted to me that people, the simple people, the unsophisticated people, all the tediously ordinary people, the members of the infamous and nefarious masses, finally realized and fathomed what all that was about. The commonplace people realized that nothing could be done any longer. That they would not allow to be fooled or placated any longer. That the end was inevitable. That this excellent ruling class was done for. Once and for all. They realized that the mutiny, any kind of mutiny, was imminent and practically unavoidable. And thus I realized along with them that in a mere moment or two through this or that door there was going to storm into this fabulous banquet hall a raucous chunk of the benighted masses. It was going to burst in here, unworthy of being here, let alone of invading this hallowed place. Of desecrating this fine place. Of profaning this magnificent place. And that frenetic and flippant mob would tear these glorious characters to pieces. Without a question. Without any even brief trial. Without a possibility of defense. And no polite words or eloquent arguments would be of any use anymore. And no barricades would be capable of stopping them. Of slowing them down. Of staving them off. And it would be the end. And it would be the irrevocable and implacable end of that wonderful hermetic elite world that I loved so much.

And thus the mixture of sinister words and no less terrifying images of a supposed tragedy of all those otherwise marvelous people materialized in my mind with surprising abruptness. It overtook my attention by force. It overtook it as well as organized in there yet another visual-aural orgy. It did that right in front of, or rather right behind, my utterly stupefied eyes. And my heart ingloriously silenced in my chest. Like a pupil who is being called up to the ominous blackboard. It silenced there waiting for any even the most makeshift relief. And my breath quickly followed in its idle footsteps, if not its inert heartbeats, threatening me with sudden asphyxiation.

Thus, I awaited that moment. That fateful moment. That

dreadful moment. I awaited the moment of the intrusive but, above all, vulgar hammering at the door. Like a debtor waiting for his creditors to pay him a hardly valuable visit. I awaited it with my whole still sprightly self. I awaited it with all my tense muscles and dilated pupils and widened veins and temporarily suspended or adjourned bodily functions. I awaited it but without even consulting it with my conscience. I waited for those hideous and coarse fists of the mob yearning to grab and humiliate these splendid and glorious people now hiding behind my back. These dazzling guests of mine. These astonishing guardians of mine. These majestic benefactors of mine. These glamorous patron saints of mine. And, above all, these ravishing masters of mine. These people occupying the most important place in my endless yet humble life. Perhaps, except for my daughter. Perhaps, except for the dainty little daughter of mine.

I was ready and prepared and willing and impatient to fall down on my oddly enthusiastic knees in front of the wild and roaring, yet still invisible, but already approaching mob. And then I wanted to give it, to offer it, in a fit of gallant, infinitely hopeless, shamelessly quixotic, and highly symbolic defiance, my bare wrinkled chest. As if it were a rather long overdue Christmas present, long past its expiration date. I wanted to order them to take me. I wanted them to take me first. To stab me and claw me and tear me to bloody shreds if needed. Me, and not them. Me instead of them. Me instead of those extraordinarily wonderful people. For in order to get to them, this savage mob, this raucous herd, would have to pass me first. It would get there but only over my infirm and tremulous and now almost already dead body.

And I was about to grab the twin lapels of my own impeccably ironed uniform and tear it open forcibly. As if I were opening a fresh bag of cereals. And I was about to tear it open along with my faultlessly starched shirt in that act of premature exhibitionism. For there was still not a single barbarian in sight. For there was still not a single sign of an impending disaster. But I already felt and relished the elegant smoothness of the gilded brass buttons, the languid dignity emanating from those little lined up sources of it located right beneath my fingers. I already felt that they were ready, adventurously ready to sacrifice themselves. They were ready to drop off, to plunge into the great unknown, and release the shirt. Like a particularly noble kind of safety pins. And I sensed the curious tingling of tension and almost irrepressible readiness in nearly all the muscles and tendons of my elderly yet still lively body. And I felt them in the regions that were most exposed to the potential stabs and blows. And I was mentally prepared, focused, internally unified on all the imaginable levels. Like a uniform and solid lump of clay. And I was also reconciled to my fate, to my unenviable plight, only to become a modern martyr to the cause of comfort, opulence, well-being, and prosperity of others.

Thus I could not do otherwise. Thus I simply could not choose any other way out of this irrational predicament. Not after so many years of mutual respect and appreciation that I had shared with those elites. It would be absurd to expect me now to turn against my generous masters. To betray them. To swindle them. To double-cross them treacherously. Or just to jeopardize their lives too much and too seriously. For I would be like a supposedly benign contraption that suddenly resolves to fight back for the surplus of kindness it received and start a rebellion to overthrow its unsuspecting creators. And their abrupt disappearance would, most probably, induce in me a severe fit of emotional phantom pains. Impossible to fight or alleviate. Impossible even to reason or negotiate with. Because I would feel like a faithful dog that loses contact with its master's playful, caring hand.

But then, as I was ready to commence my last heroic performance, I heard someone talking fearfully about some lecturer. I heard them talking about a lecturer who had come out of the always-elusive, and thus formidable, nowhere. And then, I was reached by yet another shred of a conversation. It came to me from the direction of a short and rapaciously balding man, with a few feeble strands of hair combed miserably across the expanse of his baldness. Like the lines of a stave waving and meandering across the whiteness of a sheet of paper. It was a conversation about no one else but the very same mysterious academic. And about him mostly.

An instant later, a woman spoke up audaciously from the other end of the banquet hall. She spoke up as if following the promptings of the compulsive urge to finish someone else's sentences. To complete someone else's train of thoughts. To tidy it up a little bit. And to clean up its compartments. She was of an exceedingly, if not remarkably, slender figure. But her face seemed to be strikingly incongruous with the rest of the set. For it gave the impression of being at least two or three decades more mature, more developed, far more graceful, and far more experienced, than her still adorably frail girlish body. It was as if she were an ancient statue that had been incorrectly put together by an incompetent archeologist by clumsily combining two works of art into one. Confidentially, she imparted to those gathered in her initiated vicinity, that this cunning lecturer, that this sinister scholar, kept traveling the length and breadth of the marvelous country while delivering a series of lectures. She stated that he had already managed to gain immense popularity. She claimed that he had managed to gain incredible respect. And, apparently, during those classes he instructed his listeners in the ostensibly inscrutable world of economics. He instilled in them the understanding of the essential rules of the financial world. He made them memorize the basic details about this or that aspect of the distribution of capital and profits, as well as about the division of responsibilities in modern society.

Hardly had he finished speaking and scarcely had her oddly husky voice subsided when, somewhere near me, if not right behind me, resounded a deep baritone of a tall and quite handsome young man, who was sporting a far too outstretched long neck. And due to this somewhat longish imperfection he slightly resembled a submarine with a permanently extended periscope. He deftly picked up that thread where she left off recklessly, in that conversational relay race. And then he solemnly informed a population of his decidedly more proportional interlocutors about the fact that this scholar, this fiendish academic, this beastly lecturer, taught and educated everyone who only wanted to listen to him for as long as an instant. That man evidently taught about the indubitable profits of rational capital management. He educated everyone about the advantages of proper asset management. Of income management. And of any other kind of management where money was involved. He also, painstakingly and ad nauseam, explained to his students all the pains and consequences of living beyond one's means. He explained all that, often to their unconcealed chagrin and disillusionment being painted across their commonplace faces just like a depressing kind of makeup foundation. Supposedly, he kept implanting in the minds of his beguiled listeners a complex mishmash of various rules and laws of the investment of capital. And then he taught them, no less thoroughly, no less devotedly, the creative ways of bending them and twisting them, though without the risk of breaking any of them. It was as in the case of a pencil dancing and pirouetting amid the fingers of a skilled illusionist. Apparently, he continued to disclose to them the most secret and sacred tricks of the financial trade. Apparently, he explained to them minutely the impossibly straightforward art of earning quick profits, as well as of being almost instantly and unstoppably successful in everything they wanted. In every single thing they touched. Or even dreamed of touching. And due to that, he behaved like a reckless monk who foolishly betrays the secrets of his ancient order, thus incurring the revenge of his impressively well-trained and hooded colleagues.

But, above all, there was something else. There was something seemingly much worse. Evidently far more terrifying. And thus many of my stunning companions feared it the most and all the time. For, not so much the sound of those words as the disconcerting tingling at the tip of one's tongue heralding their imminent arrival, sufficed to set into motion, and make vibrate harmoniously, out of first-rate fear, the entire priceless jewelry adorning my distinguished guests. All their gilded rings, lightly gilded signets, heavily gilded bracelets, and their diamond pendants. And all that seemed to be broadcasting, in the language of gentle jerks and sways, a kind of alarm signal. Like the howling of wolves at night. For they were in true danger. For, that academic made his listeners conscious, he made them, his enchanted followers, see and acknowledge all the instances of reprehensible injustice and equally repulsive inequity tormenting and marring the system. And these things were like an intangible form of a potentially lethal tumor growing right on the tissue of society, of whose incurable existence they had hitherto been blissfully unaware. And, as if that were not enough, he also did not shy away, not for a single dithery moment, from illustrating his points accordingly. And he did not shy away from enlightening all those poor and wretched listeners of his. From uplifting them. From instructing them. For he showed them how they could live peacefully, happily, contentedly, and in relative prosperity. For he told them about a life without any oppressive elites. For he told them about a life without any masters. Any rulers. And any powerful ones of this or that world. He told them about a life without anyone hovering above them threateningly all the time. As a kind of particularly greedy guardian angels. At least, according to his intolerably biased and unfair opinion that I begged to differ with.

Much had been said, repeated, as well as reiterated dolefully, at the backstage of this event, about this fact. Perhaps even a phenomenon. And they talked a great deal more. For, apparently, that vile man had miraculously managed to gather and unite and muster quite a sizeable group of listeners. If not an impressive band of worshippers. And it was attentive and gullible. And it was thirsty for even the most casual of his hints and tips and his guidance on the winding road to financial redemption. Many whispered furtively near this or that table, bristling with a congregation of empty glasses accurately reflecting the vacuous nature of those conversations, that he had assembled a veritable army of his acolytes. He supposedly had gathered an army of his obsessive and fanatical devotees. Whole legions of them. Entire herds of them. And they kept regrouping and reorganizing into an infinitely vulgar mass of barbarians, vicious and vengeful, posing a serious threat to our distinctly plush civilization.

And so, from then on, I knew, from that sole moment onward I understood and fully realized something. It happened in that single, forlorn, and fateful instant, in which converged the threads of my dreams, hopes, and the plans for the future. Like the skid marks on the asphalt. But not for my future. No. Because there were hardly more than a few years ahead of me. Those were the plans for the future of my one and only daughter. That delicate and infinitely frail creature. There also converged a farrago of my worst fears and doubts and nightmares. There were all the often haphazard, if not simply incidental, ingredients of some magical potion or other.

For it was then that I came to terms with the thing that I had to do now, immediately. Thus, during that single yet surprisingly capacious second I realized it. Like a posse till then following a false scent. I realized that during this second which seemed to be perfectly capable of containing whole centuries and an infinite chain of generations of people without demur. Like a sort of generational matryoshka doll. During that very second, I finally comprehended what was unavoidable for me. I fathomed what was necessary for me. I fathomed what was simply indispensable. I fathomed what was truly obligatory to ensure the unending safety and peace and bright and undisturbed future of this dazzling place. Of this incessantly glittering potpourri of remarkable people and flamboyant personalities. So I fathomed what I had to do for them, let alone for those whom I had never seen and would probably never have a chance to meet at all.

And thus I could do only one thing. And thus I could do only that last thing. For there was nothing else to be done. There was no other way out of it. Of that unthinkable predicament. Of that grotesque tragedy. Of that seemingly, but only seemingly, ludicrous catastrophe. There was no other escape from it. Like in the case of a chimney sweep rolling out of the fireplace after getting stuck in there somewhere on the way. There was no way to bypass it. Let alone avoid it in the strategically satisfying manner. And one did not need any stylish, renowned, yet overly clichéd, detective's cap, or a terribly creased trench coat, to deduce accurately what kind of thing was that. And I did not need that to guess what a ruthless and murderous idea insolently impregnated my mind. Without so much as blowing a single kiss. Or without a gentle and playful pat on my fatigued bottom. For I already knew what a cold and heartless idea boldly nested in my mind. And it filled it. And it saturated it. With unparalleled vigor. With sudden zeal and enthusiasm. I knew what a brutal idea injected a drop of flexibility and determination into my old veins. I knew what a cruel idea made my hitherto so reprehensibly neglected that nearly atrophied muscles burst with sheer kinetic power. Like an old car battery after charging. And I knew what a callous idea endowed my almost paper-thin brittle skin with enviable imperviousness and indestructibility worthy of a true armor.

From then on, I knew that I had to find that man. I understood that I had to hunt down that fanatical individual. And only then I fully fathomed, with a formidable maze of its nuances and daunting catches, the phantom of the potential consequences of that action. Of that dubious deed. Of that still unnamed crime. And from that I could not, I was simply unable, to shy away this time. And it startled me profoundly. And it sabotaged my well-being quite expertly. Like the sight of a drop dancing precariously at the end of a monstrous syringe needle.

For, considering my present knowledge, it occurred to me that it was my inalienable moral duty to catch that despicable man. It was my duty to judge him. To deliver a judgment. Even if a default one. And thus I had to hold him accountable for the atrocious crimes against humanity that had not yet come true. That had not yet taken place. But they still could do that. Any moment now. Even now. Right now. Mainly due to his Machiavellian shenanigans. Because of which I would be forced, as a one-man posse motivated by both historical and poetic justice, as a one-man jury, a judge, as well as a half of the penitentiary system, to execute such an expedited judgment. I would be forced to do that even if it were to take place in the middle of some congested street or other. I would be forced to do that even inside an impossibly crowded cafe during a lunchtime rush but before the time for dessert. Or even, inappropriately, I would be forced to do that in the vicinity of a playground suffused with the symphony of sounds and tones of the chirping, laughing, and playing children. I would do that even nearby all those innocent little creatures. Those defenseless creatures. Utterly unaware of the indomitable danger hovering above them in the form of that man. Like a curse of acne hanging above every teenager. Nonetheless, I would do that there. I would not hesitate. For, after all, they were as threatened by that man and his clandestine actions as I was. As their parents. Yet mainly, as my beloved tiny daughter. And thus, it dawned on me that I should do that there deliberately. And thus, I understood that I ought to commit that act of ultimate justice right there. That clearly shameful and unethical yet necessary, yet truly inescapable act, the mere thought of which bleached my fossilized face out of its already faint color. So I felt that somehow it would be right. So I felt that it would be perversely appropriate, and inexplicably befitting that twisted situation. Because extreme measures should be reserved only for extreme moments in history. Thus, I savored the extraordinary depth of that thought and its intensity as it resonated with me and within me. It was as though I were a music instrument whose strings are being tugged and maltreated in the name of art, and art alone. I felt that I should do it there. That righteous and justified crime. Even if only on account of the quite farfetched, tritely obvious, yet still meaningful, symbolism of it. Because that man's sinister influence on this as well as on the generations yet to come was impossible to underestimate and overlook.

And, at once, it became laughably obvious to me, as if I had known it for years, that I had to get rid of him. Definitely. Once and for all. I had to do that before it was too late. I had to do that before it was impossible to slow down the approaching cavalcade of tragic events. To stop it. Let alone to reverse all its devastating consequences. I had to do that before the damages became too great, too overwhelming, and before the number of casualties escalated and grew rapaciously to the traumatic point when it was insanely difficult to forget about them. About all those wasted lives. About all that heartlessly sounding collateral damage. I had to do that before it was impossible to refrain from starting the always-tempting, unending parade of vengeful acts of violence. I had to do that before he threw away what we had been building painstakingly for so many years. During that single lighthearted instant of his whim. For he could do that as a result of his order given by means of a single word. Of a single gesture. Of a trivial movement of his hand, of his leg, or of any other part of his body. Naturally, within the bashful limits of decency. For he could do that with an impish grin reigning supreme on his face, akin to the one on a face of a malicious boy conducting a vivisection on his sister's favorite doll. And I had to do that before he posed a threat, implacably, irrevocably, to everything and everyone to whom I had devoted my time. My efforts. And so much as a little particle of my, after all, not so short life. And in particular, I had to stop him before he became a serious danger to my child. To my fickle though adorable daughter.

Only then it struck me with the full force of realization and seriousness the enormity of that duty. I felt its weight lingering on my shoulders. I felt it, this duty, that was placed on my way, on my life path, by frivolous fate. That playful storyteller. And then it occurred to me, the range and scale of the unavoidable implications. Of the long-term aftereffects. Of the side effects. For they would greedily stretch over the whole epochs and centuries to come. Like the serpentines festooning a dance hall. They would do that even though the ignoble act itself should take no longer than a mere fraction of a second or two. Depending on the method of delivering justice that I would choose. It would depend on the fact whether it would be an old-fashioned and a rather time-consuming stab with some sharp object or other, or a far more elegant gunshot.

And I had already sensed the glares of all the past national heroes and revolutionaries watching me from invincible portraits and lofty statues. Like the night watch that is being relieved by the well-rested soldiers. I sensed them looking down on me. I sensed them observing me sternly, expectantly. As a group of unforgiving teachers examining a student. They admonished me in that nonverbal yet still painful manner. They did that while implying triumphantly that they had once done their job. They did that while implying that they had once, in their time, mustered enough courage and strength and determination to change, or, at the very least, affect, the inherently adamant course of history. They suggested that they had managed to redirect the torrent of catastrophic events by nothing else but a single decisive action. By a bold gesture. By an inflexible decision. By the sheer power of their gaze. And thus they had managed to save countless human lives. And I mean only at that distant time. For they also had saved myriads of them later on when more unsuspecting people were born solely due to the fact that their mothers and fathers had been mercifully spared tragic deaths in the carnage of this or that war. Like the books that escaped the burning stake during a radical rally. As it had happened in my case. As it had happened in my tragic case. I understood that only I, and I alone, was capable of stopping all that rampant madness galloping at us. Advancing at us. At full speed. Alarmingly. I knew that I was the only individual there, prepared enough, sane enough, if not sober enough, but surely observant enough, to notice the full scale and proportions of the mortal danger lurking behind the nearest lavishly ornamented corner. Thus I had the nonnegotiable moral obligation and the high-interest debt of honor toward those still unborn ones. Those still absent ones. And so, I had a debt toward those, theoretically, but unjustly, deprived of their right to decide for themselves. I had a moral obligation toward those stripped of their right to vote and take the floor in this informal and rather hasty internal debate of mine. For they were deprived of any say in this debate about them. About their plight. About their fate. About their future. So I had a debt toward those who soon, perhaps, even quite soon, were going to come here. Arrive here. To this perilous twisted world. And replace me without hesitation. Right on time. Like a brand new blouse taking the place of an old and fraying one. They would surely do that according to the tight schedule of the changing of the guard of generations.

And it was then that I became void of the last dregs of any social inhibitions, or the sediments of hampering conventions. And it was then that I had a clear and specified goal ahead of me. In fact, being so fixed and immutable that almost seeming to be etched in the inner side of my eyelids. Like a curse word carved on a bench in the park. And it was then that I felt that my, after all, rather senile body, received a tremendous dose of youthful energy. It did, even though it was being nibbled here and there by the loose tooth of rheumatism. Suddenly, I was driven by passion, aptly retaining and capturing the spirit, the essence of my once youthful angst. I drowned in the immensity of that irrepressible feeling. I had a kind of social epiphany. I had a social awakening. And it decimated on the battlefield of my baffled mind an overwhelming population of unspecified fears and equally vague misgivings of mine. I sensed that my muscles, even the ones of whose mysterious existence I had until then been blissfully unaware, began flexing and tensing proudly. I noticed that my insufferably sagging skin started tightening. As a tablecloth that is being spread on a table before dinner. It did that at once, remarkably, to the, considerably lowered by my advanced age, limits of endurance. It did that to the extent that it lost its otherwise irremovable crevassed topography. That unregistered trademark of it. And it did that without the fake aid of any creams or therapies. And then my whole body began growing and swelling and puffing up unknowingly. Like yeast growing in a freshly kneaded dough. And my not so much flat as sunken chest squandered belligerently, thus aspiring boldly, and perhaps also a bit too rashly, to youthful invincibility. All that conjured in my parched elderly mouth that long forgotten taste of the youthful illusion of immortality. It was neatly combined with utter and undiluted fearlessness. A quite heady mixture. And only the blade of a clock's hand, that unbeatable fencer, was capable of defeating it fairly.

Suddenly, my worn-out eyesight, my habitually squinted stare, lurking behind a pair of impossibly thick glasses perching stately at the very end of my nose, like twin icicles that had frozen there upside down, now became sharp and hawkish. Now it was as omniscient as the glare of a predator on the prowl. It seemed to be capable of spotting even the slightest movement in the bushes on the other side of the globe. And my weary hearing also sharpened of its own accord. So the two wrinkled, pale seashells of my auricles, akin to the twin broken cups, all of a sudden gained a power to hear every faintest murmur or subtle rustle or hurried thudding of blood in the temples of a terrified potential prey. If not a helpless victim.

Then my senses became deftly sensitized and improved. All of them. Without exceptions. It was exactly as if there came time for the long-planned major overhaul of my entire respectably aged self. And that seemed to be just incongruous with the pitiful general condition of the rest of my wretched body. For it had clearly overstayed its cordial welcome in this world. And due to that this singular phenomenon resembled the rather dubious practice of cramming the brand new components into a rusty bodywork of an old car, that otherwise lifeless metallic corporeal shell. Thus there was conducted only a partial restoration of me. A rather perfunctory one. If not a crude one as well. And yet I could not shake the impression that I suddenly became capable of sensing the things that till recently had been beyond my reach. I now sensed the things that till now had been nonexistent to me. For now I could even sense the vague and hardly discernible smell of fresh blood dripping sparsely from the ridiculously tiny laceration on the finger of the cook who cut himself while slicing carrots and telling a sexist joke at the same time in the kitchen three floors below. I could. I really could.

Then, it just could not escape my notice that I grew during that sole little second. For I grew more than in the course of the last half-century. I grew far more than I would have grown if my grow spurts had lasted those five long, challenging decades or more. And if the insufferable growing pains had become my closest friends. My faithful allies. And my most trusted confidants. For it appeared to me that I became at least twice as tall as before, three times more broad-shouldered than before, and nearly four times more dangerous than ever before. So I barely fitted into this enormous banquet hall. So I seemed to be rudely pressing other guests against the walls with my monstrous self. Like a piston compressing the mixture of gas and air trapped in a claustrophobic cylinder. And even I tickled an astonishingly shimmering chandelier with the top of my cap, thus turning it into an insanely expensive pendulum.

Then I immediately shed the wrinkled mask of studied civility. Then I removed the makeup of professional politeness. And I reached straight to my deeply buried and hitherto painstakingly repressed primitive instincts and atavistic urges. I wrestled with my inherent barbaric emotions. I wrestled with the ones that I shared unwillingly with all the hairy and hunched and grunting ancestors of mine. I shared them with those who had once dwelled numerously in this land, in this very strip of land, long before anyone came up with velvety drapery, silver spoons, and petite endearing chocolate mints, not much thicker than rose petals, nesting on the pillows upon the guests' arrival. Like adorable nestlings yearning for a dash of feathered warmth and care. And I was about to follow those both crude and cruel, but surely latent, instincts of mine. And I was about to start sniffing, tracking, and hunting relentlessly. And I was about to start sniffing to get him. To lay my suddenly clawed hands on him. On this despicable troublemaker. On the man responsible for this confusion. I wanted to leap at his throat ferociously. I wanted to leap at him like a feral beast with a truly murderous bent. And to break his neck. And to rip his throat open. To bite right into his unprotected aorta. Or, at least, to try doing it with the set of my frail and loose dentures. After which rather absurd attack he might have looked, with an even line of the little indentations adorning the skin of his neck, like an abortively punched ticket.

And I was about to make the first bold step on the way to realizing my diabolic plan. My hellish stratagem. The initial irrevocable step. For, as it was rather obvious at the time, the present situation required from me a dose of tenacity. A dash of resoluteness. And a dollop of insanity. Or two. But, above all, it required from me the determined and unflinching actions. For, it is a well-known fact that a road to every hotel is paved with plush and impotent intentions. Finally, I was about to avail myself of the assortment of all my newly awakened instincts, urges, and restored impulses. So I readily lifted my suddenly predatory leg, that looked as if it were capable of singlehandedly, if not singlelegedly, wiping out an entire species. But then, all of a sudden, I felt dizzy. I felt inexplicably unstable. I felt like a musician playing out of tune. And I was assailed by a tide of wild vertigos. Then the relentless blade of self-consciousness got entangled in my legs thus making me limp and walk cautiously and move awkwardly. I felt as if a spoke were being rudely put in my training wheels. And I looked around helplessly. Now to the left. Now to the right. I was like a puzzled actor hoping to use the cue cards that were supposed to be hidden discreetly somewhere around the film set, but someone hid them so well that they are impossible to find by anyone.

And then, for a single fraction of a second, I saw this entire wonderful and luxurious world orbiting around me. And me only. For the first time. Deservedly. And so I smiled in that professionally modest fashion. But then I promptly managed to mitigate my shameless contentment. For every self-respecting doorman should refrain from showing emotions to guests. Any emotions, really. And I had done that before I lost my balance. And I faltered precariously. And I tripped embarrassingly. And then I fell on the floor. To everyone's surprise. To general amusement and my own unspeakable disappointment. In the terribly abysmal silence. I fell on the floor and along with me tumbled down and was shattered to pieces my precious reputation. There was shattered that splendid and enviable outcome of the five long decades of my hard work. Of my frantic toil. Conducted in a nearly religious fervor. It was now gone. The fruit of those five long, demanding decades. Within the blink of a tearful eye. It broke instantly into a heap of little and no longer significant pieces. Like an old vase. And it was gone, gone for good.

And then I became that little, feeble, and confused old man once again.

◆ ◆ ◆

Before I had a chance to comprehend what actually happened, I had found myself out there. I was there. Right on the street. I was there, tremulous and panting heavily. I was there, swaying faithfully to the hypnotic rhythm of my insanely vicious vertigos. I was there, hugging, clinging desperately to the cool cheek of a brass barrier stanchion guarding the entrance of the hotel and holding its velvety hands with the others in line. And I stood there like a fearful seaman clutching tightly at a mast or some other element of the exterior design of a ship's deck during a storm striving hard to turn him into a feverishly fluttering yet fleshy flag.

And I stood there like that because staying inside this place, inside this otherwise fabulous place, even for a little longer, even for a little while, could have only deepened my sudden loss of balance. It could have only exacerbated it irrevocably. Like in the case of a statue of a former dictator being rocked and swayed by a no longer loving crowd. It could have led to my sloppy and downright burlesque attempts to retain that balance of mine. It could have led to my further faltering precariously in front of the habitually exacting guests, to my incurring their quietly disapproving gazes, their outwardly contemptuous gazes. And, as a tragic result, it could have stripped me completely of my hard-earned status and position. For which I had been toiling so long. So incredibly long. So indecently long. And all that could have happened, even though, for most of the time, I was capable of attaining relief and confidence only inside that place, only inside that hotel. Only when I took hold of the entrance doors, of the room doors, or, at least, of their shiny handles. Only when I caressed with the impatient soles of my feet the playfully prickly stubble of the hallway carpet. And only when I was near this very inextinguishable source of unbridled luxury. Like a little child quieting itself only at its mother's breast.

But now I feared that continuation of this futile search of mine could have drained me completely of the last drops of my precious energy. Like the home straight emptying the gas tank of a race car. It could have imperiled my already danger-ously fluctuating self-confidence, and evict me from my body. Like an overzealous landlord. It could have done that due to its being a terrible burden for my entire nervous system, straining every tiniest infirm wire and senile cable of it. For, after all, it had been focused, for so many years, on perform-ing and repeating one and the same action. Again and again. Ad infinitum. And thus it required now incomparably more energy to reawaken the long-unused parts and regions of it.

Then the garrulously rattling engine of a passing car cut short my incoherent ruminations. It cut them short as if to rebuke me sternly for clinging too insistently, and far too in-decently, to the slender barrier stanchion. As a drunk man hanging on the arm of his bitterly disappointed date.

And so I was there again. And so I was unable to see too well. I was unable to understand enough of all the things taking place around me at an insane pace. At a maddening pace. I was unable to do that, utterly blinded by that indelible bloody vision that fell on my eyes. And it fell there like an impregnable crimson curtain heralding the end of a theatrical performance. That vision of the inevitable carnage looming over this place. Over all those people. Over all those streets penciled lightly on a plan of this city. As a doodle on a news-paper's margin. And over me along with them. So I walked in a highly unsteady fashion. My hands seemed unused to the coarse texture of the walls and façades of ordinary buildings. My feet proved to be unaccustomed to the hard and rough sidewalks of the outside world. They felt disturbingly out of place far from the immensity of the polished hardwood floors. They felt pitifully adrift away from the impeccably calm wa-ters of the soft hotel carpets. And due to that, I limped like some newly born antelope or other. I teetered so tentatively that I could not help groping instinctively for any sort of firm support. Of reliable footing. Of expensive ground. Now and again I touched with my restless hands everything that found itself in my unstable vicinity. I was like a blind man who feels lost and at sea, at colorful sea, in the world bursting with delightful hues and astonishing vistas.

And so I walked in that way succumbing completely to the dictatorship of my long-unused homing instinct. I walked in the faint hope that it would manage to lead me back home. To get me out of there. To get me out of the intolerably turbulent hostile waters of the out-of-hotel reality. It was as if my now tremulous legs were twin boomerangs that, however thrown, however used or misused, would always find their way back to their owner and guardian. They would certainly find the way back to their friend and confidant. In this case, to my infinitely beloved dainty daughter.

Each step, each movement, was to me an enormous, if not downright inhuman, effort. It was as if I were wading in water. It was as if I were wading in immensely deep water, hampering and sabotaging vilely my every single move. And thus I felt as if I were a sole breakwater pole single-poledly facing an inconceivable squall.

And with every passed inch, with every traversed sidewalk tile, I sensed an increasing pressure on my, after all, quite brittle sagging chest. It nearly forced me, under an immediate threat of suffocation, to stop my breathing process. It nearly forced me to suspend it until further notice. For I felt like one of those intrepid people who try to breathe while walking against the extremely strong wind. And its roaring part was played in this case by the indomitable wind of history. From which there was no place to hide. From which I could not find any permanent and reliable shelter. Like a snake trying to escape the molting season.

Because even if I curled up right behind this or that seemingly solid, seemingly massive, and seemingly impervious façade of one of those brownstones that I was passing by abstractedly, it would be pierced by some vicious artillery shell or other. At any given moment. At any time. Because it would be destroyed by a shell apparently having it in for me, having it in for anyone, for every living human being. Or by some vagrant mortar round that would stray too far from the rest of its murderous herd. Because, even if I somehow managed to crawl agilely under this or that heavy balcony or a flight of stairs, it would be certainly smashed to pieces in no time. It would be smashed by one of the bombs that were going to shroud the sky. And they would shroud it like a flock of deadly birds. Or an even more singular fall of particularly lethal dark snow.

But even sooner I reached a dismal conclusion. An unsurprising conclusion. For I understood that staying there, right there where I was now, would guarantee me death on the spot. Right there. On that tiny patch of asphalt covered with an intricate net of little cracks akin to varicose veins. I surely would die, if I lingered there for too long. I would die there. Right in the middle of that picturesque yet already desolate street lined with the real architectural treasures and delicacies. I would die on this street bathed in the warm light. In the pleasant light. In the consoling light. In the light oozing at a leisurely pace from the glaringly modern streetlamps bowing respectfully to those historical marvels, to those miracles of past tastefulness, thus proving emphatically that contemporaneity can, after all, co-exist and form an exemplary symbiosis with history. For I could be easily reached there, right there, by any, even random and amateurish burst of machinegun fire shot accidentally by an incompetent, yet unjustly lucky, enemy soldier.

Unfortunately, even my feverish and scrupulous search for any kind of shelter in one of the nearby protective buildings could not ensure my survival of that imminent nightmare. For I still could die there. I could die beneath the rubble as easily as from a stray fragment of a windowpane, crisscrossed with duct tape like a box on a ballot paper, and smashed by an insolently roaring bullet. Against whose sharp attack I would be unable to defend myself adequately with my soft and saggy limbs.

I would not stand a chance. I would not be able to do it. Even inside those noble and proudly aging buildings and edifices that had already withstood the shattering mayhem of one war. That previous war. That still recent war. But which had withstood it due to some unprecedented stroke of luck. Many years ago. Yes still not too long ago for me. I would not stand a chance even inside the ones that had survived it more or less unscathed and unbruised. That last, distant, yet still painfully unforgettable, military turmoil. And this was because of the constant and unflaggingly relentless progress in the dubious art of killing people. For it was art, yet a peculiar kind of art, still not properly acknowledged and lavished with accolades. For this branch of art, as the only one, had a penchant for ignoring the verdicts of its staunchest critics and often implacable detractors. Completely and impenitently. And it continued to perpetrate its tasteless practices in spite of all the shrilling cries and laments of protest uttered in a tone of warranted outrage. And now nothing seemed to be certain enough. And now nothing appeared to be durable enough. And nothing was reliable enough. At least not sufficiently to trust it implicitly with my life. Or with my one-man, if not one-woman, one-girl, infinitely cute and lovable family.

And, suddenly, I looked at this pleasantly tranquil street. I looked at its spontaneously winding alleys. At its astonishing richness of details. At this entire dozing city. I looked at it in an utterly different, radically altered, and hitherto unknown to me, fashion. For, all of a sudden, it became so alien, so indifferent, and so distant to me. Both metaphorically and in the most literal manner. For even the sidewalk unfurling patiently under the now clumsy feet of mine seemed to me so oddly remote. So detached. So inaccessible. I felt as if I were gliding somewhere high up in the sky, wrapped in the downy shawl weaved out of the scenic route for scudding clouds. It was as if I were walking over a surprisingly thin glass floor beneath which was being held an exhibition of the unearthed ruins of a prehistoric settlement that thus coexisted with me at the present time. For, abruptly, all these buildings, all these dignified historical relics intertwining tolerantly with the fresh fruits of the distinctly newer architecture, gave the impression of being unusually frail. Delicate. Terribly brittle. If not just paper-thin. It was as if they were the houses of cards that could be not only seriously damaged, but also irreparably devastated, demolished, and reduced to the hardly exceptional dust, by a mere jolt, by a mere poke, let alone by my barging into one of them accidentally.

And after yet another instant I saw them as the horrifyingly lifeless piles of rubble. The piles soaring gloomily into the sky. I saw them as the things that would surely serve as a perfect building material for a mass grave of all these innocent and defenseless people. I mean all these people sleeping in them. All these people living in them. All these people loving someone in them. Hating someone else in them. Not to mention just vegetating in them unsuspectingly. And then my brand new and uncannily frightening ability became sharpened a little bit more. The eyesight of my carefully concealed mind's eye became at once capable of easily transcending the limits of time and space. Of the mostly impassable here and now. Like a deck of cards of a clairvoyante. And I not so much imagined as I simply saw these delightfully ornamented buildings in a completely different way. I saw differently these buildings in which had led their straightforward lives countless generations of now unimportant people. Of now overlooked people. Of now regrettably forgotten people. I saw these buildings eviscerated cruelly by artillery shells. I saw their walls torn down and shamelessly uncovering their intimate interiors. And along with them the most private and innermost secrets of their pitiful inhabitants. I saw them akin to the oversized dollhouses inviting everyone to turn into a brazen voyeur and take a peek inside. And I saw all these impromptu cross-sections. I saw these highly informative, amusing, yet essentially disgusting, vivisections being conducted not on one living organism, but on the lives of hundreds, and hundreds of hundreds of wretched individuals. And I saw their inhabitants. I saw them presently still living and crying and laughing blissfully. I saw them lying peacefully in the shallow graves contrived from the piles of maltreated bricks. I saw them lying in the graves concocted hastily from the debris of their own former lives. I saw them lying right under the openwork coverlets made of the bits of their own polished floors, of their own once favorite books, of their own toys, of their own beloved bric-a-brac, and of the shattered parts of their own furniture. And I saw the whole districts of this wonderful sprawling city being ruthlessly leveled by bombs and missiles. As if it were a part of an insanely radical redevelopment plan. And I saw these unique, breathtaking streets being promptly turned into makeshift cemetery alleys. With each pile of rubble, with each former building, now in heartrending ruins, having far more in common with the typical dismal tomb than a place where life had once reigned supreme.

And my mind distilled such troubling and disconcerting images, these painfully powerful visions, from the brew of my feverishly fermenting and deeply ingrained fears and memories of the horrible past. Of my horrible past. They came straight from the past still haunting me mercilessly. They came from the past in spite of all the years that had passed in the meantime. They were the half-faded but still half-heartbreaking images of my two tragically lost sisters. They showed those two cute siblings of mine who had been vilely taken away from me, who had been cruelly stolen from me. Like the life lie from a liar. They also showed my mysteriously missing parents. They showed my annihilated family roots. They showed all the tragic things that turned me into a refugee, into an uprooted immigrant in my own world. Without asking for my opinion. Without asking for my feelings. Or even for my consent.

And then it dawned on me that nothing, not a single object or tangible thing, was capable of protecting me. Of sheltering me. Of bravely rushing to my defense. Nothing was capable of protecting me in the nightmarish face of that invisible though decidedly undeniable threat. None of those imposing buildings. None of those walls. None of those superb monuments and statues triumphantly squaring their chests in the little local parks and plazas. None of those proudly glistening commemorative plaques. None of those things widely admired in the time of peace would be able to do that. For their long-past and expired splendor paled in comparison with the baleful palette of perils and menaces of our brutal times.

Then I quickly realized something. Then I realized it, in considerable panic, and to the off-key accompaniment of my frantically thudding heart. I realized that the only chance of survival, both mine and my daughter's, my gleeful daughter's, my caring daughter, was entrusting our lives to the most capricious high roller in this game. That is, luck itself. And, at once, I began recollecting, in utter terror, various situations from my own life. A whole multitude of them. I began recollecting them without paying attention to anything and anyone around me. Like a man on his deathbed no longer being troubled by the annoyingly creased bed sheet or his sweaty pajamas. They ranged from those most trivial and commonplace, like the usual morning tribulations caused by my accidental putting clothes on inside out, or by my shoelaces tearing and ripping at the least appropriate moment, to those more momentous ones like my slightly irritating tendency to forget whether I had already eaten my breakfast or not. I did all that scrupulously, and with utmost care. I did all that in order to gain absolute and irrefutable certainty, and to ensure beyond any doubt, that I was a kind of man blessed with good luck. With the best possible luck. And with all the kinds of luck, really. For I yearned to be

95

the one who had its undivided attention. For I wanted to be the one who had won its support. I wanted to be the one who could count on its favorable judgment. At any given moment. Without any exceptions. Regardless of its good mood or the lack thereof. Regardless of the flagrant presence or even more blatant absence of any extenuating circumstances. And I also wanted to find out, and I wanted that desperately, whether I was being plagued, and gnawed away at, unjustly, unfairly, by back luck. Its perverted negative. And its evil twin.

For although I could, till then, not care too much about my peculiar and not too risky weakness, about my penchant for tempting fate, now it became a matter of my survival. Now it became a matter of life and death. Suddenly, I started fearing my fondness for walking under all types and kinds of ladders. Instantly, I began worrying about my rather singular yet hopefully harmless liking for smashing and breaking and crushing all the mirrors, cups, glasses, or anything that possessed even a tiny and innocent morsel of glass in its structure. As if I were waging some savage war or other against all that could possibly capture my reflection and send it back to me. At once, I became upset due to the whole clamorous clovers of black cats that kept playfully crossing and recrossing my path to and fro whenever I stepped out of my apartment as if there were some furry conspiracy under way. For I could hitherto afford to ridicule and look pityingly, with the blatant smug smile of condescension stretching across my face, at all those counting too much, much too feverishly, and too illogically, on the favor and support of luck. I once could look that way at all those surrendering too eagerly to its capricious dictates. To its fickle and erratic whims. But now, right now, at this historically difficult moment, at this morally challenging moment, it seemed to be my last resort. It was like the last and already unmercifully crowded lifeboat that was capable of saving me from drowning. If not in the omnivorous depths of oblivion, then at least in those no less voracious ones of insanity.

Then I contemplated and sketched diligently in my be-mused mind a plethora of various possible scenarios of the future events. I sketched them frantically with the uncanny inventiveness of a seasoned raconteur. For I was like a thoughtful screenwriter preparing himself for a little chat, for the infamous pitch, with a particularly finicky film producer. But as I did that I failed to realize in time that I had veered off my previously set course too far. Too sharply. Too drastically. For I commenced to roam and wander abstractedly, farther and farther from the tirelessly pulsating main arteries of the city. With life circulating within them lively. And being suffused with the warm and inviting light. For I waded deeper and deeper into an insoluble maze of back alleys and byways shrouded in the undiluted darkness. Like the gauzy strings of a cobweb lurking in the darkest corner of the room. And this odd habit I had contracted in the, almost prehistoric now, times of my youth. But I had been failing to indulge it ever since.

And, after a little while, a few hasty and precarious steps later, I teetered to the rather singular conclusion. I came to the conclusion that the mysterious homing device installed furtively in my legs, that singular kind of contraband, did not fall prey to some ignoble breakdown, allowing for such a glaring departure from the once established path. It did not fall prey to that. But it was governed, even during this evident breach of its competencies, or rather, during this fit of its intimidating incompetence, by some secret plan. By some inscrutable plan. By some enigmatic plan. It was being governed by some imperious idea. It was being governed by the persistent promptings of some inherent yet twisted logic. And by, at least, a handful of more or less ulterior motives. For pensive, for lugubrious, for aghast, I started finding myself, by a series of strange coincidences, in a series of odd places. Just like an itinerant sleepwalker. Those were the places that I had neither seen nor visited since the distant and dark times of my youth. Those were the places of which I had nearly forgotten completely. And now I started visiting them, just like a hero of some mawkish and insufferably moralizing fairy tale. And those places were now in mortal danger. And those places I could lose now irrevocably. I could lose them, with the aching heart, even though, till then, I had not needed them for an instant. Even though I had not needed them at all.

Thus I walked through this exquisite city. Thus I walked through the shaded part of it. As if unsoiled and untouched in its dark existence by an even single stray ray of light. And I felt as though I were an astronaut who had recklessly wandered off to the dark side of the moon. I felt like a phantom of the previous epoch, that has stayed there, that has been immured in there, unable to pass away from there for some morbid reason. I felt as an ex-convict who fails to find a place he could fit in, who feels uncomfortably out of place everywhere, in every single place, even where he used to spend incomparably more time than at his recent barred home. Apparently, too much time had passed. Apparently, far too many changes had taken place in that inhospitable outside world. The very one that I kept shunning consistently. That I continued to ignore so stubbornly. That I mocked so persistently. Evidently, too much had changed in the world upon which I sneered so haughtily. I did that even though, in truth, my profound and invincible resentment toward it, as well as my earnest distaste for the laws governing it, were provoked by my mounting inability to comprehend it to a satisfactory degree. To an acceptable degree. To any degree, really. They were provoked by my crippling inability to communicate with it sufficiently. And that already immense gap only widened and grew and deepened unstoppably. It grew with every single day. With every passing second. It grew while, inwardly, I wanted to establish and maintain any form of contact, any kind of bond with it. For, after all, it was the very world from which I had come. For, after all, it was the same world from which I had originated. And the more I realized that fact, that embarrassing fact, the more I comprehended that only this thin uniform, this thin piece of fabric, along with my inseparable cap, distinguished me from it, from all the people inhabiting it, the more I hated it, the more I loathed this world unreservedly. Even viscerally. And so I was like a confused struggling artist who harbors rather ambiguous feelings toward his aged master and mentor, for, in him, jealousy freely intertwines with compassion, a desire to compete blends with heartfelt concern for his art, and a hysterical urge to surpass his teacher orbits startlingly close to respect and longing for his attention. But I refused to acknowledge it. But I refused to accept it properly. As if I were truth intolerant. And I did that even though I knew that I was fighting a losing battle.

Then I drifted deeper into my thoughts. I drifted there unknowingly while regarding in a slow and dreamy fashion the empty and impenetrable eye sockets of the surreally dark windows. They were oddly akin, at this very instant, to the horrifying holes gnawed in the buildings of a city under bombardment by the uproarious artillery. And I wondered intensely how short the memory of societies really was. And I wondered how terrifyingly little time was needed to make people forget about all the dangers and menaces and risks lurking around every corner of the human soul. Lying in wait for them. Waiting for their smallest mistake or misstep. And I wondered how little time was needed to make them, independently and of their own accord, start seeking and gravitating mindlessly toward their own, after all unforced, self-destruction. Once more. Once again. And I wondered how little was necessary to make it happen. To make it happen again despite the fact that they had not yet recovered fully from their last crushing defeat. To make it happen again despite the fact that they had not yet finished licking their wounds, profound, purulent, and smarting, from their last mistake of that violent kind. And due to that, they reminded me of a phoenix that had not yet managed to shake off all the dust from its wings before its feathers caught fire at the other end of its body. And then it struck me, without attempting to soften the blow, that, apparently, human memory, that is, of the whole nations or societies, was alarmingly short-lived. If not perishable. It was as short-lived as the footprints left in the sand by a life-guard rushing to save a drowning child that are being, later on, trampled and obliterated insensitively by the feet of the incoming inflows of vacationers. But I was still there. Right there. I still lived and breathed undauntedly. I, that incurably humble and dutiful I. The shrewd witness of both macabre and grotesque still smoldering horrors of the past. Still haunting and burdening the mentality of this fine nation. I, the one who still perfectly remembered all those traumatic events and atrocities that had been in equal measure suffered and perpetrated by the previous generations. Now absent. Now silent. Now conveniently gone. And yet, all signs showed, and they were not merely the timid symptoms of some incipient issue, that the world once again, that the world inevitably, and what was worse, voluntarily, altered its peaceful course. It did that noticeably. For it seemed that it began a spectacular turn in the same, old, proven, and catastrophic direction. It was like a man suffering from a short-term memory loss who, instead of calling the fire department, keeps stubbornly returning to his burning house and constantly forgetting why he has fled from it in panic in the first place. And that man, that devious and hellish academic teacher, was a living proof of it, of that fateful change. Of that hateful change.

And then I contemplated all these sleeping houses. And I contemplated all of them, drenched in the pleasantly dreamy languor. And I observed their walls that seemed to be heaving slightly, rhythmically. For I saw them moving in accordance with the breathing pace of their unwary and trustfully slumbering inhabitants. It was as if these houses, these sleeping houses, were enormous living organisms due to that human contribution to their existence. Yet I failed spectacularly to fathom, yet I failed to comprehend fully, despite my numerous desperate attempts and efforts, how it was at all possible that these innocently sleeping people were so naive. Yet I wondered how it was possible that they were so excessively gullible. So infinitely foolish. And so intractably irresponsible. For how could they start believing, once again, for the second time, in the same kind of dangerous gibberish? I wondered how it was possible that they started believing in the same puerile, asinine, though no less incendiary, slogans that had, after all, already led to an unthinkable tragedy at least once in the past. For, how could someone be so irresponsible? So immature? And so thoughtless? So completely thoughtless? How could someone be so carefree as to repeat the full panoply of mistakes of his fathers and grandfathers, as well as other unrelated predecessors, while making up a few new ones along the way, with such indescribable lightness and mindlessness? Like a man burdened with some embarrassing genetic flaw. How could anyone be so willing to do that? To copy the behavior of those who had been, at the time, excusably and understandably prone to make them, due to their being deprived of the invaluable benefit of hindsight? That rearview mirror of history. So I failed and kept failing to grasp something. I failed to grasp some part, some vital yet obstinately elusive part of all that. I was unable to understand, how it was possible that all these people could not wait to give up. How it was even remotely possible that they now capitulated morally. And I mean all these otherwise mostly peaceful people. And I mean all these understanding people. All these people usually caring for each other when it was expected of them. All these people habitually helping each other when it was needed. How it was possible that they surrendered ethically. Even before the first bell of the fight. Even before the first whistle of a referee. How it was possible that they listened to all those terribly momentary revolutionaries and instigators. All cursed with the exceptionally short expiration dates. All akin to that accursed lecturer. All akin to my archenemy and nemesis. How it was possible that they allowed those vile ones to fool them and swiftly deprive them of their innate and inalienable common sense. And I failed to fathom that in spite of the countless years of my often exalted, often treated with deference, endless life that amounted to my tremendous experience. I failed to do that in spite of the wide and rich assortment, the full range, of the things that I had seen and felt and adored and loved and feared during that almost interminable time.

It frightened me. It frightened me, forcing me to endure a long agony of undeserved spasms of terror. It frightened me how they proved to be capable of rejecting all that. I trembled at their eagerness to repudiate all that. I trembled at their readiness to forfeit that marvelous heritage of the last decades of undisturbed peace. That is, of peace maintained at all costs and with all one's might. In one collective effort. To forfeit it only because of a few fleeting difficulties or caprices. Only because of a few passing inconveniences. Like a rookie driver giving up the steering wheel after the first little forgettable fender-bender.

And I could already hear the staccato barking of machine guns. And I could already hear it as it quickly and deftly replaced in the recording studio of my mind the far less ominous soundtrack of the barking dogs in the dark of the night. In the impenetrable depths of this or that back alley. Then I thought that I was reached by the intimidating rumble of rolling tanks. I heard them devouring with their insatiable caterpillar tracks the smooth surface of a peaceful asphalt road. I heard them mauling an equally peaceful line of cars lounging lazily at the curb. Along with the peaceful trash cans. The calm benches. The docile food stands. And other elements of street design of the time of peace. But, in truth, it was only the rhythmical patter of a shivering loose downspout being yanked indelicately by the first and still timid gusts of the wind of history.

And I saw the large black clouds listlessly silhouetting against the sky, against the also black, the also impenetrable, yet a bit lighter, yet a dash brighter, sky. Like the fresh and ripe and intensely hued bruises germinating and uncurling their painful petals over the distinctly fainter older ones. And I saw in them the also fresh and vividly saturated portents of the fresh horrors sprouting right over the barely faded ones of the past. And then I saw them catching fire, one after another, one cloud from another, as the leaves playing a burning relay race during a murderous wildfire. And I saw them burning and curling up under the intimidating touch of the ever-voracious tongues of flames. Like children maltreated by an abusive father. And I saw them turning into ashes, without stop, without end. Like the manuscripts of rambunctious dissident writers.

And it was then that, under the constant and relentless, though no less scalding, fire of similar memories, now drastic, now lachrymose, resurrected by even the most trivial and innocent aspects of the present reality, there started resounding in my head a question. It was a particularly agonizing question. It was a question roaring like the growling of an artillery. For I asked myself broodingly whether it was really necessary for each generation to experience at first hand, and feel through its own collective skin, all the imaginable kinds of plagues, all the disasters, and tragedies of this world. For I asked myself whether each successive generation really had to suffer excruciatingly due to the same, and yet infinite, and yet immeasurable, relapses of pain. Of misfortune. Of despair. And of misery. For I asked myself whether all that was really indispensable. All those tragedies forming the notorious natural blood cycle. With unperturbed blood flowing freely from epoch to epoch. From civilization to civilization. Without a moment's thought. Without an even momentary respite. For I asked myself whether each new generation was obliged by some arcane ancient law or custom to lose its brilliant bards, its scintillating authors, its accomplished composers, its revolutionary painters, its simply ingenious minds, as well as its share of other consummate geniuses, and to risk losing its lawful heritage of the turbulent past, in some bloody turmoil or other. For I asked myself whether all that had to happen before anyone decided, resolutely and courageously, to take decisive actions against such threats. Such unthinkable perils. For I asked myself whether all that had to happen before anyone resolved to nip them in the still defenseless bud. If not a bevy of such buds for that matter. For I asked myself what was needed to deal with them when they were still only the desultorily smoldering embers of mistrust and animosity and not yet a rampantly raging fire of unbridled hatred consuming the entire horizon. And before anyone began listening to the previous and painfully experienced generations. And taking their word for it. But, unfortunately, even if it did happen, even if someone finally resolved to draw reluctantly from the boundless archive of wisdom of his predecessors, from the rich tradition of his ancestors, then, at once, as if on some unspoken command, there would briskly take place the quick rotation of generations. And then everything would start anew, afresh. And it would be exactly as if each next generation were a little endearing toddler who did not believe that fire was hot, as its parents toiled to teach it, till a persuasive burning match convinced it otherwise.

And I asked myself, was I strong enough and determined enough to do that? To prevent that? To accomplish my aim? My murderous aim? Was I confident enough to overcome the inherently venomous mental propaganda of fear, fuelling my doubts with a slew of high-octane misgivings? Would I be capable of mustering sufficient reserves of courage and inflexibility and staunchness and tenacity to carry out that task as planned? The one dominating and resounding compulsively in my thoughts? That unenviable task. That dreadful task. That horrid task? Would I manage to persevere in pursuit of that goal? Would I persevere in pursuit of that inevitably as well as

remorselessly murderous goal? And would I manage to save
the world in time? At the last minute even? But while trying
not to let that heroic act devolve into a cheap movie cliché?
Would I manage to save all those people? All those who, evidently, did not know what they were doing. Unlike me. Completely unlike me.

And then, during the moment of a tentative mental cease-
fire brokered by my reason and experience, I clumsily asked
myself a cluster of questions. I asked them without attempting
to deflect any of them subconsciously. I asked myself whether
I was capable of striking enough energy from my, after all,
rather weary, pitiful, and almost fossilized muscles. Whether
I was capable of doing it despite my age obliging even random trees to bow to me respectfully. I also inquired whether
my paper-thin and papyrus-colored skin, my enfeebled brittle
bones no thicker than a tangle of sticks supporting a fanciful
appetizer, let alone my long-overdue mentality dating back to
the previous age, if not to the former and long-replaced cen-
tury, would withstand the unthinkable pressure. And I wondered whether they would withstand the relentless poking and
pushing and elbowing. That is, all kinds of unpleasantness
that every construction has to face. Now and then. During its
working hours. And I wondered whether they would stand by
me obediently, dutifully, or rather, whether they would prefer
to shy away from their natural obligations toward me. And I
wondered whether they would prefer to boycott and sabotage treacherously all my endeavors, and to throw in the towel
sweaty with fear. And so, I wondered whether they would be-
have like a bevy of officers and simple soldiers who, seeing
the crushing enormity of the advancing enemy army, decide
to switch teams in the middle of a battle. As though it were
a friendly football match played in the backyard as a respite
from some more serious activities.

So I interrogated myself suspiciously. So I asked myself
whether there was, in the confines of my old and exhausted

body, yet another morsel, yet another little crumb, a misplaced modicum perhaps, of heroism. Of fearlessness. Or of real grit. And I looked for it being hidden and stored somewhere. Presumably, it could be hidden behind this or that wrinkle, this or that fold of my already stale flesh, serving me, from time to time, as additional and remarkably handy pockets. If not capacious pigeonholes. Of which kind of amenities all those impeccably smooth and supple and perky youths could only dream naively.

And I felt that primitive and vulgar urge thudding and pulsating in my temples at this febrile time in history. It was an urge. A primitive urge. It was an urge to fight. To struggle. To knock out my own inadequacies. To wrestle with my own weaknesses. And with those of the entire erratic nation. Yet without any bells, without any rings, and bellowing referees. And yet, in spite of all that, my mind needed and frantically looked for a sign. It looked for any sign that could, without delays, without further ado, confirm and strengthen my still fresh and fledgling beliefs and resolutions. It needed and desperately craved for any kind of symbol. It looked for anything to cling to. To trust it implicitly. To listen to its ambiguous promptings. To follow it blindly and sheepishly. To worship it piously. And I did that as if I were a hero of some incurably platitudinous fable or other.

Then my eyes leaped agilely from one lifeless object to another. They leaped from façade to façade. From lamppost to lamppost. From flight of stairs to flight of stairs. They leaped there and kept leaping as if expertly defying the laws of physics and performing a sterling acrobatic work. They did that while stubbornly scratching the reality of that dingy back alley like a cat clawing and pawing despairingly the uniform and impassive wall in a futile search of any tiny cleft, any petite crack, anything for that matter that might offer it magnanimously even a brief footing, and support it, and prevent its whole furry being from falling down from the roof.

And then, at once, I noticed right in front of me a kind of sign that I needed and that I yearned for so hysterically. I noticed it there as if in abrupt answer to those beseeching glances and unspoken pleadings of mine. Of my bewildered elderly mind. Of my trembling elderly heart. It was an almost copybook sign. It was effortlessly meeting all the possible requirements and enigmatic norms for such mysterious phenomena. And each one of them separately. And my eyes quite expertly fished it out of the often demonized morass of dull urban reality. Like a crane hunting for a smashed carcass of a car in a junkyard. It was an arrow chalked crudely on a sidewalk slab. It was there, right in front of me, lying prostrate at my feet. It was there while insolently desecrating this splendid concrete landscape. It was, undoubtedly, a cute remnant of the recent childish play, being the last vestige of the still fresh chalk-chase game, with the last faint bits of the delightful melody of giggling and chirping being inlaid in its rough and sloppily sketched surface. Like the atoms of elegance embedded into a tantalizing golden ring.

And it appeared to be drowning helplessly, its valid though utterly marginalized presence, in the formidable immensity of chaos and dangers suffusing the adult world. For that world kept towering over it patronizingly. If not imperiously. For that world kept towering over it while suppressing it and immersing it in the cacophony and rapid inflows flooding everyday adult life. Of triviality. Of sheer brutality. And that single petite arrow showed me the way to its nearby chalk cousin. And then it led me to another one. And yet another one. Thus they formed a curiously impromptu family reunion of similar drawings as well as an ideally logical straight line, invisible to both trained and untrained eyes. Like a travel destination of various bacteria to a person devoid of the aid of a microscope. They formed it as it floated demurely right beneath the surface of our mature reality. And now that odd intangible line climbed the tall and scrawny streetlamps. Now it walked the tightrope of high voltage cables. Now it ambled and

107

crawled furtively under the coverlet of untended lawns and the dying jellyfish of sprawled newspapers. And then it moved even lower, even deeper. Then it moved right under the asphalt litter of the urban jungle. As the immaterial tectonic plates. It moved there while employing to this purpose various objects and things and buildings that it encountered on its rather jumpy way. And thus, unexpectedly, meaningfully, it guided me back home.

But its distinctly childish character, its unmistakably infantile innocence, and playfulness, embedded in its imperfect, if not a bit clumsily drawn shape, invited to my mind a flurry of images of my daughter. That fine daughter. That cheerful little daughter of mine. For she was awaiting me impatiently and lovingly at the other end of that clearly perishable chalk line. And it was an alarmingly elusive guide. It was an oddly tenuous trail. It reminded me of those white outlines fringing dead bodies lounging on a sidewalk in the middle of every crime scene. As if to ensure their still not quite dead right to possess and carefully cultivate their own personal space.

And now I knew what I had to do.

Then I left a maze of dark and dim back alleys burdened with the omnipresence of filth and dirt that accumulated there furtively, that accumulated there readily, away from the revealing presence of light permeating the main arteries of this wonderful city. Like the small clumps of dust lurking under one's furniture and preparing themselves for a fluffy assault. And as I left it I found myself inside my little, cozy, and consolingly safe apartment. I found myself there to be welcomed by a warm and succinct sigh of the entrance door. And thus it tacitly approved of my recent decisions and resolutions. And thus it approved of them willingly. But perhaps it did that only out of professional solidarity between doors and doormen. And as I walked deeper into the apartment, the cracked sidewalk slabs and loose window frames of the streets gradually gave way to the invitingly soft carpet and gregarious bric-a-brac queuing on the dusty shelves. Like prisoners of war who are about to be executed by a firing squad.

But then, to my immediate surprise, not only the single door but every tiniest trinket, a neglected magazine abandoned in the middle of foreplay with an editorial page, or a long-estranged armchair yearning for a dash of human warmth, seemed to be openly sympathizing with me. They seemed to be eagerly siding with me. And they seemed to be supporting my noble cause unanimously. And I had no reason not to believe them. I had no reason not to believe that sudden burst of kindness for me, of compassion for me. Even though I watched them coldly. Even though I still watched them suspiciously. Like a poker player who intends to call his opponent's clumsy bluff. For they were not bound to me by any sort of courteous, professional obligations. For they were not like a guard dog feeling compelled to attack and bite more or less playfully every advancing mailman, its colleague and business partner. And all of them agreed with me unconditionally. All of them agreed that I had to act. And I mean act decisively.

So, I soon faced the general and still rising support and skyrocketing approval ratings for me and my perverse plan. At least, here in this congenial environment. At least here, in this informal poll conducted amid inanimate objects. For it was with that kind of objects that I got along the best. For it was with that kind of objects that I had established the firmest bonds of all. And thus I could no longer dwell on my unusually long absence of faith in humanity. Or worse yet, its full-blown truancy. For I had to get down to work. For I had to do it quickly. I had to do it ably. I had to do it discreetly enough and surreptitiously enough so as not to raise anyone's curiosity or suspicions. At least before I was fully ready.

Then, without any prior notice, without any mental warning shot, there started sprouting in my mind the whole bevies of ideas. They were as if preparing themselves for some puerile mental harvest. And I floundered. And I pondered laboriously. Thus I performed a stunning act of intellectual reconnaissance, wondering how I should go about it. I wondered how I should approach this delicate and fragile and, above all, sensitive matter. I wondered how to approach it so as not to scare it off prematurely and not to discourage and put me off at the same time. That was a question. A remarkably vital question. I wondered how I should initiate the search of that devilish academic. Of that ruler and janitor of hell in one. Of that demonic enemy and mortal foe even of all those who still remained blissfully unaware of his threatening existence.

For, after all, in order to finish all that, in order to complete my brutal task, I had to find him first. I had to find him above all else. I had to do that to execute the pre-emptive judgment issued during a hastily convened meeting of my crystalline conscience and no less pristine morality. I had to find him to do him some harm. Any harm for that matter. I had to find him to stop him. To cripple his plans. To anticipate his catastrophic moves and prevent that still not committed and still not properly envisioned tragedy from happening. Like a chaperone discerning the first timid symptoms of infatuation lighting up on the face of a teen being in her charge. But I also wondered whether I should really do that. Should I try stopping that potential nationwide eruption of violence with an act of violence? Should I try stopping that incoming madness with yet another act of madness? Can one prevent a crime with another crime? Is it really such a good idea? Is it really the right way to do that? Like a war to end all wars. Like a bomb, if not an A-bomb, to end the era of bombs. Did I have the right to do that? To try that? Did I?

Then the questions and doubts and ideas, ranging from poignantly silly to downright preposterous, busily surfaced and resurfaced on the page of my consciousness. They surfaced there one by one. Time after time. Now vanishing. Now re-appearing without any clear reason. They acted like a gaggle of children splashing impishly and ducking each other in the water. They surfaced there tirelessly, purposefully, while maintaining an almost mechanical-like precision of interval timing. With all of them obediently following their stage directions. With all of them maniacally obeying their cues. Like seasoned actors. Meantime, they frequently collided with my far more trivial and far less fateful actions. Because of which I found myself unable to undress properly. For whenever I reached for this button or that shoelace, some new and ingenious idea debuted on the stage of my mind. Thus it distracted me. Thus it rudely interrupted my previous motion. And, consequently, it inveigled me cunningly into doing something else instead, only to, quite soon afterward, force it to meet the very same pitifully abortive fate.

And it was due to that incessant yet discreetly inward wriggling of mine, due to that repeatable changes of my course, disturbingly constant in its changeability, that I might have looked to a casual onlooker, spying on me in some perverse for clearly geriatric peepshow, like a curious yet sadly incurable mental case. Or, at least, like an impassioned monologist practicing talking to himself before the opening night of his new show. For I chaotically roamed around my barren apartment. For I anxiously paced all the rooms to and fro. For I paced them without any believable purpose. Without any clear plan. Without any real necessity for doing so. I did that while defying any kind of logic or even improvised patterns of behavior. It was exactly as if I intended to break in and wear out a just bought carpet to introduce it, later on, to my friends as a valuable antique with a rich and soft history. For, whenever I started doing something, whenever I decided to focus my oddly shifty attention on some action, any action, really, it was being drastically disturbed. It was being cut short by an inexplicable urge welling up in me. And then, in spite of my making serious efforts to quell it, that urge forced me, as if reciprocating hostilities out of sheer spite, to jot something down, enigmatically and illegibly, also a dash nonchalantly, also a bit carelessly, on the edge of a napkin. On the armrest of a chair. On top of a table. And even on the kitchen windowpane. If only I did not have any more conventional writing materials at my suddenly tremulous, for extremely excited, hand.

I painstakingly contemplated the way in which I was going to harness to that, after all, tremendously exacting endeavor, the reserves of my own authority and respect. I wanted to use them as well as my own honorable position amid the younger members of personnel, in the hierarchy of my beloved hotel. Because, as common sense suggested me, it was there that I ought to start the hunt immediately. It was there that I ought to begin without any delays. At the source. Right at the very root of it. For it was a well-known fact that all roads lead to hotels. And especially to such an expensive and renowned one. To the finest one in the entire city. To the greatest hotel in the whole glorious country. Similarly, every step of a criminal, regardless of the direction in which it is being oriented, sooner or later, instinctively, guides him straight back to the stage of his crime, to the horrid crime scene.

And then I started planning something. And then I started planning a delicate process of mobilizing and utilizing a whole host of makeshift spies and agents recruited from the otherwise undisciplined herds of maids and cleaners and bellhops. I started planning it in minute detail. And then I started composing my own little and infinitely inspiring motivational speech intended for them. I started composing it while editing and revising it relentlessly. And it contained a full range of recommendations and instructions on all the things that, from then on, they should do and remember to do absolutely. For I would lecture them on all the things to which they should pay attention. For I would lecture them on the ways in which they should observe our splendid guests. Always discreetly. Always intently. Always professionally. For I would suggest them the ways in which they should look for any clues or trails or hints during the daily room cleaning. For I would lecture them on the things to look for while carrying baggage to the rooms. Of which, every single bag and even tiny suitcase should be carefully and studiously weighed and felt and groped. As if in search of some cancerous lump or other. But again, and above all, discreetly. And nothing should possibly escape their vigilant notice. And nothing should be simply ignored. Not even a sole potential bit of evidence should be ignobly neglected or overlooked.

For even a seemingly harmless lazily smoldering cigarette butt, even a haphazardly discarded towel cuddling up in the corner of a bathroom, like a victim of some ghastly crime or other, could offer me invaluable guidance. It could offer me priceless clues regarding the whereabouts of that man. Of that sinister man. And I imagined how I would be recruiting them, training them, and rebuking them. Yet always in the most tactful manner. Yet always in the most edifying manner. And I could barely withhold my excitement manifesting itself boldly in the form of a vehement shiver that set all my wrinkles and fleshy folds in motion. Like a gust of wind that turns the book's pages as if it were riffling through it incuriously. For I intended to scour diligently as well as extensively, thus availing myself of my inexhaustible patience, all the corridors and hallways and nooks and crannies on every single floor of that enormous hotel. For I intended to scour those miniature streets and squares and alleys of that hermetic multilayered metropolis. And I wanted to do that in the hope that I would finally find something relevant. I wanted to do that in the hope that I would, at last, miraculously, stumble upon something of any importance to the case. On any proof. On any bit of information. On any vital clue. For, meantime, sooner or later, someone would betray the location of his hiding place. For someone would blow the brass hotel whistle. For everyone has a breaking point. For everyone has a crumbling point. Or any other destructive point. No one was capable of hiding him forever. Even if he was curled up grotesquely behind an unsophisticated for hardly ever opened door of a janitor's closet. Or right behind an unnaturally ruffled curtain in the dining room on the second floor. No one.

So I started putting into effect this plan, this quite ambitious plan, while bringing it into this world. As a remarkably skillful mental midwife. And, meantime, I intended to derive inspiration from a wide and fertile catalog of well-proven yet imaginary methods, ideas, and most effective tactics. For I wanted to make use, on an ongoing basis, of the dubiously moral practices of fictional policemen and private detectives from countless tasteless films and even worse novels. I wanted to derive inspiration from such fictional characters fearlessly interrogating various thugs, criminals, as well as other members of the infamous dregs of society. Lingering at the bottom of every city. Unstirred by any spoon or police baton. I mean those fictional characters doing that, all that, only to find the single helpful snitch. The overzealous squealer. The obliging rat. I was ready to resort to an impressively vast array of more or less immoral, more or less dishonest, or even downright illicit, tricks and emotional gambits. I was ready to follow in the illegal footsteps of the suavest manipulators. I was ready to do it. I was ready to risk it. While not being afraid of anything. While not sparing anything or anyone. I was ready to be as a nose-diving crop duster indiscriminately sprinkling a field with a light though still disturbingly chemical drizzle regardless of whether something inhabits it or not. I was prepared to do that. To recourse to that. Only to extract and get the coveted information. I was prepared to do that while not shying away, if necessary, from numerous dirty plays, from incalculable dubious ruses, unclean shenanigans, and other evidently soiled techniques. Both those dreadfully threadbare and a few innovative ones. I could do that while willingly falling back on the utterly banal moves. As the always-thrilling intimidation and perversely exciting extortion. I could even resort to such things in the hope that, invariably, and without exceptions, the end, that noble cause, that splendid cause, would absolve me symbolically, and justify my otherwise indefensible means.

I also resolved to avail myself of the opportunity created by my fine position. By my highly privileged position. For simply, though always discreetly, I intended to listen in on the guests walking past me. For I intended to watch them inquiringly from under the visor of my professional cap. For I intended to deduce from the choreography of their moves whether they were hiding something. For I intended to deduce whether there were any sudden and inexplicable grammatical errors and embarrassing typos in their body language, betraying their distress. As if I were a stern teacher during an exam. And I intended to deduce whether, by accident, this or that frustrated limb of theirs was not quivering in that discernibly telltale fashion, urging its owner to make a brief confession, an even brisk confession, for being unable to support that insufferable weight of sheer guilt any longer. Like a fake pregnant belly of an inept shoplifter, her unreliable accomplice, which lets all her loot fall down on the floor before she manages to get out of a cashier's earshot.

In the end, if everything else failed and failed spectacularly, if all the astonishingly elaborate stratagems turned out to be failures, and nothing else but first-rate failures, I intended to take advantage of my, after all, rather significant influences and connections in wealthy circles. In diplomatic circles. In elitist circles. I would do that as their well-known regular. I would do that although I served there not so much as a full member as a breathing grease and their technician in one. For I was responsible for ensuring their spinning effortlessly and luxuriously and ad infinitum.

And thus, I strode nervously, impetuously, to and fro along and across the dim rooms and corridors of my pleasantly tiny apartment. I did that while undressing chaotically. I did that while gesticulating hectoringly. I did that while recklessly abandoning all my clothes in various often improvised and no less frequently inappropriate places. And I did that while storming into a room only to leave it abstractedly a mere instant later. It was as if I were a life-sized ball gamboling feverishly inside a lottery machine. For I repeatedly ricocheted off the furniture. For I bounced off the walls. For I did all that while imagining what I would do to him if I found him. I imagined how I would execute the verdict, I, the experienced doorman and an apprentice executioner in one. Still on a trial period. Still an improvising one. I imagined what I would do to him if he miraculously fell into my hands. Into those usually peaceful and caring hands of mine. For they now kept tightening relentlessly and with disturbing fury on some invisible oval shape, on an invisible neck, in this overture to the final act of that silly tragedy.

For a brisk moment, a disconcerting thought flitted right through my mind. It was like a moth that by passing in front of a flame casts an enormous shadow on a nearby wall. It flitted right through there. And both its improvised advent and unscheduled sojourn there lasted for a relatively short time. It was a thought that prompted me, as I listened to its ridiculously surreal theories rather grudgingly, that there existed some odd, some curious, however intractable, connection between that devilish academic, my nemesis and my foe, and that rather irritating messenger. I mean that man, that mysterious man, that terrifying man, who had turned my entire day into this unending pursuit in the first place. And I mused on that. I mused on that, striving to channel my whole available life force energy into that single action, thus seriously endangering all the biological functions of my already dwindling organism. I wondered whether it was at all possible, feasible, and imaginable. I wondered whether I had been, in truth, chasing since this very morning one and the same person. One and the same social pest. Nightmarishly incarnated in that duo. For being miraculously present in two persons. I wondered whether one, no matter how infuriating, no matter how unnerving, individual was capable of shaking and rocking my hitherto fixed and perfectly stable world to is noble foundations. And I wondered whether one person was capable of turning it callously not only upside down, but also in any other direction. Just as if it were an overgrown snow globe.

But this somewhat tempting thought was cruelly interrupted by a vehement realization. It was a realization that something was not right. That something was missing. Or rather, that something was oddly misplaced. For while trying to put my fatigued shoes by the door I could not help noticing that their habitual place was now mysteriously occupied. Their natural habitat was now soiled. Like in the case of an oil spill drifting toward a variegated reef. It had been rudely appropriated by someone else's footwear. It was also bearing all the irrefutable hallmarks of men's shoes, yet being far more sophisticated than mine. Far more elegant than mine.

And I stood there, utterly puzzled and petrified. And I stood there, suspended in the middle of a particularly deep bow. I stood there with these pitiful shoes of mine dangling hesitantly in my enfeebled hands. Like twin pendulums. And then I heard a sudden nervous rattle of the silverware coming from behind the closed door of the dining room. It was coming from the only room in the whole mournfully dark apartment that I had not yet had a chance to inspect that day. It was as though I had startled someone there with my unexpected presence. And he, or she, now shivered and panicked. Like a scared animal trembling in the bushes.

For a little frightening while I went so far as to keep asking myself whether that was it. I asked myself whether it had already started. I asked myself whether that revolution of the vulgar and barbarous masses had indeed become a fact. Like the bastardization of the fine work of art. That epitome of

117

tactlessness. That apotheosis of insensitivity. A grim and irrevocable fact. And it was then that a cold breeze of fear extinguished the flame of determination in me. For I covered my run-down face with the similarly worn-out shoes whose left sole was almost completely worn through. That rather pitiful kind of shield.

And then the till then mysteriously closed door opened with a powerful and imperious swing. It opened as a duvet that is being flung off by one who is late for work. And it opened as my gentle and frail daughter appeared in the doorframe. As if exactly on her cue. As if following some secret script. And she generously treated me to one of her adorably charming smiles. And then she spoke in that infinitely loving and caring manner, "Dad, I want you to meet someone. We've got a guest for dinner. I've met him during one of those nonsensical lectures that my friend, you know her, always takes me to, always drags me to. He's an important person. He's an influential person. He's a really important person. Don't embarrass me today." And then, while walking away, she stopped in the middle of yet another delicate step of hers. And she threw offhandedly a few delightfully melodious words over her shoulder. As if they were a drizzle of little rice grains being thrown for luck, "I almost forgot. It was his lecture. He's an academic teacher."

BOOK TWO

— ◆ ◆ —

AS THE DOOR TURNS
ON ITS HINGES...

◆◆◆

For the next several minutes I felt like an actor rehashing grimaces and gestures from his long-proven palette of old tricks and shticks to buy himself some time to recall the actual text of the play. I was so astonished. I was so ineffably bewildered. And thus, I had to prolong that rather awkward farce for a handful of scenes. And these scenes were, in that particular order: my entering the dining room, my regarding slowly and mistrustfully this young and lean and stubbornly virulent man rising from behind the table at my sight, our exchanging courtesies, our observing the formalities, and our taking seats at the opposing sides of the table. Like two avowed adversaries. Like two seasoned gamblers. And we certainly looked like them. For I noticed that it was a rather baleful kind of man. It was that odd kind of man who defied and ridiculed with his every gesture and motion the tired cliché about the ineptitude of faculty members. He did that quite conspicuously. He did that almost arrogantly. He did that, whereas I was an old man in every little, wrinkled respect.

All the time the tone of the meeting was being set by the rumble of moving furniture. It was being set by the discreet squeaking of shoes. It was being set by the gentle rustling of the tablecloth. And by the confidential tinkling of glasses and silverware. So it seemed that where the human element failed, and failed ignominiously, the initiative was being promptly seized by all the less lively inanimate objects. It was being seized by that still life. By these inhabitants of lifeless fauna. And now, at the moment, they evinced far more courtesy and good manners and warmth than all of us put together.

I noticed, after a moment of quick puzzlement, the cacophonic mishmash of little, almost imperceptible actions,

like the truculent tapping made by the knives and forks gang-
ing up on the plates. Or that playful stroking the stems of
wine glasses, which was akin to rubbing legs in dance. I noticed that ostensibly spontaneous rapping of idle fingers on
the table. I noticed them doing that right before migrating
a little to this side or that one to sketch vigorously on the
tablecloth. On that imperfect for hardly receptive canvas. I
noticed them sketching there the elaborate, though invisible,
pictures and perfunctory doodles illustrating some subject of
the current discussion or other. And it seemed to me that they
were inherent parts of an arcane dialect. It seemed to me that
they formed a barely noticeable language, existing, if not just
vegetating inconspicuously, right beneath the tepid surface of
a typical conversation. Like the whole civilization of insects
burgeoning right under one's carpet.

And I could not resist a certain doggedly nagging impression. It was an impression that this symphony of elegantly unassuming, yet still extremely relevant, clangs and clinks was a
sort of accompaniment to the incomparably less sophisticated
outpour of our loud words. A true flood of them. A veritable
avalanche of them. Especially of those uttered by this insufferable man. Mainly of those produced by this exasperating
man. For he lavished them shamelessly on my daughter. For
he showered them on her indecently. That poor as well as unsuspecting child of mine. And it was as if they were handfuls
of gifts and presents. Yet of a rather meretricious kind.

And she, that little gullible creature, that ruddy apple of
my eye, that frivolously flickering light of my life, kept looking
at him. She kept staring at him. She kept devouring him with
her eyes. To my inconsolable dismay. She kept doing that with
her enchantingly glistening eyes. She kept doing that with her
magnificent eyes whose delicate eyelids I used to kiss tenderly
while tucking her in many years ago. And she watched him.
And she observed him carefully. She did that as if in the silly
hope that she would be able to notice and pick up all that

somehow escaped the notice of her no less vigilant ears. I could not bear that. I could not fathom that. I could not accept that at all. And, what was worse, I failed to discover any reason, any cause, any believable explanation of that unendurably agonizing state of things. I failed to find the reason because of which this incorrigible parental calamity took place. Because of which she behaved in such an indescribably naive and irresponsible, but still infinitely delightful, manner. Where if not right in front of me. In front of her father and educator. In vain I rummaged cautiously in my mind as if it were a drawer of an antique cupboard whose sheer age warranted both respect and intimidating price. I did that in desperate as well as rather clumsy search of any crucial parental mistake. Any unforgivable parental crime. Or even a slight parental offense. For I looked for anything that I had once committed unknowingly, unmindful of future consequences. I did that in search of anything that I had perpetrated only to start regretting it later on. Right now. After it had grown and accumulated and fermented and then metastasized unthinkably. Like a heap of the long-overdue bills that haunts one in his impoverished dreams. And then, in the end, it had led to this profoundly devastating ordeal of mine. Where had I made a mistake? When had I overlooked the first and timid and still desultorily burgeoning symptoms of this impending fatherly cataclysm? When had I failed ignobly to act in time? And to nip it in the enchantingly petite yet still ominous bud? When had I strayed as a parent? And she as my only child? When had I become a life-sized variation on the perennial theme of prodigal fathers? When had I been demoted to the level of a laughable caricature of paternal authority? Had I missed some sign? Had I omitted some hint? Had I missed an exit ramp on the road of my conceit thus abandoning my only daughter on the roadside of it? Had I left her there, alone, forlorn, thus pushing her straight into the sticky arms of such boastful and intolerably young, and, above all, disgustingly young, virile men as he?

And thus, not hearing anything, not understanding a single thing, and in utter astonishment, I became, all of a sudden, sound intolerant. I became a deaf oddity. I became a sound-proof weirdo. As a daring diver who surfaces with his ears full of water after too many hours spent underwater. For it was as if I were suddenly and totally robbed of the ability to absorb information in the spoken form. In the whispered form. In the chanted form. Or in any other audible form. It was as if I were a clueless viewer of a silent film. And I only observed, with barely concealed revulsion, an obnoxious dance of their hands on the dance floor of a tablecloth. I observed that exceedingly, if not excessively, friendly match of their playful gazes. Alternately serving and dribbling deftly. I watched all that with truly unfeigned trepidation. Even, from time to time, bordering on sheer terror. And I watched that just like a renowned composer whose marvelous magnum opus is being ruthlessly yet unwittingly mutilated by a man humming it while mowing a lawn.

Then I noticed that I trembled and shivered inwardly. I trembled like a wild animal trapped in the headlight glare of an approaching car. I trembled along with all my internal organs that immediately abandoned, or at least temporarily suspended, their individual interests and animosities. They did that to express, in remarkable unison, their visceral outrage.

And I was hardly capable of restraining my usually obedient rumpled hands. And I was hardly capable of preventing them from vehemently taking the initiative. From, ironically, taking matters into their own, although never-revealed, hands. It was difficult to prevent them from carrying out that capital punishment. That shameful act which they had been practicing furtively and with the utmost care and diligence since this very morning. It seemed nearly impossible to stop them from doing it now. Right now. Here and now. Over the plate of soup cooked by my extremely versatile daughter. For it could have served perfectly as both his last meal and last supper. It seemed impossible to stop them from doing it here. In the presence of a witness. My beloved witness. It was as though my fingers had already stiffened implacably from the surplus of starch. And they had grown akin to iron in prison bars. For they were prepared to strangle him with my also steel, to prolong that metallic leitmotif, grip. Yet already slightly corroded by my age. The implacable age.

But then she glanced at me incredulously. Then she glanced at me. Like one's own reflection immured in a mirror that quickly reciprocates the disappointed glance at one's body contour ruined drastically by the absence of any diet. And she spoke to me in that customarily angelic voice of hers.

DAUGHTER: Did you say something? Dad? What? What did you say? Did you say anything?

DOORMAN: I didn't say a thing, I just thought...

DAUGHTER: What?

DOORMAN: I was sure... I was certain... well... that I just... that I only thought about that... inwardly... and didn't say it out loud... well... outwardly...

DAUGHTER: What? What are you mumbling there? He's always mumbling to himself and expects people to understand him... his... him...

LECTURER: His mumblings?

DAUGHTER: Yes! You're right. You're absolutely right. You always find the right word, like a real... what's the word for it?

LECTURER: Wordsmith?

DAUGHTER: As I said, you're always right.

I smiled to myself with satisfaction at the cunning way in which I masterfully evaded this inconvenient question. I smiled at the impressive maneuver by dint of which I escaped this perilous situation. This strategic ambush. I did that just as a seasoned tactician moving his troops and trenches and tanks, as if they were lifeless pawns, on the world map lying in wait on the table.

Then I was left alone after this stupefyingly brilliant subterfuge of mine, in which I cleverly convinced them of my

125

alleged inattentiveness. And I could, once again, immerse myself in the hermetic realm of my shrewd observations and no less astute contemplations. I did that like a distinguished diplomat poring over a negotiating table, and trying to see through a repertoire of intentions and desires of his incomparably lesser, more amateurish, and thus far less experienced, diplomatic opponent. I was like such a diplomat striving to construe a panoply of his opponent's true motives and yearnings and impulses from the cryptic language of his facial expressions. From the particular arrangement of his impenetrable facial features.

For there was not a faint shade of a doubt, there was not even a dithery penumbra of it, about the fact that I towered above him. And I towered considerably. Undeniably. But I did not do it only due to my formidable diplomatic experience and strategic abilities. I did not do it only due to my impeccable social graces and proficiency in the subtleties of an idiom of diplomacy. For I was like a condor that is being pitted against a feeble nestling, and that traps its rival within the confines of the intimidating shroud of the shadow of its imperious wings or something. Yet most certainly I surpassed him. I surely surpassed him in the wideness and boundlessness and sheer enormity of my horizons. For they had been stretched and expanded mercilessly right up to the limits of extensibility. They had been stretched by my eager and vigorous communing with the members of various exclusive clubs and elites. And they proved to be wide. They were so wide, in fact, that it was simply impossible to see all those horizons at the same time.

So I could not squander that rather significant, if not rather crushing, advantage of mine. It would be an unpardonable mistake to waste it now. I could not let him provoke me. I could not surrender to his unrefined games and inexhaustible reserves of his youthful impishness. I had to place my steps carefully in this subtle diplomatic chess game. Like a woman dancing with a man cursed with a pair of enormous feet. I had to calculate painstakingly my every single move and motion before even preparing myself to execute it gingerly. I had to ponder studiously my every hand and all the cards coming my way. And I had to do all that while also doing my best not to expose myself to his blows. Not to betray an array of my true feelings and emotions. Not to let him lead me straight into yet another rhetorical or logical ambush with one of his seemingly innocent arguments. And, above all, I had to pay attention not to become blinded and carried away by my undue self-confidence, if not ordinary conceit, during a fight with that less experienced foe. For it is a well-documented fact that pride comes long before a fall. Like a smug smile that runs merrily ahead of a slap across one's face delivered by a girl who proves to be immune to one's embarrassingly trite pickup lines. For history had fastidiously recorded more than a mere handful of cases in which, due to the surplus of pride, the stronger and more agile people had been ignominiously defeated by the weaker and callow ones.

And I wanted to win that hand. That match. That game. That brief and intense yet wordless skirmish of ours. I yearned to beat and vanquish him intellectually. I wanted to crush him on the illusory mental chessboard with a single staggering move. With an excellent coup de grâce. I wanted to do that right before I decided to attack him in the more physical and conventional manner. That dull and shamelessly unremarkable scholar. I wanted to do that to him, who strived desperately and a bit too obviously to disguise his tediousness as enviable athletic prowess and virility. But this camouflage was as thin and brittle as my dry epidermis. For he was nothing else but an incurably and irredeemably boring lecturer of Economics.

DAUGHTER: So, you're in the arts? You're one of those artsy men? Those artsy types? Paint-stained, chalk-soiled, and charcoal-tainted men? You're one of those?

LECTURER: Yes... you can say that... yes...

DAUGHTER: I've known a painter once.

LECTURER: Oh, really?

DAUGHTER: Personally.

LECTURER: I understand...

DAUGHTER: Even quite personally.

LECTURER: Well...

DAUGHTER: You can even say, intimately.

LECTURER: Oh... is he... I mean... was he... any good?

DAUGHTER: I said he is... well... he was... a painter. I didn't say anything about his skills or talent or anything for that matter. He was my upstairs neighbor. He is no more. Once he was.

LECTURER: But is he, was he, worthy of any professional attention?

DAUGHTER: He was, apparently he was worthy of that kind of attention. He'd made quite a stir in artistic circles at the time. But it's over now. It's long gone and over.

LECTURER: Has he burned out?

DAUGHTER: They burned him.

LECTURER: They did?

DAUGHTER: At the stake. An artistic stake made of broken easels and old palettes and disheveled brushes.

LECTURER: I see...

DAUGHTER: But my cousin has an art gallery downtown. So, I can say that I have art circulating in my veins.

LECTURER: Yes... Yes, you can say that.

DAUGHTER: I have paint instead of blood. What do you think about that? Do you like it? Huh? Do you like that expression? Paint instead of blood?

LECTURER: Yes... It's... It's quite colorful.

DAUGHTER: Just like paint! I've just said that, haven't I? Exactly like paint. You see, I also have my way with words.

LECTURER: Yes... You have...

DAUGHTER: I have my way with them.

LECTURER: More like a highway.

DAUGHTER: You're so funny! So indecently funny!

It had to be him. There was no possibility of a mistake. No matter how faint or vague. For we were not, as far as I was aware, some pitiful stock characters from a comedy of errors. Everything seemed to be right, correct, and in its rightful place. Or even better than that. For everything was correct beyond any doubt. Like all the ingredients of a complex equation.

Undoubtedly, he was an economist. He looked like one. He smelled like one. So he simply could not be anyone else than one. In any event. In any case. Because he proudly bore all the unmistakable hallmarks of a professional and thus tritely humorless economist. It just sufficed perfectly to take a quick and cursory look at his fatigued eyes. For they were frozen in that perpetual squint from observing and inspecting and exploring for a bit too long, a bit too closely, as well as a bit too incessantly, the long and winding and interminable rows and columns overflowing with cold and soulless numbers. It was as if it were some ancient code that had to be deciphered at all, even if insanely exorbitant, costs.

And so, his cold and uncaring and heartless eyes said it. They said it all. They said even more than that. They did that while succumbing, ironically, to the distinct economics of emotions. They did that after they had been infected with that intimidating and formidable lack of any feelings or compassion. Any delicacy. Any sensitivity to beauty. Any kind of beauty. For they must have been infected by those equally lifeless as well as cold-blooded numbers. And these numbers stripped him of his essential human emotions. And they robbed him insolently of any ability to feel empathy. To feel for others. And thus they turned him, discreetly and inconspicuously, yet with the economically viable efficaciousness, into an amateur criminal. They simply turned him into a dreamy murderer material.

DAUGHTER: I like your eyes.

LECTURER: You do?

DAUGHTER: I really like those deep, deep, blue, and incredibly deep eyes of yours. I like them. I could drown in them. Is that wrong?

LECTURER: No... I don't think so... no.

DAUGHTER: I like them. There's something artistic in them.

LECTURER: There is? Well, I wasn't aware of that.

DAUGHTER: I bet you were. There's this subtle touch of artistry in them.

LECTURER: I'm doing my best.

DAUGHTER: *(laughing and patting him playfully on the shoulder)* You're impossible! You're really impossible! But you should know that we women pay attention to them.

LECTURER: Is that so?

DAUGHTER: Enormous attention. Tremendous attention. Gigantic even. To the eyes, I mean.

LECTURER: Oh... I see...

DAUGHTER: I bet you do. Right through those cute eyes of yours, right?

Or his hands. It just sufficed to glance at his hands. Cold, callous, and void of the sole last chunk of that typically human tenderness. They were void of that delightful human warmth. They were void of that typically human understanding. And they gave me a gratuitous glimpse of an impending disaster. They put my little family reunion of fears in the fresh context. They made them acquire a new tailored perspective. For those hands of his strikingly resembled a part of some soulless machinery or other. They were absolutely unmoved by, and immune to, human suffering, human needs and dreams and desires. For that cruel machinery required only a fresh drop of oil here and there to ensure its long and undisturbed work. It required only a fresh drop of oil to prolong its mindless obeying the ruthless orders of his calculating economic mind, gorging itself rapaciously on a tasteless mishmash of fractions and percents and percentiles. I saw all that. I saw all that in him.

DAUGHTER: I like your hands, I really do.

LECTURER: Oh... That's nice. What's not to like, right?

DAUGHTER: I like them, but I'm not sure what I like about them most. Perhaps... that they're both masculine and artistically delicate... I don't mean effeminate, but delicate... both artistically feminine and strong at the same time. Yes, that's what I like about them... about your hands... that they're quite...

LECTURER: Handy?

DAUGHTER: *(laughing)* I'm sure they are. I'm more than sure that they are.

LECTURER: I've never looked at them that way.

DAUGHTER: Well, it's about time to start then.

LECTURER: It seems so.

DAUGHTER: I like that they look like normal hands... like typical hands... even like the worn-out hands of my father here... but at the same time there's this molecule of artistic potential lying dormant in them... that germ of genius buried somewhere under their skin... your skin... that seed of uniqueness lurking somewhere in there... invisible... untouchable... but almost palpable... I like that. I like that very much.

LECTURER: As I said... What's not to like?

But now, we sat facing each other. We sat there like two competing poker players eyeing each other over the sea of baize. We were like two generals facing not only each other, but also a rueful and agonizing menagerie of their own fears and aggravations, being personified by their staunch rival, being incarcerated unlawfully and for good in their adversary's facial features. And as we sat like that, I observed him unhurriedly and rather minutely. And it struck me. It struck me with the force of a ball being hurled by an impish burly youngster. (That accursed youth again!) It struck me that he was not as terrifying, not as demonic, as I had imagined it recently. Not even in half. He was not.

For he was nothing like that appalling mental picture, if not a quick mental snapshot of him, that I had created, developed, and then cultivated tenderly in the camera obscura of my mind. He was not like it. He was not like the one fabricated by me during a fleeting yet undeserved insidious moment of my weakness. During that brief triumph of my insecurity. He was not like the one which had been filling me with mounting concern. Which had succeeded in reviving my innermost, intimate, and long-repressed fears. Which had happened before I had a chance to not so much lay as perch my fatigued eyes on him. It had happened before I managed to get to know him properly. It had happened when he was still hiding shyly behind that large and intimidating and formidable and impenetrable cloak of mystery. Of unknown. Of a secret. Like a child playing hide-and-seek behind the trees. For then, at that time, he had been to me just a nondescript and vague being. He had been to me just a being having more in common with the hardly extinct supernatural species numerously populating all the fables, parables, as well as roaming the macabre expanse of nightmares. For although I made every jittery effort possible, although I did everything in my senile power, I could not notice in him those overgrown claws. The ones akin to a nice set of brand new scythes from a singularly baleful advertisement in some agricultural magazine or other. And this image tormented me maliciously. It tormented me and, every now and then, made a dew of cold sweat appear on my seamed back. There was also no trace, not even one, even if partly trampled, even if almost obliterated, of his, until recently, menacingly bared teeth. They were not there. I mean the ones the mere sight of which kept making my own, yet feebler, yet frailer, yet decidedly falser, dentures, vibrate disconcertingly. Like an odd and fearful version of a tuning fork that is unable to stop trembling after being set in that panicky motion by the fear of losing its jerky job. I even failed to discern any vestiges of other, more or less nightmarish attributes commonly

132

associated with all kinds of creatures of the distinctly hellish, or even insane, provenance. They also were not there. They were absent in him. The ones that, till now, I had thought that I could see in him. And which had been swelling and multiplying and magnifying rampantly with each passing second.

But now that initial fit of irrepressible self-doubt subsided and died down irrevocably. It died down like the flame of passion between a man and his effeminate colleague whom he picked up by mistake at a bar during a drunken night. And that moment of my embarrassing weakness passed away once and for all. And I felt, once again, like a full-fledged and heroic player in this odd game of appearances.

DAUGHTER: I like your manliness.

LECTURER: My what?

DAUGHTER: I like it, I really do.

LECTURER: Oh... Well, then...

DAUGHTER: I like that manly air that you exude with such effortlessness...

LECTURER: Well, thank you.

DAUGHTER: It's a rare thing. You should be proud of it.

LECTURER: I will... Thank you once again.

DAUGHTER: Yes... Men emanating such manliness are a rare kind of species these days. Believe me.

LECTURER: I do.

DAUGHTER: You'd better believe me.

LECTURER: Uhm... I do.

DAUGHTER: They're almost extinct. Long gone. Puff! Disappeared off the sad and gloomy face of the Earth with a dash of mascara smeared all over it!

LECTURER: I wouldn't say...

DAUGHTER: And all that is left are those pitiful little creatures. Those laughable residues, those miserable ruins of that once proud sex. Those men who spend their whole days on bowing to, and fawning on, others and attending to them humbly, to the point of forgetting how to straighten up and

133

look other people straight in the face. How to act instead of waiting for someone's else actions. How to alter the world instead of sabotaging every kind of change. And how to live instead of slowly dying from the fear of everything.

LECTURER: There's some truth in —

DAUGHTER: *(cutting him short)* Am I right, Dad?

Once again I nodded at least ambiguously. I nodded while shrugging enigmatically at the same time. Thus I sent out two incoherent and completely contradictory signals. And they were designed to confuse and mislead him in that wonderfully devious manner. For it also allowed me to dispatch a thickly veiled information, a camouflaged cryptic message, indecipherable, almost completely unbreakable, to my tender daughter. I sent it to her as if it were a box of chocolates. I sent it to her as she kept communicating with me in that enchanting vernacular of filial love.

But I had to pay attention. But I had to be careful not to let our intangible correspondence of quick winks and smirks and nods fall into his hands. It could not fall into the cold and mechanical hands of our genuine foe. Of the deadliest of our deadly enemies. For he could, considering his automatic and unduly calculating mind, ably decipher and break its rather unrefined code. He could deftly generate a skeleton key to it. If not a full-fleshed key. And he could use the thus gained information against me. Against us. Without a single instant of hesitation.

And yet I could not break communication with my dear little offspring. I could not even suspend it temporarily. I just could not afford that to happen. I could not leave her there. Utterly alone. I could not abandon her there. Far behind enemy lines. Far from the nearest bridgehead of ours. For she would be there alone. Hopelessly alone. In the stern and solemn face of our ferocious opponent. I had to offer her succor. I had to give her paternal support. I had to provide her with hope.

I had to. I simply had to.

LECTURER: Don't be so hard on yourself...

DAUGHTER: They say that we choose our partners, and that we then create them, in the image of our parents. But what if our parents have been to us, throughout our childhood, throughout our earliest and most vulnerable years, nothing else but the source of constant shame and disappointment? Should we then condemn ourselves to vegetation in shame and disappointment during the remaining part of our lives at the side of yet another failure? Modeled after them? Should we?

LECTURER: Well, I don't think that there's such a rule...

DAUGHTER: But what if a parent... our parent... a hypothetical one, naturally... what if such a parent constantly embarrasses us with his... or her... ineptitude and servility toward others? What if he... or she... has numerously proved to be unable to rise to the occasion... any occasion even... for he... or she... is too preoccupied with keeping his... or her... back fixed in the shape of an arch... from bowing too often to others... to anyone, really. What then?

LECTURER: Well...

DAUGHTER: What should I do then, Dad?

I had to do that. I had to do that even if I came to the astonishing conclusion that, after all, he was not evil incarnated. That he was not a lively portent of mass death and destruction. Or rather, exactly for this particular reason, I had to do that. For, seeing him now, there violently occurred to me the intolerable banality of evil. All evil to be precise. It struck me and, this curt realization, left an indelible impression on me and my soul. It was akin to a footprint soiling a freshly laid concrete sidewalk. For no one else but he, that man, that flagrantly ordinary and absurdly unremarkable man, was supposed to trigger a chain of events, the sheer enormity as well as the scale of which was, at the still blissfully peaceful time, inconceivable to me. For that very man, that seemingly harmless and innocent individual, was about to become a catalyst and a detonator and an explosive charge in one of the vehement processes that probably even he himself was unable to fathom fully. As if he were a laudable paragon of versatility. A man of lethal renaissance. For he clearly aspired to be an originator and a pioneer of innumerable future personal tragedies and national disasters. He did that as one of those modern products succumbing to the more and more common theory of multitasking. At any cost. Like a multi-tool pocketknife.

And it surprised me terribly. And it surprised me while frightening me earnestly. For, apparently, to execute this destructive task, that is, to start a fire capable of devouring and then ingesting, rapidly, effortlessly, within a mere second or two, this entire elegant and refined world of ours, it sufficed to employ someone as coy and unassuming as he was. For, apparently, he was perfect. For, apparently, he was more than enough to do that. To do the job. He was perfect to start an inextinguishable fire of social unrest. Like a burning match that lands too close to the runway of a carpet. And it would not subside or die away before the last opulent apartment, the last lavishly ornamented piece of furniture, or the last heavily embroidered velvet curtain, turned into the desultorily smoldering and charred carcass of the former and now lost splendor.

DAUGHTER: You should know I adore your extraordinariness, your uniqueness in this oppressive sea of mediocrity. I really do.

LECTURER: Well, what can I say?

DAUGHTER: Say what you like.

LECTURER: No, it's you who likes it.

(They laugh heartily.)

DAUGHTER: I hope I haven't scared you too much with my directness?

LECTURER: No... Surely not... Rather not... Presumably not... Well... I'm not sure.

DAUGHTER: I like your decisiveness.

LECTURER: Oh, really?

DAUGHTER: Yes. I like it because I'm a decisive person my-self. I'm a resolute woman. I'm a woman of character. A lot of it! I'm a strong personality. I'm not embarrassed by it, and I'm not going to be. Although men are usually afraid of powerful women.

LECTURER: I understand...

DAUGHTER: They feel intimidated by them.

LECTURER: *(a bit intimidated)* Oh... Well...

DAUGHTER: But you're not. I can see that.

LECTURER: *(pretends to be fully relaxed)* Well... I don't think that there's much...

DAUGHTER: I'm also aware of my physical attractiveness.

LECTURER: *(intimidated again)* Oh...

DAUGHTER: I know perfectly well what I look like, and what I do to men. And I admit that from time to time I take advantage of it. Why not? Why should I not?

LECTURER: I... don't know...

DAUGHTER: That's very apt. You're right. There's no reason.

LECTURER: Oh...

DAUGHTER: My mother was also a powerful woman, a fine woman, really. She knew what she wanted from life, and she knew how to get it. I also know a thing or two, and I'm going to pursue those aims of mine, at any cost.

LECTURER: I see...

DAUGHTER: Again with the lovely eyes of yours, right? *(She laughs as he looks a bit puzzled.)*

DAUGHTER: But you should know... or rather... you should be warned, that I'm not as sweet as I appear to be. I can show my claws from time to time. I can. I surely do.

LECTURER: I wouldn't even dare to...

DAUGHTER: But you have nothing to worry about. You have no reasons to worry. You don't have to worry your beautiful head over it, for I adore men in glasses. I do.

LECTURER: Oh...

DAUGHTER: I don't know why I'm such a powerful personality. Maybe it's because I can't stand passiveness and helplessness in men. I detest them. I also loathe them. And you
should know that weak men are afraid of powerful women.

LECTURER: Yes... you've already...

DAUGHTER: I really react to them in a very visceral manner.
As if my body couldn't take it.

LECTURER: Well, I don't know...

DAUGHTER: But I do know. I know. Leave it to me. You
know, sometimes I feel as if I were created... as if I were
shaped in opposition to something... or rather, someone...
someone I know... someone in my immediate vicinity...
someone who, contrary to me, is and has always been
chronically absorbed in, or addicted to, all forms of social
conventions... someone who cannot live without them...
someone who has wasted his whole life on erecting various self-inflicted obstacles and imaginary hurdles on his
own way through life while forcing himself, and his poor
family, to perform breakneck slaloms among them... even
though life is a straight and empty road, and you can roar
down it unhampered... unrestrained... to someone who
cannot spend a few minutes away from the structured
world, hierarchical world, where he knows his place... a
quite pitiful place... if not a downright laughable place...
but he doesn't want to change it... oh, no... he doesn't want
to improve his position... no... he isn't interested in any
improvement... he's pleased that the things don't worsen
too much... he's content that the things don't deteriorate
too quickly... Well... There're people like that. There're old
people like that. Believe me.

I wanted to say something. Anything, really. I wanted to say
something to back up her claims. To corroborate her theories.
To exhibit that famed family unity. To take part in their oddly
vigorous discussion of which I comprehended nothing. Or,
at least, something very close to it. And even my loyal vocal

cords started playing the first few chords of the invincible, eternal melody of paternal love. But then I silenced embarrassedly. I did that right after being curtly called to order by my infallible strategic sense. For its harsh voice with a hint of tenderness floating in it, like a drop of juice in an otherwise bitter drink, prompted me not to imperil my invaluable current position at the sidelines of all that. Of a silent referee. Of an unbiased observer. Of an unseen and unaffiliated spy, taking no sides and all sides at once.

And thus, as my initial idea was lost in the vapors of undiluted detachment, I thought that, if he really constituted such a dreadful threat to our society as well as our schematic world, if he really was such a menace, equal in terms of its ferociousness and strength to the congregation of wildest tornadoes and hurricanes, it meant that we could not sleep safely at night anymore. It meant that our peace was, from then on, irrevocably shattered and permanently jeopardized. For, even if he was taken care of, even if he was removed once and for all, it would be not only simple, but also astonishingly easy, to find someone, anyone, really, of similar ambition, determination, as well as vision, to replace him. It would be laughably easy to find someone of comparable reserves of charisma. Or even someone suppressing him considerably in all those categories. And it would be simple to find someone who was not as easy to stop and contain as he seemed to be. And thus, even I might as well turn into the far more formidable danger to the world peace than he had ever dreamed of becoming. I might, despite my shaky body. My faulty body. My body that had long overstayed both its welcome and its expiration date. I might, despite my implacable age. Which evident vice I strived to mask guiltily and compensate for with an overwhelming capital of my experience and wisdom. Like a golden crown on a shabby tooth.

DAUGHTER: You're special! Do you know it? Are you aware of it? You're really special. You're one of a kind!

LECTURER: If you say so...

DAUGHTER: Yes, you're. I know it. I feel it. I know it for I can feel it, for I'm like that, too. I'm also special.

LECTURER: That makes us two, doesn't it?

For what was superior about his hands? What was better, greater, or more wonderful about those powerful and able hands of his in comparison to mine? In what respect did they tower over my hands? Or overshadow my hands? Did they do that like a kind of multifingered eagle from some eminently hallucinational vision or an absurdly modern painting? How was it at all possible that he possessed finer hands? Better hands? Or fuller hands? Were they more comprehensively meeting the criteria of an encyclopedic definition of hands than mine? The old, weary, and indubitably creased ones? Or even, in what exactly was his impressively taut and springy neck different from mine? Was it capable of providing far greater stabilization and vibration damping for his head? And thus did it offer it a more comfortable ride over the unevennesses of life? And did it create more congenial conditions for the growth of his even most ridiculous ideas? Could his youthfully glistening impish eyes see more? Absorb more? Could they imbibe rapaciously a larger number of the usually shy details as well as nuances than mine? Was his field of vision wider, broader, higher, or even deeper than mine? Was it devoid of the pitfalls of blind spots? Dark spots? And any other spots? Was it free of them to the point of being able to observe what was happening in front of him as well as right behind his back at the same time? Were his stunningly firm and supple ears capable of hearing more precisely and correctly than mine? Could they pick up the gentle fluctuations and vibrations of air, akin to an inaudible whisper following in the light steps of an air kiss? Could they pick up all that was scandalously inaccessible not only to my ears? But also to all human ears altogether? Even for a modest fee and under the jealous eye of some abstract acoustic chaperone? Was he endowed with such, or strikingly similar, special talents and abilities? Borrowed straight from a wide assortment of magical and extraordinary powers being at every beck and call of various fantastic characters and imaginary heroes? If so, then it seriously undermined and put into new context, right before calling into question, his, till then already dubious, relations with our rather dull and unexciting species.

But then after a mere second overflowing with my deserved self-satisfaction and conceit, like a snow globe with a drizzle of little playful flakes of one's childhood memories of winter, that haughty duo readily gave way to my no less full-fledged doubts and apprehension. For I promptly noticed, to my own ineffable astonishment, how terribly weakened and tame and worn-out my hands were. They quivered slightly like a needle of a seismograph ecstatically looking forward to an approaching series of thrilling jerks and jolts. And I succumbed to the overpowering fit of nostalgia. I succumbed to it as I realized that they were now not more than a faint and blurry shadow of their former selves. Of those former, now long gone, strong and solid and diligent hands of mine. They were nothing like those hands that had never been afraid of any kind of work. They were nothing like those hands that had never shied away from any toil or challenging tasks. They were nothing like those hands that had never yielded to any inhuman effort or pain. And which now disappeared surreptitiously, under the cover of passing time. For they had become absorbed by those two mercilessly shriveled masses of bones and flesh and loose skin. It was as if they were twin succulent fruits that grew wrinkled and desiccated from lounging and basking in the sun for too long.

And I failed to comprehend, how it was at all possible that I had not managed to notice that. I failed to comprehend that while slowly coming to dreadfully seamed terms with their present pitiful condition, being, to some extent, a measure of my inadequacy. How it was possible that I had failed to discern those heartrendingly deep bite marks left on the surface of my papery skin. Like a kind of exceedingly durable stamp. That were left by an ever-voracious tooth of time. How it was possible, even though, at the present moment, I was unable to see anything but them. Yet although these marks were seemingly impalpable and ethereal and invisible to anyone else but me, I wanted to hide them embarrassedly. I wanted to hide them almost guiltily. I wanted to cover them up quickly with something. To disguise them hastily. With a stray napkin. With a lazy handkerchief. Or to slip them furtively under the rim of a plate. It was as if they were an incriminating bit of evidence that could not be left in plain view. Thus I wanted to hide them from the critical and disdainful eyes of others. Yet especially of my majestic uncouth foe. I wanted to hide those incontestable testimonies of my frailty. But, above all, I wanted to protect them against an accidental touch of some other hand. For it might easily have read from a constellation of all those intangible indentations the full gamut of my fears and misgivings. As if from an odd version of a Braille writing. And thus, I was forced to relinquish the futile dreams of my bygone youth. And, as if to add to my dismay, I had to find a place where I could conceal those treacherous hands of mine. Only for an instant. Only for the duration of this more and more agonizing meal. But then I caught my telltale hands discreetly stroking my neck that also in no way resembled my former now lost one. It also was completely unlike the one whose pleasantly springy and firm and tight skin, for some inexplicable reason, had been at some point replaced with that, certainly cheaper in maintenance, sagging substitute.

But then I looked down at my hands. Once again. With unconcealed and still mounting disillusionment. And it could not escape my notice that my eyes, along with the quality of images being obtained through them, also left much to be desired. They were terribly unfocused. They were terribly mismatched and tragically distorted. It was as though those images were captured by a broken and scratched lens. Or worse, it was as though they were captured by someone suffering from the clearly would-be artistic proclivities. Similarly a sonorous mishmash of sounds and tones reaching me all the time was not of the best imaginable kind. It was not first-rate, second-rate, or even third-rate. For it evidently was not even half as good and sharp as the plaintive cries for help uttered by an amateurish swimmer, the cries being carried into the distance by water, and riding the ripples on its stirred surface.

For, after all, and it miraculously dawned on me just now, I had a serious problem with understanding my two interlocutors. I had that problem since the beginning of this newest ordeal of mine. Their words were unintelligible to me. Their jokes were far beyond me. Their laughs seemed unwarranted to me. Their punch lines eluded me stubbornly. Their smiles gave an impression of being forced and misplaced to me. And all that looked to me like a movie in which the original brilliant dialogues have been badly dubbed over, thus ruining the pace and synchronization and timing of the entire story.

And this situation forced me to devise a particularly clever and elaborate scheme that was supposed to ensure my understanding them. For I avidly read their facial expressions. For I intently read their tireless lips. And I deduced from a flurry of their movements the moods and reactions of their owners. I divined from them when there came the appropriate moment for me to smile. To smirk. And to frown sternly. So I was like an ignoramus hanging around with erudite people who keeps nodding impatiently to everything they say, all the time, with exaggerated zeal, only to compensate generously for his own glaring shortcomings, and not to expose himself to the mortal risk of disgrace.

Then I understood something. And I was rudely overwhelmed by this sullen realization. I understood that my body, my desiccated hands, my hideously sagging neck akin to a permanently stretched-out turtleneck, my irrefutably infirm eyes and ears, and all the parts of my body altogether, were not an advantage when compared to his irreproachably smooth innocent skin. It did not help much that in every single place or spot I was marked by my imposing experience. It did not help that my every wrinkle or furrow marked some highly edifying moment or challenging trouble from my past. And it did not mean anything that from every single pore of my skin profusely oozed and emanated this precious and inimitable wisdom. Of the best vintage possible. Of the finest quality imaginable. It was as in the case of barrels in which some noble wine lounges unhurriedly. It was not an invaluable asset. A benefit. It was not a thing that it would be advisable to fight for. And even die for. Let alone brag about. But it was a flaw. And even it was an embarrassing flaw. An inhibiting flaw. That I had to be ashamed of and deny till breathless. I had to do that as if it were a body deformity being the constant source of laughter in some radically intolerant society.

And thus I lost this hand. Definitively. Indubitably. Irrevocably. I lost this little game of social chess completely and for good. And that thought left a bitter aftertaste in my mouth. It was as if I had just eaten something that was either overdone or underdone, but certainly not right. And he defeated me. And he vanquished me mercilessly. He defeated me. Yet he did it fairly. He defeated me, the old and wilting doorman. And a humble servant of all those who were wealthier and more powerful than I had ever been. But I still failed to fathom how he had managed, that vibrant man, no matter how vigorous or robust, how young, how stubbornly young, to scare so many of those unthinkably affluent people. The same ones who, under more typical and peaceful circumstances, could not be moved by any wars or cataclysms, as long as those haunted and devastated places located far away from them. The same ones who could not be touched by even the most heartbreaking human tragedies. The very same ones who had never deigned to sympathize with anyone. Let alone produce a single misplaced or miscalculated tear. And the very same ones who had never wept over the plight of all the poor and wretched and ailing ones, whom the biased cruel fate grudged luck to the point of inflicting on them a kind of luck deficiency.

But then again, I could not comprehend how this man, however manly and charismatic he might be, had been capable of gripping the minds of the, after all, boundless and inherently vehement masses. I did not know how he had managed to inspire them. I did not know how he had succeeded in taming them. And I mean them, having more in common with the wild, primordial, and unbridled force of Nature, with one of its fierce elements, than with a gathering of thinking and rational beings. And how he had managed to coax them into disobeying their both lawful and rightful, for simply much more affluent, masters was beyond me. I also did not know how he had managed to stir those lamentable dregs of society without the aid of any spoons or forks or any other silverware. I did not know how he had succeeded in promoting himself to the coveted position of their self-proclaimed leader and prophet and mentor in one. For thus he had tricked them hypocritically into swapping one stern ruler for another.

And thus I wondered how all that was possible. And I wondered that while humming to the accompaniment of the melody of disappointment that was hard, if not impossible, to drown out by the tune of clear reason. I wondered whether behind all that was merely the ordinary and relentlessly partial stroke of sheer luck. With a full range of its shameless tricks and machinations. Or rather this unexpected promotion of his was a fruit, however putrid or decayed, of ignoble collusion of coincidence and his own raging opportunism. Anyway, the precise cause and reason of it did not matter. And even, it did not matter at all. The stale aroma enveloping and permeating all those past events and historical turbulences was of no importance. It played no role whatsoever in this grand tragedy in three acts and without any epilog in sight. It was the same as with idle thoughts on, and contemplation of, the ways in which it could have been avoided. In which it might have been prevented. Into which kind of insoluble maze of alternate realities as well as scenarios there usually ventures a mind that is overwhelmed with current miseries and thus unable to cope with its present predicament. With its inescapable conundrum. For it is like with a child who in the hideous face of danger, instead of bolting away, instead of running for its barely-started life, trustingly covers its eyes, which is an insult to the self-preservation instinct and to a myriad of years of evolution that had led to its birth.

Because, sitting there, right in front of me, here and now, was he. It was no one else but he. It was he. This intimidating prophet of featureless masses. This menacing messiah of vulgar hordes. It was he and no one else. And it was he whom I had to confront now. It was he, and not some imaginary would-be stand-in of his, who, torn away from his usual activities, awkwardly strived to, more or less successfully, make the best of it. Completely unprepared for it.

And so it made no sense to wade any deeper into this kind of gibberish. It made no sense to wade any deeper into this kind of futile and always-pointless sessions of ham-fisted theorizing. Especially as they were now ineptly combined with the inevitable wishful thinking. And thus, instead of indulging myself in that kind of wasteful pastime of minds in distress, because of which I might be indicted for mental vagrancy, there occurred to me, for the first time in my eventful life, the full catalog of my failings and shortcomings. And it was bursting at its infirm seams. And it was falling apart from senility. And it was all painful from rheumatism. And it was brimful of my shortcomings ranging from those connected with age to those unjustly associated with my miserable health. And so, I was now free. Also for the first time. I was now free of my colorful glasses tinted with illusions and spurious visions, and still tenaciously reflecting the long-out-of-date self-image of mine. And so I approached this little game once more. I sat at this gaming table once again. I sat there sobered intellectually. Awakened spiritually. And with a fully realistic attitude. I sat there drained of all the sham fantasies and hallucinations about my present position. I was just like a novice mailman, who on the first day at his new job loses the last scraps and vestiges of his pants in the mouths of ferocious dogs, which are chewing and mauling them scrupulously with the air of professional detachment.

In the wake of that abrupt awakening of mine, I understood perfectly that our struggle was doomed to be insanely uneven. I understood that my already hated adversary, of the strikingly affable demeanor, was more capable than I. Far more capable than I. In terms of both physical fitness and endurance. And thus I had to avoid, at any cost, the intimate skirmishes and grand battles with him in those fields. I had to avoid them like an infantry unit ambling surreptitiously amid the jagged ruins and hiding there from enemy tanks, doing its best not to get caught in the open. So, I had to avail myself of my own unparalleled assets. As nimbly and urgently as possible. I had to avail myself of my own indubitable advantages. But they, admittedly, would not help me much, and would not be too tremendously useful, in the case of an open tussle. They would not be useful at all if it came to fierce blows. For they were of that distinctly ethereal and immaterial nature. But, nonetheless, they could assist me greatly in the process of gaining the strategic and intellectual edge over him. Over the secretly malignant him. Over this man of demonstrative stolidity. For I had, close at hand, my almost crushing experience. My astonishing tactical sense. And my overpowering wisdom. And I was not going to hesitate to use that lethal combination against him. That mental arsenal of mine.

It was because my only chance to beat him, to achieve a stunning victory over him, any victory, really, was gathering a sufficient amount of evidence incriminating him. And him only. For my every clumsy attempt at executing that judgment on him singlehandedly had to end in a fiasco. And even in a spectacular one. Like an attempt at flying a concrete kite. For my every inept try at murdering him and thus administering the, prosaic rather than poetic, dose of justice, had to turn into an embarrassing failure. Because, to my newly resurrected surprise, he was perfectly capable of fending off my every single attack. Like a cow easily defeating every fly with its tail. He was perfectly capable of parrying my every blow. Even if an unexpected one. Even if an improvised one. Especially if executed by me, in my present advanced stage of wrinkling and withering, at a relentless pace. And it was of no relevance how much time and effort I had invested in learning and mastering the intricate and sophisticated techniques of strangling and murdering various unsuspecting bolsters, cushions, and headrests. It was unimportant how able I had become in slitting the throats of countless milk bottles and turtleneck sweaters. All of them exquisitely playing the roles of imaginary necks as well as victims in general. Because the effect would always be the same. If not hopelessly the same.

Thus, any violent solution, on account of these objective and insurmountable reasons, was out of the question. No matter how indecently tempting. Or manly. Or thrilling. Or exciting. And it had to be swiftly crossed off the menu of available possibilities. But I still could, within the scope of the singularly vengeful compensation, drive him, with my incredibly cunning stratagems, straight into some cleverly devised kind of lethal rhetorical ambush. Like a geek planning revenge on a local bully. I could also force him, with my brilliant tricks and volleys of aptly formulated, shrewd, and merciless questions, to betray all the details of his schemes. Of his ignoble schemes. I could force him to impart to me all his atrocious plans of unspeakable cruelty. Not to mention his appalling motives. And with those freshly obtained yet hardly appetizing bits of information, I intended to rush to my benevolent masters. I intended to rush to those elite members of hotel aristocracy. To my informal principals. I intended to rush to them on the double. And even triple if needed. As fast as my rheumatic legs deigned to cooperate. And for this inspired act of loyalty, with certainty, a prize of some kind would await me along with an instantaneous social advancement.

But still, the most relevant and dearest to my heart impatiently approaching retirement would be nothing else but their satisfaction. Their full and undiluted contentment. Perhaps the one that would be accompanied by a lighthearted flicker of a smile conveying their boundless peace of mind and relief. The one that would flit playfully across their tense and nervous faces. And thus it would make them glow a little with excitement. Like a young ballerina at the sight of a curtain rising especially for her for the first time. Not much. But then a little more.

I had to do that very carefully. I had to execute this entire elaborate plan of mine in the gentlest and most precise fashion conceivable. I had to do that so as not to harm by accident my adorably garrulous daughter while administering to him a series of vicious and uncompromising rhetorical blows and cuts and stabs. I had to pay attention not to hurt that beloved yet now excessively insubordinate offspring of mine. For she, unmistakably, was now completely entranced by him. Like a kitten by a new ball of wool. For she was now so expertly brainwashed into believing implicitly and indiscriminately in all his gibberish. For she was now brainwashed into believing in his incoherent delusions. In his irrational theories. All bordering on, let's be frank, sheer insanity. Thus she sat there far too close to him. And thus she was well within the field of fire of my sharp and cutting arguments. I had to be cautious. I had to be wary. I had to choose my next steps wisely. I had to remain incredibly precise. I had to tread lightly, so lightly, in fact, that nearly unnoticeably. I had to be like a man playing jackstraws with hand grenades. I had to work that way in order not to inflict on her any crippling and debilitating withdrawal symptoms. Those belated though inevitable souvenirs of every past mistake. I had to demonstrate a quite unexpected level of accuracy of my fearsome arguments. Which trait was characteristic of the most seasoned ones among diplomats. For such professionals would easily use an ostensibly innocuous innuendo, a seemingly affable allusion, to throw their fierce opponents off balance. For they would know how to masterfully startle their adversaries, how to shock them, to the extent that providing first aid to them could be necessary, the same as resuscitating the last vestiges of their thus tarnished wits. And even they would know how to treat their opponents to an immediate hospitalization. And then also to a long and challenging and strenuous process of moral convalescence. And thus, my accuracy had to be comparable to, if not had to markedly surpass, that of a professional marksman. It had to be comparable to that of a sniper who is given a task of liquidating a trite political terrorist, as predictable as the second half of a Rorschach blot, hiding in the crowd of, ironically, politically indifferent people. I also had to climb, with the effortless gracefulness of my movements, to the unattainable heights of precision. And then I would be like a renowned surgeon who is forced to extricate some tiny and hard-to-reach slice of tissue, that ungrateful saboteur, that remorseless fleshy traitor, while trying not to endanger any of the neighboring internal organs surrounding it tightly. As if they were protecting it and hiding it and shielding it caringly. Out of some misdirected organic solidarity.

So I was contemplating and devising a cunning way of drawing her away from him. So I was contemplating a way of dragging her for an instant, even for a single brief yet fateful instant, from the line of fire. So I was contemplating a way of luring her out of the room. Or at least of winning her over to my safe and cozy and loving side. I had to do that before I finished him off instantly with a single inexorable coup de grâce. I had to do that before I finished him off right there.

150

Right now. In front of her. And at that insupportable act of violence, she would doubtless have taken offense, or even, begun hating me temporarily. Genuinely. Viscerally. But not for long. But not forever. Because only then she would have fathomed that it, that all of it, was for her own good. For her own widely understood yet vague good. Then she suddenly stood up, my sweet and uncorrupted little offspring, as if on some unspoken command. Like a soldier during a drill. She did that as if upon hearing my incessantly scheming thoughts. As it frequently happened in an exemplary father-child communication that we shared and enjoyed proudly. She lightly rose to her feet and moved away from the line of fire of her own accord. And then, once again, there sounded this deliciously enchanting chirping of her voice. For it was so dear, so unspeakably dear, to my elderly wrinkled heart.

DAUGHTER: I'll be back in a moment. I've got something for you. Something special. Something really special. Meantime, don't let him bore you to death with one of his outlandish theories.

LECTURER: I'll... try...

DAUGHTER: That's the only thing you can expect from him. That's the only thing you can always, and I mean always, expect from my old father. Anytime and anywhere. Being bored to death. Which, in his own case, isn't that far away.

Then she finished singing those saccharine, yet invariably moving, yet tirelessly beautiful, paeans to me. To honor her beloved father. At least, it was what I divined from the diffident tone of her voice as well as the choreography of her movements. Because the still invincible miasma of stupor enveloping my mind and stemming from that unusual situation, that unnerving intrusion of his, did not allow me to understand her words properly. Of my little girl. And as soon as she left and vanished behind the door, like an adorable nocturnal vision that is being shot down with gusto by the first sunray of the day, I was left alone with him in the room. So I mustered

151

up the strength to act, to fight, to struggle for life. I was like a mischievous pupil instantly lighting up at the sight of a teacher storming out of the classroom for he has forgotten something or other from his car.

And now, I had only to choose a way. A proper way. An adequate way to operate. I had to choose it from that wide and impressively well-stocked range of possible options. I had to choose the most suitable way for this particular situation in terms of its mood and character. I had to do that like a surgeon reaching, with that customarily sterile ceremoniousness, for a correct surgical instrument. For I did not want to overdo it. I certainly did not want to overplay it amateurishly. I did not want to spoil it like an overzealous dilettante in the demolition business, who being unable to mix and use the right proportions of highly explosive ingredients, instead of tearing down a tiny claustrophobic kiosk razes to the ground the whole quarter of the city. I also preferred not to administer too small a dose of it. For it would only infuriate and enrage him recklessly and thus incur his anarchic anger of a fierce revolutionary. For it would be like in the case of a fiery wild animal at which an absentminded hunter shoots with a water gun, slipped to him by his particularly playful little child. For if he was really prepared to topple the current political balance, if he was in truth ready to overthrow the entire world order as we knew it, what could he possibly do to me? I was too afraid to even start imagining it.

And yet I was about to part my lips. Not so much parched as serrated terribly from age, and thus akin to a pair of twin keys. I was about to do that in order to treat him to a more or less biting epithet. More or less acrid insult. I mean the one that I had been forming and shaping and kneading purposefully for some time with my still adroit tongue. But then a question began nagging me. And it assailed me and touched me insolently right to the wrinkled core of my elderly existence. It did that like an adventurous worm that sets off on

152

a perilous journey to the center of an apple. And it asked me inquisitively with interrogator's alacrity, what he was actually doing here. Right here. At our table. It asked me whether this enigmatic fact that he appeared here unasked, uninvited, and utterly unwelcome, that he intruded on us impudently during dinner time, had anything to do with those curious little species called coincidences. It asked me whether it was a mere accident. Or its close relative, a quirk of fate. And perhaps it was not she who had asked him to dinner, who had irresponsibly brought him home. To our uncorrupted family nest. To our sacred sanctuary. To our impervious refuge. Perhaps it was not she who had made that inexcusably reckless, if not downright foolish, move. Entranced and beguiled by his lecture. But, perhaps, it was he. For he was the one who had tricked her cunningly into doing that. Perhaps it was his strategy. Perhaps it was his plan. His infinitely devious masterplan. It was his strategy whose unscheduled arrival I had not expected. Whose unheralded appearance I had not taken into consideration for a single instant. Whose belligerent advent I had failed to foresee in time. For it had eluded me nimbly. For it had eluded me in spite of the innumerable decades of my faultless diplomatic training and intellectual background. And even, it had eluded me in spite of my being on intimate terms with the intricacies of world politics. Perhaps it was he who had scrupulously organized as well as orchestrated all that. Perhaps it was he who had fastidiously gathered all the bits and scraps of the necessary information. As if they were the stray and vagrant pieces of a jigsaw puzzle roaming all the nooks and crannies of a house. Perhaps it was he who had been carefully observing us. Observing her. Observing me. Observing our apartment. And now he only allowed her to think that it had been her own initiative from the very beginning. Perhaps he had somehow, if not miraculously, learned about my secret action plan. And had anticipated my moves. And had seen through all my motives. And then he had decided to get to me through my charmingly naive daughter. That only child of mine. To get close to me. To win my trust and favor. To catch me ridiculously off guard. And then, ironically, he had decided to lay his muscular, unmistakably predatory, and young, indecently young, hands on me; hands that were as if designed to wring necks and slit throats. And he had decided to do that, all that, to conduct a terrifying pre-emptive strike. It was possible. It was conceivable. And it was more than likely to occur soon. Very soon. It was even more than just possible. And with every discreetly passing second, it seemed more and more inevitable. Like a real downpour when pregnant clouds start crowding the sky and jumping all the heavenly queues.

Did he really intend to attack and harm savagely my most sensitive, most vulnerable point imaginable? The soft spot of mine that had the shape and size of a dainty childish figure and the voice of a tender little girl? Was he openly heading for a direct confrontation with me? Even more so than I had done a few moments ago? I had to get more proofs. I had to get more proven information. More undeniably incriminating evidence capable of corroborating the bold and stunningly daring theory of mine. For I could not afford to make any hasty or ill-considered move and action at this delicate stage of our still undeclared war. Besides, the top priority now, from the point of view of my safety, and of the entire elaborate operation, was establishing the way in which he had come into possession of all the dreadfully sensitive information. I had to establish the way in which he had learned about us. About me. About my, after all, still fresh plans devised no more than a few hours ago. I had to find out how he had learned about my plans that I had not yet managed to discuss with anyone outside my tyrannically balding head. Was there a leak? Had someone tipped him off insolently? Had someone spilled the proverbial beans, beads, or other adorably petite objects? But who? Who was the cause and the reason of that impertinent and gratuitous leak? Who was the cause of that lethal hemorrhage of facts? Of that secrets incontinence? Who? Who was responsible for all that? Who could be so thoroughly corrupt, ethically decayed, and void of any sediments of morals and scruples to go so far as to do something like that? Who was capable of committing an atrocious and simply abominable act like that? Who could do that, whether it was for his own benefit, or other, even if far more altruistic motives and impulses? Who could perpetrate such an act of high moral treason? Who could thus jeopardize the safety of his countrymen as well as the countless lives of those innocent and defenseless human beings? Including my own and that of the delightful progeny of mine?

So I scrutinized, without flinching, for a fraction of a second, that impenitently cruel monster. I scrutinized that beast, hiding with astonishing skillfulness and tenacity behind a surprisingly convincing and well-tailored mask of embarrassment and awkwardness. And I wondered intensely, thus overtaxing my tarnished mind that had grown stale from the long years of mindless bowing and opening doors. And I calculated in my thoughts who could possibly turn out to be the shameless culprit of all this commotion. And I strived to recollect whom I had met on my way that day. Like a taxi driver trying to remember which client has slipped him a handful of chestnuts instead of the more acceptable money. And I tried to guess to whom I might unwittingly have imparted my secret. And who could have been capable of leaking it without a blink of an eye? Either left or right one? I wondered whether it was that new brash bellhop from the fifth floor, covered with that highly unbecoming makeup of swollen pimples. He was the one who had noticed me while he was leaving one of the elevators. He was the one who had then started spying on me furtively as I had been running hectically to and fro along the empty corridors in desperate and somewhat chaotic search of that ominous messenger. Epitomizing all evil. Both already done and yet to come. For I had seen him out of the corner of my slowly retiring eye. I had noticed him even though he had thought that I could not see him through a particularly scrawny and balding fern that, at least in his ungracious mind, had offered him a rather decent cover from my glances. Had he done that? Was he the rat? Was he the infamous rat spreading the plague of death and devastation? Was he the tellingly wet source of this troubling and potentially dangerous leak?

Or perhaps it was the exceedingly amiable elderly cleaning lady from the third floor. Perhaps it was she, who used to greet me with the excited staccato rhythm of her working dentures. And whom I had run into that day on my way downstairs. It was right after my little unfortunate mishap in the banquet hall. It was right after that tragic downfall of my reputation. Had she ably deduced my latent plans and intentions from the theatrically confused arrangement of my facial features? Had she deduced it from my contorted facial features due to which I had borne no resemblance to human beings, but looked more like a real-life variation on the Cubist vision of the world? But was she to blame for it? Was she the one capable of notifying instantly, and without any delays, her unseen yet still menacing principals? Was she? Was she the guilty one?

Or, perhaps, I looked for traitors in all the wrong places? Perhaps the one at fault for all that was nothing else but the tirelessly deceitful inanimate matter? Considering the current level of technological advancement, nothing seemed impossible. Nothing was improbable. Nothing was above suspicion. So I could not trust anything and anyone. For every ostensibly innocent and ordinary-looking detail or trifle might, suddenly, turn out to be a callous informer. A malevolent snitch. A simple spy. Perhaps one of the hotel door handles, my otherwise trustworthy and reliable coworkers, had already been flipped. Perhaps it had been equipped with a handful of sensors, microphones, and detectors. Of all kinds and shapes. Perhaps they had kept sending a myriad of mostly useless and chaotic information about me to the secret headquarters of their operators. Of those insidious rebels. Of those ubiquitous revolutionaries. Perhaps they had kept sending them out of sheer habit only to get lucky that one time. Perhaps they had kept doing it to fish out of the unintelligible babble inundating them every second a single relevant detail about me. Or even, it might have been that unassuming stanchion barrier. It might have been the stanchion barrier that I had embraced, in the passing moment of weakness, in order to restore my endangered both mental and physical equilibrium. And I had done it, perhaps, a dash too trustingly. A bit too carelessly. A hint too unconditionally. And, perhaps, I had done it while forgetting to keep that customary healthy dose of mistrust and skepticism. And now, it had been, surely against its brass will, blackmailed and forced into cooperation. It had been forced into undertaking that immoral espionage activity, by the cunning henchmen of this evil mastermind sitting now right in front of me. This unrivaled colossus of corruption. This matchless giant of moral vandalism. This towering figure of tyranny. If not evil incarnated.

My internal voice kept speaking in this strain. And I rushed to the conclusion that the source of this unforgivable leak had to be summarily found out. It had to be established with utter certainty. And it had to be no less hastily put to death. It had to be put down before my far more important plans and crucial strategies saw the truculent light of betrayal and became compromised irrevocably. For thus they would sabotage all my offensive actions as well as the counterespionage ones. It would be just like in the army whose communication officers generously offer their codebook to the enemy, as a unique Christmas gift, thus crippling and revealing all the movements of their own troops.

But the worst thing was that it was I, and not he, who felt like a victim now. It was I who felt like a defenseless prey and target. It was I who felt as if I were, all of a sudden, unwarrantedly deprived of my status of a hunter. Of my strategic advantage over him. It was I who felt just like an inconsiderate zoo visitor who teases and taunts a lion through the cage bars only to discover that the cage is unlocked and its door left ajar. Or like a man standing not so much eye to eye as eye to claws with a beast ferreting in the trash cans behind his house, to realize that he has foolishly forgotten to load his shotgun after cleaning, and that he has abstractedly left all the shells in the drawer near the kitchen sink. And so, unexpectedly, we switched our roles. We switched them guardedly. We switched them as if we were two tunes etched in a record placed on a perpetually revolving turntable. And I had no other option left but to adapt to the circumstances. And I had to adapt to the new and drastically altered conditions as quickly as possible. As seamlessly as possible. And I could only hope, more or less naively or in vain, that they would promptly switch back anytime soon. I could only hope that they would return to their previous state. Or even that the elusive something or someone would mercifully suggest their brand new arrangement. Because if they did it once, why should they not repeat it and do it again?

I could only count on some surprising rescue. I could only count on some unforeseen act of grace. Perhaps even on that tasteless mechanism of deus ex machina usually specializing in ruining the otherwise impeccably written plays or stories. I could only hope that there were still left in him the vestigial human instincts. Hidden somewhere. Stored somewhere. Calmly lying dormant. Like a nest egg waiting for the hard times under the protective pecuniary wings of the owner. I hoped for those remnants of human emotions and reactions that would, undoubtedly, start protests and boycotts inside him if needed. That would raise an outraged hue and cry if the time came. If the right time came. That would prevent him from assailing me openly here and now. That would not let him put to use his markedly irrepressible fierce animal nature. And the barbarous potential it offered him. And, consequently, to murder me here. Right before the eyes of my splendid

158

daughter. And thus I secretly counted on her swift return. For it was she, and only she, about whom he cared evidently. And her eyes, those indescribably beautiful eyes of hers, could still save me from the fatal destiny. They could still save me from that unenviable fate that kept approaching me inevitably. Inexorably. To the seemingly nervous patter of his fingers on the tabletop. And, certainly, they would be the same absolutely lovable eyes that used to watch me and admire me and follow me indiscriminately throughout her blissful childhood. And so they used to learn and greedily imbibe the nuances of the world, along with its otherwise inscrutable intricacies, from the discreet pantomime of my affectionate gestures. And, perhaps, in exchange for all that, they would give me now an instant, a mere moment, indispensable to regain the edge over him. To regain the upper hand. And then they would allow me to launch a fierce counteroffensive. A relentless counterattack. I would do that just like a boxer who lets his opponent trap him against the ropes only to regroup his energy and muster the last leftovers of his strength right before starting a new thunderstorm of jabs and blows and punches.

For this present yet temporary failure of mine did not change anything between the two of us. Not a bit. Not even a little bit. It neither developed nor terribly impaired anything between us. Any emotional bond or equally profound animosity. It did not change anything. This momentary savoring by me the bitter flavor of being put in the seat of a hopeless victim. This tremendous yet only passing predicament of mine that would promptly go by and perish in the black-and-white whirlwind of the past tense. For it only reinforced my determination and zeal to put a definitive stop to his terror. To his machinations. To his tyranny redolent of the worst of times, of the cruelest of times. To the actions of that unduly wicked man. Of that heartless imitation of a cultured human being.

LECTURER: And so... I've heard that you work in a hotel... in that large hotel downtown... at least that's what I've heard...

159

what I've understood from what she's told me... mentioned to me... that is... your daughter... what your daughter has mentioned to me... Is it nice? Is it nice there? In the hotel, I mean... I think I've passed it once or twice, on one occasion or two... Is it... a nice job? Is it?

And it was then that the sound of his words, the tone of his voice, directed to me and intended for me for the first time that evening, broke that informal code of silence. And it pierced the vague shroud of my stupor. And it pierced the singular curtain of lassitude hitherto tightly enveloping my mind. For it was as if it were trying to mummify it alive. And that voice of his shocked me. That voice flawlessly stylized to pass for a dithery and tremulous one. That voice faking abashment and crippling uncertainty. Perfectly to a fault. And it shocked me unspeakably. And it astonished me ineffably. How impertinent it was! How boundlessly insolent it was! How remorselessly impenitent it aspired to be! And that as if accidental mention of the hotel! Of my dear and cherished workplace! Or even far more than that! That mention of that marvelous place forming an inherent part of me to the point of turning one of the ventricles of my heart into a cute miniature replica of its splendid lobby. That mention uttered in a distinctly offhand and noncommittal fashion. As if it were a mere building! Just some building! Just some nondescript building like many others! Like countless others! That offhand mention trying to reduce that fine edifice to a mere building that one could pass by carelessly on his way through the city to a more interesting place. That irritating mention was a kind of test. It was a kind of litmus paper slyly employed by him in order to examine and test the quickness of my reactions and reflexes. And this question suggesting, between the intangible ink-free lines and layers of it, as if I could possibly be unhappy there. Or, what seemed worse, as if anyone could feel unhappy there in any way. It was nothing else but an uncommonly sensitive barometer that was supposed to detect and probe the limits of my tolerance and mental resistance. How presumptuous of him!

A tide of unbridled anger welled up in me. It welled up in me, and a long parade of its capricious waves kept breaking insistently against the shore of my mental balance. And they kept breaking against it tirelessly although all that was nothing else but an overt tactical trick on his part. An indubitable strategic maneuver. Masked cleverly. Camouflaged vilely. Because it only posed for a harmless question, while, in truth, being designed to catch me unawares, baffle me cruelly, and thwart my own murderous plans. Which trick, unfortunately, I had to admit it reluctantly, he had managed to pull off in the best imaginable manner and style. And for which success I, once again, cursed my nearly chronic inattention. I cursed for it my lack of preparation for that kind of verbal duels. For such intellectual clashes. Because those glaring shortcomings of mine had a habit of painfully manifesting themselves on such occasions. They did that in the form of such cataclysmic mistakes. In the wake of which I was gradually, though grudgingly, inch by inch, ceding the field to my, not so much wiser or more brilliant, but doubtless quicker, opponent. It was, after all, a quite evident offensive action. It was a brazen provocation poorly disguised as an innocuous chitchat concealed right beneath that curtain of seemingly harmless platitudes. Like a child hiding amid the folds of its mother's dress. And it was not daring to veer off, not even for an inch, the beaten track, the well-proven, if not pitifully threadbare, path. Thus it was trying to lull me into a false sense of confidence. Thus it was trying to lure me into that beaten path of clichéd conversations, where, in truth, the answer to each question had been well-known for long. Even long before he had opened his filthy mouth to speak. And even for many past generations.

And so, it had started! The dismal game had begun! The first pawns had gingerly taken up their previously prescribed positions, their starting positions right on the chessboard of our conflict. Like the spouses before yet another marital battle. And I could already hear the stolid and balefully rhythmical ticking of the chess game clock. I could hear it discreetly urging us, the players, to make our moves. I could hear it silently encouraging us to act. And act resolutely. Preferably in the most reckless manner possible. I could hear it silently reminding us that it was about time to take action. To make decisions. And to make sacrifices if needed. And thus it was about time to expose ourselves to the inevitable and unmerciful blows.

Thus, carefully choosing my steps, laboriously mincing my words, I answered him in a similar fashion. I answered him in a strikingly casual fashion. I did that while mimicking his own style that made our still feeble for just sprouting conversation die there. Right on the spot. In the line of its verbal duty. And thus, the immaculate silence started reigning there, between us, during this peculiar interregnum of speech. Checkmate! After all, it was a smart move. A very smart move. It bought me some time. And at a quite affordable price. I bought me some time to think over and ponder the range of my possibilities.

LECTURER: Well... And how long have you been living here... In this city, I mean... How long have you been living in this fine city of ours? I heard... that is... your daughter was so kind to impart that knowledge to me... that you're... not from here... I mean... not from this place... not...

I listened to him patiently. I listened to him intently. I listened to him, waiting for him to finish in order to start talking myself. Like a man hoping to cross the street during the rush hour. I waited for him to finish that spurious torrent of jerking and stammering that might have fooled someone else, but less shrewd than I. That might have killed him from asphyxiation had it only been true. And then I waited for a few heartbeats of the surprisingly resonant silence. And I answered him in exactly the same strain as before. Another smart move.

LECTURER: Well... And how do you like it here... I mean... What do you think about our city... how do you find our marvelous city... our splendid city... that is... well... it's your city as well... at least now... it is now... isn't it?

162

I let yet another incoherent tirade of his pass immediately and be even more quickly forgotten. Like a footprint in the last year's snow. It met the same fate as an ignoble recital of blasphemies that he had just finished uttering in my presence. Then I told him what he wanted to know. Or rather, I told him not exactly what he wanted to know but what I wanted him to ponder and analyze laboriously in the confines of his menacing mind. And, above all, I wanted him to do that in vain. For I wanted only to distract him for as long as an instant or two.

LECTURER: And how about the weather... the weather today is pretty unusual for this time of year... don't you think... that is... sir... don't you think, sir? It is quite... quite... unusual... for this place... I mean... for this fabulous city of ours... it is... well... rather unusual... quite...

Another banal question. And a poorly concealed foot trap. If not a tongue trap. It was another trap awaiting the unaware and unsuspecting foot, or rather, the tongue of a novice. I answered him as scintillatingly as a second earlier.

LECTURER: But... how about your mission? How about that vocation of yours?

I stiffened instantly. I stiffened with fear as I was stunned by the frivolity of his subtle warnings and veiled menaces. For he looked as if he always paid attention to lace velvety compliments with threats. Did he really know about my mission? Was he indeed aware of it? Was he prepared to counteract and mar my elaborate plans? What exactly did he know, if he truly knew anything?

LECTURER: She told me about it... I mean... your daughter told me about it... about the passion and vigor with which you have been approaching your duties... your responsibilities... for decades... for long decades... at least... she said something like that... well... she did...

He spoke with a trace of distinct spuriousness ringing in his voice. Like a note played off-key during a concert. It was tickling the highest registers of my fears. It was tickling those fears that I had to suppress and quench instinctively. I had to do that before it managed to startle me and baffle me to the catastrophic point of noticeability. And so, my still nascent optimism and sense of superiority were nearly killed in the line of duty. Or, at least, they became almost incapacitated. But I dodged that danger, even if my fears still thrived unusually. Because I managed to regain my precious balance in time so as to answer him cunningly.

But then I understood that I could not count on my advantage over him, so stunning, so intimidating, and yet so fragile, so uncertain, for long. Or even forever. I understood that I could not depend on my enormous experience without end. I understood that I could not bet everything I owned and loved and cared for tremendously on such a horse. If it could even be called a horse. And if so, then a finicky one. I understood that I could not bet on such a capricious card. Because not just once during this intimate clash of ours that painful truth transpired thus straining and eventually tearing the tissue of my self-confidence.

And it was then that my suddenly nimble fingers surreptitiously ambled and meandered over the table. Like pianist's hands over a keyboard. They meandered in desperate search of a handkerchief. Of any scrap of paper. Or a stray bit of fabric. Anything, really. Any impromptu writing material. They looked for anything to jot down his inadvertent testimonies upon. And not to miss a single baleful word of them. And to use it, eventually and unmercifully, against him. And thus my fingers, moved stealthily, almost inaudibly, over the plateau of a tabletop. They moved there without any kind of supervision or anyone's control. Or assistance. Or even without asking anyone for directions. They moved over the tabletop crowded with the archipelagoes of sundry plates and peninsulas of the parts of silverware. And that sudden fit of agility was quite surprising. It was quite staggering. Even to me. If not especially to me. It was quite surprising considering their rather crippling age. But they effortlessly maintained that singular quickness even in spite of this handicap. They maintained it like a ghastly creature from a horror story that rebels against its owner and vehemently turns, not so much its back as its palm, on the far more cumbersome rest of its body.

And all that time I strived to pretend interest in the interminable and deliberately banal monologs of my opponent. I strived to pretend that while answering a medley of his equally trivial questions. I did that in an intricate idiom of studied nods as well as careful shakes of my respectably grayish head. And I did that while always paying close, if not insanely close, attention to place them at precisely the right moment. As a kind of motor punctuation marks. But it happened that my restless fingers along with my hand faithfully following in its fingersteps, wandered far, much too far, far beyond the blurry borders of my otherwise still fertile field of vision. It also happened that they indubitably lacked the energy to keep marching. To continue their quest. To hunt for the substitutes of the notepad paper. And it was then that my mind was being instantly bombarded and invaded, thus only deepening the disturbing state of my mental exhaustion, by the flood of images and ideas. Mostly gloomy. Mostly suffused with infinite sorrow. It was a mournful mishmash of them. And all of them depicted the miserable people. The helpless people. The wretched people. The lives of pitiful people. All of them depicted those whose fate was at stake now. All of them. Without any exceptions. And so, all of them depicted those who depended on my ability to move it a little further. To stretch my hand a little more. A bit more.

But then, my vigilant fingertips found and touched and inquisitively started nibbling an edge of a handkerchief. It was peeking out timidly from under my daughter's plate. Thus it resembled a diffident animal trying to hide its head under a large stone and ferreting there busily. And then they wrenched it indelicately from there. And then they brought it back to me, quickly and triumphantly. They brought it back to me. Like a retriever proudly carrying in its mouth a just-shot-down game.

And yet, my current success was only partial. If not a symbolic one. For I still lacked, and I lacked it desperately, some, any, in fact, useful writing implement. I lacked anything that could be paired off unceremoniously with that newly obtained papery trophy. I lacked anything that would be capable of putting his sinister words to paper. Of gathering that lethal dose of incriminating evidence. And thus of forming an irrefutable bill of indictment and verdict in one.

Meantime, the next ones of his unmistakable threats and disconcerting innuendoes kept raining on me. One after another. One following another. Incessantly. Tirelessly. Like the words of praise on a talented debutante. After which inescapable contact they melted and evaporated and then vanished instantly, a mere second after reacting with the habitually skeptical air that remained implacably hostile toward all one's innermost thoughts and opinions and ruminations. It was as if they were stray snowflakes, those nameless bastard children of a blizzard. And they did that without waiting for me. They did that without waiting for anyone capable of capturing them and holding them captive and immortalizing them on paper. One after another. One following another.

Thus, I panicked momentarily. I panicked as easily as a hotheaded and inexperienced youth. I panicked when my mind, after all, rather fatigued and impaired by age, proved to be surprisingly unable to cope with such an unbridled inflow of raucous information. Of his overly longish monologs. Of his excessively elaborate anecdotes. For it was as if they were deliberately defying memorization. And yet, all of them contained a hidden message. All of them concealed a second meaning. All of them guarded a no less mysterious key. And it was a key buried somewhere deep down inside each one of them. It was buried there like a belligerent blade lying dormant within the insides of a pocketknife.

And it was then that I nervously began scratching and laboriously carving my hasty notes in the tissue of this handkerchief. I began scratching them with my, fortunately, untrimmed fingernails. More or less ably. More or less successfully. And due to those improvised measures all the thus created jottings bordered perilously on the usually slippery verge of readability. And thus, equipped with the impromptu counterparts of a pencil and a notebook, I was like a child pretending to be an imaginary journalist. And only then I endeavored to catch as many useful and appetizing bits of information as possible. And only then I labored to record his words as accurately as feasible. To the letter. To the comma. To the pause. I did that to every dot as well as any other seemingly trivial and irrelevant punctuation mark that might irresponsibly have been omitted by someone even a bit less perceptive than I was. I hunted for every, even the tiniest, detail or nuance on the roadmap of his speech. I hunted for anything that could be of great importance to all those extravagantly learned specialists and other experts, being, naturally, far more intelligent than I would ever be. I mean the ones whom the insanely powerful elites would hurriedly appoint to the case. I mean those who would be hired in order to analyze and scrutinize and carefully dissect my hasty and incoherent scribbles. I mean those who would be ordered to disassemble them to the very basic ingredients. As if my notes were the stolen cars being callously eviscerated in a chop shop.

I knew that I did not have too much time. I knew that I had no time at all. I perfectly understood that the already prolonged absence of my little daughter could not last forever. It could not, even if to me time seemed to be passing rather desultorily. If not downright lazily. It could not, even if time's otherwise inexorable hemorrhage ceased altogether. And I still had to ask him so many questions. I still had to gather so much information. So many testimonies. I still had to learn so many overwhelmingly ruinous facts concerning all the frighteningly subversive plans of his. And I mean all his seditious speeches, incendiary agitation, numerous provocations, as well as the acts of ruthless sabotage. I mean all those insidious ingredients which, when mixed in the flawlessly chosen proportions, would give an unscheduled birth to a vehement and irrepressible rebellion of the masses. Of the filthy masses. Of the annoyed masses. Of the wild masses.

But I could not do that in front of her. Oh, no. I could not do that to her. Her immensely delicate nature would not withstand such a shock. Even now. Especially now. At this moment. She would not withstand it in this state of her tremendous enchantment with that man. That villainous character. That wicked antagonist of my story. And not only would she be unable to withstand it, but also, her delicate heart, beating only and incessantly to the accompaniment of her innocent love, would not take well the severe withdrawal symptoms. Those inevitable aftereffects of every infatuation. That was why I was writing fast. That was why I was writing like a madman. And with each second I was writing faster and faster. I was writing nearly at a breakneck, if not breaknail, pace. Like a seismograph striving to catch up with the most abrupt and violent earthquakes. I was writing while rapidly attaining and exceeding dangerously the limits of endurance of my long-outdated muscles and tendons. Long-untouched. Long-uncared-for. And long-unserviced properly. So I was writing while scraping my fingernails to the skin. Right to my sallow skin. I did that while clumsily cutting through the soft and frail fibers of the handkerchief. Over and over. Again and again. And due to that, I had to start my frantic espionage endeavors anew. All over again. From scratch. If not from a cut. A calamitously deep cut. Then, it repeatedly turned out that the aftermath of my botched efforts was closer to a total disaster than I had previously presumed. And I barely missed it, by a fingernail's breadth. For, every now and then, all the invaluable testimonies and unwitting admissions of guilt that I managed to extract from him adroitly and record them meticulously had been thus torn apart and destroyed beyond recognition. Beyond repair. And they were, from then on, of no use to anyone. And they were forcing me to start from the beginning on the other and still virginal part of that pitiful handkerchief. And only in the most intimate depths of my heart, bristling with the last lumps of touching naivety, I hoped that the thus created gaps and deficiencies in the body of evidence would not distort the final, and doubtless sprawling and inconsolably abstract, picture too much. I hoped that they would not contaminate the samples of his guilt too severely. Too noticeably. Too irrevocably. For one might have expected at least a dash of competency from someone with my experience.

And I could not consent to that. I could not allow that to happen. For I had only a single chance. One and unrepeatable. I had only a single chance without the possibility of any consoling replays, overtimes, or rematches. I had only a single chance to destroy this man. This impregnable personification of all that was evil and appalling and hideous and subversive in human nature. And along with that, I had only a sole chance to thwart his masterful plans, his vile intentions, right before saving humanity in the last scene of a particularly trite movie called life. And I already sensed on my shoulders the oppressive weight of this enormous responsibility. I sensed it all the time. And it was strikingly akin to that suffered by a writer who while concocting the ending of his debut novel cannot help comparing it with the endings of all the great novels from the past.

So I knew that I had to act quickly. Astonishingly quickly. So I knew that I had to move to the next set of questions. Those difficult questions. Those inconvenient questions. I had to move to all those inescapable questions, that would, inevitably, betray me and unmask me and reveal my real self as well as my true motives, if he, indeed, had not yet managed to guess any of that. I had no other choice but to take that risk. I had to take that perilous path. I had to do that, even if there was not enough time to segue into that new road of our conversation smoothly and seamlessly without raising his suspicions. For I had to switch the track without incurring the risk of derailing the speeding train of our dire thoughts. I had to move intrepidly to this unexplored and inhospitable marshy ground. And due to that, there was a danger, a rather serious and realistic one, that my hasty attempts to change the subject would sound a bit too artificially. There was a risk that they would have that air of forced effort hovering about them tellingly. Like the words of an apology coming from an inveterate hoodlum. And there was a risk that, consequently, he would come out of this present trance of his, smell an ambush, sense a trap, and bolt away. And then he also would not forget to erase all the traces of his own presence and vanish utterly. And after that strategic trick, he would doubtless pay attention not to cross the threshold of a dim and squalid hideout of his till the time of taking his place in the first row of an impending revolution. He would. Certainly, he would.

Thus I could not shy away from taking this risk any longer. I could not shy away from that even though a mere thought of it was jeopardizing the consistency of my already deficit smile. But then, once again, as well as quite surprisingly, it seemed that someone answered my hectic prayers. Instead of using that typically mute celestial answering machine of the ever-silent sky. And it seemed that someone actually answered my unspoken calls that, otherwise, might have been ringing and lamenting to the very end of the world. Or even longer. And it seemed that someone even deigned to call me back without any delays. And then someone proprietarily ordered my inscrutable adversary to give me a head start. To go easy on me. To let his well-tailored and closely-fitting mask of studied pose slide down a little. And thus it formed a gap, a cleft, a chink, in that armor of his through which I could distinctly see the unspeakable enormity of undiluted evil slumbering inside him. And through that cleft, I could see that evil and admire it in all its unabridged formidable glory. Like a wife who stumbles upon her faithless husband's secret notebook bursting with the phone numbers of his faithful lovers and casual sexual acquaintances. And, what was even more important, through that cleft I could inflict severe wounds on him. I could inflict them by stabbing and jabbing and prickling him furtively. Every now and then. Once in a while. And it made an ineffaceable impression upon me. And it made a startling impression on me. And so he started a new chapter in this thrilling game of ours.

LECTURER: ...Yes, exactly! Yes! I like the way it sounded. I like it very much, indeed. Passion. That's it! Passion is the right word! A key word! Or better, a word that is both a key and a lock! Two in one! Passion. Decidedly. Teaching art is my true passion. It's my vocation. Exactly like in your case... I mean... according to the things that she... that your daughter... what she imparted to me... And so, we have something in common after all. Isn't that great? Isn't that marvelous? Isn't that... something? But those lectures are only a warm-up. I'm not going to be hung up on them for too long. It's only a beginning. It's only an interlude to something greater... to something much bigger... and much more impressive.

I froze petrified at the sound of those words. I petrified like a tiny field mouse that suddenly senses on its hitherto unsuspecting back a gloomy coverlet of heavy shadow being cast by a majestic eagle gliding far up, high up, in the cynic sky that had seen similar atrocities so many times, in countless variants, that it does not have enough strength left to frown at it once again.

That was it. It was my chance. It was my time. It was my moment, for which I had been waiting impatiently. I had been waiting for it like a crocodile lurking right beneath the surface of the swamp, with only its eyes, those dreadful twin periscopes, emerging from the water and glancing around murderously. Instantly, I followed its lead. Just like a bloodhound whose vigilant nose has been tickled by the odor of the nervousness crystallizing on the unwashed clothes of a shaky fugitive on the run. And then, with the sensitivity of a violinist who is about to pull the right string at the right time, I incredulously inquired what he meant by all that. By something much bigger. By something much more impressive.

LECTURER: It's my grand plan. It's my master plan. It's my great dream, you know. It'll be something. It surely will be something though I'm still not sure what, that will resonate widely and loudly in society. And that's the most important thing right now, isn't it? The society will echo with it. And what echo it will be! It'll be a colorful echo! It'll be a garish echo! It'll be a real blaze of colors in this hopelessly gray, bleak, and uniformly uninspired world.

So that was it. The end was near. A total annihilation was within my tremulous hand's reach. For one did not need a particularly bright detective to put all those facts together. One did not need anyone of the kind to complete that unsophisticated jigsaw puzzle. One did not need that to read between the lines with the proficiency of a literary academic being remarkably competent at interpreting and reinterpreting and deciphering a plethora of messages and subtexts crammed in between the lines of ostensibly inscrutable texts. One just had to listen to him. That suspicious multitude of colors. That telling blaze of colors. A blaze, he said. That was exactly what he said. A blaze! Not to mention the disturbing echo! For he repeated this word more than twice. It was all pathetically obvious and simple to me. He meant blood. He, along with this feral disciples, evidently planned some kind of carnage. Some kind of unthinkable bloodbath. But where? But when? In what way? A shooting? It would be too loud. Even unpleasantly loud. What then? An attack of a mad knifer? Much too dirty. A charge of an insane bull in the crowded street? Far too chaotic. Then I got it. Then it occurred to me. Then

I got it instantly. As if I received a telepathic telegram from him replete with the constellations of disjointed stops and dots. There was no other way. The loud echo, spoke, if not screamed stridently, for itself clearly enough. It made perfect sense. Fantastic even. Undoubtedly, it was all about a bombing. He planned a bombing to gut the city and the incurably complacent, overly conceited, society along with it. But when? But where? But who would be the target? Who else was involved in this abhorrent conspiracy? I only prayed to everyone who was above me, higher than me, even if it was an impoverished deity or a stray airplane pilot or the one lingering inside a listlessly gliding balloon, that it would not be my daughter. Everyone but not my little adorable daughter. I had to know that. I had to learn that. So I asked him delicately.

LECTURER: What do you mean by alone? I'm not alone. I won't do it alone. It's absolutely impossible to do it alone! But I admire your sense of humor, so wild, so unexpected. Alone! Hah! That's a good one! Besides, I would never manage to do it alone. It's also completely pointless to do it alone. After all, I want to do it for them, for the young ones, for the uncorrupted ones. I want to involve them in it. I want to inspire them a little bit. I want to give them some kind of goal... some aim in life... A, well... some kind of... target. If you know what I mean by that. Perhaps I'll manage to discover a morsel of talent in one of them. Perhaps, under my auspices, one of them will become famous. Even if for a brief moment... Even if for an initial explosive moment of their careers.

And so he started training suicide bombers. There was no doubt about it. He began organizing and mobilizing his own youthful guerilla fighters. His own fanatic and still pimply death squads. And what could be done to prevent that inconceivable nightmare from happening other than falling straight into the open arms of hysterics? Could there still happen a sort of vehement catharsis capable of startling people out of that oppressive trance enslaving their free will and limiting the clarity of their reasoning? Was there any moral alarm clock? Could it still awake them? Even his vulgar as well as benighted supporters. Even those idle and idiotic masses remaining indifferent about everything that was taking place around them. Could there? Well, could there?

Then I heard the muted sound of my daughter's indescribably light footsteps, akin to the patter of rain on the windowsill. And I heard it, for she was, apparently, heading back to the room. I had no time. I had so little time and so many questions to ask! So I inquired interrogatively how he intended to recruit the candidates, how he intended to select them, winnow them, and turn them into the most ruthless killing machines imaginable.

LECTURER: I'd like to stimulate their minds, to broaden their horizons... I'd like to instill in them the love, the unbridled and shameless love of art, with all its colorful subtleties as well as nuances... I'd like to show them... to prove to them... to make them believe and understand that art, and high art especially, is not dead... that it's alive and kicking, kicking like a newly born horse! That art is not some mishmash of unintelligible mumblings and scribbles of some dead old men from the past... That it simply isn't true that art has no impact on, and no connection with, the artless modern world, along with its loud complexities and clamorous problems and seriously raucous predicaments... That art is, has been, and will always be, universal. That it is as readable and relevant to the current generation as it has been to the past ones and will be to those yet to come... That art, great art, magnificent art, is the only kind of currency that you can bet your money on at every single point in the history of mankind. Yes, sir!

And so he intended to start with brainwashing. Gently. Slowly. And so he intended to start all that while lacing the fatuous and plainly ridiculous arguments filling his soliloquy, that was akin to a slap in the face of every thinking individual, with the specious subtle persuasion and cajoling.

174

For, apparently, at first, he intended to befriend his carefully selected prey. Evidently, he intended to innocently win its favor and trust without raising any suspicions. And then, when its guard would be lowered and arms open wide for him, he would begin undermining everyone's authority in its eyes. Like a barker of some sect or other. He would try to erode its trust in others. In elders. In adults. In its parents. Even in its parents. Especially in its parents. And this fact was most painful to me. And he would surely choose as his targets those helpless and hopeless young people. Still gullible. Still idealistic. Still not protected by an impenetrable shield of experience. He would choose those young people still not covered with the thick varnish of skepticism and first-rate mistrust. For the invariably foolish though zealous youth will always be defeated, and defeated absolutely, by the joint forces of maturity and wisdom. It would always be defeated, just like a novice chess player who cannot defend himself effectively against a cascade of cunning tricks and moves of his much more seasoned opponent, for he does not even know what to expect when he tries to expect something. And so, it must have happened to her. This is what had happened to my petite daughter. And so, he had been callously practicing and polishing and exercising a repertoire of his unspeakable gimmicks and routines on her. On my delightful offspring. On my fragile child. As if she were his verbal sparring partner. And so he had chosen her impertinently as a test object. As an easy prey. And then he had been experimenting on her with reprehensible impunity as though she were some kind of laboratory rat, mouse, rabbit, or a deceptively mousy type of human being. That will be the day! Over my wrinkled body!

But even though I simmered and raged inwardly, I only smiled outwardly. And I spoke in the most amiable and serene voice that I could possibly afford at that stressful instant. At that unnerving instant. I spoke like that while getting rid of the last remainders of appearances. Like a snake shedding its

175

worn-out skin. I spoke in this manner while abruptly disposing of that already tattered mask of scruples and meaningless polished phrases. For there was no more time for that passionless foreplay. For there was no more time for games or charades of any kind. So I asked him directly what would be their first target. I asked him who would fall the first victim of his untamed radicalism and fanaticism. I asked him who would be inevitably punished for all the misfortunes and fiascos that had befallen him personally, thus triggering in him such an eruption of disgust and hatred for others. But, above all, for the affluent others. And although I asked him that in a fairly steady tone of voice, I trembled right behind the quickly crumbling facade of my sallow face. Like a mouse hiding behind a cardboard box. And I trembled there uncontrollably. And I quivered rhythmically afraid that I overdid it. I was terribly afraid that I went too far this time. That I blew it completely when I was so close. So unthinkably close to exposing his macabre intrigues.

LECTURER: Right in the heart! That's where we're going to hit them! Right in their insipid heart! I'd like to blow up that incredibly and invincibly gray wall of dullness. I'd like to see it crumbling and falling apart. I'd like to see people discovering in themselves at least a dash of artistic sensitivity... not much... only a dash... a little bit of it would do... regardless of their social position, wealth, or education... Yes... even education! That's why my workshops will be directed toward everyone... toward everyone who is willing to listen and feel and savor art with his or her senses as it is...

To blow up a wall! A gray wall! A dull wall! Then an image, a spine-chilling image flashed and flitted swiftly through my mind. As a belated firework flaring up a week after the New Year's Eve. Then it started circulating in my body. In my veins. In the smallest and tightest of tubes forming my cardiovascular system. Faster and faster. More and more intensely. It started circulating there to the point of bypassing my consciousness in exile completely and becoming an integral and ingrained part of my tissues.

And I did not know why but I instantly thought about a particular wall. The tall wall. The gray wall bordering my beloved hotel on one side. Like a crust enveloping a slice of bread. And thus it was neighboring the disgustingly commercial part of the city. Over which fact I lamented constantly. Over which fact I grieved everlastingly. For it was the only flaw in the otherwise unblemished exquisiteness of that place. And so he chose it as his target. He directed the blade of his anger and discontentment at that marvelous refuge of all the innocently wealthy and powerful people of this world. He directed his anger at that last bastion of elitism as well as expensive beauty in this dreadfully egalitarian world.

There was some perverse and twisted logic in it. I could not deny it. I could not dismiss it. Even if I despised it viscerally. Because, at any rate, he schemed and yearned to destroy my dearest and most hallowed place of all. Then my heart contracted painfully. Like a suddenly demolished edifice. From then on, it was personal. Definitely personal.

A spasm of genuine fear traveled through me. Now up. Now down. Like an indecisive elevator. And a tide of strong and often conflicting emotions tore me and maltreated me violently. It tore me while pulling me in one direction, then in the other. And it tore me, like a pack of well-behaved dogs assailing a trespasser and tugging at one of his sleeves, then the other, as though they wanted to be overly hospitable and show him around the property, each one of them in a different direction. I could hardly hold the handkerchief in my hand. And my obedient fingernail kept sliding and skidding helplessly on its hitherto rather cooperative surface. It was like a greenhorn, if not green-skate, ice skater proving to be unable to get even temporary traction on ice. Not much. Not even a dash of it.

And as my desperate efforts gained momentum, a series of successive waves of tears pressed and rudely pushed its way to my defenseless eyes. As if out of spite. As if to ridicule me. Of which every new one was more powerful than the former. So I could barely withstand them. So every following one threatened to bypass and overcome the flood embankments of my eyelids. And so it would make me burst into tears. Into poignant and pitiful tears of the helpless old man.

And then I was about to hit him with yet another question. I was about to follow this extraordinary blow with an even more precise and unequivocal one. I was about to hit him with that to clarify this disconcerting piece of news. To corroborate or refute those horrific speculations. To learn something more. To learn something else. To discover the details of that ghastly act of violence and undiluted barbarity, to the tiniest, to the final, and to the most irrelevant nuance. To find out the name of a potential bomber. His personal details. His description. For, after all, no one supposed that he was inclined to do it himself. Personally. Singlehandedly. I was about to ask him all that to determine the name of the explosive material. Its strength. Its quality. Its detectability. But, above all, I was about to do that to learn the number of expected casualties. And the precise date of the planned bombing. I hoped to learn that and inform the appropriate services and, consequently, save as many of those priceless, invaluable, for insanely affluent, lives as possible. But before I managed to do any of that, before I brought myself to do that, in the doorway almost imperceptibly had materialized the figure of my caring daughter. She had done it like the bailiff in the house of a chronic debtor. Instantly, she stared at me with that long and lingering gaze of her loving eyes. And it was that special gaze that she used to bestow upon me whenever I talked too long. She used to bestow it upon me to express her pride in my impressive and unrestrained wisdom.

And only then I ceased to speak. And only then the frantic delirious dance of my fingernails over the handkerchief stopped altogether. Then she approached the table with that

178

indescribably light gait of hers, hardly touching the floor. She approached it, like a moonwalker on a stroll. And thus she unwittingly mimicked the way, the exact way, in which she used to move around when she was a child of five playfully jumping over the, visible only to her, imaginary obstacles. Without a word, she took her place beside that immoral man. Then she placed in front of him a set of keys as if it were the next dish during a hardly sumptuous meal. But these keys seemed to be disturbingly familiar to me. And then there sounded her voice. Her mellow and demure voice. And every single tone or note of it was like the finest kind of candy to my fatherly heart hungering and thirsting for such filial delicacies.

DAUGHTER: This is it. That's the thing I was talking about. That's our spare set of keys. You can use it if you want. You can use it if you like.

What kind of keys were they, I inquired lovingly.

DAUGHTER: These are keys to our apartment. He'll stay with us for a few days... weeks maybe. He'll be our guest till he decides to move further with his lectures. There's no point in looking for a room in a hotel right now. At this time of night. So he'll stay here. He'll stay with us.

She declared in this enchantingly chirpy voice of hers.

A new and terrifying reality started dawning there. Everywhere around me. And my hope for a quick and peaceful solution of that farce, that dangerous farce, but a farce nevertheless, grew increasingly difficult to nourish and sustain. Meantime I was held hostage to my own previous actions and decisions. I was a hostage to it, like a funeral cortège that follows its once set morbid course and cannot veer off it even for a single

179

frivolous instant. For I could not afford to fritter away any new occasions to vanquish that man. I could not abandon my challenging task. I could not do that even though it became an insupportable burden to me. I could not do that even though carrying everywhere around with me a set of clean notebooks and freshly sharpened pencils became an incredibly troubling ritual. And even, every now and then, it could be the source of mild embarrassment to my daughter and me. For it was rather difficult to disguise it as anything or dismiss it lightly. Just like a knife being carried into the courtroom.

Once, for instance, to the ineffable delight of my dear daughter, playfully brandishing her still little fists in my honor, I joined them for a walk. I joined them for a tour around the local art galleries and museums. And it was during this leisurely stroll in the realm of high art that this insufferable radical masquerading as an insufferable charmer coquetted and flirted with her shamelessly and tried to wheedle his way into her mind. Into her lovely mind. He did all that by lavishing on her the supposedly inadvertent compliments. Like an old Christmas tree showering its dry needles everywhere around it. He lavished them on her as he was talking volubly about this or that magnificent piece of art. He lavished them on her as he was uttering a sententious punch line or two. He did that while always infallibly managing to conjure an excellent, yet in truth deeply distorted and fraudulent, anecdote about this or that painting that we were passing abstractedly. About this or that otherwise obscure installation or sculpture. However, I realized perfectly that he meant something else. I realized that behind this tight and impervious cordon of his eloquent words and learned sentences was hiding and lurking something far more disquieting than the generic tidbits about those stale products of some artists' imagination. For, in truth, all those zealous visits to these temples of human creativity were dictated by a more practical ulterior motive. A far more practical one. A far more sinister one. Because he not so much looked for some excellent work of art to feast his eyes on as he simply was in need of a large painting. And he needed it to cover a similarly large hole in a wall, which he intended to drill ruthlessly in the wall of my dear hotel. He intended to drill it there to slip in through it unnoticed. Like an eviction notice being slipped secretly under the door. He intended to plant a bomb there and slink out of the building in time before anyone noticed the surprising surfeit of paintings on the already richly adorned walls. His allegedly ingenious tricks and schemes were no secrets to me. I saw through them. Through all of them. I saw through them as easily and effortlessly as if I were a seasoned radiographer who, from watching X-ray photographs all his professional life, had developed a kind of X-ray generator in his eyes. But when I was at the point of jotting down the most relevant part, the most crucial part, of his longish and tedious testimony, the sheer enormity of whose consequences would surely tackle him as well as knock him off his feet in a single move, just then my notebook ran out of blank pages. So, I cursed and berated myself fiercely. I admonished myself for this unforgivable oversight. For this intolerable negligence on my part. And it did not help that I had, after all, been following him all the time, that vicious excuse for a human being, with the incessantly vigilant notebooks in my hand. Day after day. Week after week. Hour after hour. And thus I kept wasting the whole armfuls of similar pages. And they, to tell the truth, had to run out sooner or later, one way or the other. Like ideas in the mind of an overtaxed writer. Then, desperate, suffering an unaccountable mental anguish, I knew that I could not slacken my pace even a little bit. I could not leave them alone for a little while. I could not do that without losing irretrievably some of the most startling of his confessions. So I instinctively snatched some unfortunate piece of paper that had recklessly strayed into my nearest vicinity. And I started hastily covering it with my unintelligible notes. And thus I strived to reconstruct all that he had managed to say

181

in the meantime. Word for word. Sentence for sentence. Like a composite artist of today trying to recreate the image of a burglar from the day before. I was doing that frantically till a burly security guard helped me to realize that this new and wonderful notebook of mine was, in truth, something else. For, in truth, it was a sketchbook of a student of an academy of fine arts, who in his spare time used to come there and copy the techniques of the old masters straight from their renowned paintings. And he now demanded the return of his papery property. He wanted it back although it was by then densely covered with my frolicsomely winding scribbles and doodles, which also could be considered a form of art, yes, but with bold pretensions to the art of espionage.

Some other time, an oddly similar situation occurred. It was when, in a restaurant, in the middle of dinner, to which I took the liberty of accompanying them to their great content-ment and satisfaction, my otherwise faithful pen betrayed me ignobly. For it quit on me rudely. If not treacherously. Like an escape car in the middle of a heist. It quit on me making this unparalleled act of insubordination a case for a court martial. But having no time for such trifles, as I was anxious to finish my task, I only groaned irritably and then was forced to look for some other writing implement to fill in for it. And I found it. I found it rather quickly. Yet I did that only to discover that it was a vagrant lipstick of some elegant lady whose far less elegant husband began brandishing his fists at me. And this bizarre behavior of his put me off considerably. It put me off ineffably. For, it was our private code. Our intimate ritual. Our most sacred idiom. It was a code that had been developed and then cultivated by my taciturn daughter and me. And he had no right, no right whatsoever, to copy it or mimic it. Let alone mock it insolently. He had no right to do that even if he had learned it by spying on us at one time or another.

And yet, in spite of those and many other mishaps and blunders, I quite quickly managed to collect an impressive amount of evidence incriminating this man beyond a reasonable doubt. More or less spectacular. More or less amusing. I had an overwhelming armful of various papers, folders, notebooks, newspaper clippings, and bits of handkerchiefs. I had in my possession everything on which could be fitted, if required, a single word. A crucial word of his devastating confession. I had everything on which could be fitted anything that was capable of not so much tipping as swinging the stubborn scales of justice to my side. That only true and right side of the conflict. As if they were a wrecking ball threatening a building. I had several fragments of his clothes, parts of his garments, that I had stolen furtively from his room under the cozy cover of darkness. I had the objects that he had touched. I had the objects that he had innocently brushed against. Often inadvertently. Often unknowingly. And those objects I had then secured and described and cataloged scrupulously. Like a fastidious botanist collecting the samples of sundry plants. I had done that over the course of the first few days of his unwelcome sojourn in our apartment.

Without delaying too long, while limping and staggering clumsily under the inculpatory weight of that devastating evidence, I directed my steps to the nearest police station. For I wanted, as a result of my elaborate calculations, to try to settle the whole matter peacefully. To cope with it on the lowest possible level. I wanted to settle it without unnecessarily troubling my wealthy principals and mentors with a mishmash of unpleasant details and procedural issues. For I hoped secretly that a much greater prize and praise would await me, if I managed to resolve the whole predicament singlehandedly. It would await me there. Like a gilded trophy under a checkered flag. It would be given to me without a doubt, if I reported to them afterward that there had once been such a horrible man. Such a conniving man. Such a dreadful man. That there had been such an incomparable threat to everything that already lived and was yet to come. And who had himself died miserably. Who was no more. Who had died whether due to capital punishment or having rotted in prison. In inhumane conditions perfectly befitting such an inhuman beast as he was.

Thus, I bravely resisted the temptation to continue, most probably without end, the process of gathering various proofs, clues, and jagged scraps of testimonies. Like an avowed scavenger. For I would have continued to do so in the deceptive hope that each new bit of evidence, that each chunk of it, would have turned out to be even more relevant, even more irrefutable, even more unequivocal as well as less ambiguous, and, above all, even more valuable than all the things I had collected until that moment taken together. Then I promptly scrambled into an asthmatically wheezing bus. I took a seat, hardly managing to squeeze in there with a bulging bundle of papers resting on my thin elderly laps tremulous with excitement. As if I were carrying a baby. And I proudly looked ahead ready to set off on a new part of my adventure. Of my unexpectedly thrilling adventure.

And nothing appeared to be capable of daunting me and deterring me and startling me out of my good mood. And nothing could possibly spoil my exceptionally high spirits. In fact, they were so incredibly high that literally soaring up. High up into the sky. They were gliding high above all those unbearably commonplace and tediously ordinary people. Engulfing me. Surrounding me. Trying to drown me in their filthy mass. Like a flood of waste leaking from a busted sewer pipe. They glided above those dirty people. Those dirty people. They glided above all those dreadfully typical representatives of the proverbial benighted masses, whose incipient revolt I was going to forestall and quench and nip in its revolutionary bud. I was going to do that with this deceptively unassuming bundle of papers. Of whose existence they were not even aware. Not in the least.

And I did not even care that this or that page of the longish transcript of his extremely significant telephone conversations fell out of my hand. I did not care that it concluded its suicidal fall right in the gutter. And I did not care that I had had to both cleverly and masterfully eavesdrop on his conversations to get it by pressing my incurably curious ears, now left, now right one, to a crack in the wall marking the place where a door had once been. I did not care about that. I also did not feel obliged to weep for an instant when a faithful copy of his hasty notes and annotations to one of his lectures absconded from my embrace and flew away. Far away. I did not care that it flew away on the crest of a gust of wind, only to get caught by an outspread branch of a tree and start pretending that it was an overgrown leaf. I did not care that I had gotten those notes by laboriously shading the seemingly blank page of his notepad with a pencil thus following a quite rumpled but certainly trite example of fast-talking detectives. I did not care about that at all. Because I had already collected enough evidence, more than I really needed, to prove my murderous point. I had collected enough of it to put him away for life. If not two. Or even, several consecutive life sentences at once. If the court only decided that way. Thus I could offer him a rare and perverted kind of immortality.

I had to admit gingerly that it was quite an exciting feeling. It was a tremendously exciting feeling. It was a fantastic feeling to possess a key to the destruction of their ignoble plans. It was exciting to have it here. So close to them. Right next to them. Within reach of their cruel and crude hands. Which key they could easily have taken away from me. The elderly me. The drooling me. The tottering me. They could easily have done it if only they had wanted to. If only they had known that I had it here with me. And it added, if not only lent generously, an immensely pleasurable dash of perversity to my already satisfying mission. It resembled a quite thrilling scene from a threadbare historical drama I had seen some time ago, in which a group of haughty conquistadors was eating a meal with the members of some tribe welcoming them earnestly, with their arms open wide, with their granaries open even

185

wider, even though those same arms would be either manacled or chopped off entirely when the inevitable and ruthless conquest of paradise began for good.

Then, I noticed a pair of bums sitting a few seats ahead of me. That hardly adorable couple. Evidently very inebriated. Evidently very mumbling. And evidently very unwashed. The woman perched precariously on a man's lap. She sat there rhythmically rocking back and forth. Like an unwanted orphan. Meantime, the man kept mumbling something unintelligibly, while trying to put to use his impoverished dictionary and an equally poor excuse for a human language. He talked like that all the while stammering and spluttering mercilessly.

MAN: I won't leave you. I won't do that. I know you're afraid of that, but I won't do that. I'll be with you. I'll always be with you. I won't ever do that.

WOMAN: Stop saying that. Stop repeating that all the time. Who do you think you are? You're not that special. You're not that great! You're not! I could have been with anyone! I could have had anyone! I still can have any man I want!

I could not stop smiling. I could not help smiling wryly at the overwhelming level of pathetic delusion from which many people tend to suffer unknowingly. For many people suffer from it without even suspecting it. Faintly. Vaguely. They do that without having the slightest inkling of what is really happening around them. Like all those playing hide-and-seek still with their eyes covered. They do that even without noticing any telltale or discernible symptoms that could warn them, even out of sheer cordiality, as well as spare them the tragedy of unwitting humiliation. I smiled at those people. I smiled at the way that such nearsighted people, whose sight is clouded by the vapors of unwarranted conceit, are likely to overestimate their importance or skills or their sheer personal value as human beings. And smiling this way, I firmly grasped that slightly tattered folder. And I pressed it to my visibly sagging chest. Like an inventor cradling his most ingenious invention.

I pressed it as it was bursting with a myriad of revealing notes and careful jottings and detailed reports and records of my weeks-long conversations with the most sinister creature dwelling in my apartment.

I was going to put my devious plan into action. I was going to make use of it at last. That was why my astonishment was so enormous, so profound, and so indescribable when I finally reached the nearest police station. That was why my astonishment was so overpowering when I was escorted right from the door by a dense net of countless gazes. All curious and incredulous. All suspicious and mistrustful. It was as if they were keeping me on an invisible leash. For it was then that I encountered an insurmountable wall of misunderstanding and reluctance and apprehension separating me from those people working there. It was akin to the intractable nuances and differences separating two people from two different cultures. And nothing could possibly pierce it or tear it down. Even for a single instant. Not even one.

So, I had toiled and struggled with all my elderly might to recount the detailed description of the whole case. Of that terrifying case. Of that dreadful case. I had toiled to do that as faithfully as possible. I had even scrupulously learned all its details by my dedicated heart. I had learned that in order to be able to outline the formidable scale of the problem. In as few succinct words as I could. As enthrallingly as it was within my capabilities. I had learned all that to describe to them the complexity of the danger threatening the only seemingly immutable peace and stability and moral order of our civilized world.

Unfortunately, in spite of my best intentions I did not avoid making mistakes. I could not possibly avoid them. Like a dentist from time to time accidentally pulling out a healthy tooth or two. I did not avoid the ones like when I twisted and distorted the meanings of the most crucial sentences and arguments of his tirades. I did that, accidentally and also comically, due to the unexpected slips of the fingernail that had

187

been putting them down on a handkerchief. Thus I triggered a few brief ripples of laughter. Thus I triggered them and made them travel the length and breadth of the surface of the crowd filling the room. And to that joyful mood, I also succumbed involuntarily. Once or twice. Now and then. I did that only to silence them with the next terrifying fact about my devilish tenant.

But, regardless of my efforts, I could not help noticing a feverish exchange of bewildered and quizzical glances between my listeners avidly sporting all the shades of blue. I could not help noticing that secret communication akin to a kind of local currency. And it did not help at all that I rashly started producing from my dog-eared folder the whole handfuls of proofs of his guilt. All conclusive and indisputable. All horrid and fatal. It did not help at all that I started heaping those things, rather sloppily, rather clumsily, onto the front desk. In front of the clearly bemused police offers. I did not fail to show them, among others, an inconspicuous shot glass adorned with a curious pattern of his fingerprints. Like the wall of an ancient temple with hieroglyphs. It was from that very glass that the malicious culprit had been drinking liquor served by my hospitable daughter the previous night. I showed them a larger beverage glass with which he had been washing down the liquor. I showed them a fork with a bit of food still being cruelly impaled on it. Like the head of a defeated enemy. For with it, he had been shoveling down the splendid dinner to put some nourishing undercoat before pouring in the alcohol. And it could be used, every little chunk and crumb of it, naturally with the invaluable assistance of modern technology, to reconstruct his bite, surely as crooked as he was, and compare it with the dental records. There was also a potpourri of innumerable reports, photographs, and transcripts of his conversations with us and those that he had conducted via phone with others. And with that inflow of painstakingly cataloged evidence, I simply flooded, if not drowned utterly, the entire front desk. So it was too late to throw a lifebuoy to the documents that had already been lying there. And it was far too late to salvage a balding sergeant's coffee cup that decided to save itself from that deluge and plunged right into the floor.

To my ineffable disappointment, I talked, I explained, I labored to prove his undeniable guilt and his involvement in this repelling scheme, yet to no avail. And then even the initial curiosity and unprofessional amusement of the police officers, which they tried to conceal, with very poor results, began disintegrating into plain and ridiculous boredom. Like a promising movie that after a riveting opening scene not so much goes as runs downhill. Rapidly yet irreversibly. And it was totally unacceptable in the face of such a threat. And most probably on account of their innate, or at least trained, good manners, no one dared to interrupt me. No one dared to speak to me in the patronizing manner or make a rude gesture of dismissal in my presence. And also, most certainly, they would have started falling asleep. Without a word. Without demur. Not paying attention to any of my feverish speeches and earnest warnings. They would have started doing that, had I not, in a surge of ungovernable emotion, suddenly begun flailing my hands and shouting while trying to imitate the sounds of explosions and breathlessly repeating one and the same word. A bomb! A bomb! And a bomb once more! It did that only to interlace it, from time to time, with another disturbing one, that is, a suicide bomber.

There was nothing too strange, nothing too extraordinary, in any of those words. Perhaps apart from the horrible visions of the gloomy and sullen reality that could come true due to their explosive assistance. And yet my till then drowsy listeners reacted to them with great and unexpected animation, which, in my humble opinion, was at least slightly exaggerated. It was surely disproportionate to that situation. For a moment I was even quite impressed by, and pleased with, that sudden reaction of theirs. I was impressed with that quickness and unforeseeable liveliness intruding onto their otherwise stolid

189

and bored faces. It was like a belated guest who arrives at the party as the last one and in addition empty-handed. But it was decidedly far less to my liking, to my rather sophisticated liking, that they resolved to restrain me, me, of all people, the innocent me, the watchful me, and then they handcuffed me at once. Yet in a quite skillful and professional manner. For, it was a kind of reaction that I wanted to provoke in them. Yes. By all means. Without any doubt. But not directed against me! I was not the one to blame here! I was not a guilty party here! I was not a moral terrorist here! I did not plan, down to minute details, a bloody and brutal revolution! A veritable carnage! I did not plan anything that was intended to rock this comfortable and well-mannered world to its very foundations! So why this unsurpassed eruption of aggression? So why this unprecedented touchiness about me? Why those precautions about the presence of such a simple and innocent and basically defenseless old man who needed to swallow a hefty handful of variegated pills to be able to start urinating, and another one to stop doing that? Did I really look like someone capable of committing such appalling deeds and harrowing crimes? Did I really look like someone capable of committing them, all of them, let alone the inconceivable atrocities, of which I accused, though not groundlessly, that, contrary to me, annoyingly virile and agile young man? Did I? At my respectable age? After the unmerciful blade of time had scarred and lacerated my once youthful and supple body? After it had lacerated it to the point of turning it into a likeness of cracked and parched soil during a drought?

And although I could not condone or comprehend that kind of violent behavior toward someone who was motivated only and solely by good and noble intentions, I was impressed by the uncanny precision and sureness of their movements. For, that assured me that no one else but those people would be able to stop him. No one else but those inherently bluish people would be able to contain this unspoken threat when the right time came. But only if their attention was directed at the right target.

But, to my amazement, my desperate attempts to explain myself and appeal to their reason and convince them that I was, in truth, only a frail and doddering old man heavily affected by the unremitting curse of senility, finally began to yield the desired effects. They did that somewhat slowly even though I kept smiling to myself. Smugly. Furtively. I kept smiling at the secret fact that they were unable to imagine what I could do, and they would be surprised at the things that I was capable of. At least of which my still sprightly body was still capable. For they eventually softened the tone of their authoritarian voices. For they perfunctorily ran a few basic tests on me. As if I were a rickety jalopy that had missed its last periodic technical inspection. They asked me to blow into here. To walk over there. And then they checked my blood. Just in case. And all that time I tried to explain to them, already from behind the implacable bars, that I was merely a messenger. An innocent courier. I tried to explain to them that they made a dreadful mistake. A horrible and cardinal mistake. I told them that it was a mistake whose scale and vastness and enormity of consequences they could not possibly fathom in its tremendous entirety. And yet, history would certainly charge them for it sooner or later, indubitably. And yet, history would bill for it their progeny. The, after all, uninvolved future generations. And that bill, that clearly exorbitant bill, burdening their family for decades to come, they would never be able to settle fully. Like an avowed drunk who keeps drinking on credit till his sad and sodden end.

However, nobody listened to me. Nobody was taking me seriously even for a moment. Nobody paid any attention to my logical explanations and foolproof arguments. Not even passing attention. Not even cordial attention. For only my dear daughter believed me. Only she did it. Only she believed me when she came to pick me up in the evening. As if I were a package left at the post office. Only she believed me after being forced to listen to the insolently fake report presented to her by one of the policemen. By one of my harassers. By one of my oppressors. But he did not deign to take into consideration my version of events as the rules of a fair trial would have it. And then that uniformed tormentor of mine, only now, in her unreservedly loving presence, played that role of a compassionate and tirelessly obliging public official. But they could not fool me! Not after all the things that I witnessed here! Not anymore!

And then, all the way to the car, I sweated and labored, doing everything in my suddenly liberated power to assure her that all the things that she had just heard from them, from those blue-tinted paragons of corruption, were gibberish. A silly garbage. A worthless drivel. Like a brand new unprovable scientific theory coming straight from an eccentric yet well-proven madman. So I assured her. So I tried to persuade her. Now ceremoniously. Now in a more straightforward manner. I assured her of that while constantly incurring the risk of her looking back at me pityingly. I assured her that it was not truth. That they partly distorted the facts. And that they partly fabricated the rest of them. And all that was aimed to ridicule me. To make a fool out of me. A laughable fool of me. I assured her that their miserable theories were replete with countless logical fallacies threatening to collapse under the sheer weight not only of themselves, but also of an even cursory scrutiny. Of an even brief analysis. Like yet another excuse of an intractable adulterer. And she kept nodding to everything I said, though in that too automatic and abstracted a fashion. She kept nodding to my every word. Every sentence. Every condemnation and explanation of their harmful and unwarranted lies. Even if of the most improbable kind. And it was then that it suddenly dawned on me that I could always count on her support. On her careful understanding. On her infinite compassion. And it was also then that I

192

realized that she, of all people, was my staunchest ally in this, till then, lonesome struggle.

Then, I understood something with tremendous relief releasing my fatherly heart from a powerful grip of uncertainty. I understood that, after all, the poison of his insidious preaching as well as loathsome speeches, had not yet managed to penetrate too deep into her tissues. It had not yet infected the main organs. And it still sufficed to tighten a metaphorical band around her dainty tender hand to constrict the flow of her infected blood mixed with his subversive ideas and ideology. Like in the case of a snakebite. It still sufficed to do that in order to save her. To rescue her. To turn her, once again, into my uncorrupted lovable little girl.

Thus, succumbing willingly to this surge of fatherly affection, I resolved to impart to her my newest discovery pertaining to the case. For I suspected that the scandalous behavior of those policemen was not simply incidental. For I suspected that it could not be viewed as such. I suspected that it was a part of some larger yet sloppily painted picture. Or, at the very least, of a clearly disturbing pattern. For it clearly and explicitly confirmed my worst doubts and most daring speculations. And I do not mean those keeping me awake at night, but also preventing me from napping during my working hours. It was a suspicion that law enforcement, and, presumably, all the security services in the entire country, worked in collusion with him. For they must have been cooperating actively with those filthy rebels. For they must have been scheming cunningly with those atrocious renegades. Or even they kept receiving direct orders and instructions from their sinister headquarters. I had to admit that it sounded reasonable. I had to admit that it seemed plausible. Quite plausible, in fact. And now, all that started forming a whole and coherent and logical entirety. And all the parts and pieces of this deleterious riddle, of this baleful enigma, began tessellating and falling in the right place. They were like the pieces of an ancient mosaic giving shape to a fabulous picture that even long centuries prove unable to dissemble.

One should not belittle that too easily. One should not dismiss it too recklessly. For it explained exhaustively the enormous, if not downright monstrous, audacity and hubris, let alone incontestable arrogance, of all those revolutionaries. Including him. Especially him. Their impudent leader and mentor. For it was he who, after all, kept giving a whole series of his insolent lectures. Easily. Not bothered or disturbed by anyone. He kept giving them while traveling across the country, as if during some yet unnamed crusade, in which he continued to instigate people against the system, against its values, against its foundations, as well as against the inviolable principles lying in the very heart of it. And there was also an otherwise inexplicable fact that spoke in favor of my newest conspiracy theory. For all the evidence that I had hitherto collected and brought there was unwarrantedly detained and secured. Every little bit of it. To the smallest and least important trinket. It was detained there, allegedly in order to investigate the case that I had just laid out to them. But, in truth, it was all about depriving me of my sole weapon in this more and more hopeless battle. As if I were a predator at once being unabashedly stripped of all its claws and fangs during a routine check.

And yet in spite of such an accumulation of annoying obstacles and difficulties, I managed to outsmart them. I managed to outmaneuver them brilliantly before they had a chance to notice anything. Them, that is, all the nameless and negligible extras and pitiful supporting actors in that incipient coup d'état. I managed to do that due to my unadorned wisdom. I managed to do that on account of my spontaneous genius. For I succeeded in stealing from them a single spuriously inconspicuous object. I salvaged a single proof of his guilt from that whole, now irrevocably lost, now irretrievably appropriated, heap capable of testifying against him and all his despicable sins. It was that wretched shot glass. It was that shot glass soiled with the tapestry of his menacing fingerprints. Of that future war criminal and would-be mass murderer. It was the shot glass that I had furtively snatched from the front desk. Right from under the corrupt noses of those ignoble policemen, on my way out of there.

I was on the verge of showing it to her while carefully trying not to obliterate the precious fingerprints pockmarking it. As if they were a writing on the sand. And I could not wait to outline to her, to this beloved ally of mine, to this dear comrade-in-arms of mine, my plan of the further struggle with his still fledgling regime of unspeakable terror. I could not wait to do that when, as I scrambled into the front seat of her car, still at the police parking lot, I noticed him. This sinful man. This spiteful man. My remorseless nemesis and the constant source of my humiliation. I noticed the reflection of his eyes immured in the rear-view mirror. Like a metallic gaze of a knight framed in a slit of a belligerently lowered visor. I noticed him as he sat there in the backseat grinning at me tentatively. It was as if this unnaturally wide smile of his were produced by some unending cramp in his facial muscles. Or as if he fell victim of a highly troubling insurrection of his bowels. Then he leaned toward me daringly. He did that thus forcing me to recoil in unadulterated disgust and move away from him as far as my seatbelt allowed me magnanimously. This unrelenting shackle of mine. Firmly holding me in place as if I were a voluntary galley slave. And then he spoke to me. He spoke to me without ceasing to smile fraudulently for a single word that flew out of his habitually malignant mouth.

"We were awfully worried about you. We came as soon as they called us. We were really terrified. We came here right away. But it's over now. It's all over now. So I'm glad that you're okay. I'm glad that you're fine, Dad."

I could not help cringing instinctively at the sound of that word. For it was that word. It was that single last word of his little and thoroughly truculent speech that was also the last proverbial straw. It was the straw that not so much broke anyone's back as it shattered and tore down the last internal barriers and inhibitions of mine. Like a red cape that enrages a quite touchy bull.

And so, in truth, it was over. It was all over now, as he said it. For, apparently, if not insolently, he intended to take her place. Her cherished place in my rather cramped heart, in which there was not too much empty space left for anything else but her. Thus he tactfully declared war. A total and un-bridled war on me.

The next several days, clad in a gloomy memory of my still fresh defeat, I decided to spend by lying low. I decided to spend them by trying not to draw anyone's attention to me. If not necessary. If not unavoidable. Thus I hoped, by dint of that clever maneuver, to lull him into a false sense of calm and security. I hoped to alleviate his racing fears of me and my actions that must restlessly have been chasing one another until I would be able to resume my noble mission. And I did it like a bomber that only briefly vanishes from the enemy's radars to reappear an instant later out of the proverbial and cloudy blue, and launches a fresh attack from a different direction. To my mild surprise, it worked. And it worked splendidly.

To think of all the wonderful things that the cunning wisdom of an elderly man can achieve, when properly masquer-aded as an affable cheerful smile, that rather strong sedative, ca-pable of silencing the stray worries and misgivings hackling one.

And also now, the perfect conditions occurred to carry out my brilliant plan. For, when I least expected it, when I least counted on it, my no less ideal daughter, arranged for me a few days off. She arranged them for me to have a rest and restore some energy that I had shamelessly lost during that inordinately stressful misadventure. And due to that, for the first time in those five long decades, or more, of my professional career, I stayed at home. Sadly, it strained, if not ruined completely, my hitherto unblemished reputation and work history. As the first missed shot in the career of an infallible marksman. And that fact I grieved silently. And that fact I regretted endlessly. And over that fact lamented miserably that older, stale part of me that still opposed the idea of my getting involved in the insane realm of world politics. But now I finally could devote all my time to one and single task. I mean the task allotted to me by a joint decision of fate and history. And that opportunity could not be underestimated now. And it could not be belittled now. Especially now. Right before the next phase of our clash. And to that very moment, I had to prepare myself far less perfunctorily than before.

That was why, in the course of the first few days, I still simulated, with uncanny bravado, a complete mental breakdown, and an emotional numbness. And I did it with the laudable proficiency of a seasoned as well as acclaimed actor who has mastered, to the point of astonishing perfection, the dubious art of impersonating various characters of whose lives and life choices and living conditions he knows nothing at all. But I did not merely lie stretched out idly on a couch. For I listened to them. For I watched and observed them. For I scrutinized them carefully as well as all that was taking place around me. I was like an experienced strategist who is forced to rethink and reevaluate his original plans to adjust them to the new reality slowly starting to reign supreme around him after a lost battle. And I did that. And I did all that. And I meticulously calculated and weighed and pondered the full gamut of my future moves that were about to compensate for that recent humiliating fiasco of mine. And as I was doing that, I, slowly and patiently, rotated in my hands that accursed shot glass. I rotated it as mechanically as if I were some odd cocktail shaker. And I rotated it reflectively. That last piece of the suddenly endangered evidence that was left to me. My final card in this hand. In my elderly, yet still resolute, hand.

And it was then, between the turn of it halfway to the left and a bit to the right, that there occurred to me something. Some disconcerting thing. For there occurred to me that if all the security services of this marvelous country betrayed me treacherously and went over to the enemy camp, if all those people to whom I would have entrusted my own safety, of this country, as well as of my boundlessly beloved daughter, defected ignobly, revolted dishonorably, then there was just one possibility left. I could only turn to those who should be most interested in all that. I could only turn to those who were in real danger now. I could only turn to all those who were on the verge of being targeted by him and his acolytes. I could only turn to the potential future victims of his unprecedented actions. To the emissaries of the perennially pragmatic private sector.

But I still did not intend to trouble those greatest and most remarkable of them. The heavyweight business creatures. The eminent colossuses of profits. The veritable titans of diplomacy. No. For it was too early for that. It was too early to bother any of them. It was still too early to alarm and worry them about that, after all, still rather silly and shy tiny flame of social discontentment. There was still time before it grew and spread and swelled to the point of becoming a raging fire of consummate revolution. For there was still enough time to quench and put out this tentative flame in the lowest layers of society. For it was still nothing more than a mere cigarette butt smoldering listlessly and quite safely, though quite close to the exceptionally flammable carpet. For the truculent tongues of those flames had not yet managed to approach the highest floor, the upper echelons of society. And they had not yet started licking it belligerently. And so, there was still no need to evacuate its tenants and start a panic. For panic is always bad for business. And for hotel business above all.

So, the very next day I ventured on a quickened tour, devoid of any garrulous guides or trite souvenir shops, of all the local firms and companies in this fine city. And so, I started storming hectically into the offices of various chairmen, executives, as well as countless other business owners. I started intruding on the board meetings, the shareholders' meetings, and every other kind of meeting conceivable, while screaming from the very door that I was in possession of rare information, of invaluable information, which could decide on the life or death of the members of their families. And whenever I spoke those words, all the people gathered in those elegant rooms were struck with fear. And blood seemed to be hurriedly abandoning their faces. It was as though it were being evicted from there unexpectedly for some ridiculous reason or other. Someone usually started sobbing in the corner. Someone else fainted here and there. And this fact was heralded by the soft and muffled thud of an inert body slumping into the fluffy luxurious carpet. Like a falling tree on the grass. And I was being immediately ushered to the seats at those impossibly long tables. I was being offered a cup of lukewarm coffee. Of tea. Or, at the very least, a customary glass of water. And, not only once or twice, I saw some innocent and stunned secretary being urged imperiously to bring me some kind of refreshment as quickly as possible. Now. Right now. And this order she would strive to execute as swiftly and gracefully as she could, yet still in total confusion. She would strive to execute it while systematically losing her shoe, or both of them, in the rather hasty process. As if thus marking her way back to me.

And when I was finally provided with all that was needed, all that was customary, or even far more than that, I was being instantly surrounded by a cordon of frightened and dreadfully pale faces. They were akin to a congregation of ghosts roaming a cemetery at night. Every now and then, I saw a nervously twitching eyelid. I saw a twitching lip here and there. And they were akin to a loose exhaust pipe dancing restively under the belly of an idling car. And those people stood there in utter silence. And it was stirred only, from time to time, by the sounds of another sudden faints and collapses. And they listened to me. Yes, they listened to me! All of them! They actually listened to me! And how intensely! And how intently! What a nice change it was, after all the awful and unbelievable things that had befallen me recently! What a quality shock it was, if not a veritable culture shock, after all the unpleasant things that I had experienced till now! They listened to each and every of my words! And every single one of my learned words was being voraciously skimmed right off my parched lips. As if they were sweet nectar crystallizing and accumulating on the surface of a succulent fruit.

And, now and again, there appeared several listeners who were so impatient, so incredibly anxious, to hear the rest of my story, that they attempted to divine what I was about to say at all costs. They began the game of finishing my sentences for me. They began the game of completing my arguments for me. And then, with time, they became so advanced in it, and so restless, that they did not deign to wait for me to start them. For they had begun telling my future words from reading the movement of my lips before I managed to so much as part them slightly. It was as if they were some peculiar kind of lip-obsessed fortune tellers. And thus one could instantly notice the glaring quality gap, that nothing could possibly bridge, between the private and public sector!

But always, unfortunately, the endings of all those impromptu meetings were the same. Inevitably. Immutably. They were the same although I could not fathom and figure out the reason behind that process. Because it happened whenever I mentioned to them and described to them minutely all the grueling intricacies of that immense conspiracy encompassing the entire world. It happened whenever I started characterizing the now invisible, yet still present, yet still nefarious, revolutionaries. And those facts I corroborated by producing from my pocket the infamous shot glass adorned with a constellation of his incriminating fingerprints. For it supposed to be the ultimate and incontestable proof of the existence of this boundless scheme capable of sweeping from the surface of the market such corporations as theirs. But then, across their stunned faces, there only flitted a full palette of colors of utter confusion. Like a rainbow that is drastically out of order. Thus, once again, just as before, I noticed a rather chaotic exchange of increasingly bewildered glances among them. Meantime, I still talked and talked and still expounded undauntedly and still assured them maniacally that I was going to give that shot glass to them for free. For nothing. I assured them that they could take it even now. Right now. For I did not need it anymore. For I did not want any money for it. Because it was not about money at all. It was not about any pointless and transient laurels or prizes. For I did all that due to my great concern for them. For their unending happiness and prosperity. For, let us not pretend that their, that is, of those powerful ones living on the top floor of society, prosperity as well as commercial success remained without a vital impact on the safety and living conditions of those living at the bottom. At the lowest rung of the social ladder. To whom the barely tasted leftovers and petite crumbs of their prosperity would thus trickle down systematically, down the laboriously zigzagging and maneuvering insides as well as intestines of society. Like rainwater reaching the lowest layers of soil. To those like I and my frail daughter. For, in truth, it was all about her from the very beginning.

And I pushed that glass into their unsuspecting hands. It was the very same glass that now was apparently brimming with that invisible high-proof despair. I pushed it into their hands while beseeching them to take it away from me. As far as possible. As quickly as possible. For the sake of my daughter's happiness. For I could not take it anymore. And then, in most cases, the morbidly unstirred silence fell. It was punctuated timidly every now and then by a thin and baffled voice reaching me from the second, if not even farther, row of my listeners. And it was a voice that asked no one in particular whether it meant that their children were safe. That their beloved family members had nothing to fear now. And it kept asking helplessly what did it mean, what did it really mean, if it meant anything at all.

But the climax, as well as the following dénouement, were always similar. If not exactly the same. Because the scenario always faithfully followed the proven and a bit too threadbare pattern. It did that like a particularly clichéd pickup line. It did that regardless of the plot of that particular meeting. Of its psychological depth. Of its balance of arguments. And of various subtexts buried in that conversation. Like the highly fidgety land mines in the thus fertile field. Or regardless of its unique cast of characters. And so all those endings were strikingly alike, although a set of extremely different ways and byways and even detours led to them. For, once I was being dragged forcibly out of the conference room, kicking and screaming maniacally. I was being dragged out of there while warning them all that time, the same as before, against making this mistake. This fateful mistake. This cardinal mistake. For it was a mistake that would inescapably burden not only them, but also their closest family, and for which they would be charged at the cash register of history. Some other time I was being shown the door in the rather rude manner. It was as if they intended to insinuate that I somehow forgot how I had gotten there in the first place. Yet always, out of some residual respect for my awe-inspiring age, I was mercilessly spared the infinite humiliation of being kicked out savagely on the street. Thus I was spared the treatment of a yesterday and now stale newspaper that has been read, crumpled, torn to pieces, and from then on serves as a kind of filler in the shoes of a tramp, riddled with holes beyond recognition.

What ingratitude! What disrespect! What a scandalous behavior! What a reprehensible lack of prospective thinking! So, they preferred to shut their eyes, cowardly avert their heads, and pretend, childishly and naively, not to see or notice this problem. They preferred to pretend that this problem did not exist at all. They preferred to pretend that they could not hear that still distant and vague and muffled, yet more and more ominous, echo of the shouts of the enraged masses. It was as if they wanted to wait, idly and ineptly, for them to come right to their own doors. It was as if they wanted those masses to knock on their doors with their viciously bared rakes and scythes. But then it would be too late for any kind of defense. Far too late. Like in the case of a pedestrian who already feels a robber's switchblade nibbling at his exposed throat. Was it an exemplary display of strategic and long-term planning? Was it a way in which the business world worked? How it was at all possible that they had somehow managed to establish their exceedingly profitable companies, gain their clients, carve out a piece or two of the market, then outsmart their fierce competitors, and stay afloat in the turbulent waters of the modern market, was beyond me.

Then, as it was bound to happen sooner or later, as if out of utterly gratuitous spite, a police patrol was called. It was called to take care of that little mild disturbance of which I had apparently been the sole cause and reason. So I met these two ineffably courteous police officers at the carousel of the revolving door of the both impressive and imposing office building that I was leaving in a great hurry. I was leaving it after jogging down several flights of stairs. Panting heavily. Limping noticeably. Because I decided to choose this way out of there instead of using a perfectly functional elevator. For I knew that such cramped and claustrophobic spaces were perfect spots for ambushes and traps of every kind. Like every single nook and corner of a jungle. Luckily for me, yet only within the confines of bad luck, I recognized the already familiar faces behind these impenetrable uniforms. And so, the otherwise insufferable humiliation and disgrace, which I experienced when they cuffed my tremulous hands and pressed me to the cold and smooth marble floor of the hall, as if I were a potato stamp that had to be brutally put to paper to produce a fine and clear imprint, was a little lesser. A little more acceptable. A little less degrading. It was a little lesser than it could have been without the previous introductory meeting of ours. It was like in the case of an impotent who deliberately visits one and the same prostitute over and over again in order not to be forced to confide his debilitating imperfection to yet another uninitiated person. Meantime, the coldness and coarseness of that floor instantly brought to my suddenly apprehended mind the consoling memories of the soft and plush luxuries filling my adorable hotel. How delightful they were! How marvelous they were! And how I longed to be there again, with them, near them, and not here, in this cruel and vulgar outside reality.

Later on, through the door recklessly left ajar, I could hear the incoherent bits and scraps of a lengthy, highly emotional conversation, held between my little daughter and the duo of these bluish officers. I mean these two impertinent new acquaintances of mine, who had brought me back home this time. And I mean these two who had insolently confiscated my precious shot glass somewhere on the way. They suggested now, for some reason and in suspiciously lowered voices, that she could not allow me to keep escaping all the time. She should not allow me to spread panic and commotion with impunity. She should not allow me to wander around the city alone. Unattended. Without proper care and supervision. They insisted that I should be put into some kind of institution as soon as possible. Into some kind of permanent isolation. A quarantine maybe. They insisted that she should consider it seriously if she was unable to take good care of me single-handedly. Take care of me? Of me? How dared they! It was simply unheard-of! For it was I who had been taking care of countless august crowned heads and those, naturally, less distinguished heads of states. I was the one who kept paying insane attention not to pinch their tailcoats with the abruptly closing doors. I was the one who was careful to maintain the constant speed of the opening or closing door so that they did not produce the indelicate gusts of wind capable of ruffling as well as disheveling those esteemed heads and their coiffures. So who was qualified enough, experienced enough, or deserving enough, to take care of me? Who was qualified enough to do that, if I had been, throughout my entire career, the full five long decades of it, or more, much more, taking care of those who, in turn, kept taking care of millions of their supple subjects or vexed voters? Who was worthy of this honor? Who was competent for such a task?

Then they meaningfully repeated the suspicious word, "institution." They repeated it as if for emphasis. As if for a cheap dramatic effect. As if it were an inscrutable magic spell of some kind, capable of turning her into a frog, or their blue uniforms into something actually meaning something. And they did it in odd unison, whatever it was supposed to mean. Was it a code? Was it a coded message that they strived, using this rather bizarre and impenetrable idiom of conspiracy, to pass to him through her? Right through her? Through my darling daughter? Thus they wanted to turn her into an unknowing accomplice. Into an involuntary messenger. Into a reluctant courier. Into yet another henchman of that evil man and the mastermind of all that.

Thankfully, it appeared that she was neither pleased nor ready to assume such an unenviable position. For she rebelled and protested and fought valiantly against it. She fought like a real lioness protecting her side of the cage. Besides, everyone knew perfectly well that the only kind of institution, with or without those ostentatious quotation marks, which I respected and acknowledged openly in this downright bureaucratic world was my dear and fine hotel. It was unnecessary to comment or explain that fact to anyone. And I did not want, let alone need, any other kind of institution in my life. Both now and in the future. And so that day I was proud of her. I was extraordinarily proud of my little daughter. I was also immensely grateful to her. And my enfeebled fatherly heart was inundated with the unabashed waves of poignant and sentimental feelings at the mere recollection of her often harsh and blunt and brutal words that she used boldly in their presence. Right in front of them. For she did not shy away from them. Not even once. She did not shy away from such words while defending me against their treacherous, even though law-upholding, claws. And these words, these very words, these violent words that seemed to be strikingly incongruous with her otherwise benevolent and cheerful nature, were to me, at least at that stressful moment, far more precious and more memorable than all the best wishes and expressions of innocent childish love that I had heard from her in the course of all the years of our life together. All those that she had said to me on my birthdays. On father's days. During various family holidays. And without any special occasion in sight. And so her words on that day eclipsed decidedly, completely, a mosaic of all the cute and ineffably beautiful moments from the past. Like a new love that overshadows all the past infatuations. They eclipsed all the moments when she used to run to me breathless, early in the morning, still visibly sleepy but already smiling genuinely, to show me something that she had concocted from the web of her dreams and the thread of the first sunray of that day. They eclipsed all the moments when she used to throw her little playful arms around my neck and hug me lovingly whenever something frightened her. Or even, when she merely needed a dash of fatherly warmth. But these snapshots from the mental family album of my most cherished memories that I cultivated in my heart had to give way to her new, yet far more adult improvisation. They had to. They simply had to.

That was why, later on, later in the evening, when I suspected that she managed to cool down after that unforeseeable

verbal tussle with the law enforcement, of which I had unwittingly become the sole reason, I resolved to go to her. I
resolved to thank her for all that she had done for me since
dinner. For it was far more than other people do for each
other during their lifetimes. I felt compelled to do that. It was
imperative for me to do that. But not only because of the
fatherly feelings that I no longer could suppress efficaciously.
For I kept marinating in them all the time. But also due to
the fact that, unlike previously, this time her words had their
real worth and gravity. Noticeable and measurable. And not
a mere symbolic one. For they really saved me from a truly
disastrous fate. Like the wit of one's lawyer at the moment of
nicely fabricated truth.

And so, when the right time came, I sneaked to the door
of her room. Like the sandman on a job. I sneaked there when
it was already dark. I sneaked there when an unstirred and a
bit eerie silence started reigning supreme in the entire apartment. And I sneaked there when that malicious revolutionary
presumably believed that I really took a deserved after-dinner
nap. The door was half-open and unguardedly inviting. And,
right through the thus created gap, there listlessly kept seeping
a trickle of light. It penciled a long light line on the floor that
was as pointed as a hand's clock. It reminded me insistently
that I had not enough time. That, in fact, I had very little time
left to accomplish my task, my hunt, my sacred quest, before
it was too late. Irreparably too late.

But then, to my surprise and chagrin, the timid and muffled
sounds of weeping reached me from there. Like the scents of
freshly baked cakes wafting from the bakery. Both curiously
and cautiously, I peered in. And I saw my petite cute daughter,
perching cautiously at the edge of her bed. Like a bird on a
high-voltage wire. She was convulsing and crying uncontrollably. She was cuddled into the arms of that incumbent dictator
of fear. And I heard her talking to him and telling him about
someone. She was telling him that in the jerky and breaking

voice of hers while sobbing at regular intervals. As if these sobs were a kind of ungrammatical punctuation marks. And she was talking about someone of whom she was constantly ashamed. Who always kept embarrassing her in front of others. On whose behalf she had to make unending excuses. For whose unseemly behavior she had to apologize without end and much thought. Just as she had done today. Just as she had done right now. And she did not have the strength or guts for that. She could not keep on doing that. At least, not anymore. It was overwhelming her. It was exhausting her. It was almost killing her. This inescapable sense of hopelessness. This oppressive sense of utter pointlessness. Of all her well-meant efforts. And she went on in very much the same despairing strain. And she said that she was torn internally, emotionally. For at the same time she bore an immense grudge against that mysterious person, and she pitied him. For apparently it was a man. It must have been a man. A man who had caused her so much pain and sorrow and humiliation in the past, and who still kept doing that without end. Only now she understood finally that he had been doing that unwittingly.

Then she added, after a brief, intense silence, and in a bit more cheerful tone of voice, that, after all, I was her father. And then she added that she would never have stopped loving me, even if she had lost all her strength and will to live. No matter what. And I was enormously moved by this unexpected confession of filial affection. For, since then, I felt, I knew, I was sure beyond any doubt, for I got an ultimate and unmistakable confirmation, that my fantastic daughter was not lost altogether. I knew that there still kept smoldering in her the faint yet vivacious flame of filial feelings for me. It kept smoldering there amidst the loquacious static of his twisted ideology. To which feelings I could invariably try to appeal while detoxifying her and liberating her from his pernicious influence.

One thing troubled me, though. I still was not sure whom she discussed at the beginning of her plaintive tirade. I did not

know who ventured to cause so much distress and unpleasantness to my enchanting daughter. Who dared to do that?
Who was so morally and emotionally bankrupt to even try
something like that? Apparently, I came too late to find this
out. Apparently, my belated arrival, if not an intrusion, on that
scene, truncated her highly emotional speech. It was like when
one enters the darkened cinema right before the beginning of
the closing credits and starts asking everyone around annoyingly, how was it, who killed whom, and who won in the end.

I only hoped, and I hoped greatly, that she meant him. No
one else but him. For I was also ashamed, deeply ashamed, of
the fact that he and I belonged to the same category of species.

The last one of those strategic disasters and tactical calamities
stripped me completely and irrevocably of the last faint dregs
of my illusions. And I mean the illusions about the rather
limited range of possibilities of action that still remained
within my quite shaky reach. I could not keep deluding myself. I could no longer beguile myself with false promises or
assurances and gorge myself gluttonously on a mishmash of
spurious ideas and observations. Like a toddler greedily and
with great relish sucking on its thumb while believing it to
be the most delicious delicacy there is. I could no longer do
that whereas the reality triumphing around me had adopted
a completely different plan of action. For it had chosen an
utterly different script. For it had already begun obediently following its stage directions. Without demur or rancor. Without
looking back at the decisions and needs of the negligible supporting actors such as I. Exactly as I. And I also did not want
to become one of those miserable creatures like the would-be

singers wailing and howling cruelly with total abandon straight to the shower heads all the while bastardizing that fine art, and being unshakably convinced of their own greatness as well as that of their voices and vocal talents, yet, ironically, still unsung ones, that literally go down the drain. For, a certain dose of arrogance and conceit and haughtiness proves to be not only desirable, but also indispensable, in the case of various eccentric artists and authors. It proves to be necessary to those who are often being forced to swim against the current of transient tastes and domineering aesthetics of their times, only to, when the current of those trends eventually changes its course, swim with it. In the first row of it. While dictating the pace and speed according to their liking. But in my case, that kind of attitude could have led to a truly tragic outcome. It could have led to that in the field of perilous missions and covert operations and gathering intelligence, in which clandestine activities I had been eagerly engaged since recently. For within the blink of my mind's eye, I had taken a breakneck leap from the territory of safe amateurism and dilettantism to that of full-blown professionalism. Like an overnight sensation who transforms into a dreamy something from the utter nothing within the duration of one's sleep. But there was no place for such a distortion of facts. But there was no place for such a misinterpretation of the truth. Because each mistake in the assessment of the present conditions could have grave consequences not only for me, but also for everyone around me. And I simply could not allow that to happen.

Thus, I did not need to spend too many days on musing and pondering despondently to reach a hardly thrilling conclusion that I had already exhausted nearly all the possible means of legal action. Of acceptable action. Of feasible action. Perhaps except for that final one. That ultimate one. That last resort of mine. And I mean my turning to those sitting comfortably at the very top of the social ladder. However, if I had done it now, right now, it still would have been too early.

Too quickly. And too unprofessionally. For I would have only compromised myself irreparably and exposed my boundless and formidable incompetence in such matters. Which, otherwise, no one would have dared to point out to me. That would have been out of the question. They were far too well-mannered for that. They were too well-versed in the nuances of diplomacy to risk something like that. And yet, a kind of distaste would have remained nevertheless.

But then a brand new thought flared up unexpectedly in my lately rather gloomy and dark mind. And then it soared and glided, lightly and uninhibitedly, amid the layers of my consciousness. It soared there like a flare being shot from a distant and forlorn lifeboat, that epitome of hope to all of the involved parties. Both to the rescued and rescuers. Promptly, it dawned on me that there was only one thing that I could do. Well, perhaps, apart from hoisting a shameful white flag and surrendering the last hitherto invincible bastion of my dignity. There was only one thing. Namely, I could heavily revise my previous strategies, drastically rearrange a farrago of my aims and intents and priorities. Anew. Once again. And I could start pretending that I wanted to switch sides to become his ally. I even intended to fake my sudden conversion to his downright ludicrous ideology as well as my feverish desire to join the insane ranks of his faithful and servile followers. His fanatic acolytes. And even his mad sidekicks. And I wanted to show him that because I was unable to defeat him. To rout him. To vanquish him completely. Because I could not protect the current hallowed world order from the raging fire of an imminent revolution. And thus I decided to join him. For only in him and his preaching I saw the last faint chance of salvation and salvaging whatever would be left of this world.

And if only I was convincing enough, earnest enough, or fake enough, then he could even, without anyone's assist or vicious promptings, start trusting me. And he could even take me straight to the mysterious headquarters of theirs. To the very demon's lair. And there I would be able to work further on winning his complete trust. I would be able to make him betray me, once again out of his own free and unforced will, all the details of their elaborate evil plan. And I would remain tirelessly cautious to seize the first opportunity to copy them and replicate them and falsify them. And even to make a daring attempt at destroying his tenaciously vile organization from within. Like oil that is about to burst out of the ground while razing all that has been built on it.

And then I grew enormously excited at the thought of all that subversion. Of all that sabotaging their plans. Of all that starting a broad and resonant disinformation campaign. Of gaining time. Or, at least, of delaying the inevitable eruption of that whole revolution a mere day or two. For I hoped to give some time, the priceless time, the rare time, in that unofficial and tax-free transfer of minutes and seconds, that invaluable currency, to the proper services. To the security services. Yet I wanted to give it only to those that refused to rebel against their superiors and still remained loyal to the mighty ones of this world. For they would need it to take all the necessary actions. All the preventive actions. In fact, I was so thrilled and so enthusiastic about this new scheme of mine that I could barely sit or stand still. I could hardly tame a parade of shivers shaking cruelly my already tremulous hands. And due to that, I must have looked, to the proverbial unbiased observer, as if each and every limb of mine wanted to set off on a private trip in a different direction. Without looking back at the rest of my body. Without looking back at anything.

Therefore, the very next morning, I took a few deep breaths. One. Two. And also a third one. Just in case. Then I plunged my hands into my pockets to stop, or, at least, minimize their discordant and telling vibrations. And I ventured, with that deliciously faked laid-back and indifferent gait, straight to the kitchen. Our kitchen. For it was there that this vile creature with the centuries-long pedigree of sheer evil was ostentatiously sipping his coffee above an innocent sheet of a morning paper. Allegedly, right before leaving for work. Or rather, it was exactly what he professed stubbornly, in the hope that he would deceive me with such infantile excuses.

On seeing me, he instantly sprang to his feet. He jumped to his feet to pull a chair for me to sit upon. It was a kind of private ritual of ours. It was a kind of unsophisticated game of appearances, our harmless pastime, in which we indulged guardedly from time to time. Like two bored patrons of some bar or other. But it did not detract from the fierceness or hatefulness of our competition. Not a bit. Not even a little bit. And in the flawless politeness, with which was charged his every single move, he strived to cloak his infinite villainy. He strived to lull my innate vigilance and carefulness. But I no longer paid any attention to it. None whatsoever. I could no longer pay any attention to the complex choreography of his feigned nice gestures as well as his thoroughly sham courtesies. And I only nodded to him understandingly. And I only enacted them with him mindlessly. Then we perfunctorily went through all the motions of it. We did it like actors who have been playing their famous parts for so long that they do not need to devote any thought to them anymore.

So, I navigated ably to the table. I sat in front of him. And then I quickly laced my still shaky hands on the tabletop to allow them to cushion the otherwise telltale vibrations. And in the end, I forced a smile to my incredibly taut lips. It was as polite and disarming as I was capable of producing at that stressful moment. Meantime, he at once squared his ludicrously broad chest. He sat bolt upright. He crossed his legs under the table. Like the silverware during an interrupted meal. And then he also confidently laced his hands in front of him, as if miserably trying to imitate the dialect of my body language, and thus to ingratiate himself with me crudely.

Then, I could not help noticing that he embarrassedly brushed aside with his elbow that until now passive newspaper.

And it was in it, as I shrewdly assumed, that he had been circling and underlining with his pen the constellations of words and the whole sentences according to the strictly defined code. For it was a cunning way of communication between him and his troops. It was a brilliant way of passing orders and directives and detailed reports back and forth. Right under the, apparently stuffy, nose of the current authorities. Not suspected by anyone. Not bothered by anyone.

And, as he fiddled, with the brilliantly faked nervousness, with a floppy dog-ear of it, I told him openly what I had rehearsed earlier. I told him that in this way because I felt that such a shocking directness and bluntness, cruelly violating a mélange of tacit rules and laws of our elaborate charades replete with various ambiguities and innuendoes, would sound more credible. More convincingly. More trustfully. Even though there was not a single stray speck of truth in it. Like in the case of the supposedly homemade yet in fact mass produced preserves that have never even lain near anyone's home. So I resolutely declared that all that did not make sense. That all that did not make any sense at all. I declared that there was no point in continuing that. That we should stop fighting with each other. That none of us was going to benefit from it. That it was only a waste of time. A huge waste of time. An enormous waste of time. That, unfortunately, I comprehended it too late, far too late, that we were alike. Or, at least, very similar to each other. That we were like two blots of paint. Or that we were like two snowflakes that to an uninitiated observer look deceptively the same. That we were like two, not so much twins, but only due to the considerable age difference, as long-lost siblings, who were separated many years ago in a hospital as a result of a series of more or less unfortunate and grotesque and often downright preposterous mishaps, and who then find each other again, after many decades, and reunite, to the accompaniment of poignant music, during the scenes shot in slow motion. Preferably on the beach. And then I boldly suggested that we should unite. And then I daringly suggested that we should bury the verbal and emotional hatchet in a quiet private informal ceremony. And I told him that we should start working together, start working as a single well-lubed machinery. For we should join our efforts. And we should join our undeniable assets, my immeasurable intellect, experience, and wisdom, and his youthfulness as well as unbridled virility, to attain our goals. Our joint goals. And I meant, to lead to the, after all, inevitable downfall of this pitiful civilization of moral corruption and decay.

After an instant, I silenced. Like a kettle that runs out of steam. Promptly, I silenced. I did that uncertain whether I outdid that inadvertently. I was uncertain whether I distorted, or even overlooked, some campy line or trite one-liner or other, which I had remembered from cheap movies, and which I chose to employ now, convinced that it should appeal to him perfectly. Because he represented as pathetic an intellectual level as their makers. But he only stared at me blankly. He stared at me with the beautifully enacted incredulousness. He stared at me with his mouth wide open as if awaiting a sloppy kiss, while not daring to blink or wince even once. It was then that he probably strived to calculate and divine from my brilliantly composed and impenetrable expression how much of those things I had said were true. Even slightly true. Even infinitesimally true. He evidently tried to guess whether his previous actions and intrigues, as primitive and clumsy as they were, had inflicted such a serious loss on me. He strived to guess whether they had inflicted truly painful wounds on me. He strived to guess whether they were severe enough, and ruthless enough, to convince me to abandon my previous stance, my former ideals, and abruptly switch sides, and, understanding the hopelessness of my position, to start playing for the opposing team.

In the end, it seemed that my brilliant subterfuge produced the desired effect. Or at least he decided to take a risk and believe my rapid conversion. At least, for the time being. At least, during a trial period. For, after a brief hesitation, he kindly smiled at me. Even to excess. He smiled as extremely as if he wanted not only to make the corners of his mouth reach and tickle his earlobes, but also to let them travel farther and farther till they laced firmly right behind his evil head. As the twin strings of a surgical mask. And then I saw the ostensibly measureless reserves of his fierceness evaporating within a fraction of a second as he cleared his throat with fraudulent uncertainty. This greatest evildoer in history. And then he answered me warmly that he was not sure what I meant. But if I wanted to accompany him to the university and take part in his thrilling lectures, he would not mind that. He would not mind that at all. He saw nothing wrong with that. He would be simply delighted. And even, he added after yet another intense, meaningful moment, it would be a great honor for him. Naturally! How else! For he still did not know, he still did not have an inkling of, what he agreed to!

Then, after a quick succession of invariably homely, forced, as well as awkward smiles, that increasingly frustrating routine of ours, we parted briefly. For he was supposed to ride the elevator down, start the car, and wait for me in front of the building while honking and cussing impatiently. Meantime, I was supposed to prepare myself for this bizarre trip. This strange excursion of mine. This ultimate mission of mine. Hardly able to contain my mounting exaltation, barely capable of suppressing the unapologetic urge to scream and howl and announce to the whole large uninterested world my unforeseen triumph, I marched back to my cozy bedroom. I did all in my weakened power to retain that offhand and pleasantly casual pace of my steps. And I did all that I could not to surrender unconditionally to the overpowering desire to run up there lightly. Or even to dash down the corridor with all my quite senile might. Like a child that has just received its dreamy present.

And it was then that my laborious preparations began. For I had to consider carefully a plethora of insanely important

216

factors, aspects, and circumstances. I had to calculate the risk. I had to assess my chances with an accuracy to one decimal place. I had to choose the proper clothes as well as pick the tools that would be adequate for this highly dangerous and challenging job. And those tasks were not as simple as they appeared to be at first cursory glance. Especially considering the fact that my blood kept thudding in my secular temples. As if it wanted to get out. As if it wanted to be set free. And also a parade of various thoughts pirouetting and gamboling in my excited mind did not make it any easier for me. Not even a dash. Not even a little bit. Because for the first time, I managed to approach him. Because I finally managed to get closer to both him and his inherently malevolent organization. And also I managed to create an opportunity to methodically infiltrate its ranks. I did that like water percolating through the seemingly invincible rock only to blow it up from the inside a mere few centuries later. And due to that, I could not help berating myself. I could not help bawling myself out for not taking care of it earlier. For not finalizing such essential preparations before all this happened. Before all this started for good. Before I succeeded in fooling him that I suddenly became his favorite accomplice and true friend and comrade. Before I achieved such a spectacular triumph. And before, due to all this, my elderly head, with a face akin to corrugated iron, as well as my whole body, following its suit, threatened to burst with excitation.

In the end, I settled for a hardly fashionable set consisting of a pair of black trousers, a black yet slightly worn-out leather belt, a black shirt, accompanied by a black tie, and also obligatorily black cuff links. All that was masterfully topped with an impenetrably black sweater. It was as if it were a black icing coating a thoroughly black cake. And yet, this seemingly bizarre monochromaticity of mine was not as pointless or downright insane as it might have seemed to some. It was enforced by a duo of my clever subterfuge and a precise

217

calculation. For, dressed this way, this rather frumpy way, I could always quickly and effortlessly blend into the background if needed. I could merge visually with the surroundings if necessary. And I could always find a coveted shelter right under the invariably cozy cover of the night.

But then my already gigantic surprise became truly boundless. Like a fire in the bush. And it was wonderfully mimicked by the astonishment painted across the face of that irreverent man. Which was not that difficult to produce for such a prodigious liar as he. It became bloated to truly monstrous proportions when I rode the elevator down to discover and be confronted with the warm and sunny day, with the sky that was not soiled or marred by a single downy blot of a stray cloud. Like a delightful smile of a dentist that is not blemished by a single patch of tooth decay. And so, my elaborate and scrupulously prepared camouflage turned out to be useless, futile, as well as simply counterproductive. And for the better part of our trip, I strived to hide my undue embarrassment. I strived to mask my overpowering embarrassment both with this sartorial excess of mine and with the fact that I had somehow failed to notice in time the insane glare of the blazing sun that apparently was ready to declare total war on all that was alive and scorch the earth completely. For I had failed to notice it through the tightly drawn curtains in my room, drawn that way for fear of the mercilessly prying eyes of his crooked agents and their surveillance devices. And I hoped, I only fervently hoped, that I would not notice, out of the corner of my eye, either of them, even a faint and blurry shadow of his insufferably smug smile. Of his victorious smirk. Of his winning grin. Akin to an upturned triumphal arch. For it would be radiant with satisfaction over my mishap. For it would be expressing his immeasurable contentment with that little innocent blunder of mine. And that equally petite triumph of his. And I simply would not stand that affront. I would not. For it was as though I were joyfulness intolerant.

But all that assiduous avoiding with my eyes his supposedly smug person forced me to stare, incessantly as well as persistently, into the rather unspecified distance. And it became a direct cause of a caravan of my more or less caricatural or grotesque stumbles and pratfalls. At first, it was when I comically clambered out of the car on a crowded parking lot. For it was then that I tripped over the same curb twice. And then eagerly assaulted a trashcan. As if I wanted to hug it a bit too friendlily. And then, later on, already inside the main building of the university of fine arts, I tumbled down the same stairs three times. As if purely for effect. As if for the heck of it. I tumbled down while whining pitifully to the staccato sounds of my thudding body. But I quickly got up yet only to stumble on the perfectly smooth floor of the main corridor, to the ineffable delight of the students flocking to us from everywhere.

Each time, however, regardless of the scale and proportions of my fall and the humiliation following it as closely as a shameful shadow, I rose from the ground with complete seriousness. I rose, full of dignity. Full of gracefulness. Full of composure. I rose with that unflappable elegance that I had learned flawlessly and indelibly in the course of my performing the no less breakneck bows. For, after all, I could not let him know how tremendously ashamed I was. I could not expose or reveal to his cruel self the enormity of my disgrace. For I simply could not give him the satisfaction.

But I nearly forgot about this carnival of shame and ignominy. I nearly forgot about it as he was leading me through an impenetrable labyrinth of long and winding corridors and secret passages. All bathed in that alluring aura of mystery. All bearing that slight flavor of venerable age. All crisscrossing in every both possible and impossible manner. As the alleys of a crossword puzzle. All the way I felt that we were not alone. All the way I sensed someone's presence near us. Close to us. Even already within us. For permeating us insolently. And with unprecedented impunity. And I was right. And I was utterly right. For immediately afterward, I noticed a long procession of portraits of the splendid late lecturers and deans and provosts watching us warily from the walls of this noble institution. Like the figures of former pharaohs adorning the tomb's wall. They kept accosting us with their gazes. They kept scrutinizing us condescendingly. And they were neighbored by the portraits of their equally, if not far more, renowned graduates. And they were accompanied by these fabulous pictures and paintings that both warranted and corroborated the bright nimbuses of perennial fame surrounding them fondly. Like shawls on a wintry day.

It was then that I finally comprehended the unspeakable mastery and brilliance of his plan. Because it was an incontestable display of sheer genius to locate the headquarters of such a subversive organization as his there. Right there. Within the hallowed confines of that revered institution. Inside that veritable temple of art and human ingenuity. For it was a place where a mere policeman would not dare to venture of his own accord. For it was a place where he would not appear without a good reason, following only the promptings of his even if till then unerring hunch. And also, it was a place where he would never stray even if armed with a cartridge full of very good reasons and with a search warrant getting restive and itchy in his holster. The esteem of this place, amazing and imposing, as well as the genuine awe and respectfully lowered voices it inspired, guaranteed him and his evil organization, concealed cunningly somewhere in there, perhaps behind this gaudy painting, or that gawky sculpture, relative immunity, along with the full and unhampered freedom of its seditious actions.

That was why I could not deny him his nearly intimidating ingenuity. And that was why I could not deny him his comparably stunning slyness. Because there is hardly anything worse than blinding arrogance and a penchant for underestimating one's adversary. Those attitudes, akin to the moral gangrene gnawing at one's moral fiber, had ruined more than just one renowned general or other commander. It had ruined more than just one officer who had been forced to bolt away in shameful panic from a battleground after his overwhelming army had been ruthlessly vanquished and decimated by a surprising tactical trick executed with wonderful gusto by his numerically inferior opponent. At the last possible moment. During the injury time. And which tactical trick seemed as if it had been concocted solely with its place in history textbooks in mind.

Then there took place a few minutes of wandering through a maze of countless corridors and passages. All leading to different past epochs. All leading to bygone artistic trends. And then there came a few minutes of navigating through the archipelagoes of tables in the dining hall. Of meandering around the plateau of the dreadfully cramped university yard. Which several minutes might as well have been an eternity. But then he finally brought me to a waiting room neighboring the dean's office. He cordially pointed me to a seat nearby a little table inundated with insipid old newspapers and long-outdated art magazines. They apparently had been waiting there far longer than anyone else. And it was there that I was evidently supposed to wait for him. I was supposed to wait till he finished a brief chitchat with the dean. It was, as he assured me, an immensely affable man of my age. As though it was of any significance! How dared he! And he intended to discuss with him some marvelous cultural event. Some kind of fine vernissage that he was going to arrange soon. A special surprise of some sort.

From a verbal jigsaw puzzle of his dreadful gibberish, this impossible blend of lies and nonsensical arguments that he miraculously managed to splutter within the next few seconds, I divined that it was all about promoting a handful of aspiring artists. All of them still unknown. Yet already struggling. Yet already very promising. And already annoyingly young. Those new maestros. Those future grand masters. It was about raising funds for them. And to that event, he kept inviting me with false zeal. As a sundew asking a fly to stop by for a little sticky chat. For, as he claimed, I would certainly like it. And especially the kind of location in which it was scheduled to take place.

But then he began to convince me maliciously that, in the proverbial meantime, I would not be left alone. That I surely would not be left to my own devices. Whatever they might be. Far from it. For the secretaries, then he pointed at the two young girls glancing at us curiously, were going to take care of me. They were going to make sure that I lacked nothing. They were going to keep me company. And he would be back as soon as possible. He would be back before I started missing him. If only he knew that such a thing was a veritable impossibility! After this little pointless speech, this extravaganza of stupidity on his part, and a no less petite smile that followed it as closely as a stamp on an envelope, he moved away from me in such an abrupt manner that I should have been taken aback by it. And he promptly dissolved into the invincible darkness lying dormant behind the door of the adjacent office. He did that like a burning afterimage of an embarrassing memory of a passing day when one shuts his eyelids in the evening and tries to fall asleep. And so it was. And so it began. The final test had started.

But I could not believe that he suffered from such an intellectual drought. But I could not believe that he truly thought that I would fall, at once, there and then, for such a cheap trick. For such an incredibly unsophisticated tactic. For such an unbelievably asinine move. Yet still morally contemptible. For they were as if taken straight from poor novels and even more mentally impoverished movies, of a truly terrible pedigree. It was exactly as though he were solemnly convinced that I would lose my elderly grayish head over the, otherwise quite attractive, otherwise quite alluring, charms of these two enchanting young ladies. It was as if he really thought that I would forget myself for an instant and break the character, my meticulously polished character, and thus expose myself unwittingly as a not particularly effective double agent. Or a triple one even. For I had no doubt or the faintest illusion that this whole room was bristling with a potpourri of various surveillance devices. And they were glaring and staring at me impertinently from every dark nook. From every unexplored corner. From every clock's long face. From every cozy flowerpot. Or from every suspiciously loose sheet of paper, that not so much double as two-sided agent. For this room was, and I along with it, constantly under close observation and fastidious monitoring. I was certain of it. I was more than convinced of it. And thus I was like a curious specimen that feels a prying and paralyzing gaze of a microscope on its back. And now, he was probably sitting there, behind this impenetrable door. He was sitting there in the company of all the both soulless and heartless members of the executive committee of his menacing organization. And they watched me. And they observed me carefully. My every move. My every gesture or grimace. Even if an involuntary one. Even if an accidental one. They observed me on the large screen diluting the impassive darkness with its revealing blaze. Like a headlight of an approaching train in a tunnel. That ultimate hallmark of danger.

Thus I sat there as motionless as a butterfly pinned to a piece of cardboard, that miniature tomb. For I had to be constantly on my guard. For I had to be incessantly on full alert. For I had to maintain full control over my every single muscle and unruly tendon. For I had to either rapidly approve or dismiss the proposals and petitions, issued by various parts of my glaringly senile body, to twitch or tremble or scratch itself not so spontaneously. And, meantime, they studied me and analyzed me and scrutinized me painstakingly. They did that as though I were a missing link in their long-sought-after not so much evolutional as revolutionary equation. They did that to find out whether I was, really and unreservedly, telling him the rather trite truth. And nothing but my elderly truth. And, indeed, it was a test. A perverted kind of test at that. It was a peculiar litmus paper for our future collaboration.

Fortunately for me, the quite blissful times of my hothead-ed and hotloined youth, when a mixture of insanely attractive female charms and curves still could go to my head and befud-dle me, and intoxicate me, and disarm me prematurely, when they had any sort of influence on me, had long been gone and buried in the tomb of past tense. And now, the unquestionable assets and appetizing charms of these two adorable young creatures were sadly indifferent to me. They were as unimpres-sive to me as a slightly lopsided bench limping in a park. Or as the faulty geometry of this very table at which I was pres-ently seated. They did not make any impression on me. They elicited no reaction from me whatsoever. Well, perhaps, apart from the typical appreciation for the uncanny craftsmanship of Nature. For it was its firm adroit hand that had molded and modeled and formed them to such a spectacular end. I mean that most probably moss-covered hand responsible for creat-ing these two veritable works of art. I mean those breathing works of art who were extraordinarily congruous with both the air and atmosphere of pure artistry and unadulterated, if not unvented, genius, permeating all these rooms and halls. And this feeling was of the very same kind as the asexual ap-proval of one's neighbor's fancily cut hedge. Or of a curious cut of trouser legs in a new uniform for bellhops. I know something about these things, believe me. And so, it was solely of an aesthetic nature. And so, it was purely innocent. It was as innocent as a playful glint in the headlight of a brand new car that had not yet glared at a petrified little animal trying to cross the road in its life. And thus, I remained completely unmoved by them and their charming efforts.

Thereby, for once, my evidently and irreversibly advanced age, became not an insupportable burden, not an intolerable hindrance, but a vital asset and a valiant player in this fierce struggle of ours. Instead of interfering with my actions. In-stead of sabotaging my endeavors and compromising me at my every unsteady step, with unsurpassed stubbornness. As if out of some misdirected spite. Or due to being in some despicable collusion with him. That evil him. That was why I only smiled at them politely whenever there was a need for it. That was why I politely answered their questions whenever there was time for it. And no less politely I reciprocated their courtesies whenever it was unavoidable. But I still had some doubts and mixed feelings about their veracity. For I did not know, I was not utterly sure, how deeply they were involved in this nefarious scheme of his. So I treated them, just in case, with a certain, barely noticeable, reserve. Yet a reserve nonetheless. I treated them as if each of their utterances was both laden and lined with a plethora of catches and traps and multiple meanings. As a particularly tricky blot in a Rorschach test.

But then, all of a sudden, he materialized in the doorway. He materialized there as though out of the uncharted nowhere. Falsely content and beaming and jubilant. He was like a scientist who is far too impatient to wait for the final result of his exciting experiment and resolves to stop it and interfere with it unprofessionally. And, since the moment he crossed the threshold, he started playing the role of my savior and defender. He started playing the role of my savior who, as he apparently hoped, would win my gratitude by saving me, that old and ugly man, from the embraces of these two fine creatures. These two intimidatingly beautiful creatures. But, to his delicious dismay, nothing of the kind had happened. It was impossible. It was out of the question. For I did not feel, not in the least, particularly ugly. If not downright hideous. Let alone intimidated by the enormity of the indubitable beauty of these two lovely companions of mine. For he should know that during all those years of my career and sacrificial service in that marvelous hotel, I had grown perfectly accustomed to communing with the most exquisite and glamorous individuals gracing with their breathtaking presence this cheap vale of ugliness. It was nothing new to me. It was nothing extraordinary to me. It was nothing.

However, I must admit somewhat gingerly that the sheer force of habit created a powerful and irresistible urge in me to open and close something. It was a rather long-cultivated and long-polished habit. It was a habit that I had been nourishing tenderly for the past long decades of my exemplary duty and which had been formed during similar brief chitchats with hotel guests whom I entertained while they were passing through the door being under my care. And, on account of that, whenever each one of these chirpy girls asked me a question about this or that thing, in that incredibly melodious and polite voice being so akin to that of my little daughter, I instinctively groped for something. I groped for anything in my vicinity that could be opened or closed without delay. I did that, whether it was the cover of a haggard folder lounging on the table near me, or the lid of a box of mints lying right beside it. Like its saccharine sidekick.

However, I could not read anything from the inscrutable arrangement of his facial features. As though written in fine facial print. I could not read his reaction to my, after all, rather firm and unfaltering attitude. I did not know his reaction to my clearly victorious getting out of trouble. Out of that enchanting predicament. And, at the same time, out of that singular test that he had concocted for me slyly. Out of all the traps and ambushes that he had set for me cleverly. Out of that unintentionally beautiful interrogation. So I even started wondering whether I had botched it incidentally. I wondered whether I had ruined it unknowingly. I wondered whether I had made the best possible strategic decision on this matter. And whether I had thus dreadfully squandered an unrepeatable opportunity to infiltrate his otherwise impervious organization. I worried that I had marred it on account of my overconfidence and arrogance that emanated from me too intensely. That oozed profusely from every tired pore of my sagging body. Like holiness from a bishop. Thus, I wondered assiduously, what the final verdict of this recent clandestine meeting was. I wondered while observing his mysteriously impassive face out of the corner of my eye. I wondered while scrutinizing his whole detestably virile and vibrant self as he engaged in a tiny casual chitchat with my two gorgeous interrogators. I tried to deduce what was the outcome of the ominous conference that took place right behind this now stolid door. As if I tried counting cards at a casino. For it was then that was about to be sealed the fate of my joining their ranks. Of my being drafted into their legion of mindless as well as heartless barbarians. For it surely had been decided in there in the atmosphere suffused with the heavy, oppressive vapors of mistrust as well as skepticism. That I had to overcome. That I had to alleviate. And whose deleterious aftereffects I had to neutralize adroitly. As an air freshener battling with the fetid outcome of one's poor hygiene. But this immensely responsible task I might easily have failed to accomplish due to nothing else but that unforeseen strange spasm of my muscle of superciliousness. Or rather, of pride. And pride only.

After an instant, however, he enthusiastically motioned me to the door. Like a cinema usher armed with a flashlight, that makeshift light-sword. Then he nodded to these exquisite tormentors of mine, probably thus giving them a kind of belated cryptic orders. Some mysterious instructions. And he promptly took me for yet another stroll around the boundless insides of this immense university complex. Without a word of explanation. Without any further ado. For it was a monstrous beast of an edifice. It was akin to an anthill that had grown too much to the extent that it could start letting full-sized people in. It had never feared anyone. It had never bowed to anyone. And it had never acknowledged anything else but its own infinite splendor and grandeur. Let alone its magnificent luggage of history. And now, like a finely blushing apple that turns out to be rotten at its core, it became the nest of all that was most evil and vile and appalling in the world.

And I followed him around a maze of aortas and intestines of that imposing marble-laden organism. Like a molecule of an antibiotic chasing a bacteria. And I observed closely and carefully the bas-relief of his singularly stolid face. And I studied the tense pose of his hectically moving body, looking as though he were in such a hurry that he had no time to explain to me the simplest aspects and nuances of his recent verdicts and decisions. And as I was doing all that I knew that I should not rejoice so early. I guessed that it would be wise not to betray the irrepressible joy thudding inside my head with any unscheduled twitch of my mouth, or with any gratuitous spasm of my recklessly heaving chest. For everything could still go catastrophically wrong. Because nothing was decided yet. Because nothing was definitive yet. However, I could not resist it. And nothing could possibly help me. Not even thinking about all that was distasteful and unpleasant. Not even resurrecting in the stuffy screening room of my memory a farrago of the most agonizing and degrading memories of the past yet still hardly healed moments. All those still purulent mental wounds. All those still smarting emotional lacerations. For, soon after our swift departure from this waiting room, this intolerably amusing torture chamber, I caught myself grinning. And I mean grinning both recklessly and blissfully. For I grinned just like a child who discovers its Christmas present a few months too early.

Then, my otherwise rather listless and gracefully languid eyes leaped rapaciously from object to object. From wall to wall. From shadow to shadow. They did that with the alacrity of a professional acrobat. They slid, like zealous skiers, down the barely sketched vague contours of the renowned and solemn figures standing in the impenetrable shade of history of this hallowed place. And it was a place in which every louder grunt or foolish gasp could be regarded as the veritable blasphemy against the triumph of mind over body. They eagerly touched and groped and grazed with their insatiable gaze everything. Every single little and uninvolved thing that we happened to pass by on our way down this or that corridor. And so, my eyes were like the gaze of a child who had been locked for the night, as a kind of blessing in a particularly thick and unfashionable disguise, inside a toy warehouse. And they did that, they adroitly did all that, while seeking a place, an appropriate place, and a perfect place, where I could start right away that campaign of clandestine actions. They looked for a place where I could begin without any delays my work of an avowed saboteur. And even my usually stiff and clumsy fingers at once became uncannily nimble and agile. They began impatiently looking for, hunting for, as well as tenaciously sniffing for a thing, an even little and insignificant thing that could be promptly broken, shattered, twisted, or distorted. Or at least knocked off only to spite my devious enemy.

He, however, walked quite briskly. And so, I had serious trouble with catching up with him because of all that looking around and wriggling nervously on my part. Like a recalcitrant little boy ready to play the mischief but still not knowing how and where. Meantime, he kept consulting his watch, that invariably timely advisor of his. And, evidently, he did not intend to produce any kind of explanation. Not even any petty or paltry excuse. Not even a banal one. All the more so, he had no intention of alleviating this unnerving suspense hovering above us threateningly. This uncertainty accumulating between us fastidiously. As the first-rate hatred, that absurd side effect of a rivalry between two second-rate artists investing far more energy and far more inventiveness in it than in the creative process of their art. Perhaps he counted on the fact that by stretching to the very limits of decency that last test phase of our cooperation, as if it were a stocking on the bulbous head of a robber, he increased the chances of my betraying my real motives, of my compromising my true goals. But I did not feel compelled to give him the satisfaction. Not now. Not ever.

So, after yet another handful of minutes of heavy and lingering silence, as uncomfortable as shoes that are a few sizes too small, he led me into an impressively large lecture hall brimful of irritable and fretful students. From time to time, they grunted discontentedly. Once in a while, they sighed rhythmically. For, apparently, they waited for someone more and more impatiently. And then he discreetly pointed me to a distant seat in the last and highest row of the vast auditorium, to which promising future vantage point of mine I clambered slowly yet methodically and with the admirable tenacity of a dilapidated cable car. I did that to the, at first timid and repressed, delight of these students. I did that to their initially shy and sloppily concealed curiosity. And I did that to the rather off-key accompaniment of the respectfully muffled jokes as well as quite witty remarks being whispered by them and circulating among them. Like a singularly joyful germ of some delirious disease. And with each clumsy step of mine, with each shuffle of my feet, this din of suppressed jokes and laughs thickened and mounted and intensified and gained its momentum. It intensified till finally someone from the other end of the room, some faceless and sourceless voice, as it often happens, failed to hold back its excitement. He forgot itself. And he blurted out something that originally was not intended for external use. He suggested that apparently there awaited them so many exams and make-up exams and make-up exams following those previous make-up exams that they certainly would reach my respectable age in these noble walls before being able to graduate, in the walls that were not much older than I seemed to be. Out of the corner of my baffled eye, I noticed their lecturer and my cunning guide around this splendid temple of talent, brilliantly feigning an impromptu blush of embarrassment. Then the whole room, with equal and unbridled abruptness, as if by tacit consent, instantly abandoned the constrictive shackles of etiquette. They defied the whole artificial ritual of stifled whispers and mitigated grunts. And then they burst out laughing heartily. Gamely. Like a symphony orchestra agilely climbing the highest registers on its conductor's silent order. And I laughed along with them.

And I laughed despite myself. And then, a ripple of powerful laughter traveled, at an astonishing pace, the length and breadth of this spacious hall. And, from then on, my presence there could no longer be neglected. It could no longer be ignored. It could no longer be denied. As a shameful blunder that one commits at the dinner table and tries to blame it on someone else. I only smiled affably at the gleeful sound of all these remarks, of all these comments, after all, quite amusing ones. Quite genuine ones. Quite heartwarming ones. And, above all, completely bereft of the even residual amount of spite. Or so much as the sediment of malice.

Obediently, I took the seat that he pointed out to me. It was located on the uninhabited peripheries of that hall, on the deserted outskirts of their attention. I sat down there to watch him, imperiously and with ineffable delight, from above. I watched him, nervously stuttering and spluttering all the time, alternately apologizing for his inexcusable late arrival, and promising solemnly that nothing of the embarrassing kind would ever happen in the future. And I relished immensely the awkwardness of his feverish attempts to atone and compensate for his, after all, rather petty and insignificant offense. And this fact was the sole redeeming quality of that otherwise pitifully dreadful show. For he assured them, with all his remorseful and educated might, that it happened to him for the first time. For he claimed that it was, ironically, his quite belated debut. As he must have been a late bloomer in terms of being late for work. He convinced them that this very day it had eluded him that he was supposed to substitute for another lecturer, by the way, not a very popular one. For, apparently, the absent man had daringly broken his right hand and left leg while performing the botched acrobatics and failed stunts in a rather successful skiing accident. And he had done it so spectacularly and breathtakingly that many spectators wondered if, by any chance, it had not been his main purpose, instead of simply sliding down the slope as everyone else kept doing all that time.

And he kept lacing his tediously apologetic speech with so many stops and pauses and groans and moans till it became as maddeningly unintelligible as a ransom note composed by an illiterate person for whom even the newspaper clippings are not much help. Meantime, I glanced over not so much a sea as a pincushion bristling with the intense and focused heads of his listeners, of his intent students, sticking out of it here and there docilely. All of them horribly young. All of them unendurably blossoming. All of them intolerably promising. And I could not fend off that nagging, gloomy realization that everyone, every single one of them might, with a little extra effort on their side, or lack thereof on mine, have taken my place at my gentle daughter's side. And each one of them might have made her leave me alone in my old age. In my really old age. And I could not allow that nightmare to come true. Despicably true.

Thus, after an instant, that initial spontaneous amusement stretching and exercising my slackening facial muscles vanished irrevocably, and that inglorious relaxation in the face of the enemy, were instantly quenched. Then I segued into the full-blown discipline. And the modest thread of understanding temporarily established between them and me in the course of these several moments of joint laughter, evaporated at once. Or was momentarily cut off. Like an umbilical cord in the case of a child who wants to go its own way and not to stay with its mother forever.

Then as if wanting to spare me the unspeakable horror of listening to him any longer my muscles tautened impossibly. They tautened as he said a few things more or less sententiously. As he smiled dimly. As he strived to furnish any plausible explanation for his more and more convoluted excuses. My skin tightened thus smoothing out a handful of wrinkles and making me look at least a few decades younger. My eyes squinted suspiciously, and I instinctively bared my loose dentures. Like a bobblehead toy dog at the sight of yet another bump in the road. And I looked at those people, and I wondered, as a wave of implacable bitterness washed over me from the coast of my feet to the peninsula of my elderly head, at what things they were better than I. More proficient than I. More skillful than I. Or more glaringly effective than I. I wondered what they did or planned to do that warranted my replacement, if undoubtedly they were at the same time more naive, less experienced, far less seasoned, and decidedly less judicious than I had ever been. Without a doubt. Without any question. Then how it was at all possible that they were qualified enough, competent enough, and knowledgeable enough, to even consider ousting me from my special place by her side. To even plan such an insolent domestic coup d'état. For they were evidently considering it. How it was possible that they felt confident enough to even dare to think about removing me and impertinently pushing me off the stage of life. Along with other people similar to me. For I felt like an actor whose both face and star has long faded and evaporated as irrevocably as the ink on the already crumpled and yellowish and forgotten posters from his debut show that no one is old enough to remember, perhaps, even including himself.

I had to find a way, any way, really, to defend myself against it. I had to defend myself against this seemingly inevitable generational revolution. Like a good old silverware sensing the advent of food in pills. I had to be constantly, undauntedly, tirelessly, on guard. And I could not allow such deleterious moments of relaxation to creep into my camp anymore. I mean such loosening of the internal discipline of mine. Just like that. Just like before. Thus I had to defend myself against it gamely. And I mean now. Right now. Before it was too late. Before it was tragically too late for any kind of move on my part.

It was then that I strived at all costs to see in them, to discern in them, these alleged displays of their superiority. These symptoms of their fineness. These glimmers of their excellence. I strived to see in them all that was allowing them to tower over me and over everyone else. I strived to see in them all that would serve as a basis for my impending yet already inexorable more or less honorable future discharge from the duty in the foyer of life. Then it came to me, and I was shocked by the unprecedented abruptness of this realization, it came to me that it was them, that it must have been them, that it could be no one else but them. For it was a pack of his ardent pupils. For it was a swarm of his most avid listeners. A slew of his fanatical protégés. All these ostensibly polite and thoroughly innocent young people. And it was from this very group that he must have been recruiting, with unflagging success as well as with the connivance of the authorities of this noble institution, the members of his death squads. His undaunted guerilla fighters. His own personal suicide bombers and rabid saboteurs of every possible kind.

I felt the not so much cold as freezing sweat streaming down my cracked and wrinkled back. It streamed there while forming the impromptu brisk rivulets and the whole streams akin to the ones appearing on a cracked soil after the end of an unrelenting drought. For it struck me that I suddenly found myself among my foes. Among my adversaries. Among my archenemies. I was right in the middle of my enemy's camp. I was there like a man who while seeking shelter from the upcoming rain in the zoo recklessly wanders into a cave only to discover that he has ventured right into some kind of lair, and is now surrounded by the pride of blissfully dozing lions. At the same time, I fathomed that there was nothing particularly strange or unusual or even mildly disturbing in the fact that he had managed to draft them and brainwash them and indoctrinate them so quickly. So swimmingly. So easily. And with so little effort on his part. For they suited that ignoble purpose perfectly. For they seemed to be created with this sole hateful purpose in mind. And I understood it to the extent that I felt compelled to genuflect inwardly to his strategic genius, to bow to his tactical brilliance. For, after all, all of them wanted a change, any kind of change, really. They yearned for it. They dreamed of it. They craved it obsessively, viscerally. Each of them separately. And all of them put together. It was obvious. If not blatantly obvious. For all young people want change deep down in their inherently change-oriented hearts and souls. They desire it naively and mindlessly. They ache for it beyond limits. Like an orphan thirsty for a dash of parental attention. They lust after it instinctively with every pore of their smooth bodies. They do that even if only for change's sake. Without thinking about it. Without considering it properly. Without calculating its inevitable consequences. Without anything. Change! They had even been born with this word, with this very word, spoken in countless languages and most unpronounceable dialects, inflected in every conceivable way, circulating in their veins. For this word was like a disease capable of overthrowing the current and well-proven and splendidly working status quo. That marvelous output. That excellent pinnacle. That triumphant outcome of innumerable epochs of well-meant efforts and inhuman labor and diplomatic toil of former generations. They would do it at once only to gain an opportunity, an invaluable for terribly rare opportunity, to start something. To start anything. Anew. Afresh. They would do it unhesitantly only to have that one single chance to create something from scratch. They would do it instantly only to contribute in any relevant and memorable way to the history of mankind. Even if it meant building on the still smoldering ruins and rubble of the achievements of their ancestors. Like a particularly malicious real estate developer.

But if mostly a hint of it, a dollop of change, can lead to truly salutary effects, to quite invigorating and healthy results, this time, however, the slightest alternation, the smallest seemingly innocent deviation from the norm or the beaten standards, was potentially threatening. It was insanely dangerous. It was like in the case of tampering with a delicate balance inside some highly unstable chemical reaction by an ambitious, yet still catastrophically inexperienced, young chemist. I had to prevent that from happening at all costs. In any case, I failed to comprehend all that. I found it extremely hard to believe, even imagine, that one, anyone, really, could willingly opt for such a change. So blindly. So obsessively. So foolishly. So maniacally even. I found it difficult to believe that one could do that utterly oblivious to the costs, unmindful of the possible side effects and aftereffects and all the other effects of such an irresponsible action. Though all inevitable and truly terrifying. For I was well aware that any kind of modification or innovation, let alone transformation, could entail a great risk, a nearly palpable danger, and without any doubt, a large, if not inadmissibly large, for possibly lethal, dose of pure and crystalline uncertainty. And I mean every change. Every single one. Even the most trivial one. Even the most banal or deceptively insignificant one. Every change of the present well-established and well-tended state of affairs. And such a dose of uncertainty would be capable of killing any patient far more quickly and expertly than the long and agonizing process of decay that would be only devastating his body, slowly yet methodically, for the years to come.

I was mystified. I was utterly puzzled. For I could barely understand this urge, this bizarre craving, wild and unbridled, let alone accept it, or even approve of it. For I knew that whenever one resolves to take the risk and begin any sort of changes one ventures into the realm of the unknown whose enormity is truly overwhelming. And one does that without the aid of any moral compass. Without any ethical map. Without a dash of the highly desired and welcome knowledge. Without any relevant experience. Because whenever one enters such a terra incognita, alluringly mysterious, unattainable, and elusive, the whole baggage of one's wisdom that one had been accumulating scrupulously throughout the years turns out to be ridiculously useless and redundant. It becomes as redundant as an ability to recite poems when one is trapped inside a car that went careening down the hill.

Then, after receiving this almost cruel portion of scholarly boredom, most of which, fortunately for me, briskly went in one ear and out the other, as if I were a tunnel arching acrobatically above an informational highway, I was mercifully released. I was quickly released, along with my other inmates, from the makeshift prison cells of our student desks. I felt greatly relieved, even incredibly liberated. For right here I had very little scope to act. For right here I had no space to exercise my ingenious moves. I felt almost restrained. I could not put my undeniable potential to use, as well as the wide panoply of my innate subversive abilities. Well, perhaps, with the noble exception of a few casual attempts to disrupt the otherwise tedious lecture of his by indiscriminately shooting paper bullets from a rubber band, as well as whispering to my fellow students all the horribly wrong answers to all the insufferably correct questions he asked them. But I could hardly muster enough of the famous self-discipline of mine to contain and suppress the overpowering urge to damage and devastate his organization from the inside. That congregation of raving revolutionaries. That motley jumble of truculent lunatics. But it was absolutely necessary. But it was utterly unavoidable. For I realized, as I joined that little loud crowd pressing and pushing to the door, that I had to make a certain revision of my current behavior as well as attitude. At least temporarily. At least fraudulently. For I had to lie low, inconspicuously, unsuspiciously low. For a moment. For the time being. Because it was then that I both noticed and sensed a volley of miniature cold blades of suspicious and inquisitive glances of these official students and fanatical steadfast henchmen of his after hours. I felt them prickling and poking and accosting me. From all sides at once. All the time. Like a cutting offensive of snow during a blizzard. I instantly noticed a blatantly disgruntled and offended gaze of a boy, as pockmarked as if his face had been crushed by some higher power as a failed design only to be restored a moment later, to whom I had prompted a ludicrous answer to a question about the meaning of the symbol of a half-peeled lemon in still life paintings. For I had whispered to him slyly that it was all about promoting extremely valuable culinary skills allowing one to concoct the most excellent kinds of salads imaginable. And it amused me greatly. Though internally. I also could not overlook all the grotesquely disgusted gazes of those passing me by, ceremoniously and with ostentatious aloofness. And with a slew of paper bullets of my design still sticking to their unsuspecting backs. Like papery leeches.

Meantime he, suddenly gloomy, suddenly somber, wearing a long and discontented face that was apparently supposed to conceal the infinite reserves of his cunningness and deceit, brought me to yet another hall. It was also seemingly boundless. It was also fabulously spacious. And there was also a different group of students, hidden shyly behind the scrawny scaffoldings of their easels. As snipers lurking right behind the jagged ruins of a bombarded city. And they labored to recreate, in the somewhat crude and cruel fashion, the whole gamut of subtleties and nuances and intricacies of the soft listless curves forming the body of the rather plump, rather large, and rather nude, female model flaunting her questionable charms in front of them. She was shamelessly hubristic and bursting with her naked pride. She was like that while sitting in front of them on a bit wobbly stool. As a kind of fleshy statue. And she behaved as if she were in the vanguard of the finest God's creations, occupying a honorable place right next to the splendidly painted sunsets and mountain ridges drenched in the morning mist, which she certainly, indubitably, decidedly, was not.

So, once again, I was being conveniently seated in the back. So, once again, I was left alone at a relatively safe distance from that odious villain and devilish nemesis of mine. But still behind enemy lines. But still with enough time to act. And then, all of a sudden, without a cordial warning of any kind, I was inundated by a simply inconceivable flood of alluring possibilities for the realization of my elaborate plan. Of highly tempting options. Of blatantly promising opportunities. And they momentarily began popping up and sprouting up in front of my dazzled eyes in such an overwhelming number that, in fact, I grew seriously concerned that I might not be able to take advantage of them all. Like a thief noticing the unlocked doors of several cars on a parking lot. And then, unobserved and undisturbed by anyone, I began incorrectly mixing the paints on their palettes that were recklessly left unattended. I swiftly switched the caps on all the paint tubes whenever no one was watching. I briskly stole their pencils. I scratched their canvases. I ably extracted the balls from their ballpoint pens. I furtively trimmed their brushes till their hair looked more like an inexperienced one-day stubble. And I surreptitiously deposited in my rather cramped trouser pockets various painting tools that I managed to lay my hands on. And then they kept jingling and clamoring treacherously in there thus imperiling that entire clandestine endeavor of mine before it came to any even mildly satisfactory end.

Finally, I decided to conclude this day of first-rate and laudable subversive work with something special. I wanted to conclude it on a remarkably high note. But I still did not even suspect how high it would turn out to be. I wanted to conclude it with a kind of sweeping flourish, akin to the one complementing a fine signature. And so, due to that my choice fell, quite naturally, quite smoothly, how else, on the pivotal character of this very class, on the bare highlight of this workshop. Well, excluding him, of course. It fell on the female lead actress of that distasteful show. That rather unabashedly naked object of everyone's artistic attention. And that was why, during a recess between the classes, I approached her with feigned timidity and genuine reluctance. I approached that rather glaringly shameless creature, who, as if deliberately, even then continued to expose her dubious charms. When no one was really watching. When no one was paying any forced attention to her anymore. So it was as if she were a campaign poster from the last election. She did that while covering herself partly with a quite singular kind of tunic that was, in truth, as narrow and perversely revealing as a transparent scarf. And it generously unveiled far more than it managed to cover. Like a blabbering security guard. So then, I declared to her, in a light, ineffably light tone of voice glazed with spurious politeness, that she was gorgeous. In fact, I told her that she was so astonishingly gorgeous that the dean of this hateful place decided to take a picture of her. It was going to be an innocent picture, an ordinary picture, but at the same time a special picture, designed to immortalize her beauty. And, in this rather unsophisticated manner, it was supposed to preserve her charms for posterity. For all those yet unborn, yet vague, yet unreal, future students of this splendid university. It was going to preserve her for those who thus would be able to learn how to draw and paint proficiently, and, above all, how to resurrect with a few strokes of their brushes, her fabulous body when she was long gone and buried. But she only regarded me with that long, mistrustful, and meaningful gaze. She did that with the rigidity of a ticket collector who forgot to take with him his faithful ticket puncher yet still intends to punish others for forgetting their tickets. And it was a gaze that would not have made any impression on me, that would have failed to excite me in any noticeable way, even if I had still been trapped in the lustful snares of an unbearably youthful age. None. None whatsoever.

In the end, I noticed that this vanity of hers was apparently winning that brisk skirmish with her seriously weakened reason. For it was a heady mixture of arrogance and conceit that she kept displaying and exuding and radiating almost diligently during every single second of these workshops. Of which deplorable vice my lovely daughter was free, completely free, as well as blissfully unstained by it. And it was winning that bizarre variation on the tug of war competition with the thread

240

of conscience playing the supporting role of a rope. For after a brief moment of hesitation, she agreed to follow me straight to the conveniently sequestered janitor's closet. And it, as I kept assuring her exultantly, was a darkroom in which the alleged photo was about to be taken. In order to embolden her, to encourage her somewhat, I promptly offered to go in first. I gallantly offered that to help her overcome an initial and tyrannical reflex of understandable skepticism. That immaterial shackle hampering one's moves whenever there is a call for a definitive action. I offered to pave the way. I offered to do it like an adventurous cook venturing to taste an old piece of meat unearthed in the back of the fridge to avoid wasting food. And I paved it soon afterward. I paved it recklessly, and also a bit foolishly, as it was about to turn out.

For it was then that a cascade of odd, abrupt, cruel, and downright unfortunate events, excruciating mishaps, and critical moments, took place in quick succession. Instantly, it got out of my control. Its reins slipped through my fingers and were on the loose even though I heroically tried to get hold of them once again. Like a child who lets its precious kite fly away. And it ruthlessly brought down on my elderly loyal head a clattering and roaring avalanche of unceasing consequences. Or, perhaps, I had never had any control over any of those things in the first place. So, I entered that cramped and impenetrably dark room while groping and fumbling desperately for any solid object. For a hint of its decor. For a barely sketched contour of its cluttered labyrinthine insides. For anything revealed by an even stray beam of light. And then I tripped over a vagrant bucket. Over a lopsided ladder. Over an idle mop. Then they knocked off a nearby molting broom. And it, in turn, knocked off a few terribly emaciated easels that looked like an annual congregation of skeletons crammed into a closet. Roaring and thundering unmercifully, they quickly rammed right into a slightly slanted shelf overflowing with heady detergents. Then into yet another. And, in

241

the end, as a thrilling finale, as a riveting climax, a miniature warehouse rack overturned raucously. And it, in spite of its relatively low weight, obstructed the entrance as expertly as if it were a part of some maleficent trap heralding the beginning of an ambush, because it could not be moved at all.

Thus, I was trapped in there. I was hopelessly trapped in there. Like the last breath of life inside the coffin. I was trapped in there without a lawful sentence. Without a possibility of an appeal. Without even hearing the charges. And, above all, against my already sinister intentions. For I was stuck there in a morally ambivalent situation, in the company of a totally naked and additionally ungodly screaming art model of dubious beauty. For she was nowhere near as wonderful and exquisite as my dear wife used to be, may she rest in peace.

After a full hour, after a seemingly interminable hour, of my indescribable agonies inflicted by her agonizing shouts and tireless pummeling the stubborn door, and me from time to time, this very door was forced out of its surprisingly cooperative hinges. And then it was moved away with an inhuman effort. It was the very same door that should have been, on account of my occupation, on account of the closeness of our interests, my perfectly natural ally. Like a bartender supporting a drunk. Or like a criminal helping out a suspended policeman. But instead of backing me up, it betrayed me treacherously. For it barricaded us inside and turned this little claustrophobic closet into a real unassailable fortress with just a handful of brooms and buckets serving as the only means of defense available to me at that time. Then there materialized yet another obstacle. And it was decidedly more obstinate. Far more implacable. It was an obstacle in the form of a terrible mayhem that ensued instantly. For it was as if with the opening of that accursed door someone also carelessly opened a Pandora's box. If not an entire closet.

To my utter astonishment that promptly transformed into plain irritation when my initial bafflement subsided completely, the lecturer immediately stepped into action. He did that before I properly realized the severity of my situation. For, apparently, I had breached the prevailing code of misconduct in this otherwise thoroughly decadent place. And he leaped to my defense. And he protected me gamely. He defended me cleverly. He feverishly shielded me like a clueless lion trying to save its own hunter. And not more than a few seconds had passed after that singular outburst of his magnanimousness for me, when he began juggling, with uncanny proficiency, with extraordinary elegance, several different positions at once. For he became my unapologetically ruthless lawyer, my unfalteringly committed counselor, my manager, and my publicist. And he changed them so swiftly and kaleidoscopically that I could not tell which one of them was the real one. I could no longer tell which one was the genuine and true archenemy of mine. It was like when a parent discovers its child's secret notebook with pages covered with a few different handwriting styles implying a personality split in so many parts that it is hard to support and rear them all. For he went to great lengths to assure all the people crowding around that damned closet that there was nothing to see there. That there was nothing interesting there. That there was no need to call the police. For, basically, nothing happened of any importance. No one was attacked. No one was hurt. Both physically and emotionally. No one suffered any unacceptable losses. But, above all, he invested the impressive amounts of zeal and energy into convincing this, not so much poor as naked, soul not to press any charges against me. For, I, as he insisted, at my cruelly advanced age, would not have been able to harm her in any way, even if I had dreamed about it incessantly.

And so, it was nothing else but that unexpected and unprecedented spurt of kindness and care on his part, which instinctively instilled unconditional gratitude in me, and which convinced me irrefutably that it was he. The suddenly helpful and obliging he. It convinced me that he must have been behind all that. It convinced me that he must have planned all that. That he must have orchestrated all that from the comfortable and cozy backseat. Like a chess player ordering around all the queens and kings. Yet he had planned that not only to compromise me utterly. No. For he had also done that to curb my inherent instinct of a born saboteur and replace it surreptitiously with the boundless indebtedness for his help in getting me out of that hollering and kicking predicament, and sparing me yet another dubious pleasure of meeting with the local police officers. That was why, in his speeding car, I remained silent all the way home. As a radio that swallowed a mouthful of static. That was why I refused to look at him. I refused to glance at him, to so much as glimpse at him. I did that while restricting our eye contact to the miserable visual leftovers, to all that he managed to catch sight of in the rear-view mirror or in the windshield. And even then I defiantly averted my gaze whenever our eyes met briefly within the confines of such lustrous surfaces. For it simply must have been him all along.

And that was why all the way home, I doggedly and ruthlessly relived and replayed in the darkroom of my addled mind the whole embarrassing event. Scene after scene. Frame after frame. I replayed it while deliberately pausing at the most painful moments, and while permitting the relentless waves of remorse and sourness to wash over me repeatedly. Now and again. Over and over again. I allowed them to wash over me to cleanse me in a way. In some twisted and wicked way. Yet I did all that not out of some dreadfully misdirected desire to harm and maltreat someone, something. I did that not due to my hitherto latent and rather discreet penchant for masochism, for self-inflicting mental pain, as if I relished squashing an imaginary cigarette butt on my frontal lobe, or for torturing myself from time to time, until I reached some kind of perverse gratification. Because it is not the only kind of pleasure that remains available to one after the fierce, natural fire of lust has long been extinguished by the silvery foam of grayish hair, and after one's sex drive has discreetly driven off the bridge. I did that to savor the enormity of my fiasco. The impressive vastness of my defeat. Like a smoker relishing every puff of the bad habit that defeated him once again. And I did that to draw conclusions from my horrible mistakes. And to learn. To learn above all. To learn far more from my failure than I would ever have managed to do from the greatest conceivable victory of mine.

Somehow, I retained this rather adamantly reticent mood throughout the entire trip back home. And even later on. Already in the apartment. Like a monk who has taken a vow of silence. I retained it even while trying to dismiss that unwanted rapport with him that had been inadvertently established between us during this joint misfortune of ours. And yet, despite this reticence of mine, my beloved daughter did all the talking. She suddenly became a veritable fountain of wild and frantic accusations and admonishments and reprimands. As a mother who catches her child red-handed, and soon red-assed, committing some mischief or other. But I was not sure for whom she intended them. For he quickly took her back to her room and swiftly slammed the door behind them. Thus he insolently cut me off from the rest of her uncannily fierce tirade. Like a landlord shutting off one's utilities because of an overdue bill. So I managed to pick up only a mosaic of disjointed screams and shouts and more and more muffled plaintive cries. But they did not form any definitive or remarkably revealing picture. As the image in a kaleidoscope that can be nothing and everything at the same time.

But I had my suspicions. But I had my own ideas about that whole otherwise inexplicable confusion. Apparently, she must have stumbled carelessly upon some kind of proof, upon some piece of conclusive evidence, which brought down the last faint shroud of his elaborate lies and illusions and deception in which he had been relentlessly wrapping her, as if striving to mummify her. And she, after this startling discovery, after this catalyst of her sharp and brutal awakening, of her revelation, of her epiphany, was not going to tolerate it anymore. And she did not want to put up with his deceit any longer. It was only a matter of time. It really was.

But this time, as I supposed, this unprecedented act of open disloyalty put her at a far greater risk than I had ever managed to do by means of a parade of my more or less harmful debacles. For, nothing riles the fanatic more than betrayal in his own ranks. Not the annoying caprices of fate. Not even the devastating machinations of his most sworn enemies. Thus I had to act as precisely as possible. Thus I had to save her as quickly as possible. Thus I had to abandon this impressively elaborate and riveting though increasingly futile hide-and-seek game for good. Because there was no more time for any new brilliant moves, for any scintillating repartees, for any breathtaking last minute actions conducted in overtime. There simply was no time to waste. Not now. Not anymore.

And thus I finally resolved to do what I had been procrastinating with stunning diligence for the last several weeks, that I had been glancing at fearfully as its side effects were being magnified by the distorting mirror of my fear. For I finally resolved to apply the finishing touches to his downfall. I resolved to quicken his inevitable end. To humbly administer that coup de grâce.

BOOK THREE

— ♦ ♦ ♦ —

WHEN ONE
DOOR CLOSES...

◆◆◆

I had made up my mind. I had made the final and definitive decision. A slew of detailed orders and instructions for all my limbs and muscles and body organs had long been typed and sealed and dispatched en masse. Like cards before Christmas. And so, there was no turning back from it. And so, there was no way out of it. I was determined to do that last thing that remained within my feeble power. And yet I could not bring myself to do it. I could not force myself to execute this internal, imperious, and peremptory, order of mine. I felt like a soldier who, a second before pulling the lethal trigger, is hampered by a second of hesitancy as he desultorily wonders who is the greater criminal, he wielding his gun or the man who has sent him there while brandishing nothing more than a mere pen.

That was why a few gloomy days had to pass before I finally came to terms with my crushing and devastating defeat on all fronts. Both in the air and on the ground. Both in my mind and between us. And I was hopelessly unable to reverse it or amend it in any way now. As a child toying with a shattered family heirloom. And I had no other option but to accept it, to face its tremendous scope and almost outlandish enormity with my head held proudly high. I had to face it before I could relegate my task, my unenviable for botched mission, the very one that I had ignobly and miserably failed to accomplish, to those more powerful ones than I had ever been, to those whom I intended not only to protect gallantly but also to impress with my valiant efforts. And I mean those efforts that, in the end, came to the pretty disappointing nothing.

And that was also why, one evening, several days later, as I was brooding over the vastness of my abortive plan, over its devastated ruins and eviscerated details, I initially failed to notice that this demonic adversary of mine along with my exquisite little daughter dressed up and bustled about vigorously. They did that while hurrying each other in a rather suspicious manner. She was now visibly calmer. She was now pointedly more serene, yet with that noticeable tenseness still simmering below her delicate skin. Like water inside the kettle. Because she must have been still furious with him for all that he had done and planned to do to her. But I did not pay nearly any attention to it. And my unseeing vacant eyes gazed right through them, utterly undisturbed, as they walked hastily to and fro. I gazed at them blankly as they circulated hectically in front of me. As ricocheting racquetballs. She was putting on her best dress. He was donning his ridiculously fine jacket and helping her with an unduly recalcitrant zipper. She, once again, kept adjusting her hair and fiddling with his tie. And thus she completed that carnival of truly insufferable clichés. Like a trite kiss in the rain that can ruin even the best movie. Which things, perhaps, I subconsciously preferred not to witness at all.

But I failed to notice anything odd about it. Like an excessively well-mannered man helping the burglars met on the staircase to carry his own TV set. I failed to notice anything particularly disconcerting about it. I failed to notice that until I saw that my graceful daughter was sporting her best earrings, which her kind mother, and my genial beloved wife, had bequeathed her, and which she, from then on, wore only on not so much special as truly outstanding occasions. Was it one of them? Was it going to be a really memorable occasion? Was it going to be so special and unique that she resolved to adorn her already extraordinarily fine persona with a dash of her family's history? As if to symbolically prolong it? Was she really going to do that? Was she going to add yet another volume or chapter to it? Some singular yet nonetheless voluminous chapter? Or, at least, a mere footnote to that catalog of our family case?

Then my blood froze in my veins and stopped its circulation altogether. Like cars stuck in a tremendous traffic jam. Their elegant clothes, their furtive glances, their idiom of innuendoes and understatements, the unexpected appearance of the family jewelry, all that began forming and composing a picture, this quite frightful picture in the atelier in my mind, that I did not like. That I did not like at all. Not in the least. For it bore all the unmistakable, if not unmistakably terrifying, hallmarks of a family drama in four acts and an epilog.

But I decided not to lose my silvery head, akin to a metal ball crowning a Tesla coil. I decided not to lose my cold blood, however lukewarm it may have become in the process. And so I catapulted myself to my wobbly feet. And I stiffly marched out of the inviolable sanctuary of my room. Like a cuckoo peering out of a clock. Then, I paraded into the hall in the most offhand and indifferent manner that I could presently afford. But still at a ridiculously exorbitant emotional price. And then, watching him helping her into a coat, also her finest one, I cunningly asked her a question. A tricky question. I asked her that also in a suspiciously casual tone. I asked her whether they were going to the mall, to that mall right around the corner. And if so, whether they could buy me a piece of pumice stone to rub my cracking heels. For, since I was already home, I might as well take care of myself a little. For an instant, they regarded me quizzically. They stared at me as if I had spoken to them in that foreign dialect of insanity. Which I did not know at all. For it was merely another brilliant subterfuge that I managed to strike out of my increasingly weary mind worn out by my recent debacles. As if it were a lighter running out of fuel. And, after yet another moment of an energetic exchange of glances, as if I were watching from the sidelines an intimate and impalpable variation on a tennis match, my lovely daughter, after glimpsing inquisitively at my spiteful foe, chirped in this cheerful voice of hers that they were heading to one place. To some place. Together. And that they intended, no less jointly, to go out for dinner at some fancy restaurant. She said that it was going to be a special evening to them. A truly memorable moment. She claimed that it was supposed to be a surprise for me. Also for me. For I was supposed to be invited to join them there. For I was supposed to be a part of it. A vital part of this evening. But after all those things, those catastrophic things, those irreparable things, that had happened recently she could not imagine taking me with them. She just could not imagine allowing me to come along with them. She simply could not do that. Not now.

And so, I was grounded.

He won her over. Once again. He did that in spite of the filial love and affection that she had for me. That she still harbored in her heart for me. He did that in spite of our just, and even far more than just, beautiful history and all the equally beautiful moments whose pale reflections we cherished and cultivated tenderly in the fertile soil of our memory. Like silk flowers being a pale shadow of the real ones. He did it. I did not know how, I was not sure when or what for precisely, but he did that nevertheless. She was lost. She was lost to me. She was lost to the world. She was lost to everyone. She was utterly lost now. She was virtually gone. Like a ship which gravitates straight toward the unblinking eye of a cyclone, and which cannot be stopped or slowed down or reversed, not even by the tremendous joint effort of human hands and powers of Nature.

That was why I knew what I had to do now. I knew it pretty well. For it was still not too late to act. Not too late to pull her out of this murderous predicament, to take a certain precautionary measure, and in the end to save her. But only if I managed to act in time. And that was why I at once rushed back to my sanctuary, a little bit despondent and disillusioned. Like a child who has just discovered that chocolate bunnies are empty inside. And I felt, as if with each step, as if with each single gesture and movement of my irrepressibly tremulous limbs, I was being overcome by mounting determination. For I was surely being overcome by the unbridled will to fight and the willingness to act. And that was why in a succession of several nimble leaps and bounds I scaled a wobbly footstool, akin to a defiant bull striving to buck off an intrusive rider, which was an impressive acrobatic achievement for someone my age, that, from then on, I could take pride in. Then I reached for an oblong and dusted forgotten box lounging on top of a closet. Like a miniature coffin. And I took it down in one slow and solemn and so ceremonious that nearly pious movement, for it was there that I stored my invaluable full dress uniform of a doorman. In a parade of studied movements and ostentatious gestures, all tinged with a hint of outstanding solemnity, I barely squeezed myself into it. Like toothpaste trying to get back into the tube. I squeezed myself into it while savoring each elegant part of that ritual, while relishing every polished and smooth detail of it, and while admiring an impressive glint of refinement reflected from the rows of brass buttons that appeared to be winking at me approvingly. For they seemed to be conveying, in such shiny unison, their support for my difficult, and almost painful decision.

For I decided to go and seek help, an immediate and complex help. I decided to seek it where I should have gone in the first place, but my foolishness and boundless stupid pride had prevented me forcibly from doing it then. For there were, not someplace, not somewhere, but in that particular place, in that fabulous fairy-tale-like place, gathered all those still powerful people, those still wildly influential people. Those still omnipotent people. Like the priceless poker chips on the baize. And they were not yet affected in the slightest degree by the fierce blade of an impending filthy rebellion of the masses. And those fantastic people could still help me. They could still assist me. And they could easily turn the tables on it and allow me to get back in the game. But I had to act quickly. But I had to act efficiently. Before my daughter and her accursed intended returned from this calamitous dinner. Before they discovered that I was gone. Even for a second. And thus became insanely suspicious.

As I stormed out of the apartment, dressed in my flawless uniform, in my impeccably polished shoes, I felt for a while like a character from one of those otherwise dreadfully campy movies, who, as a retired soldier, has to execute his final order and face undiluted evil for the last time. And I only regretted that some of my characteristics detracted from this splendid vision. I mean my clumsily moving rheumatic legs, threatening to give up on me and give way beneath me and make me fall down grotesquely at every single step. I mean my cap dancing comically on top of my grayish head as I ran breathlessly while coughing and wheezing asthmatically. And I also mean my loose dentures leaping and jumping deliriously inside my mouth at that insane speed. Like clothes swirling and pirouetting inside a washing machine.

Yet it still sufficed to let me enter the cab with stunning gusto and to give an order to a stout driver. Rather curtly. Rather commandingly. For I ordered him to drive me as quickly as possible to that finest hotel in town. If not in the whole magnificent country. And then I even dared to instruct him tritely not to mind the traffic lights. And yet, in spite of my orders that gradually deteriorated to pitiful pleadings, this uncommonly obstinate driver refused to obey my glaringly cinematic voice. He remained as deaf and immune to an influx of my threats and commands as a coma victim. And, scrutinizing me closely in the rear-view mirror, he drove at an eminently crawling pace. As if to spite me. As if to get back at me. For, as it, unfortunately, turned out, I was unable to reward him handsomely for this peculiar additional service. Apparently, my frail daughter, under the supervision of my malignant foe, had ensured that I did not have enough money left to roam the city unattended. And due to that brilliant subterfuge of his, I had to give it to him, I could throw in to the basic cab fee merely a broken cufflink and a half-chewed dog snack that I miraculously dug out of my pocket, even though I had no idea how it had gotten there in the first place.

Meantime, as this defiant cab hardly roared or sped down the main street and any other street, I prayed. I covertly prayed to all gods, known gods, those approved gods, and gods certified by society and civilization, to all the official divine spirits and deities, and to a few others that I invented as I went along. And I also prayed to the mighty and superb hotel guests, that hotel elite, that there was still a chance for me of redressing my reprehensible errors. That there was still time. That it was not too late. That, despite this simply horrible and terrible delay foolishly inflicted by me, and me only, there was still enough scope left for them to act and act accordingly.

Then the cab rolled, languidly and unspectacularly, into a parking lot in front of the hotel. Like an asthmatic for whom every effort could be lethal. It did that instead of storming in there and coming to a stop with the impressive screeching of tires and the laments of slaughtered breaks. And so I was a bit disappointed. I was more than a bit disillusioned. But I did not have too much time to dwell on it unnecessarily. For I momentarily dashed to the entrance of that fine edifice. There I nearly barged into a grayish and lanky man in an exquisite tailcoat. Then I swerved to avoid a stout regal woman who blinded me impudently with her massive diamond necklace shimmering like a disco ball. And then I barely dodged a few others while miraculously avoiding a series of catastrophic collisions and crashes and even jacket benders with all those refined and impressively cultured people. Like a car driving the wrong way down the highway.

Then I halted for an instant and climbed a rather precarious vantage point of my toes. And it was then that I realized that each one of those people was an excellent part of two files of marvelously dressed respectable bodies converging seamlessly at the infinitely welcoming hotel door. They were like two strands of hair being ably interwoven into a single, firm and unbreakable braid. For, obviously, there must have been some kind of ceremony taking place inside. There must have been something. All the better, it flitted nimbly across my agitated mind, for the more of those fabulous and distinguished personages gathered in one place, the greater was my chance of succeeding. Of convincing them. Of appealing to their profoundly diamond hearts and thickly gilded minds. Of doing that during a long and moving and uplifting speech that I intended to give there. Right in front of them all. Like an inspired politician on an election rally. That was what I was determined to do. To talk to them. To show them in detail and explain to them scrupulously the breathtaking immensity of that danger. Of that civilizational disease. Of that social cancer advancing right at them. The rapidity of its actions directed at them. Hovering over them. Like a pencil suspended over a classified section of a newspaper that is ready to circle the most appetizing ads. And I meant the implacable danger that resolved viciously to sweep them off the ground. The very ground they had owned and ruled and pacified for generations. For it was going to sweep them off that ground, them, along with their majestic properties, their mansions, and fortunes. Right into the sea of oblivion.

So, I had no other choice. So, I had to do that although my petrified mind prompted me otherwise. And with each next clumsy step of my shaky legs blood hummed louder and louder in my temples. Like water splashing in a fish tank when one runs with it down the street to a pet store for his goldfish got sick. It hummed there as though to the dubious accompaniment of my heart knocking and rapping and pummeling furiously at my sagging chest from the inside. Like an escape artist who has failed to do the trick this time. And my parched elderly lips moved quickly, inaudibly. They moved while rehearsing the speech that I was going to give, while revising it diligently, while adding a word here and a word there, while crossing out mercilessly whole paragraphs and sentences, and while doing everything in my now considerably enfeebled power to make it sound as heartrendingly and movingly as my rather poor editorial skills only permitted.

But the closer I got to the astonishingly superb banquet hall, the louder and the more distinct became some voice, an impersonal voice, a nearly sourceless voice. It was an odd voice that seemed to be attacking me and accosting me on the way. It seemed to be attacking me while riding bareback on the whiffs of the finest perfumes and scents that were oozed by all those truly magnificent bodies. And it was a still unintelligible voice of someone making a fine speech in front of that congested hall. And so, apparently, it belonged to my preceding speaker kindly warming up the audience for me. He was warming it up just like a thoughtful gigolo who cooks dinner for his lady before she gets back home from work. It was warm. It was deep and deliciously mellifluous. And it kept echoing and ricocheting frivolously off the walls and the ceiling of a corridor winding and meandering ahead of me. As a long pearl necklace leading the way to an aromatic neck of an adorable lady from the upper stratum of our pitiful society. And when I was really close, truly close, temptingly close, to that coveted finish line of my spontaneous sprint, I found myself alternately devising and fabricating an array of smooth and elegant ways of intercepting the microphone from him. For I wanted to do it smoothly in order to avoid any troubling clashes. Any distressing altercations. Or even quick tussles. I wanted to avoid even a brief, embarrassing struggle over it on the podium, perhaps, by throwing in a hilarious disarming anecdote or two to soften considerably that otherwise brazen action on my part. And, meantime, as if in the background, that voice kept pestering me by sounding more and more familiar, if not disturbingly familiar, to me.

Imagine my surprise when I swiftly entered that marvelous banquet hall, breathless, panting. Like a car with a busted radiator. For I saw him. No one else but him. That spiteful him. That vicious him. That diabolical him. That nauseating personification of my worst nightmares, and now also the impudent invader of my hitherto untouched private realm of utter luxury and refinement, of which things he, the dirty revolutionary, did not know a thing. Not a single thing. And yet I saw him standing there on a dignified podium. I saw him towering over the crowd of aloof and respectable guests thronging to various works of art covering the usually bare walls. Like a rather expensive kind of wallpaper. And so, it had already begun. And so, the fight was on. And so, they, he and his comrades, had reached this place, this hermetic and price-less and symbolic place. They had penetrated to its very core. Like an insolent pest ruining the crops. They had penetrated to the veritable heart of sophistication and ultimate respect-ability, and, moreover, they had done it without any problems! Without encountering any kind of resistance! Without any effort on their part! Without the need to overcome any com-plex security measures or fortifications! Without the need to climb the barricades contrived hastily yet solidly from a herd of impressively chiseled armchairs and delightfully plush sofas! Without the need to defeat a legion of madly devoted and infinitely loyal defenders recruited from among the members of the staff! The units of murderous cooks. The companies of lethal bellhops. And, above all, the special brigades of mer-ciless cleaning ladies. For the staff ignobly surrendered the fortress. Without a single scream! Without a single bullet being shot! They surrendered it instead of fighting. Instead of shed-ding the blood of the enemy. Instead of shielding with their belligerent bodies those delicate guests, those infinitely frail creatures. And they should be punished for it. They should be whipped savagely for it. For this unthinkable treachery. And then they should be put on public display and exposed to un-limited humiliation on the observation deck on the top floor as an additional, yet a bit too harsh and brutal to some refined tastes, attraction. Without mercy. Without a trial. Without a question. Because they also had not needed too much time to make up their faithless minds and refuse to fulfill their duty. Their sacred hotel duty.

Then I instinctively started to look around, feverishly, seemingly in all directions at once. Like an owl whose head seems to be about to get unscrewed in a moment. I was glancing here, taking a peek there, while scrutinizing someone else. I strived to fish out from the thick and uniform sea of all these genteel heads any odd figures. I strived to fish out any odd elements, anything, really, that appeared to be as glaringly incongruous with that elegant mass as a smile on the face of a fresh widow. For I intended to spot his filthy vile henchmen and barbarous guerrilla fighters before they managed to do anything, before they discreetly cut off the entrances, and before they took up the designated positions and began a carnage of an inconceivable kind and magnitude. But what I was afraid of, and I mean, truly and genuinely afraid of, were the invisible squads of his terrifyingly fanatical suicide bombers. For they were ready to pull out the pin, or light the fuse, or pull the cord, or whatever they had been doing so expertly, so cruelly, and so ruthlessly, anytime and anywhere. And they could also be here. They could be lurking with impunity in here somewhere amid those fine guests. They could be prowling here blended into the background. Like an embarrassing pimple on a dappled horse. They could be only waiting to creep out of their hiding places and carry out their murderous orders. Like a trip-mine that till the moment of explosion looks deceptively similar to some exotic yet metallic type of plant. So they had to be taken down. Or at least apprehended and restrained in the first place. Before it was too late.

That was why I froze, alarmingly close to the presumed location of the entourage of his acolytes. I froze not to draw their attention to me. Like a hapless lover being spotted by a husband on top of his wife. And, seeing a young waiter advancing toward me while clumsily navigating amid those veritable archipelagoes of unbridled luxury and grandeur with a tray of wine glasses balancing precariously in his hand, I started giving him signals. I started sending him a flurry of cryptic warnings and messages by frantically winking and smiling and making faces at him. Yet to no avail. For, evidently, he did not understand any of this. And he only stared at me incomprehensibly as I toiled to communicate with him in the rather faulty vernacular of seemingly erratic winks and smirks and frowns. Like a flag semaphore who strives to fend off an intrusive bird. For I communicated to him that they were already here. That the enemy, our worst enemy, was within our borders, far behind our fortified walls. That the appalling revolution was on. And that he had to help me to stop it. To curb it. To hamper its advance. Or to do whatever was possible. Whatever was necessary. Whatever was indispensable. Even if it seemed downright impossible at first habitually myopic glance. But he was either not too bright or far too inexperienced to make anything out of that sudden influx of information. For because of that, he tried too hard and too excessively not to commit any dreadful blunder. Not to drop the tray. Not to poke or push anyone on his way. Or not to breach any of the innumerable harsh laws and rules and restrictions of an unforgiving hotel etiquette. And thus he had not an ounce, not a dash, of his attention left to so much as try deciphering my facial version of the Morse code.

Since I could not count on anyone's assistance or a good word, much less real support, I had to act alone. And completely alone. As the last tooth in the jaw of a brawler. Besides, there was a certain fact, a certain troubling and ignoble fact, for if the highly qualified and skillful and maddeningly agile officers of various security services and law enforcement agencies had kept surrendering readily and avidly going over to the enemy camp, then what could I expect from a motley jumble of cooks and waiters and bellhops? What could I possibly expect from such a haphazard bunch? Though, on the other hand, their prominent positions in the hotel hierarchy obliged them to so something, to do anything, just as I had done, or, at least, still tried to do.

Thus, I started to wander among those guests. As if nothing had happened. I wandered there as inconspicuously as possible. For I walked around as taut as a compass needle that sensed the north. I walked around while wearing that stolid expression on my face, while constantly covering my vigilantly squinted eyes with the visor of my cap. I did that as if I were shielding them from the invisible yet immense blaze, perhaps, of those people's reflected glory and splendor. And I told them, in the confidentially lowered voice and through my absurdly clenched teeth, to evacuate slowly. To casually move toward the door. Without any sudden moves. Without panic. Exactly as if nothing had happened. I told them that there was still no reason to panic. I told them not to provoke any inconvenient questions. Not to raise anyone's suspicions. Like a pupil who has forgotten to do his homework and now strives to dissolve into the oppressive air of a classroom. I told them to do that promptly. Without delays. Because their unseen foes were already here. Waiting for them. Hunting for them. And it was the only way out of this horrible quagmire unscathed.

Yet also this time I failed to elicit any kind of desired, or at least faintly resolute, reaction from them. From this herd of my noble listeners. For they hardly deigned to so much as glance at me. Or to turn they distinguished heads toward me. And they only stared at me desultorily with those looks of utter incomprehension and bafflement. Not moving an inch in this or that way. Not taking any action. Not even flinching instinctively. And on account of that mounting passiveness, I felt as if I had crept into a slaughterhouse and tried to warn the inert and sheepish cattle about the spinning and metallic danger that would, in an instant or two, turn them into the neat and even portions of fresh meat.

What was worse, after a while, when I finally began succeeding in focusing their attention, something else, some new and bizarre and unexpected factor entered the equation. Like a jealous husband storming into his wife's bedroom. And it remorselessly thwarted all my well-meant efforts. For, on their confused faces, another kind of expressions took over. And those were the abrupt grimaces and frowns full of unmitigated disgust and contempt, which I initially could not figure out, which I was unable to put my rheumatic finger on, and whose reason at first eluded me only to hit me with the full force of that odorous realization. Like the smell of a long-forgotten sandwich in a backpack, that decayed relic. For it turned out that on my way here I must have stepped, somewhat recklessly, somewhat unfortunately, into something that now started smelling cruelly and unbelievably as I stood there, in utter silence, surrounded by these very people, these splendid people, whom I desperately wanted to impress, whom I intended to enchant and win over at any cost, and who were now promptly turning their elegant backs on me, and looking away from my embarrassedly smelly shoe.

Instantly, I felt my body burn with the mighty fire of undiluted humiliation. And it burned from the split endings of my frail brittle iridescent hair right to the tips of my toes, as wrinkled as a line of corks forced out of their bottles during a party. I mean the toes hidden in my shoes, the foul culprits of my newest ignominy. And yet, in spite of those inflows of countless and erratic aromatic stimuli flooding me and assailing me from everywhere, I had not even the faintest doubt that I sensed the distinct fishy smell of his involvement in this rather stinky business. That was designed to compromise me. That was calculated to discredit me ultimately. Because he had not put our little strategic power struggle on hold. Not even for a single symbolic minute. Not even now. Not even here, in front of the ones whom I valued and respected and looked up to the most.

But there still remained one question that was not of a marginal role in the whole predicament. And by asking it, I literally stepped into a dangerous territory. For it was a question how they had possibly managed to plant that malodorous mine. That accursed mine. Whether they had done it here, on the spot, at the parking lot, using someone dressed as a parking valet or impersonating one of the guests. Whether they had set this particularly cruel trap on the stairs in the lobby, by the hands of someone posing as (horror of horrors) a gentle doorman. One of my counterparts. One of my protégés. And thus with a single poisonous act they had ruined the meticulously built reputation of the whole profession. Like a single typo gaping from the text of a fastidious stylist. Or rather, whether they had planted it on me back in my apartment. And then I had traveled unknowingly all the way up here with it lying dormant right under my shoe and waiting patiently for the perfect moment to go off like that. Like a perfectly synchronized time bomb. Gingerly, I inclined toward the latter possibility. I did that even though both of them seemed to be equally absurd and downright improbable. For what were the chances of my stepping right into it? Of our paths crossing in such an unfortunate manner? It was impossible. It was incredible, unless their tactical craft had reached such a frighteningly high level of expertise and sophistication that it soared right up into the stratosphere of subversive genius. I could not exclude that possibility too lightheartedly. I could not dismiss it too quickly. Not now. Especially not now.

But then someone fainted and fell down. I quickly realized who. I quickly recognized her. It was that disco-ball lady who slumped to the floor, unable to cope with that rather heady effluvious stimulus. And she, due to that inconceivable accumulation of jingling and rattling and clinking jewelry encumbering her every move, instantly caught everyone's attention. Like a Christmas tree tumbling down in the middle of dinner. She made the whole great vast hall fall silent. Terribly and unbearably silent. Then, the villainous lecturer, that eleventh Egyptian plague, managed to babble incoherently a few words, something about getting their signatures in those fat checkbooks of theirs and inveigling them into writing out a check or two for these excellent young artists. And then he also followed suit and became silent at my sight. He did not expect that. He certainly did not foresee that. He failed to predict that, after all, I was capable of mustering enough guts and collecting all the stray and vagrant crumbs of grit from all over my body, from its every wrinkled nook and corner, to stand up to him, to wrong-foot him, and to thwart his plans at such an advanced stage of their realization. Like a police officer who starts giving tickets left and right to the drivers at the finish line of a car race.

And seeing the thickening mixture of puzzlement and helplessness slowly yet steadily setting down on his face, like a fresh coverlet of snow, I suddenly felt proud of myself. I felt oddly proud of myself. I felt like that in spite of the insufferably hurting fetid disgrace of mine. In spite of my making a stinky old fool of myself. Right here. In front of the quite differently perfumed elites. And, when everyone stared at me in the heavy undiluted silence, he only blurted malevolently something that sounded like a particularly botched and twisted and viciously maltreated "Dad." And he even dared to adorn it with a disfigured version of a question mark lingering at the end of it. Like a drunkard loitering in front of a bar long after it got closed for the night. Then he stopped talking once again. But this time for good. And yet, every now and then, he cast furtive glances into the depths of the hall, where, following the gauzy thread of his nervous gaze, like a kitten playing with a ball of wool, I discerned my speechless daughter. For she must have been speechless due to her bursting with pride at me. At her father. At her brave and unfaltering old man.

She looked disarmingly resplendent in that fabulous dress of hers. She looked nearly as wonderfully as when she used to come to me, to run to me, all laughing and beaming lovably, still as a precocious little girl, to show off her new dress that she had bought with her mother. And now I saw on her face a constellation of a few shiny points. I saw her tears that shimmered timidly. Like a shoal of gold nuggets lounging on the bottom of the river. But those were the tears of genuine and profound emotion, provoked by the immense joy that she was an offspring of mine. Of a man who did not give up. Who did not give in. For it meant that in her veins circulated the same blood as in the body of that man who refused to bow obediently when everyone else was already lying prostrate. Who refused to drift passively with the current leading all of them straight toward inevitable death. And I felt cleansed by those tears of hers. And I felt acquitted by them. By their goodness. By their somewhat excessive and inordinate but unblemished goodness. I felt like an old bowl, dirtied over the years of its torturous life, which is being finally rinsed in the stream of pure decency. And I could see, I could distinctly see, that she welled with pride over that I did not let him insult these astonishing rich creatures any longer, that I stopped him from showing his sheer contempt for them and all that they stood for, namely, for all that was good and kind and righteous in our decaying society.

But then I noticed his increasingly nervous movements. I noticed his disturbingly erratic gestures, his tellingly shifty eyes. It all rapidly added up to a truly frightening image. And the brevity of that message was stunning. And nothing short of stunning. For I began worrying that, having his treacherous back against the wall, being pushed into the strategic corner, looking around anxiously as if he tacitly tried to summon his callous soldiers and guardians, he could decide to carry out a suicide attack personally and singlehandedly. To get what he wanted at all costs. And to win this battle in overtime. Like an overzealous coach who resolves to take part in the game himself.

So I leaped at him furiously. Without thinking. Without hesitation. I incredibly hurdled a few chairs. I knocked over a few tables. I began pushing and elbowing fiercely my way toward him. Like a forward heading toward a goal. Then I barged into several of these magnificent guests, which fact I regretted enormously. And then I was about to scale the stage and find myself next to him, right next to him. My avowed enemy. My soulless foe. And I was supposed to forestall his swift, nimble movements and prevent him from pulling the detonator's cord that was ineptly masqueraded as a part of the microphone. And when I nearly smelled his fear, like a predator on the prowl before sinking its teeth in a prey's defenseless neck, I tripped and slipped on something adhering to my sole. I immediately lost my balance. And I fell on my back from the edge of the miniature proscenium straight on a sumptuously decorated table in the first row. It was intended for truly special guests, for whom, with the aching heart, I must have ruined the whole evening. And, going down, I had a nagging impression. I had an impression that it was not I who fell into the inescapable embraces of the force of gravity, but that the ground unexpectedly shifted beneath my feet as this great enormous house of cards started crumbling and falling apart exactly as I had predicted it, to my ineffable dismay rather than contentment.

And so, I was down. I was down for good. Like a retired boxer after a lost battle with the greatest opponent in his career, his own age. Amid an ungodly clatter of crushed dishes and broken glasses, I distinctly heard something snapping in my back. And it was like when a favorite toy crashes to the floor and turns into the palpable counterpart of a shattered dream. An incredible mayhem erupted at once. A deafening cacophony of terrified cries and laments became a prevailing tone of the upcoming minutes. A symphony of hurrying footsteps reached the highest registers of chaos. And the people, all these usually dignified people, started running to and fro. Back and forth. Like glossy balls scurrying in all directions on a billiard table. I heard, everywhere around me, that recognizable and simply unmistakable patter of their elegant shoes against the marvelously polished hardwood floor. The very same floor that seemed to be pulling me and holding me back as never before. For I could not move. I could not move at all. I heard them trying desperately to revive the disco-ball lady. That innocent casualty of our little intimate total war that imperceptibly got out of anyone's control. I heard them urging everyone, here and there, now and then, to call an ambulance. Two of them. I heard the hotel staff bustling about feverishly while striving to fend off the curious prying crowd and push it away from me. Ha! Now they got to work! I heard that. I heard all of that. I heard all the shreds and scraps of audible information that inundated me as I lay there. Completely immobile. Utterly helpless. Apparently hurt in some serious way. Because I was unable to so much as twitch without causing a bolt of excruciating pain to dart right through my suddenly crippled body, through its every enfeebled tendon and muscle, let alone move properly.

And only out of the corner of my defeated eye, for I was unable even to turn my head, amid the breakwater poles of legs of these panicking and running people, I noticed my little daughter. I noticed her bolting for the door, shivering. Tears in her eyes. She ran while hiding her adorable face in her trembling hands. But this time I could tell that these tears were of a drastically different kind.

But then, the diabolical lecturer theatrically leaped to my side. He leaped there after gamely fighting his way to me. The motionless me. The suddenly defenseless me. Almost caressingly he touched my chest. Like a driver wishing to feel the soft purring of an engine underneath the hood of his car. He touched me with his right hand. The very same one that must have signed countless cruel and unnecessary death warrants which had later on been carried out by his criminal cronies, by his atrocious minions. And then, instantly, he started giving orders in a shockingly imperious manner. He ordered everyone around. Just like a skillful orchestra conductor. And through this behavior of his shined the irrepressible character of a natural revolutionary leader, of an inveterate commander, thus getting him dangerously close to exposure. He bellowed and ordered them peremptorily. He did that with the smooth gracefulness of his gestures also intended for a menagerie of his still withdrawn hateful followers. Still lingering in the shadows. Still posing a real threat. He told everyone to stay back. To leave this poor man alone. To let me breathe in peace. To make some room for me. To leave me alone. To make that accursed call for an ambulance. And all the while he kept brusquely prohibiting them from touching me or moving me anywhere for I must have badly injured my back. You wish, I thought testily before passing out.

I could recollect only a vague mishmash of disconnected and chaotic bits and fragments of what had really been happening around me from then on. All that was akin to the disorganized scenes of an amateurish movie edited by a zealous dilettante.

I remembered being carried out of that messy hall by an agile duo of sturdy paramedics, over the curious heads of the screaming and bustling and fainting guests. As if I were an enormous birthday cake. And I faintly remembered being quickly immobilized, my spine in particular. I remembered being hastily cleaned, while still lying on the stretcher. The chips of the smashed glass and plates were promptly brushed off along with the bits of food that stuck to my clothes. Like a shoal of small fish adhering to a larger one while counting on a free ride. I remembered being put into an ambulance. And

268

not too delicately at that. And it was then that someone most clear-headed of the whole medical lot suggested shrewdly to remove that faulty shoe of mine. For that stench was so penetrating and overpowering that they would surely have crashed into something on the way thus never managing to reach the hospital.

I also remembered a handful of blurry and hazy episodes from our trip to an emergency room, with the siren blaring and roaring relentlessly above me. As a loud guardian angel. For it was as if it also suffered from the agonizing embarrassment inflicted by my botched assassination attempt. And it was as if it wanted to voice its great dissatisfaction and discontentment with my presence there. For even I myself could not decide what hurt me more, the unnamed and still undiagnosed injury in my back or the burning pain of humiliation. And, due to the unnerving fact that I completely lost feeling in my back, as if it withdrew timidly from the stage not to disturb me unnecessarily, I could fully savor the scope of my newest failure.

And doing it, I passed out once again.

The next time I came around I was already in the hospital. I lay alone in one of those frightfully antiseptic and insipid rooms. As if their whole decor conveyed in sterile unison its staff's indifference to whether the patients lived or died.

Boldly fending off the hectoring fits of drowsiness, I felt compelled to follow an impromptu impulse to pretend that I was still unconscious. In order to trick them. In order to deceive them. And to wait for the proper moment to slink out of there unnoticed and finish the job that I had ignobly messed up last time.

And while fighting off sleepiness, I was defeated irrevocably.

◆ ◆ ◆

Some other time, I gingerly lifted my still anesthetized eye-lids, unsure whom and what I was going to see on their other side. I lifted them guardedly. Like a girl raising the lid of an elegant ring box and yet without being sure what she will find inside. I lifted them fearing terribly that I could expose myself and compromise my marvelous camouflage, thus losing the best kind of disguise that had ever happened to me, that of a still motionless, still nearly insensate, and still almost lifeless, unconscious man. For it was a dreamy starting point for any of my future clandestine endeavors. The best imaginable safe house. The finest inviolable refuge of mine. It was also the greatest endospore form available to me, indispensable to consider and reconsider my present pitiful position in peace.

Cautiously, I looked around. With bated breath, I scruti-nized the horizon. Like a submarine captain who extends the periscope to discover that he has surfaced in the middle of an enemy base. And then I noticed my lovely daughter, my sweet and cute little darling, curled up and dozing charmingly in the chair beside my bed. She seemed to be a bit dejected, even in her sleep. She seemed to be hiding in the doleful shade of a large curtain lurking there ominously. Like an implacable shroud of death waiting for a terminal patient to let out his last earthly growl to be able to envelop him and cut him off from the living world. She was so utterly enchanting and deli-cate, so infinitely lovable and frail, as if doing her best to help me to cultivate nostalgia for the past images that my memories had magnified and fabricated beyond any limits of decency. That veritable angel with a cherubic face! My parental heart swelled and contracted and twitched in my chest from the inflow of emotion. It did that despite the competitive deluge of various painkillers and tranquilizers bubbling and seething and circulating in my veins, to the point that I was no longer sure whether I had a single tiny drop of my own blood left in my whole dwindling body. And I felt it rising and soaring up. High up into the sky. I felt it rising like a heavily anesthetized bird that due to its erratic trajectory incurs a routine police check of an aerial patrol.

Then, she flinched nervously in her dream. Then, she flinched as if she were irritated by the intrusive nature of my incurably caring paternal stare. And she quickly pulled the covers higher, still a bit higher, she kept pulling them relentlessly until they left the margins of my peripheral vision and fully entered the frame of my sight and turned out to be a jacket, and a male jacket at that. And only then it struck me, as violently as the presence of a smoldering cigarette stub in the pocket of a secretly smoking husband, that it was no one else's jacket but his. Of this perennial source of my disgrace. Of this wayward reason of my utter downfall. And this realization instantly killed and dispelled my blissful parental mood. For he, even now, even vicariously, but always insolently, managed to mar this beautiful moment. As a drop of spit in the glass of a first-rate wine. And I felt boundless wild contempt and crystalline hatred welling up in me. Like a carbonated beverage inside a violently shaken bottle. But before they provoked the worst impulses in me, before they awakened the most dangerous instincts in me, I hesitated for an instant. I halted before launching into yet another furious internal tirade. I halted before plunging into yet another mad trance of planning and scheming and plotting elaborately. For it, the same as before, would, most probably, most certainly, lead to similar, or even much greater losses and cataclysms easily surpassing all the former ones.

And, still having in front of my eyes the more and more blurred and vague likeness of him invoked by the recent surge of anger, now gradually fading, like an afterimage after glancing at the sun too curiously, I wondered whether, by any chance, over the course of all my frantic searches and inhuman efforts and deadly pursuits I had lost something. Perhaps I had forfeited it. Perhaps I had wasted it unknowingly. Some inherently human element. I wondered intensely whether I had gone too far, whether I had strayed too far from my initial path, whether, with time, somewhere on the way, I had veered too far off my original course. Like a child being unable to stay within the lines while working on a coloring book. And I wondered whether I had really veered off it. Off my path. Off my route. I mean the one that had once been dictated to me by the eternal cadences of righteousness and justice. And I wondered whether I had veered off so far that I had long crossed that line. That infamous and mythical yet still terrifyingly real line. And due to that, I found myself on the side of my avowed enemy, the very same one whom I intended to destroy now. So, was it true that I had been chasing him for so long, so furiously, and so tenaciously, that I had, at some point, unwittingly, adopted his cruel methods? His twisted logic? A potpourri of his malicious motives? And even his perverse hateful vocabulary? Had I done it to the point of becoming a deceptive and convincing facsimile of him? A carbon copy of him? Of the very man I had set off to restrain, to stop, and to murder if necessary? That was why I wondered anxiously whether, in the capacious meantime, in the fervor of the struggle, I had become a raving fanatic myself. A rabid lunatic. A spluttering violent madman. An unpredictable radical. I wondered whether I had become someone who had to be isolated as quickly as possible, who had to be put away sooner or later and at all costs. Because I had imperceptibly become utterly unsuitable for living among cultured and good and decent people, within the confines of a civilized society. And so I had to be promptly killed off to protect others, the famous yet elusive others. And this change, this unforeseen and unplanned metamorphosis of mine, filled me with considerable fear. For it still might prove to be irreversible. If not incurable.

For it still might rob me of a way back to my former peaceful and agreeable lifestyle. Even though I had been living it for more than seven decades.

I felt a myriad of drops forming a dew of cold sweat sprouting and ripening right on my skin. I felt them being constantly prepared for harvest time. And then I felt them merrily sliding down the slope of my neck to crash against the snowdrift of a pillow. As a gang of suicidal skiers. For, if that singular and irremediable change was indeed a fact, that mental counterpart of a physical deformation acquired by one, at a bargain price, during some harrowing accident, then it was a grim fact. A truly tragic one. Even if it could be properly justified by a jumble of genuine doubts and fears for the lives and condition of everyone and everything. But if that whole unthinkable danger was not as unthinkable as I had suspected it at the beginning, if it was not even half as real and inevitable and impending as it had seemed to be, and if I had allowed them, more or less unknowingly, more or less foolishly, these wealthy and only ostensibly wonderful elites, to manipulate me, and to use me to their own ends, then it was a greater disgrace than all my previous blunders and misfortunes taken together and multiplied by infinity. For in that case I was a dangerous fanatic myself. For then I was a vital threat to everyone myself. I was one of those whom I intended to chase. I was one of those whom I intended to catch and ostracize and hunt for relentlessly. Till my last stubborn breath of the human-sized hound. And there was no forgiveness for me. There could not be. There was no chance of help or salvation for me. Or, at least, I thought so. I thought that while deluding myself in an anesthetic-laden delirium. I thought that while tossing and turning vehemently. Like a coin in the hand of a conman. I thought that till I blacked out again.

♦♦♦

Then I strived to observe my beloved daughter through my half-closed eyelids. Vigilant and slightly apart. I strived to watch over her protectively in her sleep. But, to my dismay, to my ineffable chagrin, it kept turning out infallibly, over and over again, that I was falling asleep imperceptibly and then waking up anew, unable to notice that crucial moment of transition. Like a viewer hunting for a cut in a long and ostensibly seamless take in an ably edited movie. And meantime the furnishings, namely, an incontinent drip stand, an insatiable herd of cups and dishes on the bedside table, as well as the arrangement of the drapes, changed furtively from scene to scene. As if they were the restive members of a nomadic furniture tribe remaining in undisturbed motion.

But this time my daughter was nowhere near me. She was not close to me. She was not even in the room. And only my perceptive gaze collected and organized an array of disjointed clues and hints, and, as if following a trail of invisible crumbs that she had recklessly left behind, it traveled straight to the invitingly open door, behind which, on a sterile corridor, I saw her. I noticed her with that infernal jacket hanging nonchalantly from her shoulders. Like a red cape that entraps a defeated bull. And I saw her standing there, next to this infinitely duplicitous man. I saw her standing next to a man who seemed to be branding her insolently with this insufferable jacket. For it was as if she were an unruly horse that had to be marked properly to prevent it from constantly rebelling against its owner.

But they were not alone, they were not left unattended, thank goodness. For I saw there, beside them, yet another supporting actor of this little intimate drama. He or she, for I was not certain due to seeing only someone's back, was tightly enveloped in an impeccably white coat depriving him or her of any distinguishable features, of any telling characteristics, but lending him or her the nimbus of an almost godlike authoritativeness. It was exactly like with the once pristine white bandages enfolding the mummy of an ancient ruler. And I saw him or her putting under my daughter's beautifully shapely nose a stack of suspicious papers to sign. But she demurred. But she resisted. But she fought with the idea. My little cute rebellious darling. She wrestled with it visibly even though there were no tickets being sold for this impromptu match. But then, that vile man, that wolf in not so much sheep's as jackal's clothing, embraced her with that feigned tenderness and care. And he began convincing her elaborately to do something. To give in. To yield unconditionally. But I was not sure to what exactly. He did that by trickling his hateful venom straight into her ear. And it was the very same sweet tiny ear to which I used to whisper tenderly all the fantastic stories and fairy tales while tucking her in. Then she surrendered grudgingly. She surrendered, all in tears. And with her, my paternal heart also cried.

A few days later I was finally released from the hospital. Instantly, I was trapped in the makeshift prison of a grotesque medical corset supporting my injured back. And then I was also adorned with several ludicrous "Xs" made of adhesive bandage, scattered here and there, looking exactly as if a promising treasure were hidden there, beneath my wrinkled skin, beneath the layer of my bruised skin, and right beneath my still wounded pride.

It was then that I saw her, my subtle daughter, sobbing silently. It was then that I saw her sobbing for some reason, the very reason that eluded me completely. For it felt as if I were watching some odd ritual of a distant culture that I was unable to comprehend regardless of the time and efforts I invested in that task. And, considering her recent inscrutable penchant for pouring out the immense amounts of water this way, I began seriously worrying that she secretly suffered from some kind of tears incontinence. And I saw that she took something very emotionally. I saw that she kept wrestling with herself internally over some mysterious issue. I saw that she was hurt and hurt deeply, as she stood motionless at an oddly considerable distance from her own car into which I was now being squeezed brusquely by two burly paramedics. I was being indelicately pushed into the backseat. I was being squeezed there like a bit too large bag of groceries. And this behavior of hers rather astonished me. And this behavior of hers rather baffled me. For, after all, we were not going to part for long. For we were about to see each other again. In a little while. Back in our home. Without that despicable man anywhere in sight.

Thus imagine how speechless I was, how utterly mystified I was, when I realized that not she, the lovable she, the incredibly cute she, but he, the malignant he, was going to accompany me on my hardly triumphant return home. I saw him, telling her stealthily not to join us for this trip. I saw him telling her to rather stay there, passive and helpless. I saw him telling her peremptorily to stay in front of the hospital, utterly indifferent to all that was going to happen to me. And all that I read, almost effortlessly, from the babble of his hectic gestures and incoherent expressions. I read it through the closed window of the car, my newest glass prison, my current place of confinement, in which I felt as if I were a fish immured in a fish tank, mere seconds before being flushed down the toilet, just before that vertiginous last ride of its life. I did that even though he evidently wanted to hide this little hysterical pantomime from me by deliberately communicating it to her in his treacherous whisper. But I was too smart for such childish tricks. I was too shrewd for that. And I was well familiar with all his truculent shticks and shenanigans, even far more familiar than I wished to be.

And besides, when I had been bored stiff, back in my hospital room, bored with lying constantly in an inordinately uncomfortable position, immobilized by the scandalously tight corset having more in common with a straitjacket than anything else more civilized, I had been amusing myself in a rather peculiar fashion. For I had been amusing myself by watching, through the wide open door, a TV set flickering and blinking at me coquettishly from the room at the other end of the hall. I had seen in it a figure of a suave news anchor. And I had seen him serving the freshest and most succulent news on the journalistic menu. And, although I could not hear a single sound of what he said, I had striven to read the words from the studied and polished movement of his lips. I had found it not that difficult considering that news programs in this otherwise marvelous country tended to feed us with one and the same torrent of raw and half-baked nonsense over and over again. And thus, trying to match the elegant twitching and jerking of his lips to a mishmash of usually laughable platitudes and threadbare turns of phrase that I knew so well, I had mastered, at an astonishingly unprecedented pace, the arcane art of lip riding.

Thus I understood perfectly what he said to her. And thus I understood even better how he inveigled her impudently into turning against me, into writing off the years of our tender filial relationship, and, above all, into allowing him to take care of me personally. Oh, how innocently it must have sounded! This insidious request of his. This cunning suggestion of his. How cute it must have sounded in his mute mouth as seen through the stubbornly impervious membrane of a car window, as in a movie with the sound turned down.

And then he haughtily approached the car, hardly suppressing an infantile urge to jump and hop gleefully on the way. Like an avid hopscotch player at the sight of an inviting grid. Then he swiftly got inside and eased himself into a driver's seat with that distinctly victorious air. And when he winked at

277

me insolently with that loathsome confidentiality and gave me that counterfeit smile while turning the ignition key with rather odd gusto, I had no, even passing, even generous, doubt about him. I had no doubt that it was what he had tried to achieve all the time. It was exactly what he had tried to accomplish while pestering and tormenting relentlessly my otherwise uncannily loyal offspring with various files and papers. But I could not do anything about it now. I was unable to act, if not counter-act, efficiently in any way. Crippled in the backseat. Utterly at his mercy. Like a plant glancing beseechingly at the passing gardener.

The full scale and scope of my helplessness and my hope-less position began slowly dawning on me. They did that like the first sunrays of the morning catching a burglar red-eyed in the usually nocturnal act. They dawned on me as I barely listened to him. They did that as he went to great lengths to convince me, in this forced for unmistakably fake affable voice of his, as if he really wanted to establish some kind of tenu-ous rapport between us, that we were heading to a new place, to an interesting place, and to a truly fabulous place, where there were people who would take care of me properly, who would devote to me the amount of time and attention neces-sary for my age, where I would doubtless meet new people, fine people, kind people, my respectable peers and potential acquaintances. For I would meet there the people burdened with the baggage of comparable achievements and experi-ences. And so, it was a very nice place where I would make new friends and great friends. And it was a place where, later on, we would be joined by my little daughter, by my loving daughter. But I did not listen to that shameless smug fraud. I hardly paid any attention to his smooth and eloquent words drenched in pure and high-proof vileness to the point of re-sembling verbal chocolates. For my sole presence there in the same room with him was too great a privilege and honor to him, to which I certainly did not want to add the satisfaction of my participating in his more and more miserable theater of tired games and run-down schemes. Moreover, they, in my present situation, at the present moment, had lost all their purpose. Because it resembled the unending courting of a woman even on the way to the altar when the most important binding decision has long been made and very little could be done to avoid or revert it now.

A new place. A nice place. And so, he finally decided to take me to his infamous headquarters. However, this time not to show me around its labyrinthine corridors and abysmal torture halls, or to lay out for me all the whimsical intricacies of his inconceivably evil masterplan. For he was determined to get rid of me. Once and for all. I must have become too great a risk for them. I knew too much. I suspected too much. Far too much. I was too close to them and their sinister covert actions. So they simply could not take the risk any longer. I understood that. I understood that very well and appreciated their recognition of my laborious efforts.

Then, something occurred to me curtly. And this evidently excruciating and disconcerting realization promptly terrorized my thoughts and held my attention hostage. Without so much as allowing it to use the bathroom every now and then. For, it came to me that, most surely, I would not live long enough to see the end of this trip. This sorrowful trip. This dismal trip. Or rather, its end and destination would arrive much faster and decidedly sooner than it had been previously scheduled. And then I realized that the overwhelming multitude of breathtaking vistas and bucolic scenes and shreds of lives of other people with which I inadvertently interfered now, right now, for a mere flicker of a second, while passing them and watching them abstractedly through the window, would go on perfectly undisturbed when I was no more. Without a momentary hesitation. Without an even passing mourning. For those were my last glances at this world. This external world. Those were my last glances at the world that I used to laugh at. To look down on. To sneer upon haughtily. Because it was unconnected in any noticeable or relevant way with the splendid and hermetic microcosm of my magnificent hotel. And I felt a miniature cavalcade of tears galloping down my tired shriveled face. And it astonished me utterly. If not bordered on a plain shock. It was like when it starts raining unforecasted manna in the middle of the desert for the first time since the biblical season. For, also for the first time, I allowed myself to perform such an unprofessional act as crying. I allowed myself to violate the invincible hotel etiquette so that my parched old skin started burning here and there, unaccustomed to such rampant wetness. But now it did not matter. It did not matter at all.

But then, as I had expected, my treacherous driver announced to me, in a voice poorly feigning irritation at himself, that unfortunately we were forced to take a little detour, to make an unplanned stop, and to drop by at his house on the way to that exciting place. It had to happen sooner or later. But his house! His own house! How else! How convenient! The staggering ingenuity, as well as brilliant simplicity, of his plan left me speechless, breathless. If not internally paralyzed. As if I were a mathematician who discovered that the solution of some nagging equation was too obvious and banal to be taken seriously. Apparently, as he fraudulently strived to explain himself, he had forgotten, in the breakneck rush of the last maddening events, to pack his notes and take them with him, the notes that were now absolutely indispensable to him. For he was supposed to give a more or less intriguing, more or less edifying, lecture at the grand opening of a new exhibition of new talents at the equally new local art gallery. And he was going there with my daughter. He was going there right after giving me a lift to that place. That nice place. That kind place. The place of my eternal detention.

And so, he intended to do it sooner, much sooner, than I had predicted. For, evidently, at the present mournful moment, when he could peacefully savor his unprecedented victory over me, undisturbed and unhampered, when I no longer constituted any threat or danger to him, he wanted to get it over with as soon as possible, now he wanted to move to something more interesting and far more challenging than an aged and harmless for toothless wretch. And I became to him nothing more than a former irrelevant obstacle. A past irritating inconvenience. An old nuisance that had long ceased to bother him and grate on his nerves. Like a faulty windshield wiper in a car that one has already exchanged for a newer shiny model.

There was no hope for me. Not now. Not anymore. But, with commendable humbleness, I managed to come to terms, better or worse, with a certain idea. It was an idea that brave people, all the true pioneers and heroes, always, sooner or later, have to pay for their grit, for their courage, and for their unfaltering readiness to march against the current of unyielding difficulties with their heads held high. For they always receive a receipt for that payment from the hands of those incomparably viler and meaner and far more vicious than they have ever been. And only at the checkout counter of death, only when it is all over, there comes the proper recognition and perennial, even if a bit too belated, glory. And it cannot be belittled and effaced by anything. It simply cannot. Not even by the sleeve of a clock's untiring hand.

Yet before I unanimously accepted the grim fact (I and the informal congregation of my fears), the gravel on a steep driveway of his house crunched alarmingly under the tires. It was like a viewer who while sitting in front of a TV set screams and hollers at it maniacally, trying to warn the reckless hero of some horror movie not to enter the particular room where a panting murderer lurks with an ax. Then the car immersed itself slowly and smoothly in the heavy oppressive darkness of the garage. It did that like a future drowned man diving unsuspectingly into his soon-to-be watery tomb. And, as the breaks clinked almost inaudibly, it struck me. His house.

His garden. His garage. The headquarters of all evil. Now it seemed startlingly obvious to me. Now it was so obvious, so embarrassingly obvious, although it had never crossed my mind before. And so, a disconcerted grunt escaped me unexpectedly. It escaped me like an anesthetized patient jumping off the operating table.

Then the first fall of the little specks of undiluted darkness, until then dancing and pirouetting merrily in the musty air, finally settled on the car, on its no longer shiny windshield, on the interior of the garage, and on us, also on us, above all on us. It settled there like a particularly dark dandruff. And, as soon as our eyes got accustomed to it, as if an inability to see clearly were a kind of weird acquired taste, my current tormentor and future butcher slinked out of the car. He did that with the agility of an escape artist. And, with the succession of more and more joyful bounds and hops that he no longer bothered to hide or mitigate, he walked to the door leading to the inside of the house. Then he disappeared behind it promptly. As a coin plunging into a slot machine. And even though he left the door wide open, and even though I was reached by the distinct yet muffled frivolous click of a light switch, the impenetrable darkness reigning supreme in there was not marred by an even stray beam of light. Not for a moment. It was as if this whole place, this real headquarters of his gloomy organization, were somehow contrived from all that was dark and bleak and austere in the human soul. It was as if it had sucked in all the worst vices and disgusting weaknesses of the human race and ably distilled them and extracted from them the pure essence of evil. But now, that invincible darkness was joined by unstirred silence. It was the consummate silence in which even the tones and cadences of my petrified breathing, let alone a fearful thudding of my elderly heart, seemed to be ghastly and unbearably loud. Like the laments of a maltreated rocking chair that is about to lose one of its rockers any minute now.

It was no use waiting idly for his return. Just like a snow-man heading for slaughter during a sunny day. Thus, with enormous difficulty, I clambered out of the backseat. I did that while simultaneously wrestling with the infernal corset doing its tight best to constrain my moves far more irritatingly and efficiently than any handcuffs would have done. I did that while also wrestling with a heap of various unnamed junk and unspecified cardboard boxes blocking the door. For it was as if the whole inanimate matter suddenly took his side and wanted my abrupt death. Was I so well informed? Did I really know so much? Was I, in truth, such a vital and matchless threat to stale pacts and rotten schemes wherever I turned up?

Liberated, I desperately looked for a way out, for any way out, in fact. I looked for a way out of that dark and cluttered and claustrophobic garage. To my surprise, it was invaded by a single streak of the blood-red afternoon light seeping leisurely through a little window near the ceiling. And thus this whole setting resembled a veritable vestibule of hell or a waiting room for the resurrected souls anxious to be born again. And I felt that oddly misplaced, that oddly incongruous, warm streak of light friendlily touching my elderly wretched face. It was as if some higher power deigned to take care of me. It was as if it deigned to caress me reassuringly. And due to that unforeseen act of divine compassion, the tears of my senile despair dried up completely. Like streams of money after a market collapse. I sensed a sudden surge of strength. Of invigorating strength. Of enlivening strength. I sensed a quick injection of such strength straight into my exhausted bones and muscles. As a fresh drop of oil caressing sooth-ingly the old and rusty cogs and ratchets. And, once again, the will to fight welled up in me. It did that as it was miraculously rekindled in me by that single and inexplicable spark of light.

Almost instantly, I clumsily crawled out of that corset limiting not only the pantomime of my moves but also the parade of my thoughts. I was like a proverbial butterfly shedding the shackles of its hindering cocoon. And my tremulous hands instinctively ran over the piles of dusted trifles and trinkets as well as nameless gadgets that he had hoarded in there. For, still blinded by this uplifting blaze and with blood still murmuring in my temples, I had to find something that would allow me to defeat the stubborn lock and pry open the garage door. I had to find something to defeat that unyielding guard of my death cell. Of this antechamber of hell. I had to do that. I had to get out of there, to sneak out of there, or even crawl out of there if needed. I had to do that before he returned accompanied by a death squad of his ferocious followers. Because otherwise, I was sure of that, more than merely sure of that, an unending string of tortures and abuses would await me. And during that, I would not tell them anything. And during that, I would not betray anyone. For, till the very end, I would protect and shield gamely with my humble sagging chest the splendid and wealthy and glamorous creatures of the upper classes, of the ruling caste, all the excellent mentors of mine, all the magnificent guardians of mine. And I would protect them till I let out the last breath of my adoration of them, till I died in unspeakable agony. And there was not a hint of exaggeration in all that. Not even a dollop of false or gratuitous pathos. Because that uncanny situation called for it. It called for the first-rate kind of pathos. The best one I could possibly afford at that distressing time.

Then on a curiously lopsided shelf, my watchful hand encountered some wooden object, some indistinct little affair. Apparently, it was an unspecified part of a disassembled easel. And it, due to a screw sticking out of it threateningly, could turn out to be a simply invaluable ally. It was a thing worth having on my side. For it would be my only ally during my inevitable struggle with the door lock, that metallic Cerberus, keeping me there against my will. And, besides, it formed a perfect both ironic and aesthetic subtext.

But then, I was startled by a sudden stir behind me. I flinched instinctively and abruptly turned around. And I had an indelible impression that someone halted there unexpectedly. Right behind me. As if in the middle of a step. As if totally astounded. And then I saw, only for a fraction of a second, too short to be recorded properly by my rather fatigued aged eyes, the beaming smile attached to the otherwise incredulous face of this loathsome man. It was my villainous adversary. It was he, who had managed only to blurt out a short, indistinct sound before he was cut short prematurely by a sudden blow. And it was before he fell to the ground limply as if hell finally opened beneath him invitingly. Ready to take him back home.

And only then I noticed in my a dash too shaky and unsteady hand that unfortunate leg of an easel. It still had that screw jutting out ominously like a forlorn claw. For it was with it that I must have hit him, accidentally, instinctively, utterly petrified, and in textbook self-defense. Thus, I unwittingly administered justice. Thus, I inadvertently rose to the murderous occasion. Thus, I unintentionally fended off in time the imminent apocalypse. And thus, I did all the things that I could not bring myself to do in the more careful and deliberate manner. And now his frenzied and brainwashed disciples, suddenly devoid of their leader, unexpectedly robbed of their wicked mentor and mastermind of their organization, would most probably disperse quickly. They would probably disappear into the not so thin air of the revolutionary history of called-off revolts and abortive coups and failed assassinations, of all the abhorrent things that could have been, that might have been, had they not been prevented soon enough by such spontaneous and amateurish heroes as I. And although the world was now at least a bit calmer, a dash safer, I did not feel any kind of exceptional satisfaction. I was not particularly elated or overjoyed. In fact, no such thing happened that I had expected before. And even the pleasantly surprising discovery that the valiant duo of my age and experience finally defeated the complacent and callow youth did not make my heart flutter from unbridled pride or happiness. It did not. It certainly did not. It did not, although I vanquished, without anyone's aid or assistance, the vile man. I vanquished the man who intended to appropriate my place at my adorable daughter's side. Like a commonplace pawn trying to capture the king on the chessboard of life.

But, after a brief moment of initial puzzlement, I quickly blamed it on my raving professionalism. For, apparently, it swiftly took control over me and did not allow any infantile raptures or euphorias which are the preserve of amateurs. And instead, it settled for a mild relief.

With considerable difficulty and still gropingly, I managed to find the pitiful key to the garage door. But it, as it turned out to my unceasing amazement, was affixed to the car key hanging merrily from the ignition. Like a hopeless climber dangling from the slope of the mountain. And then, as if my current astonishment was not enough, I discovered that it was not necessary to open the damned door from the inside after all. But that I simply could not have known. I could not have even supposed that. A man of my age. I could not have possibly supposed that, I, who had been sitting behind the wheel of anything other than a wheelchair five decades ago. If not more. You have to excuse the grumpy old man. Then, I ineptly got into the car and gently released the handbrake. I did that as delicately as if I tried to turn the most expensive door handle in the world. And, as it rolled back out of the driveway, I strived desperately to rein in the indecipherable deluge of various furiously blinking lights and gauges and indicators, making it look like a carnival that came too early. Far too early, in fact.

I was motivated by a thought, by a single persisting thought, namely, that I had to go back there as soon as possible. I had to go back to the excellent hotel. And I had to give the full and detailed report to my indecently wealthy masters, my marvelously beautiful leaders, and my exquisitely wonderful masterminds. I had to do that like an obedient oven that with a high-pitch ringing signals that it has performed its burning duty. But, above all, I had to go there, back there, to receive straight from their impeccably perfumed hands the prize that I deserved, the recognition that I had earned, and all that for my unequalled services.

Unfortunately, this accursed machine crashed its careless rear into a no less inattentive mailbox. It did that as if to spite me. It did that as if to punish me for what I had done to its former driver. Then it plowed right through an unmade flower bed, a disheveled shrub, and then rudely knocked over the neighbor's trashcans, akin to a set of bowling pins, and, as if it were not enough, it rammed straight into his slop-pily painted fence. Like a foolish animal from a cartoon that mistakes a fake tunnel entrance for a real one. And with this flurry of raucous catastrophes, I incurred the hellish wailing and laments and shouts of the curious people flocking to me hurriedly from the whole neighborhood. If not the entire city. Like shop sharks that smelled a fresh clearance sale.

However, I still remembered, compelled by a primitive, ir-resistible, yet irrational urge, to get out of the car. I remem-bered to do that despite all the vulgar shrieks and cries of horror. And, limping slightly from my recent misfortune, I closed the garage door behind me. I closed it for I could not, as a professional and trained doorman, pass by an open door indifferently. For it was as if it longed to be shut tenderly. It was as if it beseeched me to close it caressingly. And doing that, closing it, locking inside the still motionless body of my defeated enemy, for the first time I felt that this seemingly simple activity was laden with some hidden symbolic mean-ing. It was suddenly charged with some deep sense. And, per-haps, it was even charged with some transcendental sense. It was charged with something deeper than pampering to my most nagging urges and desires. Far deeper, in fact. For I felt as if I were closing a particularly torturous chapter of my

287

interminable life. I was closing it just like a reader who finishes reading a rather long story that has drained him and exhausted him emotionally.

The lock clicked. The door was closed. It was over.

Never before in my quite riveting, quite eventful, and quite long life, had I felt so light. I had never felt so ineffably liberated. Like a child born in prison who sees the unspeakable boundlessness of the sky for the first time in its life. For it was as if, by getting out of that dark garage, to some degree, I were born again, or as if I were born too late. I was like a long-overdue baby who has been lounging in its mother's womb for a few decades or more. And I relished it. And I savored that new element, that unexpected ingredient, which had suddenly been introduced into the goulash of my life. Even if in such a violent way. Even if in such an unforeseen way. For I was no longer at a loss. For I found my moral bearings in the world that had lost its own ones long ago. And nothing could possibly spoil this memorable moment. Nothing could spoil this new flavor that my life acquired all of a sudden. Not even the sight of the furious flashes of beacon lights lighting up the darkening horizon. Not even the rueful whining of police sirens that rent the air in the distance. And I only smiled under my breath. I smiled blissfully. I smiled with relief. I smiled at all that. For I knew that it was nothing. All that was really and truly nothing. For my daughter was finally safe now.

87809498R00178

Made in the USA
Columbia, SC
27 January 2018